M000187186

MARRYING MYSELF

A NOVEL

CHRISTINE MELANIE BENSON

Black Rose Writing | Texas

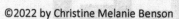

©2022 by Christine Melanie Benson
All rights reserved. No part of this book may be reproduced, stored in a retrieval system or transmitted in any form or by any means without the prior written permission of the publishers, except by a reviewer who may quote brief passages in a review to be printed in a newspaper, magazine or journal.

The author grants the final approval for this literary material.

First printing

This is a work of fiction. Names, characters, businesses, places, events, and incidents are either the products of the author's imagination or used in a fictitious manner. Any resemblance to actual persons, living or dead, or actual events is purely coincidental.

ISBN: 978-1-68513-076-3 (Paperback); 978-1-68513-146-3 (Hardcover)
PUBLISHED BY BLACK ROSE WRITING
www.blackrosewriting.com

Printed in the United States of America
Suggested Retail Price (SRP) $22.95 (Paperback); $27.95 (Hardcover)

Marrying Myself is printed in Garamond Premier Pro

*As a planet-friendly publisher, Black Rose Writing does its best to eliminate unnecessary waste to reduce paper usage and energy costs, while never compromising the reading experience. As a result, the final word count vs. page count may not meet common expectations.

For Sammy

MARRYING MYSELF

A NOVEL

Prologue

It was just before midnight, on the eve of Julia's birthday.

Asher stepped out onto the moonlit balcony of their Florence hotel, gazing at her with such tenderness and affection that Julia actually blushed. She must have known, on some level, what was coming. She'd vaguely registered the brilliant flash of diamond, the shimmering platinum band. She'd subconsciously noted Asher's uncharacteristically tentative demeanor–a far cry from the powerhouse façade he generally presented to the world–as he slowly, deliberately, even humbly lowered himself onto one knee, holding her eyes the entire time.

Yes, of *course* she must have known; how could she not? But even so, she'd felt a delightful bafflement as to what her intimate partner of nearly two years could possibly be up to. In fact, she'd had to restrain herself from blurting out, "Asher, sweetheart, what are you *doing*?"

But she hadn't. She'd remained quiet, for once abandoning her chronic– and largely futile–struggle for control of anything and everything around her (and most especially her own emotions), instead allowing the anticipation, the excitement, the beauty of the moment to build and bubble up inside her. Incredibly, this phenomenal male creature was directing his words at *her*: Julia Jones, a woman of moderate intelligence, attractiveness, and success. Your average above-average thirty-three- (almost-thirty-four-)year-old woman.

"Darling," Asher whispered. "Julia?"

She nodded encouragingly, touched by his vulnerability.

Asher cleared his throat and paused to brush a lock of his thick, dark hair from his eyes, a gesture which prompted a small smile from Julia. Asher was so commanding, so certain of what he wanted and what was important in life, and yet he could never quite tame that longish, unruly hair of his. Perhaps inspired by the works of art they'd seen today, here in the birthplace of the Renaissance, her fingers suddenly itched to paint him. Of course, she'd never be able to fully capture his essence in a portrait. He was a masterpiece–not just physically, but in every sense. She regarded him fondly, feeling herself coming dangerously close to losing herself in his deep brown eyes, yet still she didn't resist. The sensation was terrifying, but electrically so.

No more holding back, she'd thought. Finally, after a lifetime of playing it safe, she'd managed to let go completely.

"You're wonderful, Julia," he said. "I love you, I *more* than love you. I feel–it sounds preposterous, but I feel as if you saved me. You helped me discover myself–my *authentic* self, the part of me I thought I'd lost forever. And not only did you accept that part of me,"– here, he paused to shake his head in wonderment– "that's the part of me you loved the most. I can't even begin to tell you how much that means to me."

Tears had welled up in Julia's eyes.

And in that moment, she'd seen tears in his eyes, too.

"More than anything in the world," he said, "I want to be your husband. And I want you to be my wife." And then, he said it. "Will you marry me, Julia? Will you let me love you? Will you let me love you forever?"

Now, to be fair, despite what he'd said about her profound understanding of his most authentic self, Julia *didn't* feel she'd seen quite all of Asher. He'd certainly seen all of *her*; not since her beloved mother, who'd died tragically in a plane crash when Julia was only eleven years old, had there been anyone to whom she'd so willingly bared her soul. Asher, however, was a different story. Even in their most intimate moments, there seemed to be a part of him that he kept closely guarded–a part which, she suspected, might ever remain solitary.

Still, she'd felt little cause for concern. She'd chalked it up to his being an only child, a byproduct of the self-sufficiency he'd been forced to develop as a lone little boy in a world of high-powered adults. And, besides, wasn't that the nature of human relationships in general? When it came right down to it, did anyone really know *anyone*?

The point was, Asher loved her. And for those few brief moments in the moonlight, Julia at last allowed herself to *feel the love*. The love of a man who was handsome, charismatic, and successful—and, more importantly, generous, constant, and unfailingly kind. A man of character and integrity, who could have had his pick of women—his last girlfriend had been a Slovakian super-model, for God's sake—and yet, who wanted her. *Her*.

And, so, on that balcony in Florence, Julia summoned the courage to do what she'd longed all her life to do: respond to love's invitation with a joyous, unqualified, "*Yes!*"

By then, it was after midnight: June fourteenth.

"Happy birthday," Asher whispered, kissing her ardently on the lips.

"The happiest," she said, kissing him back.

They'd gone on to celebrate this, the official start of their shared forever, by making love in the canopied hotel bed in the remaining sweet dark hours of the night. Julia found herself responding to Asher's touch more fully and viscerally than ever before, that miraculous word, "*Engaged!*" reverberating gloriously throughout the deepest recesses of her heart, her mind, her very soul. Indeed, it had seemed as if every cell of her being was joyously proclaiming her newfound status to the universe: "*ENGAGED!*"

And so she had been. What she hadn't realized, however, was that engagements don't necessarily go according to plan.

PART I

Engaged!

Chapter 1

Apart from her sister, Jolene, there was no one to whom Julia was more eager to deliver the news than Kat, her best friend since their college days at Boston University. She telephoned Kat from Italy the very next day, only for her friend to beat her to the punch.

"Happy birthday!" said Kat immediately upon answering the call. "Are you engaged?"

Julia laughed, noting that the very word had the power to make her giddy. "Thank you! And yes, I'm engaged!"

"I knew it!" shrieked Kat. "Your birthday, romantic trip to Florence–I saw this coming a mile away. So tell me, is it gorgeous? Is it *enormous*?" After a moment of confused silence from Julia, she said, "The ring!"

Julia glanced at her left hand. "Oh, it's definitely gorgeous. It's a Bartlett family heirloom. And yeah, I'd say it's kind of enormous! I'm still getting used to wearing it. And I'm terrified of damaging it. Or losing it, oh my God, can you imagine?"

"Send me some photos," said Kat.

"Sure," said Julia.

A moment passed, and Kat emitted an exasperated sigh. "I meant *now*."

"Okay, okay," said Julia, laughing. She should have known; "now" was generally implicit in any demand of Kat's. She took a minute to snap some shots with her cell phone and sent them off to her friend.

Kat's reaction came only seconds later. "Wow," she breathed, atypically reverent. "It's gorgeous, breathtakingly gorgeous. And *extremely* enormous! Four carats, at *least*. Asher hit this one out of the park. Not that I'd have expected anything less. The perfect man, the perfect proposal, the perfect ring. It's all so perfect! You know, if I weren't such a wonderful person, I'd hate your guts."

"Well, thanks for being such a wonderful person," said Julia. "And yes, it's perfect. So perfect I can hardly wrap my head around it." It was true. Even now, she marveled that she and Asher had found each other–that somehow, in this over-populated, over-technologized, increasingly fragmented world, their spirits had gravitated irresistibly toward each other. Clearly, greater forces had been at work. "It could only be fate," she remarked. "Or even–a miracle."

At that, Kat–last traces of reverence gone–burst out laughing. "And to think who set it all in motion! By the way, don't you *dare* give him credit for a miracle. That's the last thing he needs for that four-carat ego of his. He already thinks he walks on water."

"Point taken," said Julia, laughing, too. Kat wasn't talking about Asher. No, in this instance, the wheels of fate had been set in motion by the most unlikely–and unintending–of matchmakers: interior designer and narcissist extraordinaire David Meadow, who occupied an office on Hanover Street in Boston's North End, just two doors down from Hartland Travel, where Julia had started working in college. David's parents were old friends of the travel company's proprietors, Carly and Franco Hart, and he often stopped in to visit with them. Over the years–and despite the fact that his personality differed from Julia's by a full one hundred eighty degrees in every conceivable respect–David had become her *de facto* buddy as well.

"Have you told your sister?" said Kat.

"Yeah, she was pretty excited," said Julia. "She said she's going out tonight to celebrate." Not that free-wheeling Jolene ever needed an excuse to party.

There was audible commotion on Kat's end of the line. "Listen, I want to hear *everything*, but I'm at a breakfast meeting with a new band." Kat worked for an independent music management company, and wining and dining the artists the company represented was a key part of her role. "But I didn't want to miss your call. I had a feeling you might have some news."

"Oh, right, I forgot it's morning for you," said Julia. "Well, you were right about the news! Good luck with your meeting. I'll call you when I get back tomorrow night."

"Great," said Kat. "Congrats again, Jules! Happy birthday! And happy—what is it again? President's Day? Veteran's Day? Something patriotic, right?"

"Flag Day," said Julia, having grown up intimately acquainted with the holiday on which her birthday happened to fall.

"Yes, happy Flag Day," said Kat. "Or no, make that happy New Year—*your* new year!"

As Julia clicked off the line, Asher walked up behind her and wove his arms around her waist. She turned her head to kiss him on the lips.

Happy New Year, indeed.

• • • •

While Asher was making some telephone calls of his own, to his parents and countless cousins, it occurred to Julia that the miracle-maker himself arguably deserved a personal notification. She sent off a text message to David Meadow:

Balcony, Florence, ENGAGED! Thanks, Cupid!

There came an almost instantaneous response: *Sidewalk, Boston, heart CRUSHED, BROKEN, UTTERLY DESTROYED. You're welcome.*

Followed by another: *But don't worry about me. I'll live. Or at least survive.*

And another: *More or less.*

And another: *But seriously, congrats, princess! He's a lucky man!*

And another: *You so owe me...*

And about a dozen more in similar veins, ranging from recriminatory to self-congratulatory to morose.

The one thing David *didn't* say was, "Happy birthday." He'd obviously forgotten—typical.

Julia sent off a final reply: *Yes, I'll owe you forever. Happy Flag Day, handsome! xoxo*

Even though she'd spoken in jest, she couldn't help but cringe slightly at the prospect; being in romantic debt to David Meadow, of all people, was not a fate she'd wish on anyone.

Asher was worth it, though.

As always, the memory of that fateful Monday morning just over two years ago brought a smile to Julia's face. At just after nine a.m., David had turned up in her office and announced, "I'm kidnapping you for a coffee." Then, forestalling any potential protest that she might be occupied with, well, *work*, he'd grabbed her hand and physically tugged her out of her chair.

David himself worked, and he worked quite hard. But because he'd also been born with a silver—make that platinum—spoon in his mouth, he tended to view other people's jobs in the same way that he did his own: as an entirely optional recreational activity. His blue eyes flashing, he'd added, "Your other option is to get drunk and let me take advantage of you."

"Hmm," Julia had said as he led her out of the office–to the amusement of Franco and Carly, who were accustomed to David's shenanigans–"six of one, half-dozen..."

David had looked aggrieved. "Stop torturing me. Coffee it is, then."

Of course, her acquiescence had been less reluctant than she'd feigned. Initially, her part-time job at Hartland Travel, which specialized in group tours to cultural and spiritual meccas like Athens, Paris, Jerusalem, and Rome, had simply been a way of earning some extra cash as an impoverished college student. The North End location was easily commutable from B.U., the work was relatively undemanding, if somewhat tedious. And there were some appreciable travel benefits.

But after graduating with a double-major in possibly the two *least* practical fields imaginable, painting and philosophy, Julia, for lack of any better ideas, had asked Carly and Franco to take her on as a full-time employee, and they'd agreed. She'd started out as an "Office Assistant," was eventually promoted to "Office Manager," and, several years later, became "Office Director." And then, just when she'd begun to wonder how many office-related titles she'd end up holding in the course of her–*ahem*–"career," she'd been struck with what had seemed at the time like a brilliant idea.

Inspired by the free plane tickets and other perks that regularly came to those in the travel business and often went unused, she'd convinced Franco and Carly to establish a small not-for-profit division, whose mission would be to bring the spiritual and cultural rewards of international travel to underprivileged youth. Hartland Travel would benefit from the myriad of charity-associated tax breaks—and she, Julia, would be able to bid goodbye to for-profit office-dom and help advance a truly worthy mission.

Now, a little over three years later, she was Director of Development (no "office" anywhere in *that* title, thank you very much) of Hartland Travel's non-profit partner, Journeys of the Heart. The title wasn't quite as impressive as it sounded, since, apart from Julia herself, JoH's sole employee was a program assistant, Whitley Fitzpatrick. Still, the agency had grown in the time she'd been there, and JoH now enjoyed funding from a variety of sources besides Hartland Travel. Although Carly and Franco were listed as the organization's joint Executive Directors, they were happy to leave most of the hands-on management to Julia, giving Julia a level of autonomy that made working for a living significantly more tolerable than it might otherwise have been. And it was wonderful to witness the positive effects of JoH's work on young people's lives.

Even so, in her quieter moments, Julia couldn't help but wonder how in the world she, an *artist*, had wound up spending her waking days writing grant proposals and reports, updating Excel spreadsheets, and coordinating travel arrangements. Only rarely did she get to accompany the kids on their adventures; for the sake of efficiency, the youth trips were linked with Hartland Travel's adult offerings, led by Carly or Franco or on-site local tour guides. Ultimately, as she saw it, her role as JoH's Director of Development boiled down to three things: (1) asking for people for money; (2) figuring out how to spend whatever money they were lucky enough to get; and (3) reporting back to the people whose money they'd spent, in the hopes that those same people would give money *again*. As much of an improvement as her position at JoH was over her "Office Director" job at Hartland Travel, at the end of the day, she was still an office hack.

Not to mention, her plan had been to paint on evenings and weekends. Somewhere along the line, *that* plan had gone out the window–along with her art. She'd scarcely painted in years.

All that to say, for a *host* of reasons, she was quite happy to be kidnapped for a coffee now and again–especially in Boston's charming Old World neighborhood, the North End, known for its cozy Italian-style coffee shops and restaurants. David loved trying anything new, and, together, the two of them had tried countless bistros and cafés. Although Julia was not a particularly (i.e., remotely) spontaneous person, David brought out in her a spur-of-the-moment side she hadn't even known she had. With him, everything was an adventure.

On that particular Monday, they'd decided to venture beyond the North End to a new fair-trade coffee shop downtown, on Tremont Street. There, inside the earthy café, David had spotted one of his interior design clients.

Who could have predicted that in that moment, her life would change forever?

"See that dude over there?" David had whispered, leaning into her and, Julia suspected, sniffing her hair; everything David did was mildly–or not so mildly–lewd. "I'm doing his house in Louisburg Square. He's loaded."

Julia had to laugh. A mansion in Beacon Hill's ultra-posh Louisburg Square was typical of David's high-end residential projects. And for David to describe someone *else* as "loaded" was rather hilarious.

She followed his gaze. "He's cute."

As soon as the words were out of her mouth, however, Julia realized what an absurdly inapt description that was. This man was not "cute." Lean and tall, with an easy, athletic grace, he had *presence*. With his dark hair, brooding brown eyes, and chiseled jaw, he radiated a quiet strength, like a tiger or a panther. His was a face with character, a face that made you want to know more. You could tell he was smart. And deep. And extraordinary. She could go on and on...

Thirty seconds later, she was still staring at him from across the room.

And then she realized that he was looking at her, too.

Naturally, the indomitable David had interrupted the moment. "Asher Bartlett!" he'd bellowed. "What's the good word?"

"Mister Meadow!" said Asher, striding toward them and shaking David's hand in an oh-so-manly fashion.

His eyes, however, had remained on Julia.

David had made the introductions. "Don't you try to weasel in," he warned Asher. "This princess belongs to me."

Julia did not, of course, belong to him. Or to anyone.

Asher had simply smiled and, seemingly as much for Julia's benefit as for David's, said, "We'll see about that."

As it happened, no weaseling had been necessary. Asher had had her heart from that very first moment.

And soon they would be married, with a lifetime of magical moments awaiting them. Julia felt nearly overcome by the ecstasy of it. What on earth had she done to be so lucky?

She could only smile to herself at the question.

Nothing was always the unavoidable answer. No one could *earn* this sort of happiness. She could only attribute it to some sort of universal grace.

Chapter 2

In the weeks after Julia and Asher returned from Italy, the wedding plans began falling naturally into place. They didn't need a long engagement, they agreed. After some discussion, they settled on Sunday, December seventh, as their wedding date.

"Lucky seven," Asher said with a smile.

Julia smiled back, unfooled by his casual tone. Logical, analytical, business-minded Asher was surprisingly—and, she thought, rather adorably—superstitious. For him, the fact that December seventh was convenient to their families' schedules and wouldn't interfere with the Christmas holidays was probably less of a draw than having the "lucky" number as part of their wedding date. But so much the better, she reasoned; in some ways, it *did* seem to make their wedding date that much more auspicious.

The wedding venue, too, decided itself: they'd be married in Thun, Switzerland, on the grounds of Schloss Himmel, the castle owned by Asher's family. The previous winter, Julia and Asher had spent a week at the white, red-roofed castle perched on the edge of a pristine lake. At the time, Julia had assumed that Schloss Himmel was a historical landmark that doubled as a luxury resort—and in that she'd been correct, except that it was a privately owned one, the thirteenth-century castle having been acquired by Asher's mother's ancestors in the early 1800s. It was a detail Asher hadn't seen fit to reveal to her until after they'd gotten engaged.

"Schloss," Julia later learned, was German for "castle." And Himmel, a German word that meant heaven or sky, was the surname of Asher's maternal grandparents.

Of course, had been her dryly amused reaction; of *course* Asher's kin had, literally and figuratively, occupied a position in paradise, above all the ordinary, earthbound humans. And for a full four days in early December, her own family and friends would get to inhabit that mountain-top position as well.

Like the venue, their wedding parties came together with hardly a thought. An only child, Asher had four cousins to whom he was extremely close: August, Archie, Alistair, and Abe–the "A-list," the family had predictably dubbed them. August, who was older than Asher by exactly three months and to whom Asher bore such a striking resemblance that people often commented that they could pass for twins, would be his best man.

Julia's bridal party would consist of her four favorite women in the world: her sister, Jolene; her stepsister, Lacey; her former roommate, Marissa; and, of course, Kat. There would be no maid- or matron-of-honor. ("How *egalitarian* of you," Lacey had remarked, no doubt having hoped to secure that prime slot for herself). For Julia, it would have been impossible to choose among the four women she loved most–and, moreover, the vacant wedding party role would serve as a bittersweet memorial to one very special person who would *not* be attending the wedding: her dearly departed mother, Josie.

Marissa, an independent clothing designer with her own shop in Manhattan, Attire by Marissa Chu, had already finished designing the bridal party's dresses. The rose-colored gowns were classically elegant, while also chic. "Trademark Chu" was Lacey's approving assessment–and anything Lacey didn't find fault with was, by definition, beyond reproach.

Julia herself would wear the wedding gown that had belonged to her mother, which her father had saved all these years for this very purpose. The dress was objectively beautiful, and knowing that it had belonged to her mother imbued it with an other-worldly sacredness. There couldn't be a more fitting way to embark upon her new life with her soul-mate.

Asher.

They spent a lazy Saturday morning in Julia's bed, going over some of the last remaining details. Regrettably, such leisurely weekend mornings were few and far between for the two of them. Asher was second-in-command only to his father at the family's century-old global communications company, BartTech, and his work required near-constant travel. BartTech's business lines included airline search engine technology, booking software, and innumerable side ventures. Julia had initially thought it quite the coincidence to learn that Hartland Travel used the company's travel software, until she'd come to realize the scope of BartTech's dealings; virtually *all* travel businesses used BartTech software in some capacity.

But right now, she realized, Asher was talking food.

"Before I forget, Pierre-Yves says we need one more option for the post-wedding brunch on Sunday." Pierre-Yves, the general manager of the Schloss, was also overseeing the wedding planning. "He suggested stuffed figs or heirloom tomato tartlets. What do you think?"

A vegan for over two decades, Julia had been delighted at the chef's innovative suggestions for their entirely plant-based wedding menu. Delectable as everything sounded, though, she found it difficult to summon strong preferences. After all, they were planning a wedding in paradise. Who really cared what you were eating when you were in paradise?

She cocked her head, thinking. "Hmm. Both?"

Asher nodded definitively. "Done. I'll let him know." He lay back in bed, yawning widely. He'd returned late last night from a business trip to BartTech's London office, uttering barely a word before collapsing into Julia's bed. The poor man lived in a near-perpetual state of jet lag.

"Is that it?" said Julia. "Anything else Pierre-Yves needs from us?"

He shook his head and yawned again. "No, that's it."

Julia frowned slightly. "It's all been so ... *smooth*. It's only August, and practically everything is all set. Is planning a wedding supposed to be this easy?"

Asher smiled and shrugged. "The Fates are on our side. We're meant to be."

Julia beamed. "That's just what I've been thinking!"

"We'd better stop talking about it, though," Asher added, "or we'll jinx it." He closed his eyes and rested his head on the pillow.

Julia laughed and propped herself up on her side so that she could look at her handsome husband-to-be. She took in his strong chest, his chiseled jaw, his captivating profile. Yes, she'd have to do a proper portrait one of these days.

Asher's eyes fluttered open, as if he'd sensed her gaze. "Sorry, I didn't realize how beat I was. We've been working around the clock trying to close this U.K. deal. In fact, Odetta's still in London for at least another week."

Julia's eyebrows went up a hair. "Oh, *really*." Odetta O'Hare, whom she'd met at last year's BartTech holiday party, was one of the company's hottest new hires–yet another Harvard MBA. While she'd been glad to see a new female executive at the testosterone-heavy family firm, she'd been far from crazy about the thinly veiled admiration with which the sultry Odetta had seemed to regard Asher–an admiration which, she strongly suspected, went well beyond the professional.

"Yeah, it's her first time flying solo on a deal," said Asher. "There've been a few bumps, but overall she's been terrific. A real go-getter, that one."

"I have no doubt," said Julia. "I'm surprised she didn't ask you to stay and help mentor her. Let me guess–did she suggest sharing a hotel suite to cut down on costs?"

Asher laughed. "Sweetheart, stop. Odetta's never been anything but strictly business. And besides, for legal reasons alone, I'd never get involved with someone at the office."

"It had better be for more than legal reasons alone," said Julia, but she was smiling as she said it. Even if she didn't fully trust Odetta, she *did* trust her fiancé. If she hadn't, Asher's extended absences would have been not merely unpleasant, but intolerable.

He leaned over and kissed her. "Legal reasons and infinite *other* reasons." He glanced at the clock. "Is it really almost noon? You must be starving. Want me to go pick up something for us? Scones? Muffins?" He grinned. "Bagels and tofu cream cheese?" Asher had only recently discovered tofu cream cheese and couldn't seem to get enough of it.

Julia grinned back at him. Yet *another* reason she adored her fiancé: even when he was so tired he could hardly stand up, he was always seeking things to do for her.

"Don't be silly," she said. "I'll go. Or we can stop somewhere on the way to the ICA." The Institute of Contemporary Art, with its lovely waterfront setting, was a pleasant walk from the North End. "You're still up for checking out that textile exhibit, right? This is its last weekend."

But Asher was already reaching for his pants. "Yes, definitely. I'm still kicking myself for missing the 'We Wanted a Revolution' show last fall."

Julia's smile widened. One–*more*–thing she loved about her fiancé was that he was possibly even more of an art nerd than she was. Although their inclinations certainly differed–she was generally drawn to the past, particularly seventeenth- and eighteenth-century landscape art, whereas Asher was always on the hunt for the latest in boundary-pushing, experimental, socially relevant artistic expression–they shared enough of an overlap that it was fun to explore together, and Julia appreciated being nudged outside her standard artistic "box." They rarely went a weekend without visiting one of Boston's notable art museums.

Asher finished buttoning his shirt. "I'll run down to the coffee shop and pick up some bagels. I'll be back in five minutes." He gave her a lingering kiss on the lips. "Don't go anywhere."

A moment later, he was out the door.

Julia lay there dreamily, already anticipating his return. He'd arrived home so drained from his whirlwind trip that there had been little opportunity for physical intimacy last night. But apart from the ICA, she realized, they had no pressing obligations later this afternoon–meaning that there was an extremely good chance that she'd soon be getting some long-overdue action.

She sighed blissfully, recalling Kat's words.

It all really *was* perfect.

Chapter 3

"You're getting married in a Swiss castle?" yelped Kat so loudly that Julia winced on her end of the phone line. "Asher's family *owns* a Swiss castle?"

"It's not a very *big* castle," said Julia–and then immediately felt guilty, because that wasn't even remotely true. In truth, she'd never seen an estate as vast and grand as Schloss Himmel, with its turrets and towers and balconies and verdant English-style gardens.

As Kat's peals of laughter echoed over the phone waves, Julia settled back on her white velvet sofa. It had possibly been her least practical furniture purchase ever, given that when she'd bought it, she'd been living with a constantly-shedding orange cat named Huck. She still recalled how, the first time that Asher had visited her apartment, he'd inhaled sharply at the sight of the massive lumberjack of a cat before emitting a massive, earth-shattering sneeze–followed by another, and another, and another.

Yes, as she'd learned that day, Asher was severely allergic to cats.

Which to her just didn't make sense. It was like being allergic to love.

Poor Huck had died last year at the age of fourteen, meaning that Asher could now tolerate being in her apartment for more than thirty seconds at a time. And her sofa was back to a depressingly immaculate shade of white–which, unfortunately, wouldn't be changing anytime soon. Given Asher's hypersensitivity, she'd reluctantly reconciled herself to a cat-less existence.

Apart, that was, from the human Kat–who at the moment was screeching like a banshee.

"*Not a very big castle*?" she practically shouted. "Jules, you do realize how ridiculous that sounds to laypeople like me, don't you?"

Julia frowned. It was possible, she thought recalcitrantly, that Schloss Himmel actually *wasn't* that big a castle by castle standards; maybe, as castles went, it was only average-sized. But she suspected that that line of reasoning wouldn't hold much water with Kat.

"What does it look like?" said Kat.

"Do you remember those pictures I sent you last winter? The place Asher and I went?"

"*That* castle?" Kat gasped. "The white one? With the towers? On the lake? "

"Yeah, that's the one," said Julia. Come to think of it, her sofa, with its creamy white cushions and cherry wood trim, was rather reminiscent of Schloss Himmel's burnt-red-tiled roof and white stone walls. "Its name is Schloss Himmel. They call it the Schloss."

"Why didn't you tell me about this before?" said Kat, clearly put out.

"I didn't know myself," Julia told her. "Asher only just told *me*."

Kat giggled. "Maybe he was testing you. He didn't want you to say yes to his proposal just for the castle."

Julia laughed dryly. "I think he was more concerned about how I'd react to finding out how wealthy he really is. I mean, of course I knew he was rich, but I'd never seen rich like *that*."

It was clear that Kat was finding this discussion enormously compelling. "So just to clarify, from what I could tell from the pictures, the castle is not small at all."

Her words were slightly muffled, causing Julia to suspect that she was talking with her mouth full. Kat was a phone eater. Not the most appealing trait, in Julia's view, but a minor flaw in the grand scheme of things.

"You're right," said Julia. "The castle's not small. It's big. Very big. In fact, it's..."

"Palatial?" said Kat.

Julia laughed. "Yeah. That about sums it up."

Yup, that was definitely crunching she heard from Kat's end of the line. Barbecue Fritos, no doubt—they were Kat's fatal weakness. When she was dating someone interesting, the Fritos tended to fade from view, but about a month ago she'd had a tough breakup, and it seemed the Fritos had made a resurgence. She liked to splash them with hot sauce, and she sometimes even dipped them in peanut butter. Julia could scarcely fathom anything more disgusting (although, to be fair, she'd never tried it), but Kat swore the combination was food nirvana.

"So who exactly owns this castle—the *Schloss*?" said Kat, her mouth obviously full. "One of Asher's brothers? Cousins? Prince Charming? Or just some knight somewhere?"

"It's been in his mother's family for something like two hundred years," Julia told her. "His grandparents were the most recent owners. And as of the day of the wedding..."

Here, her voice trailed off.

"What?" said Kat. "Tell me!"

"I'm not clear on all the legal details," said Julia. "But as I understand it, the castle is being held in some sort of trust set up by his grandparents before they died. And there's a provision in the trust that when Asher marries, ownership will transfer to him. And ..."

"*And*?" said Kat, busting at the seams.

"And, eventually, also to his wife," said Julia. "Me."

There came more stunned silence from Kat. Then, "Aaagh!"

Julia couldn't suppress a mental image of corn chip bits spewing from her friend's mouth. "Aaagh!" she agreed.

"So, in a sense, you're giving Asher a castle," said Kat, between giggles—and chews. "That's too precious."

This time, Julia didn't join in the laughter.

"Okay, what is it?" said Kat.

Julia sighed. "It's this castle thing."

Kat groaned. "Don't tell me you have prosperity guilt. Or is it just too much pressure, too over-the-top? Jules, it's *your* wedding. Don't feel pushed into having some huge elaborate event if that's not what you want. You can even just elope. You can go to Bali—it'll be perfect. Actually, I hear Fiji is better. But really, the place doesn't matter, anyway. The point is that it will just be you and Asher—oh, and me. But only if you want me there. If not, I'm totally, a hundred-percent-fine with that, too." She paused, but only for air—she was clearly on a roll.

"Kat!" said Julia, seizing upon what she knew would be but a brief lull in the homily. "I don't want to elope. I'm excited about the wedding. And I'm excited about having it at the castle. Yes, it's *totally* over-the-top, but I've never done over-the-top before. I'm actually looking forward to it. And it's so gorgeous there. You saw the pictures. It's like a dream. It's *perfect*."

"Exactly, it's perfect!" said Kat. "So what's the problem? Why is it that with you, Jules, there's always a—"

Julia didn't let her finish the thought. "It's the inheritance provision—it makes me uncomfortable. That Asher is getting a castle and four thousand acres of land."

"Holy shit," said Kat.

"Yeah," said Julia. "For marrying *me*."

"What happens to the castle if he doesn't get married?"

"In that case, Asher and his parents and his Uncle Urs would get a lifetime interest in the Schloss and then, after they die, it would go to the city of Thun as a historical landmark. Essentially it would end up a museum."

Kat paused, absorbing the implications. Then she said sternly, "Julia, do not, I repeat, do *not* go there. Do not even *think* about going there!"

"What do you mean?" said Julia.

"You know exactly what I mean! I say this as your best friend and as a recovered woman intimately familiar with the twelve steps of Overeaters Anonymous..."

At that, Julia couldn't help but snicker; the sum total of Kat's involvement in OA had been attending a handful of meetings a few years ago with a chubby ex-boyfriend, Murray, who was an OA member. It was a New Year's resolution that had lasted all of a week—actually not a bad run for Kat, who was hardly the soul of follow-through.

"... and, I don't know if I ever mentioned this to you," continued Kat, "but I even had a spiritual awakening."

Now Julia laughed out loud. Kat loved sleep possibly even more than she loved Fritos and sex—and if she'd ever been threatened with anything remotely resembling a spiritual awakening, she'd undoubtedly have pounded the snooze button until it finally retreated.

"No, seriously," said Kat. "What I learned was how insidious low self-esteem can be—it will contaminate *everything* if you let it. Now I know it when I see it, no matter what kind of sophisticated guise you try to wrap it up in. And I won't tolerate it, do you hear me? Not from you! Do *not* tell me you think Asher is marrying you for this castle. I mean, he could marry *anyone* and get the castle. The castle has nothing to do with you."

"This is *not* low self-esteem," said Julia. "It's the conflict of interest. It doesn't sit right with me."

"What are you talking about?" said Kat.

Julia considered how best to explain. "I feel like the castle, in a way, sullies Asher's and my relationship. It brings a financial interest into what should be a union of love."

She could almost hear Kat's eye-roll. "Oh, Jules. You're marrying a zillionaire and you're trying to avoid anything to do with financial interests? You're going to have financial interests all over the place, for the rest of your life—get used to it! He's rich, Julia. *Rich*! Sure, maybe the castle is going to make him a tiny bit richer, but he certainly doesn't *need* it. Again, he could marry anyone and get the castle. And he chose you! The man clearly has taste. That's priceless."

"Exactly," said Julia. "All he has to do to get the castle is get married—to *anyone*. What if that's the only reason he's marrying me? Or what if he's ambivalent and it's only the castle that pushed him over the edge? I'll never know if he would have married me if it weren't for the castle." Disconcerted to suddenly find herself on the verge of tears, she said, "Do you understand, Kat? I don't need to hear your pseudo-Twelve-Step talk right now. I need to know if you understand."

"Okay, okay, I understand," said Kat, her tone a mixture of sympathy and exasperation. "I understand *you*, Julia. You're a purist, and you can't bear the idea of anything being contaminated even the tiniest bit. And I love that about you. But I'm going to offer another perspective here. I'm not saying better or worse—just different. Okay?"

Julia sniffled. "Okay."

"These grandparents," said Kat. "Who set up the castle trust."

"What about them?" said Julia.

"What if this castle is their wedding gift to the woman Asher loves? Their way of welcoming their grandson's wife into their family—posthumously. They decided to give this gift to Asher's wife, because they knew they'd love her, in fact they probably *already* loved her. And this was their only way of showing their love. Posthumously."

Julia smiled slightly. "All right, all right. I'm impressed you know a big word. Very good."

The jibe threw off Kat momentarily, but only momentarily. "'*Love*'?" she said.

"Yes, exactly," said Julia. "Look, that imaginary scenario you created is very sweet, and maybe that was even the grandparents' intent. But *their* intentions have nothing to do with *Asher's* intentions. There's no getting around the fact that, for all practical purposes, he's getting a reward for getting married. And the castle goes to Asher, not to me. I get to live there, but it's in his name until we've been married for seven years. Then it transfers to joint ownership."

"There you go!" said Kat. "A gift of love, but with practicality. With their family's money, they weren't going to take a chance on some gold-digging skank marrying Asher for his money. They were no fools."

"It's a reward for getting married," insisted Julia. "That makes it a conflict of interest. Asher has a motive for getting married other than love. And his fiancée—me—has a material motive for marrying him and staying married to him."

"There's no conflict!" said Kat. "It's a win-win. Asher wants to get married, he wants to get married to you, and on top of getting to have you for a wife, he also gets a castle. And seven years from now, you'll have a castle, too! Jules, do you realize how amazing that's going to be? I can't wait to come visit. I'm dying to stay in a cupola. Ever since I was a little girl, I've dreamed of staying in a cupola."

For Julia, the issue was far from settled, but she was beginning to feel that there was no point in prolonging the discussion. "Fine. I'll find you a cupola."

But Kat wasn't quite done. "Julia, listen to me. You have a choice here. You're at a crossroads—a critical juncture." Kat loved the phrase "critical juncture." She used it a lot.

And, in this instance, Julia couldn't disagree. In fact, it seemed to her that life abounded with critical junctures. They were everywhere—like potholes.

"You've got a critical choice to make," Kat went on. "You can choose to believe in Asher's love—or you can choose to doubt it." Here, she paused portentously; even when, as now, Kat was being sincere, she could never resist playing things up, as to an audience. "And I'll tell you right now, if you choose to doubt it, you'll be doubting for the rest of your life."

There came another long moment of silence from Julia. Then, she said, "All right. You may have a point."

She could almost hear Kat's grin. Kat loved nothing more than winning an argument, especially when she felt she was right—which, in her book (and to Kat, that was the only book that mattered), she nearly always was.

"Believe, Jules," she urged. "Believe! If you can't believe in love, what can you believe in?"

Julia thought back to that night on the balcony in Florence. She remembered Asher's sweet, sweet touch, and what it had been like to finally let herself feel—to really, really *feel*.

And, so, she made her choice. She believed.

Chapter 4

Julia realized that Asher was eyeing her quizzically.

"What's going on?" he said. "You are somewhere else tonight."

It was Friday night, and they were lying together in the sky room of the condominium on Rowes Wharf, overlooking the Boston Harbor, where Asher had been staying on-and-off for the past year. The luxury flat belonged to Asher's mother's friends Lars and Elena Fürrer, who lived primarily in Switzerland and had offered it to Asher to use whenever the renovation work on his Louisburg house got too noisy for him to bear. Lately, the construction had been so invasive that Asher had wound up staying at the condo more often than not.

As Julia had come to find, the complimentary condo was typical of the favors so readily exchanged among the Bartlett family's uber-wealthy circles. While so many in Boston struggled to keep up with the exorbitant rents, Asher, for whom finances would never conceivably be an issue, had been granted this highly desirable space not just at a bargain rate, but for free. Why was it, she wondered, that seemed to be the way world worked–that generosity seemed to flow most freely to those least in need?

Even so, she couldn't help but love it here in the waterfront condo, a welcome respite from the hustle and bustle of the North End. This room, especially, she found highly restorative. Named for its predominant feature, the sky room had an arched window ceiling that afforded a spectacular view of the night sky.

Tonight, as always, Julia had quickly gotten lost in the stars.

She still hadn't responded to Asher's inquiry. "I keep thinking about my mom," she told him. "I just miss her. I wish she were here. That she could have met you. Known you. All that."

Asher pulled her closer. "Me, too."

He'd put on some classical music, and the joyful notes of Handel reverberated in the celestial like the soundtrack to an epic film—the movie that was now her life.

How her mother would have loved this view. Josie had had a knack for noticing tiny spots of beauty, imperceptible to anyone else until she pointed them out. She'd had that same ability with people, too, drawing out wonderful qualities overlooked by others, even themselves.

People had been their best with Josie. *Julia* had been her best with Josie. Would she ever be that good, that *whole* again?

She feared not.

With a little laugh, she patted the garish blue velvet chaise lounge they were sharing. "My mother would have loved this view *and* this chair. The Fürrers have interesting taste."

Asher chuckled. "They're not bound by convention, that's for sure. Or even necessarily by taste. But I'm not complaining."

"No, me either," said Julia.

There, safe in Asher's arms, she allowed her imagination to roam. What would her life have been like if her mother hadn't ended up on that ill-fated airplane? Would she have been less anxious, more emotionally secure? Not living in constant fear of some disaster—or critical juncture—lurking around every corner?

It was anyone's guess.

Asher nudged her back to the present. "Do you think she'd have liked me? Your mother?"

Julia smiled, touched at the question. "She would have *loved* you. She'd have all but adopted you. You'd basically have had a new mother."

His mouth twisted. "That might not have been such a bad thing."

Julia nodded understandingly. Asher's mother, Sage, could be rather overbearing. And critical. And controlling.

And those weren't even the top three.

"Well," she said, "your mother's more challenging qualities aside, we have her to thank for lining up this condo. I'm going to miss this place when we move to Louisburg Square. Don't get me wrong, I know I'll love Beacon Hill. But you know how I am with change."

"I do know," said Asher. "In that case, we'll just have to make the most of this place while we're here."

Julia snuggled in closer. "Good idea."

• • •

Some time later, they ventured out. The August night was balmy, and the sidewalks were crowded with people, like them, reveling in the final days of summer. With no particular destination in mind, they strolled in the direction of Julia's neighborhood, eventually deciding to stop in at Caffé Vittoria, one of Julia's favorite spots. The Italian café served an array of espresso drinks, liqueurs, gelato, and fanciful desserts, but it was the Old World atmosphere Julia loved more than anything else. Sleek and modern had never been her style; she'd opt for vintage any day.

Asher, on the other hand, *was* the sleek and modern type, not just with art, but with everything, and she felt a little guilty imposing her preferences on him. Still, even if Caffé Vittoria was hardly the high-power, wheeling-and-dealing type of establishment Asher typically frequented, he seemed to like it there. She hoped so, at least.

As they turned onto Hanover Street, where the café was located, it struck Julia that she actually didn't *know* many of the places that Asher regularly patronized; she only knew where he went when he was with *her*, in Boston—and he was in Boston for no more than a week or two every month. BartTech had offices in New York, Dallas, Los Angeles, and London, and Asher made regular visits to all of them. Within just the past six months, he'd also traveled to Zurich, Dubai, even Kazakhstan.

Who knew where he—and/or Odetta—went when he was in Kazakhstan?

In fact, Julia realized with some chagrin, she didn't even quite know where Kazakhstan *was*. Was in Europe or Asia? Her geographical illiteracy was doubly horrible given that she worked for a travel company. She could ask Asher, of course, but there was no need to burden him with her ignorance. She'd have to look it up when she got home.

Even at this late hour, the Caffé Vittoria was buzzing with activity. While they waited outside on the sidewalk to be seated, Asher spied a stray penny on the ground. He stooped to pick up, flashing Julia a boyish look of triumph as he pocketed the coin.

"Good job!" she told him, thinking that a multimillionaire who never overlooked a lucky penny had to be the cutest thing ever. He really was one in a million.

Minutes later, they were installed at a window table inside the café, sipping espresso. Every time the front door opened, a warm breeze wafted in.

"What a beautiful night," said Asher. "Too bad we can't order weather like this for our wedding."

Julia felt a chill just thinking about Switzerland in the dead of winter. "On that note, I know it's crazy, but what would you think about eloping? It was just a random suggestion from Kat, but the more I think about it ..."

But Asher was shaking his head almost before the words were even out of her mouth. "No, we can't do that. It's in the trust instrument that the wedding has to be held at the Schloss. Eloping's not an option."

Julia's stomach dropped. "I thought we were having the wedding there because we wanted to. Because it's the perfect place for a wedding–for *our* wedding. I didn't realize we were just fulfilling one more of the trust requirements."

Asher looked a bit queasy, and Julia sensed he was regretting the espresso. He always loved the idea of it, especially when in the North End, but when it came to coffee, things like cappuccino and café au lait suited him much better than straight espresso. She offered silent homage to the Italians, Frenchmen, or whoever it was that had first conceived of transforming such a harsh and acidic substance as coffee into something that actually tasted good. If only life were so easily ameliorated–if only it were possible to dilute all its bitter elements with something frothy and sweet.

As if reading her mind, Asher caught their waitress's eye. "Could you bring me a cappuccino, please? With almond milk."

He'd gone vegan within a few weeks of meeting Julia. She'd have liked to believe that he'd done so purely out of concern for the space-deprived, perpetually-pregnant cows who, by some morbid twist of human-inflicted fate, were never permitted to bond with their newborn calves–or out of concern for the calves themselves, stolen from their mothers at birth, the males sold for veal or pet food. And he *did* care about those things, she knew he did. But even so, Julia suspected that the foremost factor keeping Asher vegan was the visceral repulsion he'd experienced when he'd learned even just a little about the dairy industry: the artificial insemination, the infected udders, the permissible levels of pus in cow's milk sold to consumers. He likely couldn't have stomached dairy–let alone meat–now, even if he'd wanted to.

"One almond milk cappuccino, coming right up," said the waitress. She looked to be in her early twenties and had pale skin, black hair with magenta highlights, and a pierced eyebrow–probably a student at Berklee School of Music or Emerson College. Seeming to remember that Asher had a companion, she looked to Julia, who shook her head "no" to anything else.

Meanwhile, Julia's coffee had gone cold, but she wasn't thirsty, she wasn't hungry–and this castle was beginning to feel like an albatross.

She sat there in tortured silence until Asher's cappuccino was delivered.

He took a sip of his steaming drink and sighed contentedly, looking so pleased with himself that Julia couldn't help but smile.

"Good?" she said.

"Excellent," he confirmed. "So, getting back to your point about the castle."

Relieved, she nodded. Yet *another* thing she loved about Asher: he never tried to avoid a troublesome issue.

"The Schloss *is* the perfect place for our wedding," he said.

Julia sighed. "I have to tell you, I am coming to hate the idea of this castle. The *Schloss*."

Asher looked hurt. "What? Why?"

"It feels like you're being bribed into marrying me. How can I ever separate *it* from *us*?"

Asher shook his head. "It's not like that. Keep in mind where my grandparents–my mother's parents–were coming from when they established this trust. They both lost their fathers in the war. And even after they got married, it wasn't easy. For one, they had their hands full with my Uncle Urs–my mother's older brother. He made my mother's life miserable growing up. And as an adult, he cheated on his wife, paid his–allegedly-pregnant mistress hundreds of thousands of dollars to keep her quiet, only to find out she'd been lying." He grimaced slightly. "You get the idea. My parents literally can't stand the sight of him. And when they cut someone off..."

He didn't need to finish the thought; Julia knew what he meant about his parents. Sage Bartlett. with her fair hair, disconcertingly silvery-blue eyes, and elegant manner, possessed an icy Nordic beauty and an inner temperature to match. Of the pair, she was the true blue-blood, born into vast wealth.

In physical appearance, Asher favored his father, Dominic. Tall and charming and fit, Dom, now in his sixties, was still enormously attractive and charismatic, effortlessly the focal point of any gathering. But while Asher and Dom had the same coloring and the same personal magnetism, Asher had a kindness, a sensitivity, that his father lacked. Dom projected power–not mercy.

The meat issue was a case in point. Dom would never, Julia imagined, even contemplate giving up eating meat, because to him, animals–human and non-human alike–existed as resources for his own personal use; he was *entitled* to whatever they could provide him. For Asher, on the other hand, it had taken only the merest bit of information to prompt him to go not just vegetarian but completely vegan. Julia often wondered how, with his ridiculously pampered–and ridiculously high-pressure–upbringing, Asher had managed to turn out so ... *kind*.

No, she decided, he wasn't one in a million or even a billion; he was unique. She'd never find another man like him.

And, fortunately, she'd never have to.

"The point is," Asher continued, "my grandparents believed that family was everything. They wanted to help ensure that their descendants' families survived intact. And apart from my mother and Uncle Urs, their only descendant is me."

"What about your cousins?" said Julia.

"They're from the other side of the family—the working-class side. The ones who founded BartTech."

"Right," said Julia, thinking that the Bartletts had to be the wealthiest "working-class" family in history. "That's why they all work for the company."

"Exactly," said Asher. "So my paternal bloodline's going strong. But on my mother's side, it's just me."

It suddenly struck Julia what a burden he'd been shouldering this entire time. Responsibility for an entire family line—a weight that not even his "A-list" cousins could help him bear.

"Probably the best way to put it," said Asher, "is that my grandparents had a union that they felt was blessed, and they wanted to bless ours in return. Unfortunately, it's posthumously," (here, Julia couldn't help but think of Kat) "but that was their intent."

He was quiet for a moment, but Julia could tell that he had more to say. She waited, happy just to be sitting there with him, happy that they could speak so honestly with each other, about anything.

His eyes bored into hers. "Julia, I want you to know that I more than respect your concerns. I hope that you know that."

She nodded. "I do, Asher. I do." She'd soon be uttering those words in front of Asher's family and her own—at the castle in question. *Good practice*, she thought.

"But you're wrong in thinking of this castle as a bribe of any sort. It's not a bribe. It's a gift and a blessing. Can you see that, Julia? Can you believe that?"

Julia smiled. Once again, it seemed, it came down to a question of faith—not "To be, or not to be," but "To believe, or not to believe?" *That* was the question.

She said as much to Asher.

"So what's your answer?" he said.

"I believe," she said.

What other answer could she give? She did believe. She *had* to believe. Did it really matter which came first?

Chapter 5

Jolene's blue-green eyes—so like their mother's—widened. "A wedding in your own Swiss castle? You'll be like a princess! Hell, I'll feel like a princess!"

"Well, the sister of a princess is usually also a princess," said Julia.

Jolene thought for a moment. "True!"

After an idyllic week of having Asher at home, he was gone again—back to London, to sign off on the final phase of the deal he and Odetta had been working on. Tonight, Julia and her sister had gotten takeout from a Thai place in Central Square in Cambridge, just across the Charles River from Boston. They were now in Jolene's one-bedroom apartment, eating their dinner on Jolene's thrift-store couch (since Jolene had no table), using wooden chopsticks (since Jolene had no silverware apart from two forks, one of which she'd temporarily misplaced). Julia had just finished explaining about the Schloss, sparing her sister her qualms about the trust provision, since that was a subject she'd—hopefully—beaten to death with Asher and Kat.

Besides, Jolene was too trusting to question anyone's motives about anything—a case in point being her near-cultish devotion to Mrs. Catherine Lee, founder and president of SunStar Traditional Natural Eastern Remedies, whose vitamin and herbal supplements Jolene sold on a part-time basis. Like most of the company's sales reps, Jolene had started selling SunStar products simply in order to get a discount on her own purchases, and she still bought far more than she sold—meaning that the only one *actually* profiting from SunStar was the savvy Mrs. Lee (as everyone in the company deferentially called her).

In Julia's view, the situation was beyond ridiculous. But even though she was convinced that Mrs. Lee was a charlatan and that SunStar was no more than a convoluted Ponzi scheme, her sister was so committed to the holistic medicine cause as practiced by Mrs. Lee that Julia had long ago learned to steer clear of criticizing Jolene's "mentor."

Fortunately, her sister had other irons in the fire–literally. Since graduating from Massachusetts College of Art with a degree in metalsmithing and jewelry design, Jolene had also been slowly–if not very steadily–building her own jewelry business. And jewelry, Julia suspected, was the reason her sister had invited her over tonight. Jolene had been enigmatic, saying only that she had something she wanted to give Julia before the wedding.

Yes, it *had* to be jewelry of some sort, thought Julia; it had better not be SunStar supplements.

They finished up the last of their dinner, and Jolene tossed the cardboard takeout containers into the already-overflowing recycle bin. Not at all to Julia's surprise, the apartment had fallen into disarray since the departure of Jolene's most recent ex, neat-freak Nate, who'd moved out just last week. Jolene tended to attract very organized, competent men, eager to help her get her life in order. Her would-be rescuers invariably discovered, however, that not only did Jolene not appreciate their efforts to manage her life, she actually preferred to live in a state of mild chaos.

Still, if history was any predictor, her sister would have a new boyfriend within the week. "Catnip to the male species" was Kat's term for Jolene's irresistible combination of ingenuousness and sensuality. In fact, Julia had initially worried slightly that Asher, like so many other capable, high-achieving men, might wind up bewitched by her enchantingly scattered sister. But although they got along famously in a big-brother, little-sister kind of way, Asher was, by all indications, immune to Jolene's "catnip."

"I really need to start composting," said Jolene, using all her strength to shove down the contents of the trash can. "But first, I'd like to give you something in honor of your wedding. Are you ready?"

It was odd to think of a wedding gift while her sister was elbow-deep in rubbish. But then again, this was Jolene.

"I'm ready!" said Julia.

Jolene wiped her hands on her jeans, and then, possibly in response to the dubious look on Julia's face, paused to wash her hands at the kitchen sink, using dishwashing liquid since, Julia assumed, she had no hand-soap. She disappeared into her bedroom and returned a moment later with an elegant package, wrapped in black and pink paper and tied with a silvery bow. "Something old, something new, something borrowed, something blue! Here's your something new."

Impulsively, Julia hugged her. "Thank you so much, Jo."

Jolene hugged her back for only a second before pushing her away, laughing. "You haven't even seen what it is. Open it, open it!"

Julia tore away the wrapping and lifted the lid of the black box. There, inside, was a graceful, feminine bracelet–glistening rose-cut gems in a silver setting. "You made this? It's beautiful!"

Jolene nodded happily. "Jewels for a jewel–jewels for Jules! They're only rhinestones, not diamonds. But that means you won't have to worry about it as much." She glanced at Julia's left hand. "Besides, I figured you're pretty much set in the diamond department."

Julia laughed. "I am indeed. You know, this is my first wedding gift. I love the bracelet. And I love you!"

"I love you, too!" said Jolene. "I'm so glad you like it. It'll be perfect with Mom's dress, don't you think?"

Julia's eyes promptly clouded over, and for a moment she couldn't speak. She gazed down at the bracelet, still in its black box. "Yes, it will."

When she looked back up, she saw that her sister was crying, too.

• • •

Julia cringed when she saw Lacey's name flash on her cell phone at just before noon the next day. What could it be *this* time?

There was probably no one more different from her laid-back sister than her control-freak *step*sister. Lacey lived in New York City, where she held a high-level executive position (vice president, principal, Julia could never keep track) at public relations firm Mayer & Malday, on Manhattan's

Upper West Side. In the weeks since Julia had gotten engaged, Lacey had been unstoppable, hounding her about every last wedding detail. In some ways, it was helpful. In a bigger way, it was crazy-making.

But that was Lacey; she couldn't *not* take charge. When Lacey's mother, Stephanie, had married Julia's father three years after Josie's death, then-seventeen-year-old Lacey had been highly suspicious of her new step-family. She'd especially vilified Julia's father, whom she viewed as having unfairly ousted her own father, even though Stephanie had divorced him years before meeting Joe Jones. Eventually, though, as it had begun to sink in that while *she* still had both her parents, Julia and Jolene had lost their mother, and that Joe, through no fault of his own, had lost his wife, Lacey's hostility had melted away. She'd wound up becoming her newfound little sisters' fiercest defender.

And that protectiveness still remained. Even when—as in more instances than not—no protection was necessary.

Suppressing a sigh, Julia answered the call. "Hey, Lacey." Hearing a great deal of background noise, she asked, "Where are you?"

"In the park," said Lacey, her breathing brisk. "Lunchtime power-walk."

Julia had figured as much. Lacey's corner office overlooked Central Park. She often went for lunchtime walks there, sometimes even scheduling walking meetings with her clients. Lacey approached physical fitness as she did everything else: she attacked it, as if it were determined to use every trick in the book to elude her—which, naturally, only made her that much more determined never to let that happen. And her militant approach worked; Lacey was in amazing shape.

"So what's up?" said Julia.

"You may have this all worked out already, but if not, I wanted to recommend a good lawyer in Boston. She does mostly domestic and also some probate, so she's pretty ideal for what you need. She's busy, though, so you'd better get on it."

Julia was used to directives from Lacey, but this particular one baffled her. "What are you talking about? I don't need a lawyer. Or do you know something I don't?"

Lacey laughed, since of *course* she did. "I meant for the pre-nup."

"A pre-nup?" said Julia. "Why on earth would I want a pre-nup? If anyone should want one, it's Asher, not me. I have no assets." It was true. Apart from a savings account she'd been contributing to since she first started working at Hartland Travel, which now contained just over eighteen thousand dollars, and a modest retirement fund through JoH and Hartland Travel, she had nothing.

"Jolene told me about the castle," said Lacey, her athletic shoes making whishing sounds as she strode over the park trail. "And how it'll become yours in seven years. That's a valuable material interest. You shouldn't mess around with it."

"But–" said Julia.

Her stepsister proceeded as if she hadn't spoken. "Plus, you're getting married to an extremely wealthy man, and that gives you some legitimate lifestyle expectations. You need to make sure your interests are protected in case Asher fucks you over."

"Lacey!" said Julia. "I'm not even married and you're worried about me getting fucked over? I thought you liked Asher. Why would such a possibility even cross your mind?"

Lacy sighed. "Julia, *everything's* a possibility. I'm not saying I think it's going to happen. I'm just saying, cover your ass–and your assets!"

Julia spoke firmly, knowing that her stepsister would seize upon any perceived weakness. "Lacey, there's no pre-nup, and there's not going to be one. Like I said, if it would make sense for *anyone* to want one, it would be Asher, and he's never even *touched* on the subject. And I know it's because he feels exactly the same way that I do about our wedding and our marriage– that it's meant to be. And it's forever."

She braced herself for a counter-argument. Married at twenty-seven, divorced at thirty-one, Lacey had plenty of reasons to doubt the "forever" part of marriage.

But there came only a long pause, during which Julia caught the sound of birds chirping and wind rustling through the trees in Central Park.

At last, Lacey replied. "Fair enough, Jules. I'm a cynic, but even I can see that what you and Asher have is special." She laughed. "Who knows? You guys might even make me a believer. In love, I mean. I doubt it, but we'll see."

Julia smiled. "Thanks for looking out for me, Lace."

"My specialty. And ironically, now that I've finished my walk, I've gotta run. Talk soon?" Before Julia could respond, Lacey added, "And let me know if you change your mind about Denise, the lawyer. I've already discussed your situation with her, so she'll be able to crank out a draft pretty much on the spot."

"No pre-nup!" said Julia–*again.* "And no Denise. But thanks anyway."

She was talking to a dead line, she realized. Lacey had already ended the call.

Chapter 6

Tuesday morning, Julia was at her desk at work when she heard the front office door swing open–probably one of her bosses.

"Good morning!" she called from her tiny corner office.

Sure enough, a moment later, Carly appeared in front of her desk. Sunglasses perched atop her windblown blonde head, her makeup impeccable, the co-founder of Hartland Travel looked glamorous even in leggings and a tunic-style top. She also looked mildly distraught.

"Good morning," she said. "And I'm so sorry, but we're not going to be able to come to Switzerland for the wedding. Can you ever forgive us?" She thrust a bag at Julia. "Here, they're vegan. And they have gluten. That means you can have them for breakfast."

Julia's face fell. "Oh, no! I was really hoping you'd be able to make it." She peeked inside the bag–double-chocolate chip cookies. "Thank you, these look amazing. But no, I'll never forgive you."

Carly looked even more distraught. "Oh, don't say that! Franco will explain. He's right behind me–he ran into someone on the street. His family is planning a huge family reunion in Sicily in November, and another trip so soon after–"

Again, the front office door opened, and, a few seconds later, Franco himself strode in. He was wearing slip-on shower shoes, black gym pants, and a black T-shirt. Unless they had in-person client meetings, the Harts kept a very casual work environment at Hartland Travel. Franco gave Carly a peck on the lips, coming away with a smudge of bright red lipstick on his lower lip.

"Yes, yes, blame it all on me. It's always all my fault." He thrust yet another bag at Julia.

"What are these?" she said.

"Vay-gahn, glutton-free, chocolate-beet muffins. That'll work, right? I always forget what you are, so I figured I'd cover all the bases."

"I told you, honey, she's just a regular *vee*-gun," said Carly. "And it's *gluten*-free, not glutton-free."

Franco looked at Julia. "See what I mean? I never get anything right. It's a wonder I've made it this far."

"It really is," said Carly.

"Well, thank you, these look fantastic," said Julia. "I definitely won't be glutton-free this morning."

"Julia says she'll never forgive us for not coming to her wedding," said Carly.

"She didn't mean it," said Franco. "She only invited us to be polite. Right, Julia?"

"Is that true, Julia?" said Carly. "You're not mad?"

"I *did* really want you there, and I'm incredibly bummed you're not coming," said Julia. "But since you brought me muffins and cookies, I guess I can forgive you."

Franco looked at his wife. "See? *Now* who's right?"

"You, dear, you," said Carly. "Thank you for understanding, Julia. We'll do a special post-wedding celebration when you get back."

"That sounds super," said Julia. She took a muffin out of the bag and offered it to Franco. "Want a muffin? They're vegan and gluten-free."

"Pass," said Franco, absently scratching at his large belly. "But I guess I could try a cookie."

Julia gave the muffin to Carly and handed Franco a cookie.

"Thanks," he said. "Now get to work."

"Tyrant," said Julia.

"Show some respect," said Franco.

The Harts gave her one last wave and left.

Julia took a muffin for herself and put the remaining baked goods in a desk drawer. She'd been working for Carly and Franco for so long that she'd almost come to think of them as her adoptive parents. She'd really hoped that with their travel connections, they'd be able to manage the trip to Switzerland—but apparently not. Her father and Stephanie would be there, as would her ninety-two-year maternal grandmother, Sophie—her only living grandparent. But the rest of her budget-constricted friends and extended family had declined due to the expense.

At this rate, the large majority of the wedding guests would be from Asher's side of the family. Gratuitous hops across the ocean were far more achievable for people in his world.

Oh, well.

Julia pushed the wedding thoughts out of her head. Time to get to work.

Fall was her busiest time of year at Journeys of the Heart, in large part because October thirty-first was the application deadline for JoH's Travel Sabbatical scholarship competition—TS, for short. The TS winner would take a trip abroad for up to a full year, all expenses paid, for the purpose of cultivating spiritual growth and deepening understanding of the arts, science, and the humanities. The program had been established just three years ago, thanks to an unexpected fifty-thousand-dollar grant from a private donor, an eccentric Silicon Valley retiree now living in Concord, Massachusetts, who had renewed the grant every year since. Following its unanticipated, serendipitous beginning, the TS program had quickly become one of Julia's most time-consuming projects.

Unlike most of JoH's offerings, the TS program was merit-based. From the initial pool of applicants, Julia and Whitley would select three as finalists; these final three would then be interviewed by Julia and the five members of JoH's Board of Directors, who would ultimately select the winner. Julia had had the daunting task of creating the application process from scratch, as well as a system for rating the applicants on their character, scholastic accomplishments, and the cultural merit, originality, and social value of their proposed travel plans. That had been a relatively manageable task for the first year's small pool of applicants, but the number of applicants had been growing by leaps and bounds every year, making it that much more challenging to select the winner. While it was a thrill to be able to offer a deserving young person such a unique travel opportunity, Julia had lost plenty of sleep over all of the worthy students who *didn't* win.

Compounding the difficulty of selecting the TS winner was the financial pressure she felt to procure sufficient funding to keep the program going. Although the TS benefactor seemed committed to continuing the program, she had no idea the extent of that person's resources. This year, she was working on a proposal to secure funding from another deep-pocket donor, The Boston Cultural Foundation, to ensure the survival of the TS program.

In other words, there was no end to the TS-related work in sight.

For the third time that morning, Julia heard the front office door open, and she could tell from the clatter that it was her program assistant, Whitley. Barely five feet tall, with a tumble of long red curls, green eyes, and an exceptionally large nose, Whitley looked more like an elf or a leprechaun than the serious-minded, socially conscious woman she was. She would soon be completing her master's degree in social work at UMass Boston. Julia had no idea how Whitley managed to balance grad school with her full-time job at JoH, and she almost didn't want to know; she needed Whitley too much at JoH.

"Morning, Whitley," she called.

"Morning, Julia," Whitley called back.

Seconds later, she was in Julia's doorway, fidgeting anxiously. "You have a minute?"

"Sure," said Julia. "What's up?"

Whitley took a seat in the chair across from Julia's desk. "I don't know what we're going to do. Eliot has completely exploded."

"Eliot?" said Julia.

"That's my nickname for the TS program. As in T. S. Eliot. Get it?"

"Cute," said Julia.

"Based on what I've seen," said Whitley, "we're going to have at least triple the applications we had last year. And tons more are still coming in. Twenty-three just this morning! And it's still almost two months until the deadline. Julia, it's too much! How in the world are we going to pick someone?"

Julia found it endearing how avidly this smart, motivated young woman seemed to crave her professional guidance. For all her flurries of panic, Whitley was highly competent. She would be more than capable of taking over Julia's job if Julia decided not to keep working after the wedding.

The thought was humbling. Here was she, Julia, at thirty-four years of age, with over a decade of office experience—and she could be more than adequately replaced by a fresh-faced grad student in her first real job. Not that she'd ever harbored any illusions about the expertise required for her role at JoH. But if it wasn't rocket science, it was all for a worthy cause.

Whitley was still awaiting her response—as evidenced by the twitching of her notable nose.

"Okay," said Julia. "Here's what we'll do. We'll divide the applications between us, and we can't spend more than twenty minutes on any single application. Based on that initial assessment, we'll tag each one as great, good, mediocre, or no way. Most of them will fall into the good and mediocre categories."

"But what about your ratings system?" said Whitley, aghast. "We were going to rate all the applications based on those ten criteria and rank them ..."

"Out the window," said Julia, more casually than she felt. "Maybe we'll use it next year. So after you and I get through our respective piles of applications, we'll switch, and we'll rate each application a second time without knowing how the other person rated it. We'll keep the double-great ones and the great-good ones, and we'll discuss any that one of us thinks is great and one of us thinks isn't even good. We'll eliminate the no-ways."

"Got it," said Whitley, as if these scattered directions represented a carefully conceived course of action. "I'll create a shared spreadsheet to keep track of our individual ratings."

"Perfect. And if you have any other ideas, let me know."

Whitley brightened. "In fact, I do! I really think it's time for us to get an intern."

Julia instinctively recoiled. She loved the homey feel of their small office. And she was less than eager to take on an intern who'd require guidance and attention.

Sensing her reluctance, Whitley pressed on. "Eliot—that is, TS—is going to totally dominate our time for at least the next few months, and we can't just forget about the other grants. We have major reports due to the Giovanni Group and the Marilyn Fund in October, and we also have some grants that are coming up for renewal this fall."

"Yes," said Julia, "but things will slow down once the TS winner is selected. I don't know if we'll have enough work to keep in intern busy."

"That's not going to happen. Besides, if we run out of work, Carly and Franco can always use some help at Hartland Travel. Come on, what do you say? It won't be a paid position, so we really have nothing to lose. I can post an ad on some job sites today."

"Okay," said Julia, trying to feel more enthusiastic. "Why don't you see if you can line up some interviews for next week."

Whitley was already out of her seat, all four feet, eleven inches of her raring to go. "I'm all over it."

Chapter 7

By that evening, after another full day of TS applications and spreadsheets, Julia had a clear vision of what the rest of her week was going to look like. Maybe an intern was a good idea after all.

But right now, work was the least of her concerns.

She walked the few blocks home, tossed her bag onto the couch, and resolutely began stripping off her clothes.

Tuesday night was yoga night: her weekly six o'clock yoga class at a studio on North Bennet Street in the North End. It was Ashtanga yoga—a vigorous, supposedly energy-stimulating style. A "yang yoga." What it *actually* was, though, was torture. And she'd learned it was dangerous to delay even a moment in changing into her workout clothes.

She threw on a T-shirt and yoga pants and headed out the door.

Kat had come with her to her very first Ashtanga class about a year ago. Kat, however, had lasted barely fifteen minutes into the ninety-minute ordeal—at which point, she'd shot the teacher an insulted look and muttered, "You've got to be kidding me." She'd taken her time rolling up her brand-new (never-again-used) magenta mat and accidentally (or not) side-swiped one especially limber woman with it on her way out, entirely unembarrassed at her early exit.

However, if Kat had no shame, Julia had enough for them both. She'd not only finished out that first excruciating class but had continued going back every week for more. The staff at North Bennet Ashtanga now considered her a regular and greeted her with the camaraderie of fellow yogaphiles–while not-so-subtly urging her to come more often than once a week. Ideally, they'd explained, Ashtanga was meant to be a daily practice.

Daily Ashtanga? Julia had thought. *Could there be a more awful notion?*

But she hadn't had the heart, or the courage, to reveal to the studio staff or other yogis that she wasn't truly one of them and that she kept coming back simply because she felt that not being very good at yoga, and hating it, weren't sufficient reasons for abandoning a supposedly worthwhile practice.

Minutes into tonight's class, Julia realized she'd forgotten to take off her engagement ring. She'd done that last week, too; she still hadn't acclimated to this diamond-ring-wearing thing. She slid it off her finger into the zipped pocket of her yoga pants for safekeeping, and the Ashtanga session proceeded as usual: an hour-and-a-half of awkwardness, discomfort, and outright agony, replete with burning arm, thigh, and ab muscles, failed attempts at difficult poses, and plenty of corrective nudges from tonight's teacher, Pepper. All of which finally left her in her standard Tuesday-night post-yoga position–on her back, on her mat, eyes closed, breathing heavily, in a half-conscious, sweaty fog.

Free at last, she thought. *Free at last.*

At least until next Tuesday.

She was still lying there when she heard a voice.

"Julia? Julia Jones? Is that you?"

"Yes, it's me," she replied automatically, her eyes still closed. *Like a patient etherized upon a table*, she thought–and then realized she'd spoken the words aloud. Maybe it was the TS overload at work; she had "Eliot" on her mind. This wasn't the first time she'd noticed that Ashtanga seemed to impair her usual thought-speech filter. The effect tended to persist for several hours–another item to add to the list of annoying things about yoga.

"A poetry quote I actually recognize," said the voice. "T. S. Eliot, right? Maybe high school wasn't a complete waste after all."

Julia opened her eyes. The face into which she found herself staring seemed vaguely familiar. That, together with the high school reference, helped everything click into place.

"You're Sean Harris!" she said.

He laughed. "I am! This is so bizarre, running into you here, like this."

"More bizarre for me to run into *you*. I don't think I've ever seen a guy in yoga class. A guy like you, I mean." She immediately blushed, but she was so hot and sweaty that hopefully it didn't show.

"A guy like me?" Sean said innocently—but could that be a note of flirtatiousness she heard in his voice?

Of course not, Julia told herself. "Oh, you know—non-student. Over the age of twenty-five. Heterosexual." She grinned. "Hot."

They both burst out laughing.

Sean looked down at her, still lying prostrate on her mat. "I have to say, I kind of like meeting women this way. Sprawled out in front of me, at my mercy."

Julia promptly scooted up into a sitting position.

"That class kicked my ass," said Sean, sounding a bit dazed. "I've been going to this yin yoga class that's totally chill. But I missed it this week and I figured, hey, a yoga class is a yoga class. I had no idea I was signing up for *this*."

Julia nodded vehemently. Keeping her voice low so that no one would overhear, she said, "It's horrible, isn't it?" She felt a subversive rush of relief at finally expressing her long-hidden yoga secret.

Sean laughed at her intensity. "Yeah, I'd say so."

He gave her a hand up, and Julia immediately noted his strength. Asher was strong, too, but in a subtler way. Sean's manliness was very marked. It intimidated her a little—it always had. In high school, she'd seen him around in the hallways, occasionally they'd spoken a few words. Of course she'd been attracted to Sean Harris, of course she'd been mildly obsessed with him—what heterosexual Jefferson High School girl *hadn't* been? His family had moved to town from Iowa just in time for him to join the freshman class at their high school in Syracuse, New York, where he'd quickly become a superstar—quarterback of the football team, with the beautiful head-cheerleader girlfriend (Anne-Marie Amoroso), and on top of that, he was smart. Was there anything sexier than a scholar-athlete? After high school, he'd gone back to Iowa for college, on a football scholarship.

Julia, on the other hand, had been a largely unnoticed, nose-to-the-grindstone, "good student"–honor roll, track team, Arts Journal, but she'd never been valedictorian or class president or head of anything. Her one fleeting moment of Jefferson High School fame had been when her design was chosen from hundreds of entries for a community art mural which, for several heady years, had graced an entire wall of a little league baseball stadium, until it was painted over to accommodate a ten-foot-by-twelve-foot Doritos ad. Apart from the mural, Julia's high school existence had been largely behind the scenes. Introspective and imaginative as a child, during high school, without her mother to turn to, she'd been even more terrified of the opposite sex than she was now. In short, she'd been a socially awkward, good-girl nerd–and so she remained at her core.

Yes, of *course* she'd been attracted to Sean Harris. He'd also been completely out of her league.

Mr. Out-of-Her-League was still holding her hand, she realized. As if sensing what she was thinking, he dropped it.

Julia's palm felt warm–which made sense given that she was still dripping with sweat from the Ashtanga session. Sean's palm had been moist as well. It occurred to her that she and Sean Harris had exchanged body fluids.

Stop it! she ordered herself. *Be normal. Or at least pretend.*

"You feel like grabbing some coffee?" said Sean. "It's so crazy running into you after all this time. I want to hear what you've been up to."

"Sure," said Julia. It was on the tip of her tongue to add, "I'm surprised you even remember me," but then she recalled Kat's number-one commandment: no self-deprecating remarks. She pictured Kat saying, "You're a gorgeous, funny, *amazing* woman; of course he remembers you!" Substituting Kat's imagined attitude for her own, she said, "I'll fill you in over a cappuccino."

Sean's eyebrows went up. "That might be all right for you, but real men don't drink cappuccinos."

"I beg to differ," said Julia, thinking of Asher. She almost elaborated, but for some reason left it at that. "Besides, that's sexist. But no worries, I won't force one on you. Anything you need to do to preserve your masculinity." She grinned. "Yoga boy."

Sean shrugged. "Touché." Then he shook his head. "Oops, I don't think real men say that, either."

"Definitely not," said Julia.

As they left the studio, Pepper called to them. "See you next week, guys. Or maybe sooner?"

Julia smiled and waved noncommittally. She and Sean clambered down the steep stairs from the fourth-floor studio.

As they stepped out into the comparatively cool night, they were greeted by a glowing pink sky, a fireball of sun sinking just below the horizon.

"Wow," said Sean.

"Wow," Julia agreed, noting how the last rays of sunlight accentuated the golden tones in Sean's dark blond hair. "It's like a scene from a movie."

A *romantic* movie, she thought. Funny that she would be feeling romantic *now*, with her hair frizzy from the un-air-conditioned yoga studio (further humidified by the yoga victims' evaporating sweat), wearing her most rag-tag workout clothes (dingy green t-shirt, black yoga pants with a hole in one knee; she did own cute yoga outfits, but this wasn't one of them). And then, of course, there was the fact that she wasn't with her fiancé. In other words, she had rock-solid reasons for not feeling romantic.

Well, she reminded herself, she was human. Feelings didn't always follow rules. She was a sensual adult woman, her muscles had been physically relaxed by an hour and a half of targeted yoga torture, and she was on a survivor's high at having made it through another round of Ashtanga. It was a sultry late-summer evening, and she was walking alongside her high school crush, Sean Harris. It was only natural that her skin was tingling, her face was flushed, and her heart was beating slightly faster than usual.

Of course, none of that meant that these romantic feelings had any substance. They were merely the remnants of teenage nostalgia—nostalgia for experiences never had, wishes never fulfilled, the rather pitiful side-effect of her—and maybe every red-blooded American woman's —longing to go back in time and fulfill her adolescent fantasies, to be everything she hadn't been during those self-conscious teen years: confident, sexy, *cool*. And she could enjoy these feelings for what they were: a pleasant puff from the past, a dreamy diversion from adult reality. She felt extraordinarily mature for noticing her feelings without judgment, while at the same time recognizing their disconnect with reality. Apparently she'd absorbed something from her Buddhist studies course at B.U.–maybe even from yoga itself.

"Where to?" Sean was saying. "Paradiso? Vittoria? Mike's?" he suggested, naming a few of the nearby cafés. "Or if you feel like getting out of the North End, we could head over to Newbury Street. We could even go to my place. I'm at Comm. Ave. and Gloucester, not too far."

The mention of the Commonwealth Avenue location practically stopped Julia in her tracks. *Sean Harris* was inviting her to *his place*?

It meant nothing, she admonished herself. *Nothing!*

Her left hand suddenly felt very bare. She reached into her pocket for her engagement ring and slipped it back on. Sean didn't seem to notice.

"Let's do Vittoria," she said, doing her best to block out any thought of the private dwelling space in which Sean Harris lived his life.

"Perfect," said Sean.

They proceeded down the street, Julia thinking, if Anne-Marie Amoroso could see her now...

Chapter 8

"Anywhere you'd like," said the same waitress who had served Julia and Asher just a few days before, easily recognizable by the magenta streaks in her dark hair.

What prompted a person to dye her hair pink? wondered Julia. Come to think of it, Marissa—to the consternation of her conservative Chinese parents—had had pink hair at one point. She'd have to ask her.

She and Sean chose a small round table by the window. Julia ordered a soy cappuccino, which seemed faintly sacrilegious after yoga. Pepper drank only herbal tea—when she wasn't following a strictly raw-food diet, that was. Sean ordered a regular latte; apparently *that* was manly enough for his taste.

She gave him a look, which he accurately interpreted.

"Totally different from a cappuccino," he said. "No froth."

Julia had to laugh, despite her disappointment that, evidently, Sean Harris was not a vegan. Well, she caught herself thinking, she'd managed to convert one man, she could always convert another.

In the next instant, though, she reminded herself that she wasn't going to be converting—or doing *anything* to, or with—Sean Harris. Other than having an innocent non-alcoholic drink after yoga class.

"I don't remember you being so ridiculous in high school," she said.

"I've always been ridiculous," said Sean. "You just didn't spend enough time with me to notice."

Julia considered this an extremely generous remark. To suggest that during high school, spending time with *Sean Harris* had ever been an option for her was an extraordinarily expansive gesture. She wasn't fooled, of course; she'd never been part of that select group. But it was nice of him to pretend for her sake.

The waitress reappeared at their table. "One cappuccino and one latte," she said, setting down their drinks.

Dusted with milk-chocolate flakes, Julia's cappuccino looked very pretty—and very white. Soy milk usually had a creamier, more vanilla-toned hue. "That's a soy cappuccino, right?" she said.

"Oh, sorry, I thought you said skim," said the server. "Do you want me to bring you another one?"

"Yes, please," said Julia. "And no chocolate on top." Accustomed as she was to the day-to-day challenges of being vegan, she hated coming across as high-maintenance—and in front of Sean, no less! But neither was she going to ingest the bodily secretions of an ill-treated, unconsenting cow, no matter how beautifully frothed and presented, merely to avoid some momentary social discomfort. After all, after thirty-four years, she ought to be pretty comfortable with social discomfort.

"All right, give me just a minute," said the waitress, taking back Julia's drink and leaving Sean's.

Maybe she was being paranoid, but Sean seemed to be eyeing her questioningly.

"I'm a vegan," she offered by way of explanation.

Sean looked intrigued. "Oh, yeah? For how long?"

She shrugged. "A long time. Since I was eleven, actually."

"That *is* a long time," said Sean.

He seemed to be waiting for her to say more, but Julia only nodded. In her experience, nothing sent men running for the hills like hearing about why she'd gone vegan—Asher, of course, being the one notable exception.

"Come on," Sean prompted. "There's got to be a story there."

He was regarding her with such open and genuine curiosity that Julia couldn't help but respond. "My parents were kind of New Age hippie types," she told him. "What are the odds—two born-and-raised Catholics meeting at a Zen commune in upstate New York? We didn't talk about it much, but we were pretty much vegetarian when I was growing up."

Sean chuckled. "A little different from *my* family. Before we moved to Syracuse, I lived in Iowa—not too many vegetarians there, I can tell you. In fact, that probably would have been considered worse than being a communist."

"I bet," said Julia, a little reluctant to continue. It had been such a pleasant evening thus far (apart, of course, from the yoga class itself); she didn't want to ruin things by getting too heavy. But Sean was looking at her with that same inviting look, so she plowed on. "I'm not sure if you knew this, but my mother died in a plane crash when I was in the fifth grade." The tragedy had been big news in Syracuse, but since it had happened before Sean moved to town, it was possible he didn't know.

"I did hear about that," he said. "I'm so sorry. I can only imagine what that must have been like for you."

Julia was glad he could only imagine; she'd never wish the experience on anyone. She took a deep breath and continued. "A few weeks after my mom died, my class went on a field trip to an organic dairy farm. My dad thought it might help me to be around the animals."

"That makes sense," said Sean.

Julia smiled wryly. "He thought so. Well, they took us to see a newborn calf. He was barely a day old, and he'd already been taken away from his mother. He was in this tiny stall, all alone, and he just looked so ... *lost*." Even now, the recollection made her wince. "And I found out that's how the dairy industry works. Once the cows give birth, they take the calves away from their mothers because if they let them nurse, there wouldn't be enough milk left to sell. The male calves go for veal or pet food. And the females are raised in isolation until they're old enough to get pregnant and start producing milk. And the cycle just goes on from there. None of the babies ever get to be with their mothers."

She supposed she'd been expecting some sort of reaction, but Sean only nodded. "Yeah. I'm from Iowa, remember? I know about dairy. I guess we just tried not to think about too much." He cast a guilty glance toward his latte.

Julia immediately felt guilty for making *him* feel guilty. But then again, he'd asked!

"I guess more than anything," she said, "it was the timing that made it really get to me. Seeing that tiny little calf, all alone..."

Sean finished for her. "And since you'd just lost your own mother, you identified."

"Yes. Exactly." Would she have empathized so deeply with that forlorn-looking little creature if not for the trauma of losing her own mother at an early age? She liked to think so–but in reality, she'd never know. "I came home that day and told my sister, Jolene, about the dairy farm and the calf, and she was just as horrified as I was. The two of us essentially ambushed my dad, and we all ended up going vegan." She smiled. "My poor father. He had no idea what he was in for when he sent me on that class trip."

She shook her head slightly, thinking back. What a time it had been. Fresh from her mother's death, everything had seemed surreal. Within just a few short weeks of that fateful class outing, the Joneses had gone from being a fairly typical two-parent American family who just happened to eat a lot of pasta and declined pepperoni on their pizza, to being an utterly *atypical*, single-parent, vegan family–before anyone even really knew what "vegan" was–who ate tofu scrambles and cereal with soy milk and bran muffins made with flax seed instead of eggs. The dietary shift, and the skeptical responses it had evoked from their neighbors, had, in many ways, unified their new, three-person family when they were still raw with grief. It had given them a focus and a mission–something to think about besides the great gaping hole left by Josie's death. Now, twenty-three years later, they still ached from the loss, but, incredibly enough, they were doing okay. And vegan living remained a family bond.

That said, it still pained her that she hadn't been able to help that little calf–hadn't even tried, really. Not that there was anything she could realistically have done. She'd been eleven years old, for goodness' sake.

Sean touched her knee, obviously feeling an instinctive urge to offer physical comfort.

Julia flashed him an appreciative smile. Who'd have thought that studly Sean Harris would turn out to be such a sweetheart?

Then again, she reminded herself, she'd been talking about her dead mother; a person would have to be made of stone not to respond sympathetically. Sean was just an ordinary guy, responding to a sad story just as any normal man would—well, any normal man apart from David Meadow. In fact, it suddenly struck her, not once in all the years she'd known him had David ever asked when or how or why she'd gone vegan.

And that right there was why she wasn't with someone like David, but with Asher, who wanted to know anything and everything about her—*and* her mother.

"So your dad went along with the vegan thing?" said Sean.

"Yeah, crazily enough, he did. We had some pretty wild adventures trying out new recipes. Which were often disastrous." Julia grinned; finally, some happy memories. "Like our first time making almond milk—we made such a mess of the kitchen! I think that was the first time we'd laughed since my mother died."

At that moment, the waitress returned with her cappuccino.

"Sorry for the wait," she said, setting down the steaming drink. "One soy cappuccino, no chocolate."

Sean, who'd politely left his latte untouched while Julia awaited hers, now requested a green tea.

Yes, Julia decided; he was definitely feeling guilty. "Please, you don't have to ..."

He gave her a sweetly tolerant look. "Stop. The latte would've kept me up all night anyway. And besides, you made a valid point about lattes. They're not super manly. Unlike, say, green tea."

Julia laughed, relieved at the return to lighthearted banter. "My thoughts exactly."

"Oh, so who's sexist now?" said Sean.

"Hey, nobody's perfect," said Julia.

Once the waitress had brought his tea, he raised his cup. "Cheers!"

As they clinked their mugs together, Julia wondered whether the other café patrons could possibly intuit the profundity of what was taking place at this tiny table: the heretofore-unimaginable deliverance of high school non-entity Julia Jones into the celestial social stratosphere of Jefferson High School VIP Sean Harris. It was truly a landmark moment—one which possibly only Jolene, who'd been two years behind Julia in school and thus had a sense of their high school pecking order, would be able to fully appreciate.

She sipped her cappuccino, which was delicious and well worth being high-maintenance for. "You know, I kind of wish I'd discovered coffee in high school. It could have made all the difference for me–made me feel sophisticated, suave. I could have had a totally different high school experience."

Sean looked intrigued. "So what *was* your high school experience?"

Julia immediately wished she hadn't said anything; it was not an experience she was eager to revisit. But she'd already told Sean about her mother's death. Compared to that, what was a little adolescent angst?

"Oh, pretty much just stress," she told him. "My father remarried when I was fifteen, so I was getting used to having a new stepmother and stepsister. I was always worrying about my grades. And track. And my social life–I stressed over something that was basically non-existent. Honestly, it's amazing I didn't completely burn out my system. I got worked up when guys didn't ask me out–and even more worked up when they did. Which fortunately hardly ever happened." So much for avoiding self-deprecating remarks; she again blamed Ashtanga for her uncharacteristic level of self-disclosure. It made sense, though–yoga left her muscles extremely loose, and wasn't the tongue technically a muscle? "And having a boyfriend was the most stressful thing of all."

Sean smiled–really more of a smirk. "Oh, yeah, Harper, right? Really short? Funny? Super-smart? Complete lunatic?"

Julia thought she might die of embarrassment right there and then–although if it were possible to die of embarrassment, it would surely have happened in high school. Jesse Harper, the rebel genius whom even teachers had called by his last name, had been her one and only high school boyfriend. Their "relationship"–a nonsensically elevated term for what they'd had–had lasted a whopping three-and-a-half months. But at least, for that brief period of time, she'd been a girl with a boyfriend.

Oh, it was all so incredibly humiliating! But she was the one to have raised the subject. All she could do now was face it with as much dignity as she could muster.

"Harper was short," she allowed. There was little debating that point; five-foot-four was generally considered short for a teenage boy–particularly for a senior in high school. "And yeah, he was a maniac. His parents were divorced, and he lived with his dad, who was away all the time. He got wasted every single weekend–and he considered Thursday and Friday part of the weekend. Basically, he was completely out of control. A perfect match for an innocent like me."

Although, on second thought, it hadn't been *all* bad. Harper had certainly livened up the Arts Journal, which he'd joined his senior year on a whim–unlike Julia, a devoted staff member since her freshman year. "He was very passionate. And he really was brilliant. We had some of the most fascinating conversations I've ever had in my entire life. Of course, I didn't realize at the time that was probably the result of his being stoned. But somehow we managed to connect." She sighed. "If only he hadn't been so short."

Sean was obviously finding all of this extremely entertaining. "Weren't you like a foot taller than he was?"

"No!" said Julia. "Only a few inches. Well, five inches. More with heels."

He was laughing outright now. At her, but not meanly.

"How can I even look you in the eye?" said Julia. "When for me, high school was basically one prolonged exercise in humiliation?"

"Well, look on the bright side," said Sean. "You'll never be able to live down those high school days, so you don't even have to try. You can just relax."

Relax, thought Julia. What a concept.

"So tell me what you've been up to since then," said Sean. "Do you still paint?"

She smiled, flattered that he remembered that much about her. "A little bit, on weekends. Not enough. For years after I graduated from college, I painted practically every spare second I had outside of work. I thought I was finally getting somewhere about six years ago when a gallery in the South End started showing some of my work. But then the gallery's lease expired and the management company sold the building to developers. And not long after that, my dealer retired. At that point, I kind of lost my fire."

"So what *do* you do?" said Sean.

But Julia decided she'd done enough talking. She hadn't heard a thing about Sean. "You first," she said.

He shrugged. "Okay. Well, let's see. I went back to Iowa for college. I played football. That was great for a while, and I had all kinds of professional ambitions, but I ended up with a bad concussion my junior year and had to leave the team. I was crushed at the time, but in hindsight, it probably saved my life."

Julia nodded, strangely relieved. She wouldn't want anyone she cared about playing college football.

Sean continued, "And then about two years after I graduated, I got married."

"You're married?" Julia heard herself exclaiming in what sounded like, well, *horror*. She threw in a hasty, "That's great!"

Sean looked at her wordlessly for a moment, his expression inscrutable. "Well, no, not exactly. Not anymore." He glanced down at his drink. "That is, I *was* married, but my wife died. Just before our four-year anniversary."

For a moment, Julia could only stare. "Oh," she finally managed. "I'm so sorry. How awful."

"Yeah. Pancreatic cancer. It was bad. At that point, I was working as a sportswriter in Sioux City, but after Jenny died, I couldn't stand being there anymore. I got a job in L.A., and that's where I've been for the past eight years."

"L.A.," said Julia. "Nice." She felt ashamed to have assumed that she was the only one to have experienced personal tragedy. Sean might not have experienced the loss of his mother, but the death of a spouse? That was something *she* could only imagine.

"Yeah," he said. "After a while, though, the earthquakes started getting to me. And the drought. And the egos. Then my editor, Jimmy, left the *L.A. Times* for a job with *The Boston Globe*, and he started pestering me to come work for him here. Finally, after the Red Sox won the World Series–twice!– I couldn't resist. I've been here since March."

Julia nodded. It made sense that Sean was a journalist; he was obviously good at getting information from people. She herself had revealed more to him in the last twenty minutes than to anyone else in recent memory. Maybe it wasn't entirely the fault of Ashtanga.

"Do you have any kids?" she asked.

"No kids." Sean's expression suddenly changed; he was clearly done discussing his marriage and his wife's death. "So now you know about me. Tell me about you."

Compared to Sean's impressive achievements and emotional upheavals, Julia's own life seemed so—mundane. She toyed with the handle of her mug and began reciting her post-high-school résumé. "I went to B.U. for college..."

But before she got any further, Sean interjected. "Holy *shit*! That is a *rock*!"

Julia followed his gaze, which had landed, of course, on her left hand— on her engagement ring.

She found herself staring at it, too, with a strange detachment—as if that ring weren't on *her* finger, on *her* hand. For the first time ever, she wondered if her ring was tacky. Could it be that she, the epitome of understatement-bordering-on-invisibility, had somehow crossed the line into *crass*?

"It is big, isn't it?" she said.

"*Big*?" said Sean. "That thing has more carats than..."

"Bugs Bunny?" she said.

"Something like that. I was going to come up with some really clever pun, but I was blinded by that massive hunk of ..."

"Diamond," said Julia, stating the obvious. And not just any diamond— the *quintessential* diamond, of impeccable quality and clarity, in a stunning platinum setting dusted with multiple smaller diamonds, creating an overall effect of moonlight on hard-crusted snow.

Sean gave a short laugh. "So I take it you're engaged. Either that or you've got really weird taste in jewelry."

His tone was snide, even bordering on—*rude*.

Julia inhaled sharply. "I have exquisite taste. As does my fiancé. Even better than me, probably!"

"Well, good for him," said Sean. "And for you. That's important in a life partner."

She bristled at his condescending tone. "What's your problem, Sean? Do you have diamond envy? Is it a size thing?"

"Oh, trust me, I have no issues with size," he shot back. "I'm all set there."

Julia could only look at him, confused. Clearly, they weren't talking about diamonds anymore. And sweet, studly Sean Harris was being kind of a jerk!

She just couldn't understand why.

She glanced down again at her engagement ring, a precious treasure that had belonged to Asher's great-grandmother. It wasn't crass; it was *gorgeous*. How dare he make her feel ashamed, even for a moment, of her breathtakingly beautiful ring?

In the next moment, though, she had a flash of understanding. Her indignation instantly dissolved into sympathy. "Oh, Sean, I'm so sorry. It didn't even occur to me what a sensitive issue marriage must be for you. After losing your wife. Jenny."

In that moment, Sean, who'd looked on the verge of spewing forth another biting remark, simply deflated.

Yes, thought Julia with some satisfaction, she'd hit the nail on the head. That was one of the advantages of being an introvert, the additional insight it offered into human nature. Not to mention being a vegan—a way of life that invariably deepened one's connection with all living creatures, with the earth itself. She looked at Sean, doing her best to convey only compassion and emotional support, to invite his trust. To let him know that he was in the presence of a sympathetic soul. A friend.

He was silent for a few moments. Clearly, this was an extremely uncomfortable subject for him. Understandably so.

You're safe, Sean, she mentally telegraphed. *You can talk to me.*

Her telepathic reassurances apparently had their intended effect, for he finally spoke.

"Umm, well, that's very understanding of you." He gave a little laugh and shook his head. "Oh, Julia, you're sweet."

Julia immediately grew suspicious. "Why am I sweet?"

Sean laughed again. "For misinterpreting my self-serving male motives. My wife died over ten years ago. I mean, I still miss her every day, but it's not exactly a fresh wound. So yes, marriage *is* a loaded issue for me, but that's not why I was being a prick about your ring."

Now Julia was even *more* confused. "So why ..."

He shrugged. "Oh, it probably *was* diamond envy–no, it definitely was. I felt threatened by the size of that thing. It aroused my primitive survival instincts, and I attacked. I'm sorry," he said, reaching across the table and squeezing her hand for emphasis–the hand with the rock. "Really sorry. Please accept my apology. I shouldn't have insulted your ring. It's beautiful."

Thrown by all the sorrys, Julia felt embarrassed that her intuition had been so off-base. She should have learned by now that people–especially *men*–were almost never as emotionally complex as she imagined.

And what could possibly have aroused Sean's primitive survival instincts?

Sean looked sheepish. "I guess I was just disappointed to find out that you're spoken for. That I wouldn't be able to get..."

Here, he hesitated, and Julia wondered if he was going to say "into your pants."

The thought caused a surge of energy in, well, her pants.

"Anywhere with you," he finished. "After all these years, I was finally getting a glimpse into the mysterious Julia Jones. I was hoping I'd get to spend some more time with you."

Julia, on her part, was dumbfounded to hear that her relationship status mattered one iota to Sean Harris. *Sean Harris!* Jolene would never believe it.

"Oh," she said.

Sean smiled, his eyes very blue. Julia wondered if they changed color, depending on the weather or what he was wearing. She'd bet they did.

"Can I at least walk you home?" he said.

"Sure," she said. "That would be nice."

Sean insisted on paying the check, and they stepped outside.

Julia's yoga pants were sticking to her, and the breeze on her damp clothing made her shiver. Sean wrapped a friendly arm around her, just to warm her up. As they walked the few short blocks to her apartment on

Salem Street, Julia reflected that the people they passed on the street would almost certainly assume that she and Sean were a couple.

Appearances could be so deceiving, she mused. So much existed beneath the surface that she sometimes wondered why the surfaces existed at all, when their only function seemed to be to confuse or mislead. Although, she had to grant, on certain rare occasions, appearance and reality did happen to coincide. In those unusual instances, things were precisely as they appeared.

A few minutes later, they reached her apartment building. They paused in front of the entrance.

"Well," said Sean, "see you at yoga, I guess. If I ever go back to that class, that is." He looked at her for another long moment and said, "God, I wish you were single."

Julia gazed into his blue eyes. "Technically," she said, "I still am."

And that was all it took for him to lean forward and kiss her.

His lips were warm, a fiery contrast to the cool night air. Julia was no longer chilly; in fact, her whole body felt hot—as did Sean's. She wondered vaguely whether they might spontaneously combust.

When they finally parted, he looked at her questioningly, as if searching her face for her reaction to this sweaty encounter.

But as much as Julia didn't want to lose the moment, it was too late. She was already back in her head, thinking.

Glancing down, she saw that her left hand, ring and all, was resting casually, familiarly, on Sean's arm. She snatched it away. Over the course of the evening, she realized, she'd told Sean he was cute, she'd told him he was hot, she'd discussed her mother's death, and she'd freely admitted her high school loser-dom. Essentially, she'd laid *everything* out on the table—so not her style. How ironic that she'd been heading off to an Ashtanga class, determined not to let her emotional aversion deter her from persevering in an unpleasant but physically beneficial practice, only to be confronted with her own susceptibility to temptation.

"I shouldn't have done that," she said, making herself look at him. His eyes were indeed a different color now—more of a slate-gray, almost black. "But I couldn't resist kissing you at least once."

Sean smiled faintly. "At *least* once?" He leaned toward her again, but this time Julia held him off.

"*Just* once. For old times' sake."

His smile faded. "We had no old times."

Julia shrugged. "Yeah, well, anyway. Okay then. Good night."

Sean was staring at her in seeming disbelief, as if waiting for her to change her mind. Now, his blue eyes were almost impenetrably dark.

She could only look back at him helplessly. What else was there to say?

At last, he sighed. He smiled a poignant but genuine smile. "I am happy for you, by the way."

"Thank you," said Julia, touched.

"Although, I have to say, you were kissing me like someone who really wanted to be kissed."

She bristled. "Trust me, Asher kisses me—just, well, anyway. Thanks for walking me home." She turned pointedly away and went to unlock the front door of her apartment building.

"You're welcome," she heard him say.

As she turned her key in the lock, she couldn't resist a backward glance. Sean Harris was already walking away.

. . .

Julia trudged up the stairs to her apartment, a whirlwind of emotions distracting her from the first hints of post-Ashtanga muscle soreness (which, she'd learned, would hit full-force in another eighteen hours or so). So this was how it felt to be flirted with, lavished with attention, *kissed*, by Jefferson High School dreamboat Sean Harris—something she'd longed for for most of her high school years.

The only trouble, of course, was that she *wasn't* in high school anymore. And even *more* importantly, she wasn't single, except technically. She was engaged to a man she loved—*the* man she loved. She wasn't supposed to be kissing people simply because she felt like it, in some pitiful attempt to relive high school glory days that never were. Her lips were spoken for!

She paused on the staircase, not ready to be home, where she'd have no choice but to face herself. How could she have done this? She'd betrayed her own character, and Asher, by wanting Sean so intensely. She'd hesitated hardly a moment before succumbing to his overtures.

Pathetic, she thought. So starved for high-school-level coolness that she'd sunk to this adolescent behavior.

That lovely romantic glow she'd experienced was already but a distant memory. With a contemptuous shake of her head, she climbed the remaining stairs to her apartment. Once inside, she retrieved her cell phone and sent a text message to Asher, who was still in London. Texting had become the easiest way for them to stay in touch when he was away.

I miss you, sweetheart! she wrote. *xoxoxo*

A minute later, her phone flashed an incoming message from him.

I miss you more, angel! Back Monday. Love you. xxx

Her heart swelled, and for a second she felt okay again. But a moment later, her mood plummeted further still. Some "angel" she was. How could she have jeopardized *this*, all that she and Asher had—for *nothing*?

She fired off a second message, this time to Kat.

Meet me tomorrow after work? I really need to talk.

Never-unplugged Kat responded almost instantaneously, as Julia had known she would.

Sure, 6:30 @ CSP? I'll bring us dessert from VG.

By "CSP" Kat meant the Christian Science Plaza, a park a few blocks from Kat's condo on Massachusetts Avenue. It was a favorite after-work meeting spot of theirs. And "VG," Julia knew, referred to Veggie Galaxy, a diner in Central Square, in Cambridge. The shorthand was typical of her and Kat's communications; there was nothing like a friend with whom you didn't have to spell everything out, thought Julia thankfully.

Great! she texted back—even though she wasn't feeling great about much of anything.

Still, the right course of action was clear. She owed it to Asher to steer clear of Sean Harris–at all costs.

She set down the phone and tried to draw some consolation from the evening's one positive ramification: she was *more* than morally justified in never going to yoga again.

Chapter 9

Kat was already sitting by the Reflecting Pool when Julia walked up to the Christian Science Center Monday evening. Her attention absorbed by the two containers in front of her, each containing two half-slices of vegan cheesecake (one regular, one chocolate), drenched in a thick peanut butter sauce and topped with gobs of whipped coconut cream, Kat didn't at first notice her friend approach.

"Don't you dare eat my whipped coconut cream," said Julia.

Kat looked up. "Good timing! And I was only going to eat mine, I swear." She handed Julia one of the boxes. "I couldn't decide between regular cheesecake and chocolate, so I had them give us each some of both."

Julia took in the desserts. "Peanut butter sauce? This looks incredible. Thanks."

She took a seat next to Kat on the bench. Although it was still warm out, there was an underlying coolness to the September air. Fall was on its way.

"No problem," said Kat. She wasted no further time in tasting her whipped coconut cream. "Oh, my God. *Heavenly.*" She gazed appreciatively upon the expanse of water, which shimmered with the sun's waning rays. "You know, I don't know much about Christian Science, and I probably wouldn't be a fan of it if I did, but you've got to admit they nailed it when they created this place. It's so tranquil here. It makes me feel contemplative. That's a word, right? Contemplative?" Julia nodded, but Kat, who was now sampling the butter sauce, paid no attention. "Mmm, *beyond* heavenly. Orgasmic."

Kat was enjoying herself so immensely that it took her a moment to notice that Julia was crying.

"Jules!" she said, clearly baffled. "Cheesecake is supposed to make everything better, not make you cry! What's wrong?"

Compelling as the desserts were, Julia had been thinking of little but her romantic transgression. She sniffled and took a forkful of whipped coconut cream. It *did* seem to stem the tears a little, probably because all the saturated fat was now clogging her tear ducts. "What's wrong with *me* is the question. I'm engaged to an incredible man, I love him, I have *the* most beautiful ring in the world, and the most beautiful dress..."

"And soon a beautiful castle," put in Kat.

"Exactly! And soon a castle. So why do I go and fuck everything up?"

Kat paused mid-bite. "What are you talking about? What'd you fuck up?"

Julia's lip quivered slightly. "I cheated."

Kat's face showed her shock. "With who?" she said. Her cheesecake bite teetered precariously on the edge of her fork until, just in the nick of time, she delivered it safely to her mouth. "Whom?" she hastily amended, not wanting improper verbiage to distract her friend from more interesting matters.

Julia dabbed at her eyes with a napkin. "I guess it wasn't exactly cheating. I mean, it was, but I didn't have sex."

At that, Kat couldn't quite suppress a roll of her eyes. It was clear what she was thinking: dear, maddening, Victorian-minded Julia. "Jules, it's not cheating to have a lewd thought. To be attracted to someone else. Not if you didn't actually *do* anything."

"I *know* that," said Julia. "I *did* do something, that's the problem." She drew a deep breath and spoke her truth. "I kissed Sean Harris."

While it was apparent that Julia considered this monumental news, the name meant nothing to Kat. "Who's Sean Harris?"

In a torrent of words, Julia recounted the story of Ashtanga and Sean—and their kiss.

When she'd finished, Kat grinned. "Sounds hot."

"That's it?" said Julia. "That's all you have to say?"

Kat had probably never in her life answered "yes" to that particular question—nor did she do so now. "Well, no. I mean, okay, it probably wasn't something Asher would have wanted you to do. Probably not what you *should* be doing if you really intend to get married."

"Of *course* I really intend!" said Julia. "Do you think I'm playing here? That I just wanted a diamond ring? Or a castle?"

"No, no, of course not," said Kat. "Calm down. What I meant to say is that it probably wasn't the best thing you've ever done, but seriously, Jules, a kiss is just a kiss. It's different from having sex. Not to mention, there were extenuating circumstances. It's only natural that you'd be more susceptible to the charms of your high school crush, who's so built up in your mind that what real-life man could possibly measure up."

"Built up not just in *my* head," Julia felt important to clarify. "The heads of probably ninety-nine-point-nine-nine percent of the female alumni of Jefferson High School."

"Got it," said Kat. "Let's face it, Jules, you're about to make a lifetime commitment. It's a big deal. It's not surprising you felt compelled to act out."

"Haven't I already made a lifetime commitment?" said Julia. "Isn't that what being engaged is?"

"I would say that getting engaged is more like making a *commitment* to make a lifetime commitment. No, an appointment—an *appointment* to make a lifetime commitment. It's not quite the same as the commitment itself."

"I don't know," said Julia. "I think the marriage ceremony is more a public ceremony honoring a commitment that's already been made."

By now, Kat's patience was wearing thin. "Jules, you're engaged. You're not married. There's a difference. If there weren't, there'd be no need for anyone to get married. So stop with the over-analysis. You were a little impulsive, Asher wouldn't be happy, but Asher doesn't know, and he never *will* know. You got to kiss your high school crush, and it was fun and no real harm done, except to your over-sensitive conscience. Your guilt, your *disproportionate* guilt, is not going to do your fiancé any good. So *let it go.*"

Julia was quiet for a long moment. Then she said, "You're right."

These were possibly Kat's two favorite words—to hear, of course, not to utter. She grinned and took another bite of cheesecake.

Julia frowned. "It just bothers me, though. What Sean said after we kissed."

"What did he say?" asked Kat.

"He said it seemed like I'd been wanting to be kissed."

"Oh, whatever," said Kat. "That's just the male ego. They always like to think that you've been languishing away from unsatisfied sexual desire, like some horny Sleeping Beauty, until you're rescued by them and their enormous cock."

Julia looked indignant. "I didn't touch Sean's cock. We only kissed!"

Kat laughed and patted her leg, clearly finding this all very middle-school. "I get it, I get it. So are you going to be okay about this, Jules? You're not going to get all weird, are you? Oh God, you're not planning to *confess*, are you? To Asher, I mean."

Julia shook her head. "No, I don't think that's the right thing to do. I guess what I'm worried most about is that I'll do it again. I didn't stop myself the last time—what's going to stop me the next time?"

"It'll be different," Kat assured her. "You were caught off-guard last night. And besides, who knows if you'll ever even see him again? You're not planning on it, are you? Now, that would be pushing it."

"No," said Julia. "Sean doesn't even have my number. If I don't go back to yoga, I doubt I'll ever see him again."

It was the truth.

She only wondered why saying so made her slightly sad.

• • •

Fortunately, the rest of the week passed quickly. Julia's sister had been satisfyingly blown away to hear how she'd run into *Sean Harris* at a yoga class, of all places. Otherwise, the Jefferson High heartthrob had been mercifully out of sight and out of mind.

And for that, she had work to thank.

By Friday afternoon, Julia and Whitley had gotten through most of the TS applications they'd received, and Julia was now entering still *more* data into *more* spreadsheets.

Immersed in busywork, her mind began to wander. Kat's mention of confession had stirred up something in her head. Even if she couldn't unburden herself to Asher, she *could* confess to a priest. She hadn't been to confession–or Mass, for that matter–in years, but she'd been raised Catholic, and, on some level, the rituals of Catholicism remained ingrained in her. As morally dubious as it might be to return to a church she'd forsaken long ago for the selfish purpose of lightening a heavy load, it was the best option that had occurred to her thus far. And desperate times called for desperate measures!

There was a small church right around the corner from her apartment– St. Ignatius. An internet search easily turned up the scheduled hours for confession: Saturday, from one to four p.m., or by appointment.

She would do it, she resolved. This very weekend.

The decision made Julia feel a little strange. Proudly heretical Kat would be appalled. She wondered if she ought to confess her planned confession to her friend.

She decided against it. Kat didn't need to know everything.

Chapter 10

Saturday dawned bright and crisp. Julia went for a morning run along the Charles River, which was dotted with colorful sailboats. On sunny days like today, the river took on a magical cast, comprising seemingly infinite shades of blue. Today, though, the sparkling waters only served to remind her of Sean's eyes.

All the better that she'd soon be confessing. It would help her put their brief interlude firmly behind her.

At shortly before one o'clock, Julia left her apartment and set off down the street toward the church, so intent on her mission that she walked directly into another pedestrian who was talking on his cell phone, similarly oblivious. When they collided, he was startled into noticing her.

David Meadow's gaze pierced hers.

"Gotta go," he said into his phone. "A really hot woman wants to talk to me." He slid his phone into his pocket. "Julia! This must be my lucky day."

"When do you *not* get lucky, David?" said Julia.

He tittered. "True."

His maple-syrup-colored hair gleamed in the midday sun, and the faintest hint of scruff lent him the perfect touch of devil-may-care. That, together with his trendy designer jeans and impeccably tailored, open-collared burgundy shirt, gave him the look of a playboy out for a stroll–which made sense, since that was essentially what he was.

He was so preposterous in so many ways, thought Julia. So ostentatious and slick, so ADHD–but for all that, there was something endearing about him, a tiny nugget of sweetness at his core.

"What are you doing now?" said David. "You look thirsty. You look hungry. Let me buy you something. A drink. Lunch. Dinner. More drinks. A diamond ring–no, you've got one already. Okay, a diamond necklace, why not, you're worth it. What do you say?"

They had collided right at the edge of the footpath leading up to St. Ignatius Church.

With a start, Julia recalled her moral errand.

"Umm," she said.

"What? Other plans?" said David. "Don't tell me you're meeting *him*. Billionaire Bartlett."

Asher wasn't quite that–but close. Julia smiled. "Imagine that. Meeting up with my future husband. How risqué to have a date before we're even married."

David frowned for just an instant, before his face settled back into its typical, chronically good-natured expression. Nothing ever got him down for long. "Right. No, that's cool, you know I'm all about Asher. After all, I was the one to introduce you. Biggest mistake of my life, no thanks necessary, but glad to be of service when I can. He's not worthy of you, no question about that, but then again, who is, is the sad reality. Except for, well, you know–yours truly. But I'll grant you, he comes closer than a lot of guys–hell, *most* guys. I support your decision. Okay, 'support' is too strong a word. I accept your decision. I won't stand in your way."

Julia smiled wryly. "Thanks, David. Your endorsement–or acceptance, whatever–means the world to me. But actually, I'm not meeting Asher. I was just about to go in"–she gestured toward the stone building to her left–"here. The church."

David recoiled slightly, clearly unable to fathom any reason for intentionally entering a house of worship. "The church? Why?"

A number of plausible explanations flitted through Julia's mind: spiritual counseling, volunteer work, she was considering becoming a nun (that one would have been a joke). But lying on her way to confession seemed inappropriate. "I'm going to confession."

David's eyes widened.

Julia noted the slight dilation of his pupils, the flush of his tanned face.

Yup, she diagnosed: he was turned on. Not that it took much to get David Meadow's juices flowing.

"So," he said offhandedly, "anything in particular on your mind? Probably just the usual mundane stuff, right? Not going to church? Taking the Lord's name in vain?" With a casualness that didn't fool her for a second, he added, "Impure thoughts, maybe?"

Outwardly, she was grinning, but inside Julia was feeling quite tortured. Suddenly she felt as if she might cry.

"Oh, David," she said.

The next thing she knew, she was in his arms, yes, crying, and he was holding her, stroking her back, murmuring comforting words. "Jules, it's okay. It's fine. You're all right."

She instinctively leaned into him, savoring his warmth, at the same time thinking in the back of her mind that she must be crazy. She was not a crier, she was not a drama queen, and, of all the people in her life, David Meadow was probably the *least* appropriate—or logical—person to turn to for emotional support.

"I don't know what's going on with me," she said, as much to herself as to him. "This wedding has just brought up so much *stuff.*"

David massaged her neck. "I think that's normal. I've never been married, but it must be overwhelming to be about to give yourself over to someone else—for life."

Julia nodded, or tried to, but ended up burying her head deeper in the crook of his shoulder. He drew her even closer.

David continued, his voice a little husky, "And for someone like you, so sensitive, who feels things so deeply, of course this is going to affect you that much more. You wouldn't be you if it didn't."

Julia lifted up her head to look at him. She must look terrible—mushed hair, smeared makeup, tears accentuating her laugh lines and the circles under her eyes. But what did it matter? "David, I kissed another man. That's why I came here, to church. To confess."

His mouth twitched. "Oh. Interesting."

He thought this was funny, Julia realized—a big joke! She wanted to pummel him. "Just shut up. My mistake for actually trying to talk to you about something real. Just forget it." She attempted to extract herself from his arms and push past him toward the church, but he pulled her back.

"Jules, come on, I'm sorry. I didn't mean to..."

"Look," she said, cutting him off, "maybe to you, marriage, commitment, *love* aren't a big deal, but to me they are. I know I haven't been living up to those standards or I wouldn't be here now. But I'm trying, okay? For you, a little dalliance here and there might be acceptable, but to me, this commitment"—she thrust her left hand directly in front of his face—"this ring, is real. And if I can't honor that..." She crumbled. "I don't know what I'm going to do."

David nodded, seeming to grasp what she was saying. "Julia—and please don't take this the wrong way. Do you want to be a wife at all?"

She stared at him dumbly.

"I'm asking seriously, Julia. Women have traditionally gotten the short end of the stick when it comes to marriage. And I know you. You're not pushy about it, but you have an independent spirit. You know who you are. Could that be what's going on here? That completely apart from Asher, it's the institution itself you have reservations about? Because marriage is *not* the only option for two people who love each other."

David Meadow...philosopher, sociologist, *feminist*?

The notion was so absurd that it took Julia a moment to collect herself.

"I'm not here for premarital counseling, David. Especially from you. No offense."

"Ouch!" he said. "But fair enough. I just want you..."

Julia waited for him to finish the thought, but he didn't say anything further.

"You want me?" she said, smiling faintly, if nothing else grateful to him for sparking her sense of humor—which, she sometimes she felt, had all but evaporated the moment her engagement ring had appeared.

David chuckled. "Well, *that* goes without saying. But what I was going to say was, I want you to be happy. You *should* be happy. You're engaged."

"I *am* happy," said Julia. "So happy I can hardly believe it. I almost feel guilty for being so happy!"

His eyebrows went up. "I won't say anything about protesting too much."

Julia's smile faded. "Look, I need to go in and get this off my chest."

The image of forbearance, David nodded. "Okay, go do your thing with the priest, and then come talk to me some more."

"Talk to you about *what*?" said Julia.

"I can't leave you hanging like this. Come meet me at Vittoria when you're done. I'll buy you a cappuccino. Or a drink if you're up for it. I'll take your mind off all your worries, at least for a little while—promise."

"Fine," said Julia, knowing it would be too much trouble to put him off. She'd been spending an inordinate amount of time at Caffè Vittoria lately, but then again, there were certainly more unpleasant ways to spend time (yoga immediately came to mind).

"Outstanding!" said David. "See you in a few."

• • • •

When Julia entered St. Ignatius Church, it was totally empty, apart from an elderly woman hunched over in the very first pew, praying. Julia spied the small wooden confessional booth at the back of the church and walked toward it. Upon stepping inside, she was immediately flooded with Catholic-girl memories.

You can take the girl out of church, but you can't take the church....

She heard a stirring on the other side of the confessional screen—the priest.

"Bless me, Father, for I have sinned," she recited. Catholicism was like riding a bike, she thought; it all came right back to you no matter how long you'd been away.

"What's that?" barked the priest.

She started, wondering if the confessional script had changed. She tried again. "Bless me, Father, for I have sinned," she said, a little louder this time. "My last confession was, umm, I can't remember exactly. A long time ago."

"Have you left the Church? Coming back to wipe the slate clean? What, getting married, are you?"

"Actually, yes, I am!" said Julia. "How did you know? Is this a common thing?"

"Pretty much," said the priest. "All these folks, worried about their past relationships, flings, affairs, infidelities. The men with their mistresses and one-night stands, the women with their indiscretions and boyfriends on the side, wanting to enter this new phase of life, conscience clear. Not a bad idea, of course, but not how this sacrament was intended to operate. It works better if it's a regular part of your life. We're humans, we're sinners, we sin all the time, *all* the time. Silly to think that going to confession once every ten years is sufficient to stay on top of your sin."

"Staying on top of your sin," said Julia. "Like dirty laundry."

"No difference," said the priest. "Same exact thing."

She couldn't resist asking, "Father, what about the sanctity of the confessional? You're talking quite a bit about what happens in here."

The priest laughed apologetically. "One of my biggest shortcomings. Gossip, no two ways about it, you're right, my dear. I can assure you, though, I never talk about individuals. I'll tell tales, which is wrong, no argument, but it's all generalities. Tell me, have I repeated a single name, a single description, given you any insight into the actual identities of these philandering folks?"

"No," said Julia, feeling cross-examined.

"And I won't to anyone else about you. Not one word. Besides, I can't see you, I don't recognize your voice, and I imagine you're not one of my parishioners."

"Well, geographically, maybe. But no, I'm not a regular parishioner."

"Well, there you go," said the priest. "So enough about everyone else. Tell me, dear, what brought you in here today? What is it you're worried about?"

Julia took a deep breath. "For the record, I'm not a philandering wife. And I don't intend to become one."

"Good, good," he said. "A marriage has to be built on trust. It's the only way. There's no substitute."

For a moment, she felt too ashamed to speak.

The priest was used to this, Julia reminded herself. He'd heard it all a million times before–and much worse than this. "I know. That's why I'm here. Father, I haven't been worthy of my fiancé's trust."

"I knew it!" he said. "What, pre-wedding jitters? Did you sleep with someone else? One final fling? You can tell me."

It was discomfiting that this North End priest seemed worldlier than she. "No. There was no–intercourse. We kissed. It was someone I knew from high school."

"Ah, old boyfriend," said the priest.

"He was never my boyfriend. More like an old crush."

"Ah, even harder," he said sympathetically. His "harder" was pronounced "*haahd-uh*," in the traditional Boston twang. "Old crushes are hard" ("*haahd*") "to get over. What might have been and all that."

"Exactly," said Julia, relieved at feeling understood. How foolish to have thought that she was unique in this regard. "But that doesn't make it right, what I did."

"No, of course not," said the priest. "At the same time, though, we must recognize our humanity and our inherent propensity for sin. It is for this reason that we must rely upon our Lord and Savior Jesus Christ to redeem us. Tell me, dear, was this *liaison* planned or premeditated in any way?"

"No, Father, not at all. It was completely spontaneous. I just ran into him."

"And no plans for future meetings?"

"No, Father," she said. "Of course not."

"Fantastic. Fantastic. My child, you have sinned, but with sincere repentance and penance, our sins are forgivable. You did the right thing by coming here. Your transgression was not a mortal sin, you know this, yes?"

"Yes," said Julia.

"As I see it," said the priest, "this incident represents an opportunity for heightened awareness. Entering into the sacrament of marriage entails a solemn vow. It changes not only your last name, but your relationship with the world. And especially your relationship with other men. I know, these days men and women are all supposed to be buddies, co-workers, pals. But you must remember that, as a wife, you have a responsibility to avoid placing yourself in situations where you may be more likely to stray. Your husband, of course, will have a corresponding responsibility."

Julia, having anticipated such an admonition, had her response at the ready. "I know. I'm never going to yoga again."

"Yoga?" said the priest, confused.

"That's where I ran into Sean," she explained. "The guy from high school."

"Ah," he said. "Well, no need to go that far. Marriage doesn't mean giving up all your favorite activities. Just use your judgment."

Julia frowned, disappointed at this lack of priestly enthusiasm for her intended renunciation of yoga. Then again, she was here for forgiveness, not enthusiasm. "Yes, Father."

He seemed to sense her reservation. "What is it, dear? Why are you so troubled?"

She hesitated. "I'm not sure."

"Do you love your fiancé? Do you want to get married?"

"Yes, of course," she said. "Of course I do."

The priest was silent for nearly a minute, gathering his thoughts. When he finally spoke, his tone was warm. "Remember, dear, that doubt is part of life. It's our lot as humans to doubt. Jesus himself experienced doubt–look at his dying words: 'My God, my God, why have you forsaken me?' That wasn't the divine Jesus speaking, it was the *human* Jesus. What I'm saying is, don't attribute too much significance to doubt. That's not to say that you should ignore it completely, but you don't have to let it ruin your day. Or your life."

"Right," said Julia softly.

"My dear, keep God close to your heart" ("*haaht*") "during this important time," he said, his brusque Boston voice reassuring. "Remember, everything you need is right there, in your heart."

He made it sound so simple, thought Julia. "Thank you. I will."

He gave her some prayers to say as her penance, and that was that. She was forgiven.

Julia left the church pleased that she'd taken some action, no matter how unorthodox–or orthodox–it might be. She hadn't waffled, she hadn't wasted time spiraling into morbid reflection. Wasting time, she reflected, was probably the biggest "sin" of all.

She walked into Caffé Vittoria and spotted David at a table by the window–the very table she and Sean had occupied only days before. In a show of ostentatious chivalry, he stood up and pulled out a chair for her. No one did "too much" like David.

"Thanks," she said.

Their waitress appeared, and Julia recognized her from her last visit there–and the one before that.

"I remember you," said the girl with the magenta-streaked hair. "You have a lot of –friends."

Julia ignored the remark, which she thought quite tactless. Yes, she'd been here with three different men in less than a week, but one was her fiancé, and the other encounter had been completely–well, mostly–innocent. As was today's, with David.

David ordered a soy cappuccino for her and an Irish coffee for himself. Then he looked at Julia expectantly. "So? How'd it go?"

"It was interesting," she told him. "The priest was very...pragmatic. No, salty, that's the word. I liked him."

"Did he forgive you?" said David dryly.

"Yes," said Julia. "In fact, he guessed my situation right away! He said it happens all the time."

David chuckled. "I bet. So what was your penance?"

Julia looked at him, dismayed. "I forgot to do my penance! Three Hail Marys, three Our Fathers, and the St. Francis prayer. Which I'll have to look up online. I'd better go." She pushed back in her chair, preparing to leave.

"Jules, Jules, take it easy," said David. "It can wait. You've got a cappuccino coming."

"No, I won't be able to relax. Let me just run over there really fast and I'll be back."

He sighed. "You know, if you weren't so fucking gorgeous, I'd be out of here. Hold on a sec." He pulled out his cell phone and clicked it a few times, and then handed it to her. "Here you go. The St. Francis prayer."

"Perfect, thanks!" said Julia. "I'll be right back."

She hurried back to the church and knelt down in a pew.

"Hail Mary," she whispered. It seemed silly, but a deal was a deal. A slew of insincere prayers couldn't possibly eradicate her misdeed–but then again, her *intent* was sincere, if not the words themselves. She sincerely regretted kissing Sean.

Right?

She considered. No, she didn't exactly regret *kissing* Sean; what she regretted was *when* she had kissed him. She regretted *not* kissing him when she was in high school (not that she'd ever been presented such an opportunity)–and she regretted kissing him *now*.

Her timing had been backwards. That's all.

She finished her prayers a few minutes later with a sense of relief.

Now she was *really* forgiven.

Chapter 11

Julia returned to the café and gave David back his phone.

"Thanks for the technology," she said. "It's a beautiful prayer. The St. Francis prayer, I mean."

He nodded. "Good to know. I'll have to check it out."

Right, she thought.

He smiled. "Hey, do you think having one prayer in my search history will cancel out dozens of porn searches?"

"Dozens?" said Julia.

"Okay, hundreds? Thousands? Hundreds of thousands?"

She shrugged. "Sure, why not? If prayers can't do that, what are they good for?"

"I wholeheartedly agree." David leaned back in his seat and sipped his Irish coffee. "By the way, I told them to hold your cappuccino until you got here. I knew you'd want it hot."

Julia eye him warily from across the table. With David, she was sensitive to comments she wouldn't have thought about twice coming from anyone else, making for a conversational obstacle course of double-entendres. In some ways, it was fun. In other ways, it was exhausting.

"Which brings me to my next subject," he said. "While you were doing your thing at the church, I was able to give your situation some real thought."

"My *situation*?" said Julia.

"Just hear me out. And keep an open mind."

Now Julia was *really* wary. Keeping an open mind around David Meadow was generally not the most advisable course of action. She had a strong sense that it would be best to cut off this line of conversation at the pass. She began making her excuses. "Listen, David, I can't stay long. I've been meaning to get in some painting." Which was true–even if it was something she'd been "meaning" to do for over a year now.

He laid a firm hand on her forearm. "Your painting can wait. This is important."

At that moment, the pink-haired waitress returned with Julia's cappuccino.

Julia sighed internally; apparently she wasn't going anywhere just yet. "Thanks," she told the waitress. She stirred her drink and waited for David to continue.

"You promise you'll listen?" he said. "With an open mind?"

Him telling *her* to listen–hilarious.

"I'll listen, I'll listen," she told him.

He looked satisfied. "All right then. I wanted to discuss what happened with that high school classmate of yours–Sean, was it? I get the sense you've been feeling extremely guilty over that little incident. Am I right?"

Julia brightened. "Actually, I'm feeling a lot better about it now that I confessed. Talking to the priest sort of helped reset me. Not that I think he has any special forgiveness powers or anything. I mean, I'm not a practicing Catholic–I don't even really believe in God! But I think it helped just to take some action. There really is power in action, you know?"

"Right, right, the power of action," said David, sounding supremely uninterested. "But you *were* feeling pretty horrible about it, right?"

"Well, yeah. I felt guilty enough to go to confession."

"Maybe even *excessively* guilty?" he pressed.

She shrugged. "Maybe. I definitely felt pretty awful about it. I don't know if I felt guiltier than I *should* have felt, though. Kat seemed to think so, but that's pretty typical. My guilt sensors are much more robust than hers–yours, too, probably," she added with a smile.

But David didn't smile back. He nodded very seriously, as if she'd just confirmed an important point. "Exactly. On that note, let's talk for a minute about your background. I think it would be helpful to take a look at your relationship history."

It was all Julia could do not to laugh out loud. "David, I didn't realize you'd become a life coach."

He looked miffed. "Please, Julia. You promised to listen with an open mind. Enough with the joking around."

Mr. Let-Me-Entertain-You telling *her* to stop joking around? Again, hilarious. This was going to be good, she could tell.

"All right," she said. "Go ahead."

But it seemed David was going to make her wait a little longer for the punchline. He took a final swig of his drink and, in one fluid motion, signaled the waitress, who scurried over, annoyingly eager to do his bidding.

David ordered another Irish coffee. "How about you, Jules? Refill?"

"Sure, why not," she said. At this rate, her blood would soon be fifty percent soy milk, fifty percent espresso, but if this was going to be an extended conversation—and it seemed that it was—she'd need the sustenance.

"Another soy cappuccino, please," David told the waitress. "And can you make it an extra-large? We're going to be here a while."

Julia suppressed a groan. Just as she'd feared.

"We don't have any larger mugs," said the waitress. "How about this? I can ask the barista to make it in a teapot, and you can pour from that."

"Perfect," David answered for Julia.

A few short minutes later, David's mug had been refilled—and between them rested an enormous ceramic teapot, filled with steamed soy milk and espresso.

"I'm never going to be able to drink all of that," said Julia.

The comment seemed to delight David. "And that, in fact, is the *perfect* segue into what I wanted to discuss with you."

"Oh?" said Julia. Yes, this was going to be *really* good.

David leaned forward in his chair. "I'd like to share a theory. You haven't had many serious relationships, have you, Julia."

She shifted uncomfortably. "That's your theory?"

"No, no, I'm just laying the groundwork. I'm right, though, yes? You don't open yourself up to just anyone."

Julia shrugged. "You could say that."

"And sexually," he said. "You haven't been with many men, have you?"

Julia was less than crazy about the direction this conversation seemed to be taking. "Is that a question, or just another assumption you've made about me?"

He gave her a tolerant look. "It's my own deduction. I would like to ask you a question, though. I hope you feel comfortable enough to answer me honestly."

She rolled her eyes. "Go ahead."

David leaned in even closer. "Julia," he said, his voice practically a whisper, "were you a virgin when you met Asher?"

She leaned forward as well, so that her face was only inches from his. "David," she whispered back, "I was thirty-two when I met Asher."

He continued to hold her gaze. "And?"

She looked away. "Not that this is *any* of your business. But no, I was not a virgin when I met Asher."

If she'd hoped that would be the end of it, she should have known better.

"In that case," said David, "tell me–how many men had you been with before Asher?"

Julia blinked. "This is *so* not your business."

"Just tell me," he said.

She took a moment to pour herself some more soy cappuccino. It actually *was* kind of nice having a whole pot-full. "Been with, in the biblical sense?"

He nodded.

"Two," said Julia. "Two men. I dated other people, of course. And fooled around. But there were only two that I actually slept with."

"Tell me about them," said David. "Who were they?"

"What, you want names?"

"Just tell me, Julia," he said wearily. "I'm your friend."

As much as she wanted to stonewall him, Julia knew it was useless to even try; there was no derailing the David Meadow train once it had left the station. "The first guy was Chris. I met him on line–that is, on a real line!– at a coffee shop on Newbury Street. Remember when things like that used to happen?"

"And when exactly was this?" said David.

"I was twenty-four. So now you know. I lost my virginity at age twenty-four. Probably twice the age you were when you lost yours, am I right?" If there *was* a way to derail the David Meadow train, it was by giving him an opening to brag about his sexual escapades.

He didn't take the bait. "What was your relationship like with this guy? Chris? Your sexual relationship, I mean."

Again, Julia wondered futilely how in the world he'd gotten her talking about her sexual history. But she'd already told him the worst of it–Julia Jones, the love-starved twenty-four-year-old virgin. No point holding back now.

"It was wonderful," she said. "He was really sweet. We had a lot of fun." She paused, trying to find the words to best explain. "I will say, though, it wasn't quite what I'd expected. After holding out for so long, I thought that sex would be cosmic, totally mind-blowing. And don't get me wrong, I loved being with him that way. But it just didn't seem very, *important*, I guess is the best way to put it. My expectations were probably too high. I'd waited so long that maybe I'd just built it up a lot in my mind and was destined to be disappointed."

This explanation clearly held no water with David. "That's ridiculous. You *should* have high expectations. Sex *should* be mind-blowing and cosmic. And more. How did it end?"

Julia sighed. "Really suddenly. We dated for almost three years, and it was pretty serious–or at least so I'd thought. And then one day, out of the blue, he told me he was getting back together with his ex-girlfriend. She'd tracked him down on social media, and he realized he'd never stopped loving her, and that was that."

David nodded, still all business. "Okay. So that was guy number one. Now tell me about guy number two."

"The second guy was Noah. I was twenty-eight. We met at Harvard Bookstore. A doctor was giving a talk on a book he wrote about medical research and the problems with animal testing."

"A vegan thing," said David, already bored. "Got it. How long did you date him?"

"A little over two years. He was finishing up a Ph.D. at MIT, and he got offered a tenure-track position in Kentucky that he felt he had to take. And that was pretty much it. I went to visit him once, but it just kind of fizzled out after that."

"And the sex?" said single-minded David.

Julia thought about it. "Honestly, it was better with Chris. Sex with Noah was–pleasant. Just not very exciting. Kind of how I feel about pasta. I enjoy it when I'm eating it, but I don't think about it when I'm not. I don't dream about it. And I wouldn't miss it one iota if I never had it again in my life."

Julia suddenly realized she'd revealed far more than she'd ever intended; David was going to think she was a cold, *cold* piece of work. And maybe she was. Maybe she just wasn't a very sexual person.

There were worse things, she assured herself. There were rewards to an intellectual life.

"So there you have it," she said, forcing herself to meet his gaze. "Inhibited, frigid, repressed–go ahead, jump to any conclusion you want. I don't know why you're asking me all these questions, but there you go. That's my sexual history in a nutshell. Two guys, two mediocre sexual relationships. So what? I have nothing to be ashamed of."

David's eyes widened. "Of course you don't. I wasn't suggesting that you do."

Julia was suddenly embarrassed at her overreaction. Again, protesting too much, anyone?

"Honestly," said David, "nothing you've told me comes as a surprise. It's all pretty much what I imagined." He allowed a pregnant pause to build. "And now for my theory. Are you open to some advice?"

She shrugged. "Sure."

"Again, just keep an open mind. And know that I have your best interests at heart." He made a little V-sign with his fingers and tapped his heart twice for emphasis. "Now, I'm not normally an especially unselfish guy—no, I take that back, I am pretty generous. But keep in mind that the subject we're discussing here is my number-one area of expertise."

Julia smiled wryly. "What's that? Marriage? Infidelity?"

David gave a smug toss of his handsome head. "Sexual satisfaction, sweetheart. You've got some serious exploration to do."

It suddenly dawned on Julia: he was going to recommend a sex toy. David loved gadgets, and it was no secret that he loved sex—and what other sort of guidance could he possibly have to offer?

In the next instant, though, another possibility occurred to her. "Are you going to tell me to try having sex with a woman?"

He looked startled. "No, that's not what I was going to say. Why, is that something you've –"

"Stop it!" said Julia. "Look, I want to make absolutely clear that I have no complaints about my sex life with Asher. He's ..."

Here, she hesitated. Again, this was *so* not David's business. Was he simply fishing for information? Could that be what this conversation was really all about—lurid details for him to jerk off to later?

"Asher is amazing," she said. And it was true. They didn't make love that often, maybe a few times a month, but certainly not due to any lack of desire on either of their parts—far from it. It was just that Asher was so incredibly busy, and he was away so much. And, most of all, he liked to do things right. When he made love to her, he invested heart and soul. She could feel it, the way he gave her *everything*. If it weren't so wonderful, it might even be overwhelming. And she was certainly happy to forgo a little quantity in favor of some serious quality.

David was right about the validity of high sexual expectations, she realized. Sex with Asher *was* cosmic and mind-blowing—a true union of bodies and souls.

Although, it now occurred to her, a little more spontaneity might be fun. And she played a part in this, too; if on-the-fly fooling around was something she wanted, she could–and would–encourage it. After all, when had she ever asked anything of Asher and been denied?

Never.

She took a moment to consider the circumstances in a new light–using that open mind that David had urged upon her. Yes, poor Asher was a perfectionist of the highest order. No doubt the pressure he put on himself to perform in *every* capacity, including sexual, took an enormous toll. His overly demanding mother had made him feel inadequate in countless ways. As his wife-to-be, it was *her* responsibility to let him know that with her, he didn't have to be perfect–that their sex life didn't always need to be a perfect union of spirits. Sometimes it could just be fast and fun and furious.

Julia smiled to herself at the thought. Who knew? Maybe this would even mark the start of a whole new sexual chapter for her and Asher. She'd certainly never expected inspiration or wisdom to come to her through David Meadow, of all people. But she'd take it where she found it!

The unwitting source of inspiration had apparently gleaned that her thoughts were elsewhere. David patiently sipped his Irish coffee, waiting for her to return to earth.

Noting his avid expression, Julia could tell that whatever it was that he had to say, it was extremely important to him. She forced herself back to the present. "I'm sorry. Go ahead. What's your theory?"

He grinned, obviously eager to continue. "My theory has nothing to do with Asher. It's about you. About your sex life *before* Asher."

"Okay," said Julia. "My sex life before Asher. What about it?"

"It wasn't good enough," he said forcefully; indeed, he all but *pronounced* it. "Not good enough for you."

Julia laughed. "I appreciate the sentiment. And you know, you're probably right. But so what? That's the past. Now I'm set for life. Sexually speaking." She smiled flirtatiously, a tactic that in the past had always succeeded in distracting him, no matter what the topic.

This time, though, to her astonishment, it didn't work. In fact, David looked downright pensive. Clearly, big things were brewing inside that boy-toy head of his–which didn't bode well. David and deep thinking didn't mix.

"Think of it this way," he said. "Imagine an orphan girl who's grown up in abject poverty and has never gotten enough to eat—*ever*. She's hungry *all* the time. She's never *not* had a gnawing feeling in her stomach."

Julia nodded, humoring him.

"And then," he continued, his blue eyes brightening as he warmed to his story, "the orphan girl is adopted by two wonderful, well-to-do parents. For the rest of her life, she'll always have a warm bed and three wholesome, nutritious meals a day. She'll never again have to worry about where her next meal is coming from."

Julia had no idea where David was headed with this parable—she assumed it was a parable. "Sounds great. Are you suggesting that I adopt an orphan girl?"

"No, no, that's not my point. Although you would be a great mom. But yes, it's a happy ending for the orphan girl." He paused portentously. "But it's *boring*. If that's all she gets, I pity her."

"What are you talking about?" said Julia.

"Think about it," said David, his tone urgent. "The orphan girl needs to make up for a lifetime of deprivation. She needs a family friend who'll take her out and spoil her rotten, who'll give her potato chips and ice cream sundaes, who'll let her eat cookie dough and frosting straight from the bowl until she's sick to her stomach. She needs decadence, over-indulgence. She needs to experience what it's like to have *more* than enough." He sat back in his chair, allowing the suspense to build before he revealed what was clearly intended to be the penultimate lesson of the orphan-girl story. "Or a lifetime of enough will never *be* enough."

Julia looked at him, still not comprehending. Clearly, he was discussing more than food, but she had no idea the point he was trying to bring home. "Why can't her new parents do that for her?"

"Not their job," said David. "They're supposed to help her learn healthy eating habits and make sure she's eating her vegetables. They don't want her stuffing herself on junk food. No, this sort of task requires an outsider. It's an outsider role."

The hairs on Julia's arms prickled; suddenly, every cell in her body was on high alert. When David reached for her hand, she nearly jumped out of her skin.

"It's *my* role, Julia," he said solemnly. "I can help you find the closure you need in order to fully commit yourself to Asher after a lifetime of sexual deprivation. It's what you need. And I think, if you get past your puritanical notions about sexuality and fidelity, it's also what you *want*."

For a moment, Julia was too shocked to respond.

She snatched her hand away. Who knew where that hand had recently been? Or more to the point, she could make a pretty good guess where that hand had been.

"You douchebag!" she said. "You self-serving, manipulative *asshole*!" In her peripheral vision, she noticed the pink-haired waitress staring. "You're sick, David. Sick! To betray my trust, to take what I told you in *confidence*"– to her chagrin, she was now choking back tears–"and twist it around and use it to try to get me to sleep with you–it's borderline sociopathic. No, scratch the 'borderline.' It's *full-on* sociopathic."

She stood up from the table, so outraged she was tempted to swipe their coffee mugs–and that ridiculous, cappuccino-filled teapot–off the table, her fury rivaled only by her shame at having been idiotic enough to confide in this … *cretin*. Suddenly fearing she might dissolve into a puddle of angry tears right there in the café, she looked to her feet–a grounding technique recommended by Pepper, the yoga (yes, blasted yoga) teacher.

And ground her it did. In the next instant, the rage rushed right out of her, leaving in its place only an icy resolve to get very, *very* far away from David Meadow and his self-serving sexual maneuverings.

She put those two feet of hers to excellent use and walked out the door.

Of course, David wasn't one to give up so easily. He tossed a handful of bills onto the table (probably hundreds, thought Julia contemptuously, knowing the casualness with which David spent money) and came chasing after her. "Please, Julia. It's not like that at all. I want to *help* you."

"Thanks but no thanks," she said, not slowing her pace, not even looking at him.

Undeterred, he continued walking alongside her. "Jules, sweetheart, don't be like that."

Like what? she thought. *Sane?*

"Oh, come on, Jules," he said, a note of playfulness creeping into his voice. "I'm offering you the opportunity of a lifetime here. After all, don't you want to find out if the grass is greener in...the *Meadow*?"

Julia stopped in her tracks and stared at him.

He looked hopeful. Yes, she realized incredulously, he *still* thought he had a shot.

David's mouth curled upward in a suggestive half-smile. And then, in the next moment, he was leaning toward her...

It wasn't until his lips were mere millimeters from hers and she'd caught a whiff of whisky and coffee and expensive cologne that Julia grasped that he actually meant to *kiss* her.

Instinctively, before she even knew what she was doing, she'd slapped that handsome, hopeful face of his.

The resulting *whack!* was satisfyingly resounding—and effective. It took the wind right of him.

She walked swiftly on, and this time he didn't try to follow.

Chapter 12

Julia closed her apartment door behind her, her head spinning. It just went to show, there was no telling what offers might come your way in a day.

Not to mention, pouncing on her after confession–*confession!* David had truly plumbed new depths.

Her stomach still churning from the teapot of cappuccino she'd ingested, she decided to brew some tea. Hot hibiscus tea never failed to calm her nerves, and the vivid pink color alone always lifted her spirits.

Settled on the couch a few minutes later, warm mug in hand, she did feel a bit better. She wondered what Kat would make of David's offer. She'd so often found herself in the position of defending David to Kat that she was almost reluctant to tell her friend the story. Then again, at this point, she hardly needed to worry about sullying David's good name!

It was the tea, she decided; it always helped clarify things. Coffee was good for getting things done, but for understanding, tea was best.

She needed to talk to Kat.

Julia reached for her cell phone and dialed her friend's number, but the call went immediately to voicemail. She disconnected and sent a text message instead.

Just got an offer I COULD refuse. You will love this.

As she leaned back on the couch, thoughts still swirling like a hurricane in her head, her gaze came to rest on the easel set up next to the west-facing window across the room–the easel she'd all but disregarded of late. She'd chosen that spot for the beautiful natural light it received, especially in the late afternoon. But lately she'd been so caught up in work–and love–that she'd hardly been painting at all. In fact, she couldn't recall the last time she'd made any art.

The blank canvas now stared back at her reproachfully. Today, it seemed, the easel was not so easily ignored.

Julia sighed resignedly. She'd jinxed herself by telling David she'd been meaning to get in some painting; she hadn't meant *today*. But with Asher out of town until Monday, her time was her own, and she had no plans for the rest of the day other than to meet Jolene later for a bite to eat. No more excuses; she'd take an hour this afternoon and paint.

Just then, her phone buzzed–Kat, calling her back.

"Tell me," said Kat. She was panting.

"What are you doing?" said Julia.

"Running. Well, run-walking. Josh at work talked a bunch of us into doing a marathon."

"A *marathon*?" said Julia.

"Well, a marathon relay. There are five people on the team. We each have to run just under five-point-three miles, and the race is the first weekend in November, so we have eight weeks to train. We have a training schedule and everything. I'm supposed to start with twenty-one minutes of run-walking–walk two minutes, run one. So, you can talk while I'm running or walking, but if you need me to respond you'll have to wait till I'm walking."

Julia was still processing the notion of Kat exercising. "Okay. I can do that."

"So what's this offer?" said Kat. Noisy breathing and jarring noises indicated that she was now jogging.

"The offer was from David," said Julia. "You're not going to believe this. He hit on me."

"Why wouldn't I believe that?" said Kat, her breath ragged.

"Well, get this–he did it on my way back from confession."

"*Confession*?" gasped Kat. She was definitely running now.

"It was the Sean thing," said Julia. "I wanted to get it off my chest. So I decided to go to a church and confess to a priest, and I ran into David on the way and ended up spilling everything to him."

"Did you cry?" accused Kat.

"A little," said Julia.

"Well, there you go. No wonder he hit on you. David can't resist a crying woman. He can hardly resist *any* woman, let alone a crying one."

"Actually, there's more to it than that," said Julia. She gave Kat the full account, orphan-girl allegory and all.

Kat was silent–speechless, or maybe just breathless; Julia couldn't be sure.

"Kat?" she finally prompted. "You okay? You're not having a heart attack, are you?"

"Nope, I'm done," said Kat. "I was at fifteen minutes when I got your message. I just hit twenty-one."

"That's fantastic! How do you feel?"

"I feel fucking great," said Kat, laughing. "Shit! I really do."

Julia laughed, too. "Well, good!"

"I'm actually right around the corner from you," said Kat. "Want to meet on the Greenway in about five minutes? I'm just going to grab some coffee first."

"You got it," said Julia.

• • •

A short time later, they'd claimed a bench near one of the fountains lining the Greenway, the tree-lined walkway installed after the seemingly never-ending Big Dig construction had finally finished. Julia had brought her mug of tea, and Kat had an iced coconut milk latte, plus enough napkins and sweetener packets to accommodate at least a dozen people. Kat never traveled light.

"So David wants to give you sex therapy. That's rich." She grinned wickedly. "There's not, maybe, any chance that you might take him up on this, is there?"

"Kat!" said Julia. "Be serious."

Kat shrugged. "Well, he *is* hot. And I know he's a total player, but come on, can you really blame him? He's definitely got animal appeal."

Julia hadn't anticipated this line of "reasoning."

Kat continued, "I mean, if he weren't kind of your boy, I might've taken a roll in the hay with him myself."

Julia gaped. "My *boy*? And when, precisely, have you been scoping out David Meadow?"

Kat groaned. "I haven't, that's my point. And this is exactly why. You wouldn't have liked it."

"Have you had, umm, the *opportunity*?" said Julia. "To be with him, I mean?"

Kat cackled. "Are you kidding me? Every attractive woman–no, make that every *woman*–within a five-hundred-mile radius has had the opportunity."

Julia nodded slowly. "You know, you're probably right. I wouldn't have liked it. I don't know why, I have no claim on David. And I'm certainly not *interested* in him. Especially after today!"

"I know, I know," said Kat. "And I'm not interested in him, either. Well, except sexually. But I figured, why upset"–at the look of protest on Julia's face, she corrected herself–"*disconcert* you, just for a slimy pretty-boy."

Julia gave a short laugh. "Well, thanks. I guess."

Kat looked up at the sky. "Much as I hate to admit it, I *have* been tempted on one or two occasions. Like last summer–remember that night we all went to the Liberty Hotel?" The luxury hotel, actually a renovated prison, had an always-happening outdoor bar.

"I remember," said Julia.

"David and I ended up sharing a car home, since he was heading back in my same direction, to the South End. And when we pulled up to my place, he started getting out of the car, like it was just assumed he was coming in."

"What did you do?" said Julia.

"I told him to get back in the car, and that if I'd *wanted* him to come in, I would've asked him. He just kind of shrugged and said, 'Your loss, babe.' Oh, and then he said, 'It's just a matter of time–you know you want me.' Or something along those lines. He was pretty drunk. And so was I, for that matter. But fortunately not drunk enough to actually invite him in." Kat laughed and shook her head. "Anyway, that's just one of a million examples I could give you. Good old David–testosterone on steroids."

Given this new information, Julia felt extremely foolish that it had ever made her feel even remotely special to be the constant target of David's overtures. In reality, it just made her ... *typical.*

Kat chugged the last of her latte and gathered up her used napkins. "Listen, I'm supposed to meet Josh and the other guys for dinner, so I need to go shower. That's what people do after running, right? I don't know the etiquette."

"Yeah, it's good etiquette not to get too stinky," said Julia.

"I've also started doing green smoothies," said Kat. "I'm not messing around here."

"Clearly," said Julia. "Want to do brunch tomorrow?"

"Twist my arm," said Kat, never one to turn down brunch. "Hasta la vista."

•　　　•　　　•

On her walk home, Julia wondered idly whether someone might possibly have broken into her apartment while she was gone and painted something inspired on the canvas that had been sitting there, untouched, for longer than she liked to remember. After all, why should break-ins necessarily be deprivational? Maybe, as human consciousness continued to evolve, even crime would become philanthropic. Burglars would break and enter people's homes not to vandalize or steal, but to express their creativity and leave gifts, Santa Claus-style. Granted, today's episode with David seemed predictive, if anything, of a *downward* ethical trajectory for humanity. But even so, Julia managed to get herself enthused enough over the idea of compassionate crime that she was mildly disappointed to return to her apartment and find her front door securely locked–and the canvas still painfully blank.

Oh, the daily agony of being an artist! Not since a little over five years ago, when her then-art dealer, Stuart, had gotten a few of her paintings into the now-defunct South End gallery, had she had any identifiable measure of artistic accomplishment. The unfortunate irony was that the artistic agony never ended–even when, by all indications, one had ceased being an artist.

She sighed aloud. She'd learned, of course, that the only time she ever stopped agonizing over painting–or not painting–was when she was actually painting.

Fine, she thought irritably. *I'll do it.*

It took some time to gather up her paintbrushes and oil paints, and to locate the pencil sketch she'd made nearly a year ago which was to serve as the basis for her next piece. She changed into some paint-spattered lounging pants and a T-shirt, and cracked open a window to help diffuse the paint fumes. She thought wistfully of Huck, who would have been launched into a state of exuberant hyper-stimulation by the unfamiliar activity.

As she picked up a paintbrush and got to work, Julia felt an unexpected rush of joy. She'd missed this even more than she'd realized.

Don't get too excited, she warned herself. *You'll only be disappointed.*

But, in fact, she wasn't. As had happened too many times in her lifetime to count, once she began painting, the painting took over. She abandoned her pencil sketch and her preconceived notions of what the piece should be and allowed herself proceed intuitively, more abstractly than was typically her style. How could she have gone nearly an entire year without doing *this*, the thing that, more than anything else, made her feel truly alive?

At the peak of her artistic ecstasy, she caught herself–and laughed. She'd experienced this sort of artistic elation before. And it usually meant that the work itself was crap.

Fortunately, though, when she was in this mode, she tended not to care so much about results. Such was art, such was life: bliss, inspiration, crap, all mixed up in one glorious, ridiculous mess. Granted, it might be a bit pathetic to not be particularly gifted at the activity that she felt she'd been born to do, but there wasn't much she could do about that. Besides, painting was more stimulating than watching TV, it was more enjoyable than yoga (not that *that* was saying much), and it had no calories. And much as she hated to admit it (because it meant she'd have to keep doing this), she did relish this feeling of being alive.

The next thing Julia knew, it was well after seven-thirty. She'd been painting for over four hours. She was ravenous.

She stepped back for a moment to consider the work-in-progress. To her pleasant surprise, it actually wasn't too bad. It was bolder, more daring than her usual naturalist style. She could almost, *almost*, envision it in its final form. She would see it through; she owed it that.

Childishly happy, she grinned proudly to no one. She was an artist again.

Glancing at the clock, Julia realized she'd never make it to Cambridge in time to meet Jolene at eight. She texted her sister to let her know that she was running late, only to learn that Jolene had forgotten about their dinner plans but was still up for getting together. It was annoying but hardly surprising; Jolene considered plans and schedules more like suggestions than actual commitments. They arranged to meet instead for a late-night movie in Kendall Square, near M.I.T. Jolene wanted to see a Turkish documentary about cats.

As Julia cleaned up the mess she'd made in her living room—the kind of mess artists were *supposed* to make—it struck her that Asher had never seen her paint. To her, her job at JoH was merely a temporary diversion from her true vocation, but by this time, Asher probably thought of it as her career. With his connections, he could easily have pulled some strings to get her paintings into a decent gallery, and he'd offered to do so many times. But she'd always declined, determined to make it on her own rather than rely on his influence.

Of course, she *hadn't* made it on her own. She hadn't made it at all.

But right now, when she was still flush with the thrill of painting, none of that seemed to matter. As Julia headed to the bathroom to clean herself up, she gave her work-in-progress one last glance—and smiled. Even if the finished piece didn't end up being any good, she decided, the time she'd spent painting had been *more* than worthwhile.

Because in these past four hours, she hadn't once thought of David Meadow, the Schloss, or Sean Harris—or yoga.

Chapter 13

Kat dumped an entire pitcher of maple syrup onto her French toast before realizing she hadn't left any for Julia. With a guilty glance at Julia's still-dry pancakes, she said, "Sorry, I got a little carried away. Carbing up, you know, for the race."

"The race that's two months away?" said Julia. "Good thinking. No point waiting until the last minute."

"My thoughts exactly," said Kat.

They were ensconced in a booth at Veggie Galaxy, which, in addition to its life-changing cheesecake, offered a diner-style vegan breakfast menu. It was their brunch spot of choice.

Kat signaled to their waiter, who brought them more maple syrup and refilled their coffees.

This sort of excess, Julia noted, she had no trouble enjoying.

Kat grinned. "So any change of heart since last night about David's offer?"

"You must be on sugar overload," said Julia. "Because you're obviously not thinking clearly."

Kat looked offended. "Maple syrup isn't sugar. It's different. It has all kinds of nutrients that actually enhance brain functions. And I need to get quality carbs now that I'm a long-distance runner. A marathon runner."

"Right," said Julia. "Now that you're a marathon-relay run-walker."

"*Anyway*," said Kat. "The more I think about it, David probably *would* show you a really good time. And what's the big deal? It's just sex. Asher's not the jealous type. Maybe, if you express your needs to him sensitively and honestly, he'd be okay with it."

"*Please*," said Julia. "He's not overly possessive, no, but come *on*."

Kat laughed. "Yeah, okay, maybe that *would* be pushing it. In my–not insignificant–sexual experience, even the most powerful men tend to harbor secret insecurities about their sexual prowess."

"Why don't *you* sleep with David?" said Julia. "Maybe, if you express your needs to me sensitively and honestly, I'll be okay with it." She recalled David's parting words. "After all, don't you want to find out if the grass is greener in ... the *Meadow*?"

"Oh, my God," said Kat, setting down her fork. "Did he actually *say* that?"

"He did indeed," said Julia. "So I say, go for it, Kathleen–graze those greener pastures. You don't need a roll in the hay, you need a roll in the *Meadow*!"

They both burst out laughing uncontrollably, drawing looks from people sitting nearby.

They did their best to get a hold of themselves.

"Good God," said Kat, clutching her stomach. "That man is out of this world."

"He's like a different life form," Julia agreed. "But seriously, if you're attracted to him, and sex really *is* no big deal, why *don't* you sleep with him?"

Flippant as the inquiry had been, it was immediately apparent to Julia that she'd succeeded in flustering the normally unflappable Kat.

"Because that would be a bad, *bad* idea," said Kat. "I know his type, and I know me. If I had sex with him, he'd own me."

"Really?" said Julia, intrigued.

Kat sighed ruefully. "Yeah. It kills me to admit it, but it's true. I'm pretty hot for the guy. It's too dangerous. I don't play at that level. He'd eat me alive."

"What's with the self-deprecation?" said Julia. "Are you turning into me?"

"Can we change the subject, please?" said Kat.

"No way," said Julia. "Are you seriously interested in David Meadow? I had no idea!"

"I'm *not* interested," said Kat. "That's what I'm trying to tell you."

"You're not interested because you intuitively know he's not right for you? Or you're refusing to be interested because you're afraid of being hurt?"

"Neither. Both. I intuitively know he would hurt me, and that's not the right man for me. Anyway, it's irrelevant. We're not talking about me and David, we're talking about *you* and David. Remember?"

Julia was enjoying the unusual feeling of having the upper hand with Kat. "Yes, but all of this about *you* and David is *much* more interesting." She grinned. "In fact, now, knowing all this, I could *never* take him up on his offer. Not that I was ever going to," she added hastily. "But I would never take your man. Even temporarily. I mean, not that I could, even if I wanted to."

"Of course you could," said Kat. "Look at you—tall, blonde, funny, artsy, legs up to your neck. You're like the girl next door, with edge. You could get just about any man you wanted."

"You're crazy," said Julia. "I never get men. Not good ones, anyway. I mean, *now* I did, with Asher. But you're the kind of woman men love to be with. You're easy. Not easy, slutty—well, that, too—but easy, low-maintenance. You and Jolene are the man-magnets, not me. And you can *definitely* play at David's level."

Kat groaned. "Look, enough already. We're *both* man-magnets, and we've already spent *way* more time on David Meadow than he deserves. Can we declare the subject officially closed?"

"Agreed," said Julia. Her stomach felt unsettled; for that, she blamed not the (approximate) gallon of maple syrup she'd ingested, but the nauseating David Meadow.

"On another note," said Kat, "have I mentioned that I'm getting ridiculously excited for your wedding? A vacation in Switzerland with you and Asher and his glamorous friends—in a *castle*? I mean, when again will I ever get to hang out in a castle?"

Julia grinned. "Anytime you want! Mi casa, tu casa. Or I guess I should say, 'Mi castle, tu castle.'"

Kat looked startled. "Oh, right! Of course. I keep thinking it's like we're going on vacation and then it'll be over and we'll go back to real life. I keep forgetting this *is* your real life."

Julia's smile faded. "You're telling me. Do you think this will change things between you and me? My being married? Being..." She couldn't bring herself to say it.

Kat laughed. "Rich?"

Julia nodded, embarrassed.

"Nah," said Kat. "After all, we've survived your poverty all these years, working for those misers at Hartland Travel." Julia opened her mouth to defend Carly and Franco, but Kat cut her off. "And we'll certainly survive your being part of high society. Even if I'm still just a regular working-class schlep."

"Yeah, right," said Julia, knowing that Kat had done quite well for herself in the music business—especially lately, since an artist her agency represented had become a worldwide sensation following the release of his groundbreaking bluegrass album. Of course, Asher's wealth was in a different realm.

"Besides," said Kat, "the solution is obvious. I'll just marry one of Asher's rich friends. One of his *hot* rich friends."

"That *is* the perfect solution!" said Julia.

"And fuck David Meadow," added Kat.

Julia laughed. "Or not."

Chapter 14

Monday morning, at her desk, up to her ears in Travel Sabbatical applications, it occurred to Julia that for all of their wedding planning, one issue she and Asher *hadn't* settled was whether she'd go back to work at JoH after the wedding. She wouldn't *need* to work, of course, and Asher had urged her to take some time off or at least scale back to part-time, but they'd never reached a final decision.

She suddenly felt rather desperate to talk to him. But he was still in London, and wouldn't be back until tonight.

She impulsively sent him a text message.

Hi honey! I think I should keep working. At least until after the next TS round.

Her phone buzzed an incoming message.

Angel! Was just about to text you. I'm back early—just landed. Want to talk tonight, Paradiso, 6:30?

Julia grinned at the pleasant surprise. Since Asher flew everywhere on BartTech corporate jets, he wasn't bound by flight schedules. He was referring to Caffè Paradiso, a dark and exotic spot that she loved as much for its name as for its murky vitality. Inhabited at all hours by artists, locals, crusty old Italian men, and the inevitable tourists, it was a North End institution. And finding out that she'd get to see Asher a day earlier than expected had instantly boosted her mood.

She immediately sent off a response.

You just made my day! Can't wait to see you, sweetheart.

At shortly before six-thirty, Julia left work and walked over to Caffè Paradiso, where Asher had already claimed them a corner table. He rose to greet her, and they kissed and hugged tightly before taking their seats.

Julia inhaled deeply, breathing in the rich coffee aromas. "Caffè Vittoria is romantic, but Paradiso is...sexy."

"Oh, you think so, *sexy*?" said Asher, running his fingers lightly up her wrist.

"Yes, I do, *sexy*," she said. "I am so happy to see you."

He played with her fingers. "The feeling, my dear, is mutual."

Eventually, a waiter arrived to take their drink orders, his only response to their requests a curt nod. Julia and Asher exchanged amused looks. North End institutions were sometimes long on atmosphere and short on service.

Just then, Asher's cell phone buzzed. He glanced at the display. "I'm sorry, sweetheart, I need to take this."

"Don't tell me," said Julia. "Odetta?"

Asher laughed. "No, nothing to do with work. I've been waiting to hear from Gareth about an issue we're having with the contractor."

Gareth Knight was the architect handling the renovation of Asher's Louisburg Square house. Lately it seemed that new issues were popping up almost daily—and Julia felt more than a little sympathy for Gareth in that regard. Her detail-obsessed fiancé was undoubtedly as high-maintenance an architecture client as there was.

"It's fine," she said, but Asher was already off to talk in the relative privacy of the café entryway.

Several minutes later, he was still engrossed in conversation. Julia picked up an abandoned *Boston Globe* from a nearby table and began leafing through it, looking for the arts section, which seemed to be missing. She was about to set the newspaper aside when she noticed a familiar byline on the front page of the sports section: Sean Harris.

Her pulse quickened. Her efforts to put her post-yoga encounter with Sean behind her had been so successful that, in some ways, it almost seemed as if it had never even happened—which made it that much more disconcerting to come across this tangible evidence that he not only existed but was, indeed, living and working right here in Boston. Not that she'd thought he'd been lying about working for *The Globe*. But seeing his name in print made it that much more real.

She scanned the article—something about a pre-season Celtics game and the team's prospects for the season. It featured quotes from some of the players and the coach. Julia got the sense that, for all his casual ways, Sean Harris was hob-knobbing with some pretty big names—big, at least, to people unlike herself, who had even a modicum of knowledge of professional sports. She was so absorbed in the article that she didn't even notice when Asher returned to the table.

"You're reading the *sports* section?" he said. "I'm sorry, sweetheart, that tells me how bored you must have been. You're a real sport," he quipped, giving her an apologetic kiss on the lips.

Julia smiled. "Oh, it's fine. I was reading the sports section because I recognized the reporter's name. I went to high school with him."

Asher glanced at the byline. "Sean Harris? That's a pretty common name. You sure it's the same guy?"

If he only knew, thought Julia.

"I'm sure," she said. "I ran into him last week at yoga."

"Nice," said Asher, exhibiting the merest polite interest in yoga, professional sports, and Sean Harris—for which Julia could hardly blame him.

"So is everything okay with the contractor?" she said.

"The contractor? Oh, yeah, it was just an irregularity with the tile installation in the kitchen. No big deal. We got it worked out." Asher grinned. "Gareth was telling me this hilarious story about Rusty."

Julia's smile turned plastic. In her estimation, she'd heard one too many stories about Gareth's high-strung Irish setter, Rusty, of whom Asher was inordinately fond. She couldn't help but resent that he'd never had nearly the same affinity for Huck. Of course, that hadn't been Asher's fault, but simply the unfortunate result of his allergies, which had made both his physical and emotional closeness to Huck—or any cat—impossible.

"Oh yeah?" she said, doing her best to summon some enthusiasm.

"Yeah," said Asher, his expression keen, and Julia braced herself for yet another Rusty tale. They varied in the details, but the theme always involved Rusty's ingenuity, inventiveness, and/or unparalleled brilliance. Asher proceeded to relate the dog's latest antics: this time, Rusty had faked a limp in order to get special treatment from Gareth, who, between Asher's Louisburg Square project and another large project in the Hamptons, had been working nonstop. "She knew just how to manipulate him," Asher finished, his laughter reverberating in the small café. "And people say Irish setters are stupid! Not even close."

Julia laughed along with him, doing her best to get into the spirit. She knew that her weird jealousy of Rusty was illogical, but she envied the bond Asher and Gareth shared in loving the same animal. "That *is* pretty funny. Dogs are great." And it was true; dogs *were* great. "*So* great," she added for emphasis.

"Aren't they?" said Asher. He reached for her hand. "But enough about Rusty. Tell me what's on your mind, sweetheart."

Relieved that they were done discussing the dog, Julia smiled. "It's just beginning to sink in for me that this is really happening. We're getting married—and everything is going to totally change. For both of us, but even more so for me. I'll be moving, for one. And I need to figure out if I'm going to keep working."

He nodded, waiting for her to continue.

Suddenly self-conscious, she said, "I did some painting this weekend. It's not finished, but if you're lucky, I might give you a glimpse of the work-in-progress."

Asher's eyes lit up. "Terrific!"

Julia hesitated, unsure how to tackle the subject of her art. She couldn't let it fall by the wayside again, as she had for most of these past several years. But at the same time, it seemed rather nonsensical to suddenly assert the vast importance of something she'd managed to do almost entirely without in the time she'd been with Asher.

"On that subject," she began, but she again faltered for words. Asher held degrees from the finest schools, where he'd excelled both scholastically and athletically, even earning a spot on the men's Olympic rowing team the summer before his senior year at Yale. Then, after graduating first in his class from Harvard Business School, he'd worked for several years for a London-based communications company before taking on an executive role at his family's already phenomenally successful business—the profitability of which had continued to skyrocket under his leadership.

In short, Asher had succeeded at virtually everything he'd ever set his mind to. Whereas she, a supposed "artist," had managed to support herself—barely—through a job at a nonprofit that had only the remotest connection to art. *That* was the sum total of her professional accomplishments. She had no credibility.

She stared down at her lap, feeling small.

"Honey, what is it?" said Asher. "You can tell me."

Julia forced herself to look at him. "In our time together, you haven't seen me very active as an artist. That's partly because when I met you, I pretty much forgot about everything else."

He rubbed her leg at the implied compliment.

"And also," she said, "my art seems kind of trivial compared to the huge deals you're always putting together."

Asher regarded her seriously. "I hope I've never given you the impression that I think your work, or your art, is trivial. I don't at all. Not in the slightest."

"No, you're wonderful. It's my own doing—or non-doing. But this past weekend, I realized that I've got to make my painting a priority, or it's going to slip away from me forever. And I can't let that happen. It's too important to me."

He nodded, his hand still on her leg.

"The other thing," said Julia, "is that painting is what makes me feel most connected to my mother. Even if I'm not any good at it, I need it for that."

Asher smiled tenderly. "Sweetheart, I understand. How could you possibly think I wouldn't?"

She nodded, for a moment unable to speak. For all his good intentions, Asher *couldn't* understand, not completely. He'd never known Josie, who'd been so open-hearted and warm, a veritable beacon of love—the polar opposite of Asher's overbearing mother. Asher had grown up the constant focus of Sage's exacting attention, forever falling short in his efforts to be what she wanted him to be.

These days, of course, Sage Bartlett had nothing to complain about. Asher was perfect.

"I've seen the photos of the paintings you had in that South End gallery," Asher was saying. "And the mural you did way back when. Julia, you have something special. And even more importantly, it's special to *you*. I think it's wonderful that you're committed to focusing on your painting. It would be wrong for you to let that passion go to waste."

Julia preferred to ignore the subject of her artistic aptitude. "You're away so much that on a practical level, you probably won't even notice if I do more painting. But maybe, once in a while, I might pass on an event so that I can stay home and work. You think you can fend for yourself now and again?"

She'd been avoiding his gaze, wanting to get out the words before she took in his reaction. Now, with some hesitation, she looked directly at him— to find that, of course, her trepidation had been entirely unfounded.

"Julia," he said, "it's *fine*. I won't take it personally if you decide it's a better use of your time to stay home and paint than to come out with me for a night of small talk and schmoozing. And yes, I can entertain myself if need be. I just want you to be happy. That's it."

"Thank you," said Julia. "I know you want me to be happy. And it just so happens that you make me happy. So it all works out." Her tone was light, but her words were heartfelt. "Just so you know, I'm aiming to make you pretty happy, too."

He squeezed her hand. "You do an amazing job of that. And speaking of jobs, what are you thinking about work?"

Julia's expression darkened. "We're just so busy at JoH. The TS project is taking up all of my and Whitley's time. She nicknamed it 'Eliot', after T.S."

"Cute," said Asher. "Although, you know, T. S. Eliot wasn't the healthiest guy. He had all kinds of weird physical ailments."

Julia laughed dryly. "Well, I hope the TS program itself doesn't end up giving *me* all kinds of weird ailments. I don't think I've ever felt so overwhelmed at work."

"If that's the case," said Asher, "why would you want to keep working after the wedding?"

It was a logical question.

Julia shrugged. "They need me. Besides, I can't just become a housewife. You don't even *need* a housewife. You have Angela." Angela, who'd been the Bartlett family's maid for most of Asher's childhood, still came every day to cook and clean for him, bouncing between the Louisburg Square House and the Rowes Wharf condo. "I can't just be a kept woman."

Asher smiled. "I think being married disqualifies you from being a kept woman. Look, I'm not saying you shouldn't keep working. But I want you to get it through your head that you can do anything you want—paint, write a book, go to grad school, play tennis, stay home and eat bonbons. You could even volunteer at the foundation." He was alluding to BartTech's non-profit foundation, which made grants to many non-profits, JoH included. "*Anything*."

Julia's face had paled. "Eat bonbons? Become some society matron? Is that really the sort of life you envision for me? The kind of *wife* you envision me being?"

Asher frowned. "Of course not. My point is just that you have all kinds of options." He eyed her questioningly. "Or is this really about you? Do *you* have doubts that you're projecting onto me?"

She blinked, surprised at the question. "I don't think so."

"You're an incredible woman, Julia. Am I enough of a man for you?"

"I should think so," said Julia. Then she recalled Kat's words; apparently it *was* true that even the most charismatic, confident men harbored deep-seated insecurities about their sexual prowess. "Sweetheart, I love being with you in every possible respect—physically, emotionally, intellectually, spiritually. And I have a feeling I'm going to *love* being with you in that castle of yours—ours."

Asher's face relaxed, and Julia found herself captivated by his smile, his full, sensual lips, his strong jaw.

Was he enough of a man for her? He was the man of her *dreams*.

"You've just been saying you want to focus more on your painting," said Asher. "So instead of going back to work after the wedding, why not do that?"

Julia nodded slowly. Talking things through with Asher always helped clarify them; he was like tea in that regard. "I really *do* need to focus more on my art." With a private glow, she thought of the no-longer-blank canvas at home. "I know it sounds grandiose, but once I stop procrastinating and actually *paint*, I feel as if I'm doing what I'm meant to do."

"Well, there you go," said Asher. It was evident from his tone that he considered the matter decided.

It wasn't, though–not to Julia. "I'd feel awful abandoning Franco and Carly."

Asher's face showed his skepticism. "They're businesspeople. And for what they're paying you, I'd say you don't owe them a thing."

Kat had made the same point. Still, Julia hesitated. "It's not just them I'd feel bad about leaving. It's the kids we help. I'm the only one who knows what's going on with all the programs. And even though the main reason Franco and Carly founded JoH was to get a tax break, we've helped a lot of young people. I'd hate to see it all disintegrate."

Even so, Julia found herself unconvinced by her own protestations. She'd always hated being chained to a desk. And JoH wouldn't fall apart with Whitley still there.

She finally began to absorb what Asher had been trying to convey: *she would be able to do whatever she wanted to do.* Her life would be one of her own choosing, no longer dictated by financial constraints. Daunting as it was to contemplate fully focusing on her art and finding out what, if anything, she could achieve if she really set her mind to it, it would be sheer cowardice to stay in a dead-end office job simply out of fear of attempting greater things.

Her mother would have wanted more for her than that. *She* wanted more for herself than that.

Thinking again of the partially finished painting at home, she said, "You're right. There's no point in continuing to stay in a job I never intended to make my career. I'll need to wrap up this next TS cycle, but that'll be winding down by December, just in time for our wedding. Then in January, when we get back, I can try painting full-time for a few months and see how it goes. After that, if they really need me at JoH, maybe I'll go back part-time or something. Or maybe not!"

Her announcement prompted a wide grin from Asher. Julia again thought how lucky she was to get to kiss that mouth, those lips, every day for the rest of her life—at least those days he wasn't thousands miles away on business.

"So no more doubts about work?" he said. "Or the wedding? For real?"

Julia found herself quoting the confessional priest. "Doubt is part of the human experience. But I don't doubt in you."

"Good," Asher whispered. "*Good*."

•   •   •

On their way back to Julia's apartment, Julia and Asher ambled hand in hand up Hanover street. A large construction project was underway, marked by bright orange traffic cones that surrounded the mechanical equipment that would crank into action the next morning. Absorbed in thoughts of work and the wedding, Julia scarcely noticed the heavy machinery—until Asher, still holding her hand, veered off the sidewalk so abruptly that her arm was nearly torn from its socket.

"What's wrong?" she said, rubbing her shoulder.

In the next instant, though, as they passed a flatbed truck, on which was mounted a cherry-picker crane extending toward the high-rise building above, Julia put it all together. By abandoning the sidewalk for the narrow shoulder of the busy street, Asher had prevented them from walking beneath the crane. She burst out laughing.

"Asher, honey, you *do* realize that's not a ladder?"

Not until they'd returned to the sidewalk, the ladder-like crane safely behind them, did he reply. He grinned and gave a little shrug. "Why take chances?"

Julia shook her head at him affectionately. "You're bonkers." As she well knew, Asher's superstitious nature extended far beyond avoiding walking under ladders and picking up lucky pennies: he meticulously avoided cracks in sidewalks, never opened an umbrella indoors, and had knocked on more wood than perhaps any human in history. She only hoped that, as his wife, she'd succeed in making him feel safe enough in the world that he could abandon some of his superstitious rituals.

She clutched his hand protectively.

Yes, she would make it her personal mission to make sure that Asher felt safe—always.

Chapter 15

On an otherwise-innocuous Friday morning in early October, Julia answered her ringing office phone—only to find trouble on the other end.

The caller, speaking in a very thick French accent, immediately launched in. "Mademoiselle, I am so very sorry."

"It's all right," said Julia automatically, although she had no idea what she was forgiving, or even who was offering the apology. "What's wrong?"

"It is the Schloss. I am afraid, mademoiselle, that there is a problem. The wedding."

In a flash, Julia realized who it was. "Pierre-Yves?" A born Frenchman, the Schloss Himmel manager was fluent in both German and French—and not quite so fluent in English. Julia had met him when she and Asher visited Schloss Himmel, before getting engaged.

"Yes, mademoiselle," he said. "I am Pierre-Yves."

"What's this about the wedding?" she said.

He sighed a deep, weary French sigh. "Mademoiselle, there has been an error. Schloss Himmel was promised...I apologize, mademoiselle, *I* promised, I gather full responsibility for the error. For the photography shooting in December."

Julia felt a wave of dread. As she'd learned from Asher in recent months, the Schloss was not merely a vacation destination for the Bartletts; it was also a substantial source of revenue for the family. They regularly hired it out for everything from film productions and travel calendars to fundraisers and other special events. She now vaguely recalled that Asher had mentioned that in early December, the castle was to serve as the venue for a photo shoot and songwriting talent competition–something to do with *Cosmopolitan* magazine and a country music television show, if she remembered correctly. Why in the world anyone would want to film a Nashville-based drama at a Swiss castle, she had no idea–but then again, logic wasn't exactly a prerequisite for television. At the time that Asher had mentioned the *Cosmo* event, she'd barely registered the details, probably because the concept of a magazine photo shoot had seemed so far removed from her real life, and the event wouldn't be affecting their wedding in the slightest.

And in fact, the photo shoot *still* seemed far removed from her real life. But the castle manager's anxious, overly apologetic manner suggested that some aspect of it might be affecting their wedding after all–and not in a positive way.

"What's wrong?" she said, trying not to panic. The wedding invitations had been printed and were due to go out next week.

"Mademoiselle, it was my error *complemente*," said Pierre-Yves. "I believed the shooting to be enduring for one day only, but I was incorrect. It will endure for one week. And we will require at least one complete day following the shooting to prepare the grounds for the wedding."

Julia was beginning to have a dreadful inkling of what he was getting at. "And when is the shoot scheduled to start?"

He hesitated, obviously reluctant to tell her. "Five December."

"And it lasts for one week?" Julia thought out loud. "Meaning that the grounds won't be ready by December seventh. They won't be ready until..."

"Thirteen December, mademoiselle," said Pierre-Yves. "It is a Friday. We may conduct the wedding on that day."

From *lucky* seven to *unlucky* thirteen.

"Friday the thirteenth," said Julia. "What better day for a wedding?"

If Pierre-Yves caught her sarcasm, he didn't let on. "I apologize from the bottom of my heart, Mademoiselle Julia. We can cancel the photo shooting. There is nothing more important than your wedding."

Julia was beginning to wonder if that was really true. "Have you told Asher, Pierre-Yves?"

"I thought it best to inform you first, mademoiselle," he said.

Meaning that he'd been hoping she would break the news to his boss.

"It's all right, Pierre-Yves," she told him, even though it was anything but. "I'll talk to Asher."

As she clicked off the line, she thought, not talk *to* him, talk him *down*—from his superstitious emotional ledge.

• • •

For all his understanding ways, Asher tended to get rather uptight about scheduling hiccups, last-minute changes, and administrative errors. He'd confided to Julia that as a teenager he'd suffered from mild OCD. (*Mild?* she'd thought. *Used to?*) She herself wasn't crazy about the idea of a Friday the thirteenth wedding; how her superstitious fiancé would respond to the news wasn't something she wished to contemplate long.

She felt a quick burst of hope; maybe it would spur him to elope. But then she remembered the trust provision. Asher might be superstitious, but even he wouldn't forgo a castle simply to avoid a Friday the thirteenth wedding—at least, she was pretty sure he wouldn't.

She took a deep breath and called him.

He answered immediately. "Pierre-Yves told me."

"Oh," she said. Apparently the conscientious manager had felt too guilty to leave it to her to convey the news. "So how are you with this?"

"Me? Don't worry about me," said Asher. "I don't want you to worry about anything."

"Too late," said Julia. "Asher, I know how you are. I know that getting married on Friday the thirteenth has got to be your absolute worst nightmare."

He laughed dryly. "First of all, we're getting all of this information third-hand. It may have been a mistake to let Pierre-Yves deal with *Cosmo*. I'll talk to them myself, and I'm sure we'll be able to figure something out." He paused. "And Julia?"

"Yes?" she said.

"I'm going to marry you. I'm not going to let a silly thing like this stand in our way. Friday the thirteenth may just turn out to be the luckiest day of my life. *Our* life."

Julia let out an enormous sigh of relief. She should have known that, when push came to shove, Asher would rise above petty superstition. She realized, once again, how much she truly loved and admired this man—and how ridiculously lucky she was to be marrying him—on Friday the thirteenth, or any day.

"I love you, sweetheart," she said. "And I feel the same way."

•   •   •

Asher called back a few hours later. "Okay. We've got a few different options. The first is to have the wedding on that Friday the thirteenth. Unfortunately, we can't postpone it until Saturday or Sunday, because the museum auction is that weekend."

"Right," said Julia. Not only was the Schloss booked for *before* their wedding, but the Thun Art Museum had arranged to host a gala there right *after* their wedding. She hadn't given that event much thought, either, since she and Asher had expected to be long gone by then, on their honeymoon. "So what are our other options?"

"Well, other *option*. I talked to the event coordinator at *Cosmo*, and they're willing—not just willing, interested in—incorporating our wedding into the photo shoot."

Julia's chest constricted. "What do you mean? I thought this was a contest to find some up-and-coming country music star. What do we have to do with that?"

"It would be a buildup to the wedding," Asher explained. "They'd do a feature on you and me, and then as the grand finale, the winner of the songwriting competition would sing at our wedding reception, while you and I have our first dance. That way we'll be able to have the wedding on December eleventh instead of the thirteenth."

Julia could scarcely believe what she was hearing. "Since when are you into country music? Do you even know any of these people? In the contest, I mean?"

"Well, no. But whoever wins is bound to have some talent."

"So you're totally fine with this," said Julia. "You're totally fine having some random person selected by *Cosmo–Cosmo!*–sing at our wedding. And having our wedding day be the grand finale of a country music songwriting competition and *Cosmo* photo shoot. You're absolutely, totally fine with that."

"I'm just letting you know what our options are," said Asher. "So what, *Cosmo*, who cares? They'll also cover *everything*. Not that expense is an issue, but if we agree to this arrangement, they'll not only pick up the entire tab for the wedding–food, flowers, photos, favors–but they'll make our wedding part of their feature story and actually *pay* us for participating. It's a win-win."

"A win-win?" said Julia. "You're actually referring to our wedding as a *win-win*? I'm dreaming, right?"

"What's wrong with us getting something out of this? Or is this another conflict of interest for you? A magazine feature and romantic photo shoot will preserve the whole event for posterity. We'll be part of history."

"Right," said Julia. "Mainstream country music history. In *Cosmo*. *Cosmo!*"

"I see," said Asher. "So if it were *Town and Country* you'd be okay with it, but *Cosmo* isn't high-echelon enough for you?"

Much as Julia had tried to fight them, tears were now streaming from her eyes. She was glad that Whitley was in the other room. "So sue me. I don't want to be a *Cosmo* cover girl, is that so hard to understand? And no, I don't think I'd feel differently if it were a different magazine. I don't want this to be a publicity event, or a business proposition. Is that really so ridiculous of me? And is it really so hard to understand?"

Asher was silent.

"And do you have to be so mean about it all?" she added, hating how whiny she sounded.

The silence continued for so long that for a horrible moment Julia thought Asher had hung up on her.

But then he said, "I'm sorry, Julia. No, it's not so hard to understand." He gave a little laugh. "I'm so used to mixing business with pleasure, killing two birds with one stone, so to speak, that for a second I lost sight of the bigger picture. But you're right. Our wedding can and should be just what it is. Our special day. We don't need to turn it into a *Cosmo* event."

Julia knew she ought to leave it alone, but she couldn't. "But if it were up to you, you'd go ahead with the *Cosmo* plan."

"Well, I'd at least consider it. But I understand your perspective. I'll talk to the *Cosmo* people. I'll make it clear that we're not to be part of the shoot. That we want it to be our day, and our day only."

Julia smiled wryly on her end of the line. "Our day. Friday the thirteenth."

"Umm, right," said Asher, and she could hear the smile in his voice, too. "Yeah, I guess Friday the thirteenth it is."

Chapter 16

Incredibly, by the following Friday, they'd managed to work out the scheduling ramifications of the wedding date change.

Seated at her desk at work, sorting through the latest round of TS applications, Julia marveled at how satisfactorily the situation had been resolved. Not only had Pierre-Yves handled the bulk of the logistical details, but he'd made the *Cosmopolitan* executives feel so guilty about disrupting their original wedding plans that the magazine had insisted on picking up the tab for the entire affair–even *without* their participation in the photo shoot. Talk about a win-win! Again, it was just the sort of munificent financial favor regularly bestowed on people like the Bartletts. Apparently there was no price to be put on the family's goodwill.

Perhaps best of all, she and Asher had even figured out a way around the dreaded Friday the thirteenth wedding date: they would exchange wedding vows at the stroke of midnight on Saturday, December fourteenth. It was such an obvious solution that she wondered that it hadn't occurred to them sooner.

Julia's cell phone was buzzing like crazy.

Her face darkened. David Meadow, no doubt.

Rivaling the frenzy of the latest flurry of wedding planning had been the barrage of incoming communications from David. Some were contrite, some indignant, some lighthearted, others despondent, but all conveyed the same overarching message: her being angry with him was torture (for him), and it was up to her to relieve his suffering. She couldn't–simply *couldn't*–keep doing this to him.

It had gotten old fast. Julia had taken to deleting his voicemail messages without listening to them. But that still left his text messages, which were rife with tragic emoticons: broken hearts, teary faces, sad-looking puppy dogs, and, his particular favorite of late, a steaming cup of coffee.

She turned off the still-buzzing phone without bothering to check the display. She had much more pressing matters to attend to. The Travel Sabbatical applications had continued flooding in, and Whitley, as promised, had posted an ad for an intern. Three candidates were coming this afternoon for interviews.

An excited Whitley now poked her head into Julia's office. "So, are you ready to pick the person who's going to save our lives? Or at least our sanity?"

"That's going to be a tall order on the sanity part," said Julia. "Speaking for myself, at least."

"No kidding," said Whitley. "Speaking for you, that is."

"What time is the first interview?" Julia asked.

"Eleven-thirty. If all goes well, your sanity could be saved by noon."

By eleven o'clock, though, the first candidate had canceled, explaining that she'd gotten a paying job. The second candidate, scheduled for two p.m., failed to appear. That left only one remaining intern prospect: a North End local named Byron Knowles.

"The good news is, I think he's the best one, anyway," Whitley told Julia. "He even has his own consulting firm. He sounded really on-the-ball."

•   •   •

By all indications, Byron Knowles was indeed on-the-ball. Whitley greeted him when he arrived at the JoH office at four-fifteen, fifteen minutes early for his interview. By the time Julia stepped out of her office to join them, Whitley and Byron were settled cozily on the couch, drinking coffee from a neighborhood coffee shop, Boston Common Coffee, and chatting a mile a minute. Julia felt like she was interrupting two old friends.

Noting a third, untouched, steaming cup on the conference table, still in a cardboard carrying tray, Julia looked at Byron in astonishment. "Did you bring us coffee?"

He jumped to his feet and extended a hand. "So you're the famous Julia! Byron Knowles, how do you do." About six feet tall, in his late twenties, Byron presented an extremely dapper appearance: starched and pressed white shirt, checkered maroon bow tie, and trousers in the rosy shade known in the Northeast as "Nantucket red." "And I couldn't come empty-handed."

"That was so thoughtful," said Julia.

He smiled an ingratiating smile. "I know you ladies like it sweet." Running a hand lightly over his perfectly coiffed blonde pompadour he added, "And for that matter, so do some of us boys. So they've got plenty of cream and sugar."

Before Julia could say anything, Whitley looked sorrowfully at Byron. "Julia doesn't take cream *or* sugar. She's *vegan*."

Byron's eyebrows shot up. He peered at Julia from beneath heavy eyelids. "Of *course* you are. I should have known. How's this, Monday I'll bring you a special goat's-milk-laced coffee—oh, wait, that's not *vegan*, is it? I meant a rice-milk-laced coffee—organic, of *course*—since I'm sure you don't do *soy*." He smiled to suggest he was joking, but something in his tone made Julia's skin crawl.

Whitley, though, was giggling delightedly. "Oh, don't worry, Julia's not one of those *annoying* vegans. Seriously, I bring burgers in here all the time for lunch. And meatball subs, chicken masala, you name it. We are in the North End, after all! Julia has no problem having meat around."

"I wouldn't quite say *that*," said Julia.

The others seemed to take that as a joke, which perhaps was best.

"No worries," said Byron. "I'll be extremely considerate of your eating disord–I mean, *veganism*." Laying his right hand on his chest, he said, "I hereby pledge, veal parmesan only once a week–and *never* on Fridays. And no foie gras *whatsoever*." He glanced coyly at Whitley. "Except when Julia's out of the office."

Whitley was cracking up.

Julia forced herself to let it go. "Shall we get down to business?"

Julia and Whitley proceeded to tell Byron about JoH's mission to bring travel and cultural opportunities to underprivileged youth, focusing particularly on the help they needed with the Travel Sabbatical program. Byron, in turn, told them how his newly established consulting firm had worked with a Beacon Hill architectural society to design a software program to track and assess applications for a prestigious architectural fellowship. Much as Julia had—secretly—hoped that Byron's skills wouldn't mesh with the type of work JoH did, or the TS program in particular, that clearly wasn't the case.

"Byron," she said, "if I can be blunt..."

"Oh, please, Miss Julia, be blunt," said Byron, to Whitley's giggles. "I can take it blunt. And *hard*."

Again, Julia's skin crawled. Again, she forced herself to let it go. "I'm just curious as to why in the world you would want to be an–*unpaid*–intern." She felt a sudden ray of hope; perhaps Byron had the misimpression that the internship was a paid position.

He smiled patiently, obviously having anticipated the question and deemed it sophomoric. "Two reasons. First, I try to do what I can for the community. I used to be very involved in campaign work for the Tea Party, but I lost my taste for national politics a few years back." He made a face. "You know, after our prize candidate was robbed of his rightful Senate seat by a certain conniving Marxist *bee-yotch*. Who shall remain nameless."

Julia couldn't quite conceal her surprise at that last remark. Even Whitley was giving Byron a questioning look.

"I know, I know," he said with an unrepentant shrug. "I've blown your minds. A gay man who's a social and fiscal conservative, now you've seen it all." He puffed out his chest. "You're never going to figure me out, ladies. Get over it."

Whitley guffawed, clearly loving the show.

Turning his attention back to Julia, Byron said, "And the *other* reason I'm interested in the intern position is that my humble little consulting firm is branching out into online travel services. I can certainly find ten to fifteen hours a week to help you all out, and it'll give me additional experience with the world of online travel. And if, down the road, Hartland Travel ever happens to be in need of some consulting expertise, I hope that they'll keep me in mind. I see it as a win-win for us both."

Julia's shoulders tensed. The notion of her wedding as a "win-win" had triggered her and Asher's ugliest disagreement ever. And now it seemed that "win-wins" were infiltrating her work environment as well. So why was it, she wondered, that she didn't feel that she was winning much of anything?

Whitley looked expectantly at Julia as if to say, *"Well? What more do you need to hear?"*

But Julia wasn't ready to welcome Byron Knowles into the JoH fold just yet. She stood up from her seat. Byron and Whitley took the cue and rose as well.

"Thanks so much for coming in," Julia told Byron. "We've got a few more people to see, but we'll be in touch."

Whitley looked again at Julia, as if to say, *"What?"*

Byron either didn't notice or ignored the non-verbal exchange. "Thank you, ladies," he said. "It's been a pleasure." He gave Whitley a final intimate wave on his way out the door.

After he'd gone, Whitley turned to Julia. "Why did you tell him we had other people to see? For one, we don't, and for two, he's perfect!"

Julia shrugged defensively. "I didn't like him. I got a bad vibe."

"What, because of the foie gras crack? You can't hold that against him. He was just joking around!"

Julia exhaled, trying to come up with a logically persuasive reason for not hiring Byron to do unpaid work, when JoH could really use the help. She couldn't.

"I just didn't like him,' she said again.

Whitley looked on the verge of despair. "Come on, Julia, he's *perfect*. Before you came in, he was telling me he could get started on reviewing some of the Eliot applications this weekend. He said we can even use his consulting firm's tracking system, which will be perfect since we're not using yours." She gazed imploringly Julia. "*Pleeeeease*? We got along so well. I can tell we'd all have so much fun working together. And we really, really need the help."

Something about the wild red hair and big nose made Whitley tough to dissuade.

"Okay, okay," said Julia. "You're right, we do need the help."

"Yay!" said Whitley, jumping up and down, a tiny, gingery bundle of energy. "I'll call him right now and let him know." She all but skipped out of Julia's office.

Ten hours a week, Julia reminded herself. How bad could it be?

Chapter 17

As she walked to work on Monday morning, Julia did her best to focus on how the sunbeams danced on the waters of the Boston Harbor, rather than on the fact that Byron Knowles would be invading her workspace that afternoon.

Not *invading*, she corrected herself.

Contributing. Collaborating. *Helping*.

And in the meantime, she had a Byron-free morning to look forward to.

"Great news!" said Whitley when Julia walked into the JoH office. "Byron said that since we're so swamped these next few weeks, he's happy to come in for more than ten hours a week. He'll be in around nine-thirty."

"That *is* great news," said Julia. So much for her Byron-free morning.

Then, from directly behind her, she heard Byron's own voice. "And I bring still greater news: I'm here *now*. With coffee!" He set down a large cup on Whitley's desk. "Hazelnut latte with whipped cream for Whitley. Sweets for the sweet!"

As Whitley gushed her appreciation, Byron unloaded a drink more closely resembling a hot fudge sundae than anything remotely related to coffee and placed it on the worktable that Julia and Whitley had set up as a temporary work station for him. "Iced caramel latte made with heavy cream, with *extra* whipped cream for me. Sweeter sweets for the sweeter sweet!" He smirked at Julia and Whitley. "Haven't you heard? Saturated fat is *back*!"

Finally, with a flourish, he handed Julia the one remaining–comparatively austere-looking–drink, along with an entire tray of condiments. "Last but not least, one large black coffee with *no* whipped cream for Miss Julia. Your choice of coconut milk, almond milk, rice milk, and fake sugars. Artificial sweets for the—well, you know." He flashed her that "just kidding" smile of his, which Julia was already coming to loathe.

Whitley, naturally, was out of her mind with delight.

Julia pasted on what hopefully passed as a smile. "Thanks, Byron. You're the best!"

She sounded artificially sweet even to her own ears. Maybe Byron was onto something.

Whitley, who'd discussed the TS project with Byron over the weekend, dove right in to the intern training. Apparently, Byron had already reviewed over a dozen applications. In addition, he'd tweaked the software program his firm had designed for the architecture competition to use in assessing the TS applications.

A few hours later, peering over Byron's shoulder at his computer screen as he entered the pertinent data, Julia had to acknowledge, "This system of yours really is fantastic. Thanks to your help, we'll get 'Eliot' in shape in no time."

At Byron's questioning glance, Whitley explained, "That's my pet name for the TS program. As in T. S. Eliot."

Bryon's impeccably groomed eyebrows shot up. "Well, now that I've performed my intervention, hopefully it will continue to be 'Eliot' rather than 'TS'—as in *Total Shit*."

That one had Whitley rolling in the aisles.

Julia left the new BFFs to their merriment and returned to her own office. She left her office door open—although she wasn't sure how long she'd be able to stand the sound of Byron's resonant voice.

Fortunately, the newest batch of TS applications quickly captured her full attention. The first one of the day was from a sixteen-year-old girl from Quincy, Massachusetts, Tatyana Kozak, whose Ukrainian-born mother had died during childbirth. Tatyana hoped to travel to Ukraine to meet her extended family and do genealogical research into her mother's background. In her own words, Tatyana wanted, more than anything, to get to know the mother she'd never met.

Anyone would have been touched by the girl's story, but having lost her own mother, Julia found herself especially moved. Had it been within her power to do so, she might have awarded Tatyana the TS prize on the spot.

However, Tatyana's was far from the only compelling submission. The next was from Wayne Jackson, a seventeen-year-old student from Boston's Roxbury neighborhood. Wayne had won a scholarship to Berklee School of Music but wanted to first spend a year researching native rhythm and dance in West Africa. Then there was Niall Crowley, a senior at Boston Latin High School who hoped to travel to Ireland to meet the childhood acquaintances of his father, a first-generation Irish immigrant who'd died of alcoholism when Niall was only eight years old—another child who'd lost a parent at a cruelly early age. And those were only the first three applications of the day.

Transfixed as she was by the TS applicants' personal stories, Julia only vaguely registered the telltale squeak of the front office door as it swung open. Immediately thereafter, however, she was jolted from her reverie by possibly the one thing more distasteful than another foie gras joke from Byron Knowles: the sound of David Meadow's voice.

"Whittles!" David was saying in his grandest, most expansive, world-is-my-oyster manner. "My bonnie leprechaun lassie! And guest of Whittles—who are you, my good friend?"

There followed a brief but evocative silence, and then—second-most-distasteful sound—Byron's voice, saying, "Your good friend is *exactly* who I'd like to be. Byron Knowles, at your service—and I do mean *service*."

David cackled. He was such a narcissist, thought Julia, that he was a sucker for flattery from *anyone*—male, female, gay, straight, educated, illiterate, you name it. Anyone who offered lavish, hollow praise spoke the preferred language of David Meadow.

Byron spoke that language, of course. And he did so in a voice even sleeker than his modish pompadour.

"And I'm David Meadow," David was saying. "So, servant boy, can you please help me find a princess named Julia Jones? I'm rather desperate. You could say I'm jonesing for Julia! She has flowing blonde hair the shade of daffodils, no, no, more like buttercups, and her skin is creamy—"

"I think you mean soy-milky," said Byron, triggering hysterical laughter from "Whittles."

"Right again, my friend!" said David. "That soy-milky vegan skin makes me..."

Julia had had enough. She tore herself away from the wholesome, heartfelt, inspiring writings of students keen to learn more about the world and themselves—and walked into the main office area to address the man who represented the polar opposite of all those things: all that was impure. Unwholesome. Insincere. Uninspiring.

Etcetera.

"Hello, David," she said coolly. "Can I help you?"

David regarded her forlornly. "You're still peeved with me. I don't blame you."

Julia noted that the others' interest was irritatingly piqued. David took the opportunity to gaze soulfully at Byron. "I'm sure that by now you've gleaned that Julia is a woman of extraordinary gentility and refinement."

"I have indeed," said Byron dryly.

"And she's breathtakingly beautiful, is she not?" said David.

Byron shrugged. "Oh, I *suppooose* so," he said, drawing out the word. "In a watery, Gwyneth Paltrow sort of way." (*Screw you*, thought Julia.) "Not exactly *my* type, of course." A barely perceptible smile graced his lips. "If you don't mind my saying so, David Meadow, you're a little breathtaking yourself."

David smiled modestly. "Oh, stop. We can talk—in depth—about me later." He drew himself up to his full height (six-two and change) and said, "But first, Whittles, Byron, I have a confession to make. The other weekend, I got carried away by Julia's great beauty. Her fairness had such a powerful effect on me that I momentarily lost my wits—yes, Whittles, I was witless! In my delirium, I failed to recall that this princess is spoken for. And I tried to tempt her to run away with me."

Whitley gasped. "For real, Julia? He came on to you?"

"That's one way to put it," said Julia.

David looked sad. Which, of course, didn't mean that he *was* sad. Just that he had decided it suited his purposes to appear so.

"Can you blame me?" he beseeched his enthralled audience of two, plus Julia. "I was overcome by her loveliness and charm. I'm only human. I am but a man! But surely that's not an irredeemable act. Surely she should forgive me. Right?" He looked pleadingly first to Whitley, then to Byron, then to Julia herself. "Please?"

The act had obviously worked on Whitley, who'd always been a soft touch for David's charms. "Julia, he's groveling. I do think that merits some leniency."

"*Pleeeease?*" said David, groveling even more.

Julia had seen it all before, of course; David Meadow had no new tricks—except maybe in the bedroom, and she had no interest in seeing those.

Meanwhile, Byron was staring at *her*. "You are *loving* this, aren't you, *Princess* Julia. You cold, heartless..."

Julia wondered vaguely if he was going to call her a "bee-yotch."

David, that paragon of maturity and honor, raised a hand to silence JoH's new intern. "Now, now, Julia's not the one at fault here. That's me. Julia found her Mr. Right. I'm her Mr. Wrong. All I ask is to be forgiven."

Julia felt the chastening eyes of Whitley and Byron on her. It was clear that David Meadow wasn't going anywhere without her absolution.

"Fine, David," she said. "You're forgiven."

"Yes!" he said, with a fervent pump of his fist. "*Yes!*" He embraced Julia in a huge bear hug, lifted her up, and spun her around and around.

Byron, who'd been watching jealously, leaned in close to David and said in a stage whisper, "You're too good for her anyway, hot stuff." He winked at Julia to show he was "only kidding."

Meanwhile, Whitley was laughing and jumping around in the sheer excitement of the moment.

Julia's feet had yet to touch the ground.

Once David had—finally—set her back down, she said, "Can we talk privately for a minute? In my office."

David cast a triumphant look at his Byron, his new biggest fan.

"Go get 'em, tiger!" said Byron.

David growled ferociously as he ushered Julia into her office.

She shut the door, using all her self-restraint not to slam it.

David meekly took a seat.

"That wasn't exactly fair," she said. "You know Whitley can't resist you. And Byron—well, no comment on Byron."

"What else could I do?" said David. "You were ignoring all my messages. Extreme measures were called for. I figured if I caught you while you were with Whitley, I'd get the benefit of your general reluctance to humiliate people in public. I didn't know about Brian—"

"Byron," said Julia.

"Whatever. He was just a serendipitous addition. Gay men love me."

"Well, you figured right," said Julia. "Obviously. Or we wouldn't be sitting here right now."

David looked cowed. "Julia, I'm sorry. Really. My...*offer* to you wasn't something I'd plotted and planned. It popped into my head after I ran into you on your way to confession, and then after a whisky or two—okay, more like three or four—at Vittoria, while I was waiting for you, it started to seem like a truly inspired idea. I won't blame it entirely on the booze. But the booze did help."

Julia felt her outrage fading. David was inarguably the king of spontaneity and stupid ideas. And he held his liquor dangerously well, at least superficially, which explained why she hadn't surmised the extent of his intoxication.

She couldn't help but believe him. At least partially.

He gave it one final push. "At the end of the day, Jules, I'm a horny, self-serving asshole who saw a potential opportunity to get you in the sack. And failed miserably. And not to mention, completely disrespected Asher—and you—in the process. Look, I know I don't deserve your forgiveness, but I'm asking for it anyway. Please? Can we go back to being friends? Pretty please?"

Julia sighed, knowing that her forgiveness was probably a preordained event. She never wanted to believe that people were entirely bad—even when it was true. "You promise never to do it again?"

"Promise! Unless, of course, you want me to."

"In that case, we're safe," said Julia.

"Ouch!" said David. "So am I still invited to your wedding? I've been lots of places, but never to a Swiss castle."

"You're still invited," said Julia. Among other things, it would have been too complicated to explain to Asher why she'd suddenly removed David Meadow from the guest list.

Mission accomplished, a beaming David jumped from his chair. "Brilliant! And now I'm afraid I must dash. Noon conference call with Gareth and two of our clients—a couple of obscenely wealthy nutcases."

"Oh, yeah?" said Julia, as she escorted him out into the main room, where Whitley and Byron were seated, pretending to be working. "Big project?"

David rolled his eyes. "Aren't they all. But yes, this one is big even by my standards. These two have a place in the Hamptons, and they hired Gareth as the architect, but only on the condition that I'd do the I.D. So he has me to thank for this one."

"I think Asher mentioned something about that project," said Julia. "Poor Gareth, I'm pretty sure Asher's had him running around in circles on the Louisburg Square renovation. You, too, probably."

David gave her a long-suffering look. "You've got that right. These past few weeks, our project calls have been more like therapy sessions than interior design."

Julia smiled affectionately. "That's my Asher."

"Have you heard about the latest design drama?" said David. "The color scheme for the master bath? We'd decided on a Tuscan beige, but now he's thinking maybe we should go with a shade called 'bittersweet,' kind of a burnt orange. He loves it, but..."

"He's afraid the name will bring bad luck," said Julia, laughing. "Oh, yes, believe me, I've heard all about the bittersweet."

"All things considered, compared to your man, these two clients are a walk in the park," said David. "They're crazy, but they pretty much let Gareth and me do whatever we want. Which always works out best for everyone in the long run." He glanced at his Rolex. "And now I *really* must dash." Pausing only long enough to gaze intently into her eyes one last time, he said, "Julia, you're the best. The *best*. I promise I'll make it up to you, all of it."

And then he was gone—but not before shooting Byron and Whitley a thumbs-up on his way out the door.

"Sorry you guys had to witness that," Julia told her coworkers.

"No problem," said Whitley. "Most exciting thing to happen here all week! He's such a sweetheart. I'm glad you guys worked things out."

Byron was fanning himself. "What a hottie! Did I hear him say he's hanging with some obscenely wealthy couple in the Hamptons?"

"Always," said Julia. "David Meadow, interior designer to the stars."

Byron gave her a strange look. "Life is rough, eh? You're not only engaged to a millionaire hottie, you have all the other richest, most eligible hotties after you, too. Everyone wants a piece of Princess Julia."

There was that snaky smile again. It was becoming quite evident to Julia that, for whatever reason, Byron did *not* like her.

"How did you know about my engagement?" she said. "And Asher?"

Byron looked at her like she was an idiot. "Honey, how could I miss that rock on your hand? Four carats, am I right?" He waggled his fingers disconcertingly. "Quick Google search and all the facts were right there, at my fingertips. Asher Bartlett, David Meadow, their respective financial states. You are one lucky lady."

Somehow, when Byron said it, it sounded like a crime.

But Julia only smiled. "No argument here."

Chapter 18

By one o'clock, Julia's stomach was rumbling, and with each passing minute, Byron's cackle seemed to escalate in pitch and duration. She grabbed her jacket.

"I'm heading out for lunch," she told Whitley and Byron. "You guys need anything?"

Byron didn't miss a beat. "One extra-large cheeseburger, please? Or wait, no, make it a lamb-burger instead. Oh, and bacon! Lots and lots of bacon."

"Got it," said Julia, stepping out of the office before he could say anything else.

She closed the door firmly behind her and paused on the sidewalk.

I hate him, she thought. *I fucking hate him!*

She tried not to wonder how she was going to make it through the rest of the afternoon.

Fortunately, the midday sun was warm on her face, and the gentle breeze seemed to temper reality just a bit. Boston wasn't known for fabulous weather, but every now and again, nature came through. It was a glorious day to be in the North End.

She made her way toward Lewis Wharf and followed an unmarked gravel path which led to a "secret" garden, where she hoped to find an empty bench to relax and people-watch. Evidently, though, she hadn't been the only one with that idea; when she reached the garden, she found that all the benches were taken.

No matter. It was a perfect day for a stroll.

Julia walked along the HarborWalk to the waterfront, allowing the briny ocean scent to lift her thoughts from petty office concerns to daydreams of the high seas. Then, lo and behold, she spied a just-vacated wooden Adirondack chair–prime real estate on a day like today. She hurried to claim it. As she reclined back on the roomy chair, she noted how brilliantly her engagement ring sparkled in the sunlight. She smiled down at it, feeling, in that moment, that she was sparkling, too.

A shadow then fell across the bench, and her ring.

Julia looked up, shielding her eyes from the sun.

"Well, hello," she said to Sean Harris.

He was wearing khakis and a navy blue polo shirt, his blonde hair gleaming in the sunshine–the all-American boy. In this light, his eyes were more steel-gray than blue. "You're everywhere," he said.

"Or you're stalking me," said Julia.

"You wish," said Sean. He gestured to the space beside her. "May I?"

"Sure," she said. The wide wooden chairs were designed to easily fit two or even three people. She slid over to make room.

Sean took a seat and stretched out his long legs. They sat in companionable silence for a few seconds, watching the sunbeams dance on the ocean surface.

"By the way, I just wanted to tell you I'm sorry about what happened the other week," said Sean. "I know you're engaged, and I should have respected that."

Julia was glad she didn't have to look him in the eye. "You don't need to apologize. I was just as much to blame. I think we were both caught off guard, seeing each other after all these years. We lost track of reality for a minute."

For some reason, her choice of words made Sean smile. He turned his head to look at her. "We did, didn't we?"

Julia wasn't sure how to respond.

He laughed, letting her off the hook. "So don't you have any work to do? Or do you just sit by the water all day, basking in the sunshine?"

"Someday," said Julia jokingly–although, in fact, that day wasn't far off. "My office is right down the street." She told Sean about her job at Journeys of the Heart–and her newfound nemesis, Byron Knowles. "I also live right down the street," she concluded. "Essentially, my world is very small."

Sean grinned. "Fortunately, you have a *very* large diamond to make up for that."

"Yes, exactly," said Julia. "The diamond makes everything else okay." She felt glad that they were joking about her ring–a marked improvement over the volatility of their last conversation. "So what about you? Don't *you* have any work to do?"

"Plenty," said Sean. "But I had some time between appointments, and I figured I'd swing by here to check out some sailboats. My brother has a place on the Cape, and I'm thinking of buying one to keep out there. Want to come take a look?"

Julia was about to say no, she had to get back to work, but she suddenly felt defiant. What reason had she to rush back to the office? She'd been blindsided first by Byron's early arrival, and then again, just a few hours later, by the groveling David Meadow. Running into Sean was her first *pleasant* surprise of the day.

"Why not?" she said. "I can take a walk."

They meandered through the marina and stopped at a food cart for hot pretzels, which they ate as they strolled around, looking at the boats. It was refreshing how *normal* their little outing seemed, thought Julia–just the sort of thing you did when you ran into a friend unexpectedly. And Sean *was* a friend, she felt. That awkward tension was gone; they were just two people enjoying a sunny autumn day by the harbor. Maybe, after the wedding, their friendship would continue to grow. She wondered if Asher would like Sean. They didn't have a huge amount in common, but who wouldn't like Sean? Or Asher, for that matter?

"*Serendipity*," said Julia, pointing. "That sailboat over there. In the third slot from the right. That's its name–*Serendipity*."

"Slip," said Sean. "Not slot."

"Oh, excuse me, captain," she said.

He gestured toward a graceful, forty-plus-foot sloop. "I like that one. *Agápe*. You know what that means, right?"

She shook her head.

"It's Greek," said Sean. "The highest form of love."

"Oh, yeah?" said Julia. "And what do *you* know about love?"

The words were barely out of her mouth before she regretted them. She hoped Sean didn't–mistakenly–think she was flirting. Or worse, insulting his dead wife. She tried to read his expression, but he'd put on sunglasses, and she couldn't see his eyes.

He shrugged. "I know a little bit."

Rather abruptly, he stopped walking and turned to face her. "Speaking of which, when's the big day? You're building up some serious muscles in that left ring finger of yours, you realize. It's like twice as big as your right one."

"No!" said Julia, holding up her two hands to compare–and finding, of course, that her left ring finger was no larger or more muscular than her right. "You almost had me going for a minute there."

Sean laughed. "More than almost. Seriously, when's the wedding?"

The wedding, thought Julia. "December. December seventh. No, actually it's the fourteenth. We had to change it."

Sean flashed the little-boy grin that had consistently enraptured the entire female student populace of Jefferson High School, Julia included–and probably some male students as well. "Maybe, if you're really nice to me, I'll let you come out on my boat. When I buy one, that is. I mean, I'm sure your fiancé's a great guy, but can he really compete with that?"

"No, not really," said Julia. "I mean, there is a castle, but I wouldn't say that castles actually *compete* with boats. It's like trying to compare apples and oranges; they're two totally different things."

If she'd been intending to floor Sean, she'd succeeded. He'd pulled off his shades and was staring at her.

A moment later, his face relaxed into a smile. "Oh, I get it. You're just messing with me because of what I said about your muscular ring finger."

Julia already wished she hadn't mentioned the castle. "No, believe it or not, there really is a castle. It's in Switzerland. It's part of a family trust. But it's small. Very small." She shook her head, frustrated with herself; why did she always feel compelled to describe the Schloss as small? "No, I take that back. It's actually a big castle–very big. But no boat."

Sean was looking extremely amused.

Then Julia remembered. "Wait, come to think of it, there *is* a boathouse by the lake. Obviously there are some boats in there. But just some kayaks and a scull; Asher rowed in college. And in the Olympics one year. There's a small motorboat, too. But no sailboats. Nothing like this," she said, gesturing toward *Agápe*. "Nothing nearly as nice as your boat. Your future boat."

By now, Sean was laughing–hard. "Right, of course. I should have known." He tossed his last bit of pretzel in the direction of a lurking seagull, who snatched it up. "Well, I'm glad you'll be getting a castle, Julia. And some water vessels. You deserve nothing less. Sounds like you're marrying the right man."

She looked at him uncertainly, trying to gauge whether his words contained some sort of hidden barb. "Yes, I think I am. Not because of the castle, though."

Sean put his sunglasses back on, and the gesture seemed so final that Julia wondered oddly whether she'd ever see his eyes again.

It was silly to have thought that they might become friends, she realized. This recent intersection had been but an anomaly. Their lives were headed in completely separate directions.

"I should get going," he said, suddenly formal.

Julia nodded. "Yes, me too."

"Good luck with the nemesis, by the way," said Sean. "Hope that works out."

"Thanks," said Julia, although she couldn't imagine the situation with Byron ever "working out"–other than by her leaving JoH.

Which, of course, she would be. Soon.

"Well, I guess this is goodbye," said Sean. "I probably won't see you again before the wedding. Or after the wedding. I imagine you'll be spending a lot of time in Switzerland. And wherever else the other family castles happen to be."

"There's only one castle, that I know of, at least," said Julia. "But yeah, you're right. I guess this is goodbye."

She stood there silently for a minute, and then she opened her arms. They hugged for a long moment.

And then, before she knew it—for the second time in two months—she was watching Sean Harris walk away.

Chapter 19

The weeks that followed brought gray clouds and cold and rain, and for Julia, the atmosphere in the JoH office wasn't any brighter. Working closely with Byron on "Eliot" had merely confirmed her initial assessment of him as arrogant and generally horrible to deal with. And his obnoxious comments at her expense had only escalated.

The bond between Byron and Whitley, on the other hand, had only intensified. Byron demanded a constant audience, and in Whitley, he'd found an ardent and devoted fan. Even more frustratingly, Byron had managed to dazzle Carly and Franco as well. They were now having him divide his work time between JoH and Hartland Travel. Within just a few short weeks, Byron had gone from being an unpaid intern to being a rather well-compensated part-time employee—and for Byron, "part-time" meant thirty to forty hours per week.

Seated at her desk, as usual, one Thursday morning, her office door shut in defense against the sound of Byron's incessant chatter, Julia felt like a prisoner in her own office. How had things gotten so bad, so fast? Her sole consolation was knowing that she'd have to endure Byron for only a few more weeks. Carly and Franco had agreed to the three-month leave of absence she'd requested for after the wedding.

And every additional day she spent in Byron's presence served to reinforce the likelihood that her temporary leave of absence would end up being a permanent one.

At this rate, she thought morosely, the others would hardly even notice she was gone.

She turned her attention back to the applications of the three Travel Sabbatical finalists, which she was reviewing in preparation for the final interviews next week. As usual, the TS competition had turned up some amazing kids, but they'd managed to decide on these final three: Tia Lovett, Cruz Costa, and Tatyana Kozak. Tia, a straight-A senior (after skipping her junior year entirely) at New York High School for Art and Design, aimed to spend her first year of college studying classical architecture in Rome. Cruz, a seventeen-year-old boy from Albuquerque, New Mexico, wanted to work with a non-profit water protection group, En Esencia, in Mexico. And the third, Julia's personal favorite, was Tatyana Kozak, the motherless Ukrainian girl who hoped to travel to Ukraine to discover her ancestral roots.

Julia's cell phone buzzed, distracting her. She checked the display. Kat. She clicked to take the call. "Hey, what's up?"

"Sorry to bug you at work," said Kat. "I just wanted to make sure you're coming to cheer me on this Saturday."

"Cheer you on for what?"

"My race," said Kat. "The marathon. First weekend in November, I told you!"

Amidst all the goings-on at work. Julia had completely forgotten. "Oh, right, your marathon relay! It's here already?"

"Marathon, marathon relay, same difference," Kat was saying. "A total of twenty-six-point-two miles is being run, I think is the main point. And the weather's supposed to be gorgeous—clear, sunny, in the sixties. In November! Just how I like it when I run my marathons. Can you believe we've been training for over two months?"

"Not really," said Julia, who'd assumed that Kat's race plans—like the majority of Kat's health-related pursuits—had evaporated into thin air. "So you're actually going to do it?"

"*Yes*, I'm going to do it," said Kat, sounding offended. "You think I've been swigging green smoothies for nothing? Five-point-two-four miles, here I come!"

"I didn't mean it that way," said Julia. "I'm impressed you've stuck with it."

Kat laughed. "Honestly, I am, too. I'm up to four and a half miles without walking, so my only goal for race day is to run the whole way. Without dying, that is."

"That's a great goal!" said Julia. "Especially the not dying part."

"Well, considering what happened to the original marathon runner, I figured that was key. He ran from Marathon to Athens to deliver the message that the Greeks had won their battle against the Persians. And then he croaked."

"You've really done your research," said Julia.

"I wanted to know exactly what I was getting into when I agreed to do this marathon thing," said Kat. "And I have no intention of getting into death."

"I'm glad to hear it," said Julia. "You know, I'm going to have to bring Asher to the race. Because otherwise, he's never going to believe it."

"*What*?" shrieked Kat. "Your confidence, babe, is a bit underwhelming. But yes, by all means, bring the Ash-man."

At that moment, Byron's shrill laughter pierced Julia's office door, startling even Kat.

"What the heck is *that*?" said Kat. "A fire alarm or something?"

"If only," said Julia. "No, it's *him*. You know—*Byron*."

"Ah, the nemesis. No wonder you want out." Kat chuckled. "Well, honestly, if he's what it takes to get you to break free of your low-budget, dead-end job, then that might not be such a bad thing. You should be thanking him."

Could it be, mused Julia, that Byron *had* given her the nudge she hadn't even known she'd needed to close out this chapter of her professional life?

"Thank you, Byron," she said, testing the concept out loud.

"There you go," said Kat. "How'd that feel?"

"Terrible," said Julia.

Kat laughed. "How about adding in a goodbye?"

Julia tried it. "Thank you, Byron—and goodbye."

"Well?" said Kat.

"*Much* better," said Julia.

Over dinner that evening, Julia told Asher about Kat's race. Angela had cooked for them tonight: three-bean chili with butternut squash and Angela's specialty pumpkin cornbread, made with walnuts and maple syrup. "I told Kat you'd have to come watch in person or you'd never believe it."

Asher laughed and reached for another piece of cornbread, the bottom of which was gooey with maple syrup. "That's probably true. What's funny is that I was planning to be there anyway. Gareth's running, and I told him I'd bring Rusty."

Julia felt a twinge; there it was again—that weird jealousy she had of Rusty. "Were you going to invite me? Or is three a crowd when it comes to you and Rusty?"

"Of course I was, sweetheart," said Asher. "It's just that you've been painting Saturday mornings, and it slipped my mind. But this is perfect. I'll swing by your place and pick you up, and we can head over together to Gareth's to pick up Rusty."

Julia had a sudden image of being trapped in Asher's car with the high-strung dog. "Maybe it makes more sense for me to meet you there."

"You're probably right," said Asher. "That way I can take her for a nice long walk so she won't be a bundle of nerves at the race."

"That makes a *lot* of sense," said Julia.

"So since when is Kat a runner?" said Asher. "I had no idea."

Julia laughed. "Yeah, me, either, really! It's a fairly new thing. I didn't know Gareth was a runner, either."

"Oh, yeah, he's practically a pro. He generally does longer races, but he decided to do the marathon relay with a men's group from his church."

"Gareth's religious?" said Julia, surprised. She'd pegged him for a secular intellectual skeptic.

Asher rolled his eyes slightly. "Very much so. He was raised Christian Fundamentalist, but now he goes to a Unitarian church."

"Interesting," said Julia., thinking that she really ought to take the time to get to know the architect who, after all, was creating their future home.

"It's too bad he can't make it to the wedding. You two have gotten so close during this renovation."

"Yeah, well, that's the downside of a destination wedding. But it'll be better for him to stick around here, in case anything comes up with the house." Asher chuckled. "Plus, Gareth's a huge cheese snob. He says it's sacrilegious to hold a vegan wedding in Switzerland." Catching Julia's look, he said, "I know, I know. But I never expected him to come to the wedding, anyway. We've got more of a business relationship."

"You're going to cheer him on in a race," said Julia. "That's more than just a business relationship."

Asher laughed. "No, no, I'm just the person bringing *Rusty* to cheer him on in the race. To Gareth, I'm just the dog's chauffeur."

"Got it," said Julia. "So you'll take care of the dog—and I'll handle the Kat."

"Exactly," said Asher. "And I'm pretty sure who'll have the easier job."

$$• \quad • \quad •$$

Saturday morning, Julia took the T to Kenmore Square and walked to the section of Commonwealth Avenue where Kat had suggested she wait. To her disappointment, since Gareth was running the final leg of the race for his four-person team, Asher—and Rusty—had opted to watch the race from a spot closer to the finish line, meaning that Asher wouldn't get to see Kat actually running.

And that she was here alone.

It wasn't fair, she thought petulantly. If not for Rusty, she and Asher could have watched the race together. Once they'd spotted Kat, they could have hopped on the T and made it to the finish line in plenty of time to cheer on Gareth. But that plan would never have worked with the rambunctious dog by their side. Rusty wasn't even Asher's dog! Why should she, Rusty, come before *her*, his fiancée?

Her resentful thoughts of the copper-colored canine were interrupted by the pounding footsteps of the first approaching runners. The lead runners were focused and warrior-like in their intensity. The next wave was a hodgepodge of men and women of varying ages and body types. Then Julia spied a woman in a slim-fitting magenta top and black running tights, chestnut hair pulled back in a serious ponytail.

Kat!

Julia used her cell phone to snap a photo, screaming all the while, "Go, Kat! Kat, Kat, Kat!"

By sheer chance of spacing, Kat was running almost solo on this stretch of Comm. Ave., a smattering of runners ahead, others some distance behind. With no one else to root for, the nearby spectators picked up Julia's cry, chanting, "Kat, Kat, Kat!"

Hearing her name from the small but enthusiastic crowd infused Kat with a visible burst of energy. She raised her arms victoriously, giving Julia–and several others–a high-five as she ran past.

Her chest swelling with pride, Julia texted Asher the photo she'd taken: incontrovertible evidence that Kat was, indeed, a runner.

• • •

Later, amidst the post-race chaos, Julia rendezvoused with Kat and her teammates. Out of a hundred-plus teams in their category, they'd come in twenty-fourth.

"Respectable," said Kat's stoic teammate Taylor.

"I'll say!" said Julia. "Top twenty-five percent. You guys did great! And *you*," she said, looking at her friend, "were incredible. You're an athlete–a Kathlete!"

"Kathlete!" yelped Kat. "I love it. Hey, we're doing a pub crawl up Newbury Street. Want to come?"

"Let me check what Asher is up to," said Julia. When she pulled out her phone to call him, though, she found that he'd already sent her a text message. The crowds had proven too much for Rusty, and he'd left to give Gareth and Rusty a ride to their home in Brookline.

Disappointed, Julia looked back up at Kat. "He left."

Kat grinned. "That means you're in for the pub crawl!"

She had no reason not to, realized Julia. "I'm in!"

She and the others bumped and jostled their way down the crowded sidewalk toward Sonsie, the first stop on their pub crawl list. The celebratory post-race glow was contagious, and Julia's mood lifted. Much as she wished that Asher could have been there to share the experience, she'd have hated for the two of them to be one of those couples who were joined at the hip, with no lives of their own. Today, they'd both been here to support their friends—something she hoped would never change.

Chapter 20

The Journeys of the Heart office was buzzing on this November morning, the day they'd been building toward for the past four months: today was the first of the interviews with the three Travel Sabbatical finalists. Tatyana Kozak would be coming at ten-thirty to meet with Julia, Carly, Franco, and the other two JoH Board members, Carter Evans and Sally Watson.

Lean, six-foot-six, no-nonsense Carter was a fifty-eight-year-old veteran who taught auto shop and coached track at Madison Park Technical Vocational High School in Roxbury. Sally, a former teen mom and domestic violence survivor, was the executive director of Angel Whispers, a transitional housing program for women and families in Jamaica Plain. Both African American, Carter and Sally jokingly claimed credit for giving JoH some street cred–and for saving it from being not just lily-white, but *blindingly* white.

It was sadly true. Diversity was hardly a strong suit of Boston, and even less so of the North End. Julia had met Carter and Sally at a conference on travel, multiculturalism, and global philanthropy, and she felt lucky to have gotten them to agree to serve on the Board.

She joined the others in the conference room. "You guys ready?"

"Ready as rain," said Carter.

"*Right* as rain, big man," said Sally. She liked to give Carter a hard time. "Don't make us look stupid in front of this sweet little Ukrainian girl. And try not to scare her, either."

"Yes, *ma'am*," said Carter. "Right as rain, and not stupid–or scary. Got it."

The five of them animatedly discussed Tatyana's background and qualifications. Then, at shortly after ten o'clock, they heard the front office door swing open: Tatyana, arriving early for her ten-thirty interview.

They looked at one another and grinned. This was it!

As they'd planned, Whitley and Byron greeted Tatyana and entertained her in the outer office until the official interview time. Eager for a glimpse of the young woman whose application had so touched her heart, Julia cracked open the conference room door and peeked outside. Byron, naturally, was holding court, regaling Tatyana with what sounded like a story about Ukrainian Easter eggs, while the young woman listened with rapt attention. Tatyana was short and a little chubby, with chin-length brown hair, a round face, and wide brown eyes. She gave the impression of a puppy dog, guileless and eager to please.

Julia quietly shut the door and returned to the conference table.

"Well?" said Sally.

"She's adorable," said Julia. "I have a good feeling."

At ten-thirty on the nose, Whitley ushered Tatyana into the conference room, Byron trailing close behind. Once the introductions had been made, the Board members took turns asking Tatyana about the genealogical research she'd done into her mother's family and the motivation behind her proposed trip to war-torn Ukraine. Whitley and Byron looked on, taking notes.

Tatyana proved to be a delight, every bit as sweet in person as she'd seemed on paper. It was clear that this proposed pilgrimage to her mother's homeland was not some impulsive notion conceived out of casual curiosity, but the culmination of a lifelong yearning to connect with the mother she'd never known. As the young woman talked about her family and the loss she'd never been able to quantify, Julia had to consciously rein in her own emotions. She felt a desire to call a halt to the contest right then and there and award Tatyana the prize on the spot, but of course she couldn't do that. She could only hope that Tatyana was having a similarly profound impact on her colleagues.

She glanced at the others, trying to gauge their reactions. The Harts had wanted children but had never been able to have them, and Julia could tell that they were deeply moved by Tatyana's story—and could that be a tear she saw Franco wiping from his eye?

Perfect, she thought.

Julia looked next to Carter, but could not read anything from his standard friendly, open expression. Sally, though, was leaning forward, nodding enthusiastically at something Tatyana was saying. Whitley, transparent as always, was sitting bolt-upright, transfixed by Tatyana's story. Even Byron was uncharacteristically subdued.

It couldn't have gone any better, thought Julia as the interview wound down. They concluded with warm goodbyes and promises to stay in touch. Julia walked Tatyana out, impulsively giving her a heartfelt hug on her way out the door.

She then re-joined the others in the conference room.

Carly's emotions were written all over her face. "What a sweetheart. In a way, I feel just as sorry for her mother, never getting to know that lovely girl."

Julia blinked back tears. "I know. Wasn't she sweet?"

"*So* sweet," said Sally. "I wanted to adopt her myself!"

"You found a good one, Julia," said Carter. "Nice work."

"*We* found a good one," said Julia, not wanting to deprive Whitley and Byron of their due credit.

Byron's forehead furrowed. "*We* found *three* good ones. Keep in mind, folks, the TS party has only just begun."

He was right, of course; they still had two more candidates to interview and evaluate.

Even so, Julia was certain that neither of the two remaining finalists could possibly hold a candle to Tatyana. Tatyana had this in the bag; she could feel it.

•   •   •

The next day, their same group reconvened in the JoH conference room to welcome the second TS finalist, aspiring architect Tia Lovett, who'd taken the train in from New York City. Dressed to the nines in a professional-looking business suit, her black hair in a neatly trimmed afro, Tia exuded confidence and enthusiasm. Incredibly poised for an eighteen-year-old girl, she was also almost impossible not to like.

Carter, an architecture enthusiast himself, took the lead in Tia's interview. Tia recounted how spending time at her grandfather's historic estate in Millbrook, New York, had inspired her passion for classical architecture. She went on to discuss how under-represented African Americans, and especially African American women, were in the field. Noting wryly that she'd heard that, contrary to popular opinion, the world didn't begin and end with the United States, she emphasized her determination to see something of the world and expand her professional horizons before committing to four years at an American university.

Tia was clearly a young woman who knew what she wanted and would undoubtedly get it, thought Julia. She could tell that Sally was especially taken with her. Even so, hearing about Tia's dreams and ambitions didn't touch her heart the way Tatyana's story had. As they ended the interview, Julia felt confident that, if it came down to a choice between Tia and Tatyana, the JoH board would go with their *own* hearts–and choose Tatyana.

Meaning that there was now only one person standing between Tatyana and her personal Travel Sabbatical: the third candidate, Cruz Costa.

• • •

The interview with the third TS finalist was scheduled for Friday afternoon, via videoconferencing, from Cruz's home in New Mexico. When the young man's image appeared on their computer screen in the JoH conference room, Julia's heart sank. His hair was shiny and black, falling nearly to his shoulders, and his features were strong and well-defined. Most striking, though, were his onyx-black eyes, which, even via video, were mesmerizing.

She glanced at Byron–no surprises there. His jaw had dropped slightly, and he was wearing a look of imbecilic adoration identical to the one she'd seen any number of times on David Meadow's face. It couldn't have been any more obvious if he'd shouted it from the rooftops: Byron Knowles was smitten.

It wasn't a pretty sight.

The others on the panel jumped in with their questions, which Cruz answered with intelligence and ease. He discussed the national and international water shortage, the devastating effects that the worsening drought had already had on Mexico and the American Southwest, and the disparate effects of environmental degradation on indigenous populations around the world. He was down-to-earth, funny, and well-spoken, and the hour-long interview flew by.

As they wrapped up the discussion and watched Cruz's visage vanish from the monitor, Byron let out a self-satisfied sigh. "Well! He blew *that* out of the water, so to speak."

His remark prompted chuckles and words of agreement from the others.

Still swooning, Byron added, "Not to mention, *Cruz Costa*? I mean, come *on*. Could there *be* a cooler name?"

"Well, let's not be hasty," said Franco. "This is an important decision, and do we have two other candidates."

After some discussion, they all agreed that Tia, while impressive, didn't best represent the spirit of the TS award, which emphasized spiritual growth and public service over professional ambition. And, so, as Julia had anticipated, the choice came down to Tatyana and Cruz. She felt compelled to speak up on Tatyana's behalf.

"As some of you know, I lost my mother when I was eleven. I know from experience that nothing can compensate for growing up without a mother, like Tatyana did." Her breath caught for a second. "But this trip would help."

Carter nodded. "Plus, family history is so important. Young people today have no sense of where they come from, their roots. Genealogy is a great thing to encourage."

"And she was *such* a sweetheart," said Carly.

"I know," said Sally. "Didn't you want to just hug her and tell her how proud her mother would be?"

That was *exactly* how Julia had felt.

Franco looked thoughtful. "Taking action and creating something positive from her loss—that takes character. She's a good girl, you can tell."

Now Julia was extremely encouraged. Being a "good girl" was the highest possible praise from Franco. They were only moments away from awarding the Travel Sabbatical to Tatyana—again, she could feel it.

Until Byron ostentatiously cleared his throat. "So, umm, *guys*? I hate to bring everyone down from this cloud of maternal emotion, but *someone's* got to be the voice of reason here."

Right, thought Julia. As if she and the others were useless, blabbering, blubbering blobs.

Franco looked amused. "Go ahead, Byron. What's on your mind?"

He frowned, looking ultra-serious beneath his coiffed blonde doo. "Frankly, what's on my mind is money. At this point in time, we do not have annual funding for the TS program—correct?"

All eyes turned to Julia.

"Somewhat correct," she said. "I expect that our same individual donor will renew the grant for next year, but he makes those decisions at the end of first quarter of every year, so we won't have an absolute guarantee until March. He's pretty quirky, so I didn't want to push him. In the meantime, I'm working on a new proposal to The Beantown Stash, and we have proposals pending with several other potential donors. I'm very hopeful that something will come through even if the original TS donor doesn't decide to keep funding the program."

Byron's perfectly groomed eyebrows shot up. "When it comes to funding, I've learned never to be *hopeful* of anything. But from my consulting experience, I can tell you that the best way to get people to invest in something is to be able to sell them on the *last* product you put out. And we can *sell* Cruz—*I* can sell Cruz. This global warming stuff is *hot*, no pun intended—well, partially intended. I say we get on that bandwagon and market the TS program as encouraging young environmentalists like the delectable señor Costa. We'll be beating off the donors with a stick."

"Let me guess," said Whitley. "You'll take on that job."

"Beating them off with a stick?" said Byron, with a suggestive eyebrow-raise. "You got it, gorgeous."

"You know, that's not a bad point, Byron," said Franco. "Thanks for thinking in terms of fundability."

"Why I'm here," said Byron oh-so-modestly.

"And the water crisis could use publicity," said Sally. "Everyone's heard about climate change, but most people aren't aware that there's a water shortage."

"I had no idea myself," said Carly. "Not until he started talking about it."

Byron, though, had more to say. (*When didn't he?* thought Julia.) "Again, to be the practical one here–you'll thank me later for not giving a rat's *ass* about political correctness–oops, sorry, vegan Julia, you probably *like* rats' asses–it can only help our cause to give the TS award to a candidate of color. When's the last time that happened?"

Once again, all eyes were on Julia.

"This is only the third year of the program," she said. "Meaning we've had only two winners. But yes, they've both been white."

Byron nodded. "There you go."

Julia felt like a convicted bigot.

They were all quiet for a moment.

Franco broke the silence. "All right then. Are we all in agreement on Cruz Costa as this year's Travel Sabbatical winner?"

Everyone in the room nodded–except for Julia.

"For the record," she said, "I think Tatyana is the most deserving candidate. My vote is for her."

Franco nodded. "Anyone else?"

No one spoke.

"I'm afraid you're out-voted, Julia," said Franco. "Cruz Costa is the winner. We'll make Tatyana the runner-up, meaning that she'll get a five-hundred-dollar prize, and if something comes up and Cruz can't go, she'll get the trip."

"Fair enough," said Julia, reminding herself that she shouldn't hold it against Cruz that Byron Knowles liked him. (Craved him. Desired him. *Pined* for him.) "I'll notify the candidates on Monday."

After the others had dispersed, Whitley and Byron huddled together like schoolchildren. Julia heard Byron murmur, "Cruz-a-licious! Who knew a water-loving tree-hugger could be so scrumptious? I may have to go green—or green*ish*." He smirked at Whitley. "You realize, of course, seventeen's well past the age of consent. It would all be *completely* legal."

"You've thought of everything!" said Whitley. "So are you going to help Cruz-a-licious dig some water ditches?"

"Oh, I'll irrigate his fields any time," said Byron. "Any time at all!"

Whitley giggled exultantly. "B, you are too much!"

In this instance, Julia couldn't disagree. Byron really *was* too much.

• • •

Julia returned to her own office, grateful for the quiet. It all but killed her that Tatyana wouldn't get to go on her trip to Ukraine. What stung most of all, though, was that it had been Byron—right-wing, non-environmentalist, foie gras fan *Byron*—to turn the TS tide in Cruz's favor.

And all because he had the hots for an admittedly striking high school boy.

Still, she couldn't fault the others for their choice. She'd also been extremely impressed with Cruz; after all, she'd helped select him as one of the three finalists. If not for Tatyana's story, which touched so pointedly on her own experience, Cruz would have been her top pick as well. He was inarguably a deserving winner. She just wished that the TS competition had felt...*cleaner*.

She sighed, mentally taking stock: an imperfect process, not quite the outcome she'd hoped for, but, all told, "Eliot" had been a success.

And best of all?

Eliot was over.

Chapter 21

Marissa checked the hem of Julia's dress. "Perfect. You, my friend, are ready to get married!"

That weekend, they'd set up a makeshift fitting room in Kat's living room for the bridal party's final fittings. With short, funky black hair and dark eyes, Marissa was organized, energetic, and unfailingly level-headed—the perfect counterbalance to the rest of the bridesmaids.

Julia gazed at the image reflecting back at her from the mirror. "It's really happening," she said, scarcely able to believe it. "A week from now I'll be married."

"*Yes*, it's really happening!" said Marissa. "And you look amazing."

Jolene drained the last of her fourth glass of champagne. "So the dress is addressed? Do me next, Miss Mariss! Address my dress!"

"*Mrs.* Mariss," corrected Kat. Last year, Marissa had married her longtime partner, Clyde, a filmmaker in Brooklyn. They made an adorable, Mutt-and-Jeff-like pair - Clyde, a six-foot-three Jewish man with wild, Einstein-like white hair, and Marissa, five-foot-four, Chinese American, and ten years his junior.

"*Ms.* Mariss, please," said Marissa. "And yes, Jolene, I'll address your dress. Come over here."

Jolene climbed off the couch and stood unsteadily as Marissa made adjustments to her rosy pink gown.

"Thank you so much for coming up to Boston for this," Julia told her friend. "You really are the best."

"I think you mean the *bess*," said Jolene. "Ms. Mariss is the bess!"

Julia and Kat exchanged looks. What had they been thinking offering Jolene alcohol before noon? Julia only hoped that her sister would manage to hold it together for the actual wedding.

"No big deal," said Marissa. It was her standard response to just about everything.

"I know my place is a bit of a comedown from Fort Greene," said Kat, referring to the Brooklyn neighborhood where Marissa's shop was located. "Hope we're not cramping your style, Mrs. Marississ." She grinned. "Sorry, that just sounds so much better than 'Ms.'"

Jolene hooted. "Mrs. Marississ, oh, that's good!"

"Please, Kat, don't encourage her," said Julia.

"To answer your question," said Marissa, "you guys are *not* cramping my style. My style is way beyond cramping."

"Right on, sister!" said Jolene, attempting to high-five Marissa as she re-pinned a hem.

"Stop moving, Jolene, so I don't prick you," said Marissa.

"Ouch!" said Jolene.

"Did I prick you?" said Marissa.

"No, that was ampissatory," said Jolene. "Anticipory. You know what I mean."

The rest of them were laughing.

"Jolene, you're a cheap drunk," said Kat.

"Frugal!" said Jolene. "I'm a frugal drunk. By the way, how was Lacey? Tell us the truth, Ms. Mariss, did she drive you bat-shit crazy?"

Lacey's fitting had happened last week, in New York, but she would be arriving in Boston this afternoon, to help kick off the bachelorette festivities—the planning of which she'd naturally domineered.

Marissa laughed. "Lacey? No, she was cool. She liked the dress. It fit. All good." She patted Jolene on the shoulder. "Okay, you're all set. Good job, Jo!"

"Thanks, Mariss!" Jolene collapsed onto the couch, seemingly exhausted from the exertion.

Meanwhile, Marissa had moved on to Kat—and was eyeing the substantial gap in the bodice of the supposedly form-fitting dress.

"Kathleen! You went and got skinny on me. Don't you know that everyone always *tries* to lose weight before a wedding, but no one actually *does* it? What the hell?"

Kat looked sheepish. "It happened by accident, I swear. My plan was to try out this running thing long enough that I could legitimately deem it a total waste of time. But it turns out it's had a marginally positive effect on my life. So it gets to stay. At least for now." She cocked her head. "So in your professional opinion, Marissa, would you say that I'm too svelte to be a bridesmaid? Maybe I should I be the bride instead?"

"Excuse me!" said Julia. "That slot is taken."

"And are you suggesting that the other bridesmaids are fat?" said Jolene. "That's a little harsh, Kitty Kat–calling me drunk *and* fat? One or the other I could deal with, but both? That's just plain mean."

Julia groaned. If they didn't get her sister under control, it promised to be a *very* long day–and night.

But Marissa had thought of that, too. She was already handing Jolene one of the dozen bagels she'd brought up from New York. "Jolene, you *are* drunk, but you're not fat. Now get something in your stomach before you puke all over my beautiful dresses."

"Thanks, Mariss," said Jolene, obediently tearing off a chunk of bagel and stuffing it into her mouth. "I don't think you're fat, either."

Marissa had almost finished with Kat's dress. "I'll get this fixed up tomorrow, before I head back to the city." She looked at the others and grinned. "In other words, we're good! Dresses addressed."

They changed back into their regular clothes, refused Jolene more champagne, and set out for the restaurant Lacey had booked for lunch, which was just a few blocks away, in the South End.

Marissa wrapped an arm around Julia as they walked. "Only a week until the big event! You ready for a midnight wedding in a castle?"

"I'm ready!" said Julia. "And what better time for a wedding in a castle?"

"*No* better time!" said Jolene. "Let's just hope Asher doesn't turn into a frog after midnight."

Julia laughed. "I think you're getting your fairy tales mixed up."

"What do you mean?" said Jolene.

"There's the one about the princess who kisses a frog who turns into a prince. And then here's the other one, where –"

"Oh, right, Cinderella," said Jolene. "Her stagecoach turns into a pumpkin if she stays out too late. Well, pumpkin, frog, whatever—let's aim to avoid *both* those scenarios."

"Good thinking, Jo!" said Kat. "Only happy fairy tales from here on out."

It's really happening, thought Julia—again. "I'm getting married!"

Her sister stopped dead in her tracks and hugged her tightly and drunkenly.

"*Yes!*" screeched Jolene. "We're getting married!"

PART 2

(Almost) Married

Chapter 22

"Julia," said Lacey. "You're...*luminous*."

"Thank you," said Julia, smiling. Hardboiled Lacey wasn't someone who ordinarily used words like "luminous."

Of course, today was far from ordinary.

As she had only a week before, Julia gazed at her reflection in the mirror. People had told her often enough that she was beautiful, but tonight, in her mother's dress, Jolene's bracelet on her wrist, her hair piled on top of her head, a few delicate tendrils spilling down around her face, she *felt* beautiful. A stylist had done her makeup, which was impeccable, but she knew it wasn't the cosmetics giving her face this special glow.

It was love–the love radiating from her heart.

Kat was beaming sappily. "It's true, you *are* luminous! In fact, I'd say we're *all* looking pretty luminous."

"Very much so," said Julia. "Most luminous bridal party ever!"

Amidst the joy of the moment, she felt an incongruous jolt of sadness. She looked instinctively to her sister.

The ever-intuitive Jolene was already by her side. She leaned in and gave Julia an awkward hug, not wanting to muss her dress.

"She's here with us," whispered Jolene. "I know it."

No, she wasn't, thought Julia–or she wouldn't feel this gaping emptiness inside her, like the unhappy eye of a blissful storm. "I just wish..."

"I know," said Jolene, squeezing her tight, not worrying anymore about the dress. "Me, too."

They both pulled away, wiping at their eyes.

Marissa immediately swooped in to fix their smudged makeup and straighten their gowns.

How petty all of her worries of these past few months now seemed, thought Julia. To think how unnecessarily worked up she'd gotten over the Schloss, the Travel Sabbatical competition, and Byron Knowles. At this point, her workplace was but a distant memory. It was quite conceivable that she'd never return there again, other than to visit.

Today, of course, was also the dreaded, legendary Friday the thirteenth. The notion that that "unlucky" date could possibly have tainted this perfect day now seemed laughable.

"Friday the thirteenth isn't so bad after all," she said with a smile.

"Maybe you'll start a whole new trend," said Marissa. "Friday the thirteenth will become known as a *lucky* day. At least for weddings."

"Very possible," said Julia.

Jolene was fidgeting with excitement. "It's almost time, Jules. Dad will be here any second to walk you to the chapel—and then down the aisle!"

Then came a knock on the dressing room door.

Lacey opened it, and Julia's father poked his head inside. His eyes welled with tears when he caught sight of his eldest daughter. "Oh, Julia. My precious, beautiful Julia."

Julia smiled, unused to such sentimentality from her intellectual father. Then it occurred to her that while this was the first time her father had seen *her* in this dress, it wasn't the first time he'd seen this dress. Her mother had been wearing it on their wedding day.

"Your mother would be so happy to see you now," he said.

Julia nodded, not trusting herself to speak.

Her father offered her his arm, and she took it, feeling that she suddenly understood what people meant when they said that everything in their lives had been preparing them for one particular moment. It was as if her entire life had crystallized in this one day—the day she'd been awaiting her entire life.

A buzzing sound was coming from the corner.

"Sorry, that's probably me," said Lacey. "I forgot to turn off my phone. One second."

But the sound was coming from Julia's handbag–the stunning white Stella McCartney purse that had been an early wedding gift from Carly and Franco. She reached for it.

"Leave it, Jules," said Kat. "It's your wedding day!"

"No, it might be my grandmother," said Julia. "Her flight was delayed in Charleston."

"Sophie made it in just fine," her father told her. "We picked her up at the airport a couple of hours ago."

Julia, however, had already retrieved her phone. She saw that she *had* missed an earlier text message from her grandmother. But the incoming message was from Asher.

She smiled. Superstitious Asher had pledged not to see her before the wedding–but, presumably, a text communication didn't count as "seeing." She touched the screen to view the message. "*I love you*" was what she was expecting to see.

And the message did say that. But that wasn't all it said.

I love you, Julia. But I can't do this. I'm so sorry.

Julia stared at the phone. And stared some more.

Her father touched her shoulder. "Julia? Everything okay?"

To Julia, from that moment on, everything looked, and felt, fuzzy. She simply couldn't understand. These words, these letters–could she be reading them in the wrong language? Would the message make sense in French, perhaps? Or Chinese?

But no matter how many times she read and reread the message, its text kept conveying the same inconceivable reality: Asher wasn't coming. Asher wasn't getting married. Which meant that she wasn't getting married, either.

Unless, of course, she was planning to marry herself.

"Looks like I may be marrying myself," she said. She meant it, she supposed, as a joke, but it didn't sound even remotely funny.

"What are you talking about?" said Kat. She snatched the phone from Julia's hand.

The screen had gone blank from inactivity, and for a moment Julia wondered if she could have imagined the whole thing.

But then Kat touched the screen, causing the same message to reappear.

"You are *shitting* me," said Kat, glaring at the display. "No fucking way."

"Kat," said Julia. The obscenities seemed inappropriate on her wedding day.

Except, she remembered, it wasn't. Not anymore–apparently.

A dark, creeping blob of awfulness was spreading through her gut. She felt as though she might throw up.

"This is insane," said Kat. "I'm calling him, Jules. This is just some sick, twisted, cold-feet thing. I'm not standing for this. I'm not." She clicked the phone screen to pull up Asher's number and held the phone to her ear. "Pick up, you jerk-off. What kind of man are you?"

All of this, naturally, had piqued the others' interest. They all hovered over Kat, craning to hear what was said.

Rubberneckers, thought Julia.

"Voicemail," said Kat contemptuously. She ended the call, looking as if she was about to throw the phone against the wall, until she evidently remembered it didn't belong to her.

Meanwhile, the others crowded around her, wanting to see Asher's message. Kat pulled it up and showed them.

This was getting out of hand, thought Julia. It had to be some sort of crazy misunderstanding. Asher wouldn't just not show up. Not her Asher.

She retrieved the phone from Kat and dialed her fiancé.

The call went immediately to his voicemail, and she found she had no idea what to say. "Sweetheart, what's going on? Where are you? Please call me. I love you."

She clicked off, feeling foolish for having declared her love to someone who was abandoning her if not quite at the altar, only a short distance away. Thank goodness she'd checked her phone. Otherwise she might have been waiting indefinitely at the altar itself.

Her father steered her to an armchair in the corner. "Here, honey, sit down. Don't worry. We'll get this straightened out."

Julia mutely obeyed the instructions, at least in part.

She sat. But she had no idea how she was supposed to not worry.

At some point, there came another knock on the dressing room door.

Julia's head, and everyone else's, pivoted sharply toward the door. It was clear they were all thinking the same thing: *Asher?*

The door opened, and there came a gasp of happy relief from Marissa.

But it wasn't Asher in the doorway; it was only his best man, August. Julia realized that her New York friend, who'd met Asher only a handful of times, had seemingly mistaken his lookalike cousin for Asher himself. She stood to greet him.

"August," she said, both in greeting to him and for Marissa's benefit.

"Well?" said August, sounding excited and impatient all at once. "What's going on, ladies? It's that time–in fact, it's *after* that time! Or are we aiming for fashionably late?"

"*Well?*" said Kat. "You tell *us*! You were on the plane with him." August and Asher had planned to fly to Thun from London, after a week of taking care of more BartTech business.

August looked startled. "Asher? No, Odetta needed one more hand on deck to wrap up this U.K. deal, so he decided to take a later flight. He told me he'd get a car from the airport, but I haven't seen him. I figured he must be in here. With you."

"He'd never have come to see me before the wedding," said Julia. "Bad luck."

August gave a short laugh. He well knew Asher's superstitious nature. "Right, I didn't think of that. So where the hell is he?"

Julia handed him her cell phone, and he read the text message.

His face reddened. "Julia, I have no idea what this is all about. I'm so sorry."

"Hey, Julia?" said Lacey. "It's almost twelve-twenty. People must be wondering what's going on. How about I go let them know?"

"No, I should do it," said August. "I'm the best man."

Joe Jones was already heading toward the door. "No, guys, I'll take care of it."

At that moment, the only sensation Julia had was a slight itching along her spine, from the detailing on her dress. Although other people's emotions were clearly running high, her own suddenly seemed to have evaporated entirely. It occurred to her that she could use the numbness to her advantage.

"Dad, I'll handle it," she said. "It's my wedding–that is, it *was* my wedding. I should be the one to call it off."

"Are you sure?" said her father.

Julia nodded, feeling slightly woozy but grounded by the rock that was now her heart. Without another word, she departed the dressing room. Her would-be bridal party, and August and her father, unsure whether to stay or follow, straggled indecisively behind. A few minutes later, she entered the main chapel, where the two-hundred-plus guests–and the non-denominational Swiss officiant–were gathered.

She made her way down the center aisle, alone.

At the sight of the beautiful–and belated–bride, someone burst into spontaneous applause, triggering a joyful, thunderous standing ovation from the crowd.

Julia paused in the aisle, touched by the show of support.

Then then she realized that, of course, they had no idea.

She reached the altar and turned to face the guests. The clapping quieted.

Julia took a deep breath and took care to speak clearly and audibly; she certainly didn't want to have to repeat herself. "Thank you so much for being here. It means the world to me that you came all this way to share in what was going to be such a joyous event." Her breath caught, and, for a horrible moment, she wasn't sure she'd be able to continue. She straightened her back and forced herself to go on. "Unfortunately, there's been a change in circumstances. There will not be a wedding tonight. But please, stay and enjoy the Schloss, and the food, and each other. Apart from the actual wedding ceremony, everything will proceed exactly as planned."

The last remark prompted a lone startled chuckle from one of the guests, and Julia realized how ridiculous her comment must have sounded.

Oh, well.

"Thank you all," she finished. "Really."

With that, she made her way back down the aisle and out of the chapel. Pandemonium had all but broken loose. She could hear the guests barraging the bridesmaids, the groomsmen, and her father with questions, but she'd leave it to the others to explain. She'd done her part. She'd made the official announcement.

She stepped out into the hall, feeling empty but strangely proud. She hadn't broken down. She hadn't cried. She hadn't turned ugly or rageful or hysterical. She had done well.

And what if she had? was her next vicious thought. What if she *had* maintained her dignity, at least to some extent? What had it accomplished? Where had it gotten her?

She tried to ignore the thoughts tearing around in her head, but they grew only more insistent. She walked faster, desperate to escape them, only to realize a few minutes later that she had no idea where she was going. She turned down first one hallway, then another, trying to find her way back to her room. She succeeded only in getting more and more lost in the Schloss.

At last, she stopped short. This had been supposed to be the best day of her life. Instead, here she was, lost, alone, in a grand, vacant hallway, without an inkling as to where to go or what to do next.

That awful feeling in her gut was back. And it was now lurching into her throat.

She sprinted to the WC she'd just passed.

Kat found her there, heaving into the toilet. Her friend knelt beside her, stroking her back, until she'd expelled the contents of her stomach.

A few more dry heaves and she was done–for now.

Julia stood up, feeling dizzy.

Kat flushed the toilet once, and then again. "Oh, Jules. Are you okay?"

Julia swished some water around in her mouth and spit it out into the sink. "Sure. I'm great."

"Oh, Jesus. I mean, as okay as you can be? What do you want to do?"

Julia looked at her friend. "Get married. That's what I wanted to do. I didn't have a backup plan."

For once, Kat seemed truly at a loss for words. "Okay, look, we need to get ourselves together. Why don't you change, and then we'll go up to my cupola. We'll get the staff to bring us some tea." She smiled encouragingly.

"After all, isn't that Julia Jones's number-one rule of life? When in doubt, tea?"

Until Kat's mention of changing clothes, Julia had all but forgotten that she was still wearing her mother's dress. What a wretched figure she must make, roaming the Schloss in her dead mother's wedding gown, like a maiden in some particularly grim fairy tale.

She glanced down now at the dress. It was tearstained, makeup-smeared, and wrinkled from kneeling on the floor. Her mother's gown deserved so much better.

The next thing she knew, she'd collapsed onto the toilet seat, her body heaving with ugly, guttural sobs that sounded too savage and animalistic to be coming from her. For what seemed like an eternity, Kat rubbed her back and said things Julia didn't hear.

Eventually, Julia's sobs slowed, her jagged breathing evened, and the tears ebbed to a sporadic trickle.

Kat handed her a tissue, and Julia blew her nose.

"Okay, let's try that again," said Kat, nudging her up. "Let's get you changed and then we'll go upstairs to my cupola, drink some tea, regroup. Or maybe you want something stronger than tea? Like espresso?" When Julia didn't respond, she added. "That's a joke."

Julia tried to smile. "Good one. Yeah, sure, tea's good."

Aided by Kat's unerring sense of direction, they quickly made their way back to Julia's room, which turned out to be right around the corner. There, in the room she'd been meant to be sharing with Asher, Julia changed out of her mother's dress—that was how she was thinking of it, she realized, as her *mother's* dress, not her own—into a pair of pajama pants and a T-shirt. So much for her sexy wedding night lingerie.

She and Kat then headed up the windy spiraling staircase to Kat's cupola.

Romantic as the notion of the cupola had been, however, it proved in actuality to be cramped and unsuitable for lounging. And, so, they made their way back down to the main floor, to Lacey's spacious suite. There, they were joined by Julia's father and her stepmother, Stephanie. Marissa, Clyde, and Jolene arrived minutes later, Jolene armed with booze: several bottles of wine, brandy, and Irish whisky. They had a sleepy-looking Sophie in tow.

Her grandmother looked about to drop, noted Julia. "Nana, you didn't have to come. Please, go get some rest. I'll see you in the morning."

Sophie hugged her, then nodded. "If you're sure, honey. It has been quite a weekend."

Julia had no response.

Clutching the mug of tea Kat had made her, she sat on the sofa, flanked protectively by her father and stepmother. Lacey, too, seemed determined to stay close; she'd squeezed onto the couch on the other side of Stephanie.

"I know this might sound weird, Jules," said Marissa from the loveseat she was sharing with Clyde, "but despite the circumstances, thank you for bringing us here. I don't think I've ever been anywhere so beautiful. I hate the situation, but I love this place."

Julia nodded wordlessly, unable to feel more gracious. Right now, Schloss Himmel's shameless beauty seemed almost a personal affront. But for someone as aesthetically-minded as Marissa, this visit was truly a once-in-a-lifetime opportunity—literally, Julia realized. None of them would ever have occasion to come here again. Including her.

In fact, it struck her, when Asher returned to the Schloss, he, too, would be doing so as a guest. The castle was like his version of her mother's wedding gown: without a wedding, it wouldn't become his.

"I guess Asher wanted a castle, but he didn't want it *that* much," she said.

Kat looked stricken. "Jules. Stop."

"Or else he *did* want the castle, but he *didn't* want to marry me so much that it was worth giving up the Schloss."

The others exchanged glances. Julia's father and stepmother, in tandem, rubbed her legs consolingly. Jolene, who'd curled up next to Marissa and Clyde on the loveseat, raised the bottle of whisky, offering another sort of consolation. For Jolene, of course, tonight's tragedy represented, as much as anything else, an opportunity to drink.

Julia shook her head, unwilling to risk losing what semblance of composure she'd managed to regain.

Jolene shrugged and refilled her own glass. "Jules, there's got to be an explanation. This is the kind of thing *I* would do. Not Asher. Asher's solid."

There was a loud rap on the door, startling all of them.

A ray of hope pierced Julia's heart like a lightning bolt: this time, it *had* to be him.

Her thoughts raced. It was after one a.m., meaning that it was technically the next day, Saturday, the fourteenth. Friday the thirteenth had more than lived up to its dire reputation, but it was over, and Asher was here, and the guests couldn't have gone far. They'd call everyone back together and proceed with the wedding only slightly behind schedule. Marissa could help her fix up the wedding dress; it was just a little makeup, no blood or vomit or anything worse–and moreover, what did it even matter? She'd happily marry Asher in Kat's pajamas!

She jumped off the couch and flung open the door.

She was greeted by the sight not of Asher, but his parents.

Julia's tenuous emotional control dissolved, and, once again, she was sobbing with terrifying abandon.

Dom hugged her to him. "Julia, I'm so sorry about this. I don't know what happened. We talked to him this morning. Everything seemed fine."

Julia wiped at her eyes, trying–again–to get herself together.

"Something must have come up in London," said Sage. "But this behavior is unacceptable. This is *not* how I raised my son." Her eyes were blue, frosty, unfathomable–the antithesis of her son's.

Julia wondered if she'd ever get to stare into Asher's warm brown eyes again.

Dom said, "We still want you to be part of our family, Julia. You *are* part of our family."

"Quite honestly," Sage added, "at this point, we'd rather have *you* in our family than Asher." Noting that Julia was still sniffling, she offered her a monogrammed handkerchief.

The small kindness only had the effect of restarting the flow of Julia's tears.

"Thank you," she murmured. "You both mean a lot to me. No matter what."

Julia forced herself to relax her hands, which were clenched into fists. As she flexed her fingers, her diamond ring caught the light, undimmed in the slightest by the recent turn of events.

Her ring. Her breathtakingly beautiful ring—mocking her with its cheerfulness.

She suddenly hated it and everything it represented.

She slid it off her finger; it came easily, as if it knew it no longer belonged there.

"Here," she said, handing it to Sage. "I know it's a family heirloom. It should be back in your family."

Sage made a show of reluctance, but then accepted the ring. "Just for now. For safekeeping. Until we get things straightened out."

She was spared the need for further excuses by the appearance in the hallway of a visibly shaken Pierre-Yves.

The Schloss manager anxiously cleared his throat. "Mademoiselle Julia, my condolences. I know that this is difficult. I will take care of everything. Everything. Just—yes? Tomorrow there will be a private breakfast for you and your close family. The remaining guests will be located in another room."

Even though she knew he was only trying to help, it sounded to Julia as if she was being quarantined. "Thank you, Pierre-Yves. That will be perfect."

He smiled, relieved. "The guests are very happy tonight, Mademoiselle Julia. That is, they are not happy with the state of circumstantial events, but they are being well attended and are enjoying themselves as much as possible in this given situation."

Dom nodded approvingly. "Good. Thank you for looking after our guests, Pierre-Yves. What with everyone's crazy schedules, we don't often have the chance to gather *en masse* like this. I want people to be able to make the most of this opportunity to be together."

Under the state of "circumstantial events," Julia had little sympathy for the logistical challenges faced by a clan of modern-day aristocrats when they tried to get together. She bit her tongue as Dom rattled off, in French, a string of further instructions for Pierre-Yves.

Dom then turned back to Julia. "Take it easy, okay? We'll take care of the guests."

Pierre-Yves again cleared his throat.

"Yes, Pierre-Yves?" said Dom, a tinge of irritation creeping into his voice. "What else?"

The Schloss manager shifted uneasily on his feet. "There is just one other matter. I spoke with the inns, and I explained the–*situation*. I fear that they were not overly accommodating. With great reluctance, the lodgings on Oahu, Kuiai, and Hawaii complied to cancel the reservations, but they would grant but a partial refund. However, the inn on Maui stated that they reserve their especial honeymoon suites at least one year, sometimes two, in advance, and they do not permit cancellation within six months of the reservation date, under any circumstances." He frowned. "I tried to explain that this was not 'any circumstance,' but they would not hear me."

At first, Julia had no idea what Pierre-Yves was talking about.

Then it hit her like a tidal wave: the honeymoon. Asher had planned a dream tropical vacation for the two of them–a full month in Hawaii. They'd been scheduled to fly out on Monday, arrive in Honolulu the following morning, and catch a local flight to Maui the next day. After a ten days there, they'd planned to island-hop, doing week-long stays on Oahu, Kauai, and, finally, the Big Island.

The thought of it now made her want to cry–again.

Pierre-Yves looked as if he, too, might burst into tears, so terrible did he feel for bringing up such a sensitive subject.

"It's all right, Pierre-Yves," said Julia. "Really. I'm all right."

Sage touched her arm. "Julia, the honeymoon was to be our wedding gift to you and Asher. Please, let it be our gift to *you*. We've got the reservation anyway, so take a couple of weeks and enjoy Maui." She pressed a credit card into Julia's hands. "The hotel is covered. Use this for any other expenses. Really, this trip's on us."

Before Julia could respond, Pierre-Yves, whose indignation had clearly been building, burst out, "So callous was this luxury resort! Never in my lifetime have I heard such coldness, such heartlessness—*never*! 'Use it or lose it,' they said! I could not believe my own eardrums."

At that, Kat, who had been witnessing everything from an armchair across the room, piped up. "We're using it, Jules! We're going to Hawaii!"

PART 3

The "Honeymoon"

Chapter 23

Even on the luxurious BartTech jet, it was a marathon trip from Thun, with refueling stops in New York and Los Angeles. Now, after a whirlwind twenty-four hours in Honolulu, Julia and Kat were on the beautiful island of Maui, where they'd finally have a chance to settle in and relax.

The concierge of the Island Gem Hotel led them up a majestic, curving staircase to the honeymoon suite. Smiling graciously, he opened the door of the suite and gestured for them to enter.

Julia's eyes were immediately drawn to a bamboo table covered with red rose petals arranged in the shape of a heart. Resting on top was a white vase overflowing with dewy red roses. Next to the flowers was a bottle of champagne, chilling in a silver bucket of ice.

Kat caught her look. "Oops," she muttered. "Guess they didn't get the memo."

Julia nodded vacantly. It was barely noon. The day had to get better.

"Is everything all right?" said the concierge, sensing something was off. "Anything I can get you?"

"Thank you, we're good," said Kat, dismissing him.

He nodded politely and left, shutting the door behind him—the resulting breeze stirring up an entire *cloud* of rose petals.

Julia now noted a path of petals stretching from the doorway to the bedroom.

"They really went all-out," said Kat.

"They sure did," said Julia. She walked to the window and pulled back the curtains. The view was like nothing she'd ever seen—a stunning expanse of cliffs, sky, sea, and black sand beach. Another world.

Kat, eager to explore their lavish surroundings, wheeled her suitcase through the spacious kitchen and lounge area into the bedroom. She called to Julia a moment later.

"Jules, I think I've discovered heaven! I'm never going to leave this bed."

When Julia didn't respond immediately, she said again, "*Jules*! Come see."

Julia tugged herself away from the window view and walked into the bedroom, stopping short at the sight of the largest, gauziest, most inviting canopied bed she'd ever seen. She gaped, awed at its sheer immensity. Bigger than king-sized, it seemed to scale a full city block. Lying on it, Kat looked like a little girl. Clearly, this was a bed meant for other-worldly dreams and passionate lovemaking—for a honeymoon with the love of your life.

Its very presence seemed a cruel practical joke.

"Come on," urged Kat. "There's plenty of room for both of us!"

"That's for sure," said Julia. "I think this bed is bigger than my entire apartment."

The apartment in which she'd be continuing to live, she now realized—no more Rowes Wharf condo, no move to Louisburg Square. Instead, she'd be returning to her solitary existence in her tiny, lonely, one-bedroom apartment—and her tiny, lonely life.

A fresh wave of despair threatened to overwhelm her.

"Come *on*," said Kat. "Check it out!"

Julia climbed onto the bed, a veritable island unto itself. For once, Kat hadn't been exaggerating. The mattress was soft yet firm, cozy yet invigorating, dreamy yet sensual, peaceful yet passionate—in short, ecstasy-invoking.

"Mmm," she murmured. "This *is* nice."

"Umm, *yeah*. And check out that view," said Kat, nodding toward the window. "Nothing to sneeze at, eh?"

Julia glanced over—another other-worldly beach scene. A storm seemed to be brewing, and the crystalline sky had darkened to a charcoal gray, occasionally pierced by shafts of sunlight. She could hardly tear her eyes away. "Nothing to sneeze at," she agreed, brushing a stray rose petal from her arm; they were sprinkled all over the bed. "I get the sense Pierre-Yves didn't explain quite everything to the hotel."

Kat shrugged. "Well, hell. We'll let them think we're a hot lesbian couple who just tied the knot. So what if Asher turned out to be, well, more of a *dasher*? We'll have a great time!"

The look on Julia's face made Kat realize she'd gone too far. "Oh Jesus, Jules, I'm sorry. It's too soon to be cracking jokes about this, isn't it?" She brightened. "Hey, why don't I pour us a drink? That champagne is chilling, after all, for a reason!"

Without awaiting a response, she hopped off the bed. She returned a moment later with two flutes of champagne, one of which she handed to Julia. "Dom Perignon–fancy! We have to make a toast."

Julia looked at her. "And what, exactly, are we supposed to be celebrating? Heartbreak? Abandonment? Betrayal?"

Kat, however, would not be dissuaded. After some back-and-forth as to a suitable–and sincere–subject for a toast, they finally settled on...dolphins. In this tropical setting, marine mammals were certainly relevant. And who didn't genuinely want the best for dolphins?

They clinked their glasses together.

"To dolphins!" they echoed.

And so the "honeymoon" began.

• • •

The storm broke a few hours later. Julia and Kat watched, mesmerized, from the bed as raindrops pummeled the enormous bedroom window and lightning flashed across the sky. For a brief interlude, the fierce majesty of their natural surroundings managed to take Julia's mind off her desolate state.

Not long after, the rain slowed, and rays of sunshine began to pierce the cloud cover.

"One more toast!" said Kat, topping off their glasses with the last of the Dom Perignon. "And this time it's got to be something better than dolphins."

"What's wrong with dolphins?" protested Julia. "They're so smart, and sweet, and brave."

"You know what I mean," said Kat. "Let's toast something *real*."

"You want real?" said Julia, raising her glass. "To the wedding that wasn't! And the love story that wasn't. And the soul-mate that wasn't." She knew she was wallowing–but surely, after all that had happened in these past forty-eight hours, she was entitled to a bit of wallowing.

She set down her drink and shut her eyes against another threatening storm–this one of tears.

Kat watched helplessly as her friend sat rigidly, using every ounce of energy she had not to cry. The ridiculousness of the effort only made Julia's suffering that much more poignant.

"Oh, Jules," said Kat. She set down her own glass and hugged her friend tightly for a few long minutes.

They pulled apart, Julia wiping at her eyes.

Kat retrieved her champagne and again raised her glass. "Cheers, take two. Not to the wedding that wasn't, but the vacation that *is*. To friendship. To the future. To us!"

This time, Julia didn't resist. "Cheers!"

From the bedside table, Kat's cell phone flashed. She grabbed it and looked at it, and her face lit up–causing Julia to wonder whom she'd heard from.

She didn't have to wonder long.

In the next instant, a familiar voice–as commanding as Moses parting the Red Sea–boomed from the hallway. "Ladies! I have arrived! I bring tidings of good cheer and enough Christmas spirit to make you forget all your cares–and any unmentionable exes."

Julia looked at Kat–who looked away.

"But sir," called Kat in her best damsel-in-distress voice, "we don't even know who you are. We're just two helpless, hapless females, all alone in this big, big bed."

She was really getting into this, noted Julia.

"There's no cause for alarm," said the voice. "I'm a heartless, hopeless *Homo sapien*, and I'll fill any gaps in your life–and your bed."

"Oh, that sounds wonderful," simpered Kat. "But we wouldn't *dream* of imposing."

"The imposition is all mine," said the voice. "You just focus on your *position*–or positions. Yes, multiple positions are best."

"Downward dog?" said Kat with a glance at Julia, who was impressed that her friend had retained even that much yoga language.

"How about downward *doggie-style*?" said the voice.

Unable to contain herself any longer, Kat leapt from the bed and ran out of the bedroom to open the door of the honeymoon suite.

A moment later, in bounded–who else?–David Meadow.

He promptly wrestled Kat to the bed, in the process jabbing Julia in the ribs with his elbow. She poked him back, which incited a bout of tickling. In the agony of torture-compelled laughter, Julia thought simultaneously how much she hated being tickled and what a relief it was to feel like a kid again, before she'd had to think about things like proposals and engagements–and castles.

Come to think of it, she *had* noticed David and Kat huddling conspiratorially at the Schloss.

"Just tell me," she gasped, "how long have you been planning to crash my honeymoon?"

David shrugged. "Hey, some unmentionable person's loss, my gain." He'd finally halted the tickling and had settled himself on the bed between Julia and Kat, a well-toned arm wrapped around each of them. "I lucked out last-minute on an ocean-view room just a few doors down."

Julia looked around him, at Kat. "I will *never* forgive you for this!"

"Settle down," said Kat. "Have some champagne."

"Screw champagne," said David. "Let's have some *real* drinks. I came prepared."

He proceeded to fix them a round of beverages from the stash he'd brought: margarita mix, tequila, even limes. Then, he re-joined them on the gargantuan bed, his head resting on Julia's lap, his legs stretched out across Kat's torso.

"They've got an incredible-looking hot tub downstairs," he murmured, eyes closed. "We should check it out later. Everything in Hawaii is clothing-optional, you know. I'm like ninety-nine percent sure."

Kat wriggled out from underneath his legs. "Look, the sun's out! Who's up for getting some air?"

David sighed. "Why does it have to be go, go, go all the time? I just got here. Let's all just chill out for a bit. Together. On the bed."

Kat rolled her eyes—and off the bed. "Is it just me, or is it getting a little close in here? I think we could *all* use some air."

Julia looked at her accusingly. "You're the one who invited him! What did you expect?"

"You're right," said Kat apologetically. "My mistake."

Unperturbed, David shrugged. "Well, Kathleen, you know what they say—if you can't stand the heat, get out of the kitchen."

"And here I didn't even know you could even cook," said Kat.

David smiled suggestively. "Oh, I have *many* talents you don't know about. Maybe, someday, if you're lucky, I might show you a thing or two. In the kitchen, that is."

Kat was already heading toward the door. "Great, I'll look forward to that." Over her shoulder, she added, "Don't burn anything, Dave." She knew, of course, that David hated being called "Dave." "And don't catch anything, Jules. I'll be back in a bit."

Not until Julia heard the hotel suite door click shut did it fully hit her that her "friend" had left her alone, in bed, with *David Meadow*.

She jumped off the bed and chased after Kat.

She caught up with her just as Kat was about to step into the elevator. "What the hell? You spring this on me and then leave me here? Alone? With *him*?"

"Oh, relax, he's harmless," said Kat. "Although, definitely use protection if you decide..."

"Are you *insane*?" said Julia. "I won't need *protection*. What were you thinking to invite him here?"

Kat shrugged defensively. "It was his idea! He convinced me it would help take your mind off things. And in a moment of weakness I agreed." She sighed. "Look, I'm sorry if this was a bad, *bad* idea. He's only staying a few days. He'll be gone soon."

"It's fine," said Julia, suddenly exhausted. "I think I might go take a little nap."

"Good idea," said Kat. "You're probably still jet-lagged. And seriously, if David's being annoying, tell him to go back to his room. He's a big boy. He can take care of himself."

Kat stepped into the elevator, and Julia returned to the bedroom. There, she found David lying on the bed, contemplating the bottle of tequila he'd brought.

He grinned proudly. "Duty-free! I got it at the airport."

"How thrifty of you," said Julia.

David nodded. "That's me. Thrifty." His expression turned reflective. "Look, Jules, now that Kat's gone, we can really talk." He patted the bed beside him. "For real. Just between us."

Ordinarily, Julia would have thought twice–no, thrice–about joining David Meadow on a bed. But this one was so huge. It would be fine.

She took a seat next to him and stretched out her legs.

David gave her a searching look. "How are you doing, Jules? I mean, how are you *really* doing?"

She shrugged. "Okay, I guess."

He smiled sympathetically. "Well, considering the circumstances, I'd say okay is pretty good. You know, you don't have to be so *strong* all the time."

Julia laughed darkly. "I don't feel strong at all."

Smiling tenderly, David touched her cheek.

The sweetness of the gesture struck a chord in Julia that none of his flirtatiousness ever had.

And the next thing she knew, he was kissing her–more of a question than a declaration.

To her surprise–and probably even more so to his–she found herself kissing him back.

Why *shouldn't* she enjoy the pleasure of physical contact, she thought rebelliously. If the warmth of his lips and the heat of his touch could reach that numb place deep inside her, maybe she'd feel that she wasn't completely dead inside after all.

"Julia," he breathed, now kissing her in earnest, "I've wanted…"

But Julia didn't want to talk. She kissed him to make him stop talking and felt his excitement, which excited her even more. David pulled her tank top over her head, his hands gliding down her body.

How long had he been wanting to touch her this way? How long had *she* been wanting him to touch her this way?

"Oh, Julia," he said, his voice rough. She shivered as he reached beneath her floaty beach skirt, which wasn't covering up much at this point. "If only I could make you mine. *Really* mine."

Meanwhile, Julia had undone the buttons of his shirt and was enjoying the benefits of David's gym/spa obsession, namely, his chiseled, waxed, muscular–but not overly so–chest. She smiled faintly. "Well, why don't you give it a shot?"

"Oh, you're just toying with me," he said, in between kissing her neck and nibbling her ear. "Having some rebound fun. It's like makeup sex. Except that what you're making up for is sleeping with Asher these past few years instead of me. It doesn't count."

"What's wrong with rebound fun?" said Julia, reaching for his hand and guiding it between her legs. This was it, she realized; after all her protestations, she was going to find out for herself whether the grass was greener in…the *Meadow*.

And then, to her astonishment, David pulled away.

He sat upright in the bed, his breathing agitated, that lazy, languorous expression gone–leaving Julia completely confused.

"What?" she said. "What's wrong?"

David looked pained. "Oh, Julia, I would love to do this–you have no *idea* how much I'd love to do this. But I can't. It wouldn't be right."

Julia could only stare. To think that she'd let him touch her this way, that he'd succeeded in affecting her so viscerally–only to turn her away? "*You* of all people are trying to protect my *virtue*?" Suddenly realizing that she was more than half-naked, she grabbed for her tank top and pulled it back on. "Why? Because that's all I have left?"

"Of course not. It's just–" David fumbled, at a rare loss for words. "I'm not who you were meant to be with on your honeymoon."

Julia hated him for being so handsome, his golden-brown hair disheveled from their tussling, his dark blue eyes sparkling like the Boston Harbor on a sunny spring day. He didn't deserve his own physical attractiveness; it should have been bestowed on someone more worthy. "You came all this way to tell me *that*? In case you haven't heard, the man I was 'meant to be with' on my honeymoon apparently had other ideas."

David's only response was to wrap his arms around her and pull her close.

They were still half-naked and sweaty, but their connection now felt oddly innocent, even fraternal. Any sexual overtones had vanished.

"What happened, David?" said Julia, cursing the tears that were now streaming down her cheeks. "What went wrong?" With dark amusement, she watched him scramble for a diplomatic response until he realized–to his almost comical relief–that she wasn't talking about *him*. "Why did he just disappear?"

David sighed and shook his head. "For the life of me, Julia, I have no fucking clue."

• • •

Some time later, Julia came to. David's face was buried in the back of her neck. She'd fallen asleep in his arms.

She pulled away and rolled onto her other side.

Only then did she see that David's eyes were open. He'd been watching her.

She smiled dryly. "And to think that just a few months ago you were offering to make up for everything I'd missed out on sexually my whole life. You were the one toying with *me*."

He looked rueful. "I know, I know. It's just, well, a few things have changed."

Julia laughed bitterly. "Right. I'm available now. That's what changed."

David shook his head. "No, that's not it." She watched, morbidly amused, as he summoned every ounce of maturity he had (two, maybe three, total?) and forced himself to meet her eyes. "Tell me this, Julia—could you be with me? I mean *really* be with me?"

Why not? she thought defiantly. So what if David wasn't deep, if he lacked Asher's quiet intelligence, his sensitivity? And so what if he wasn't her soulmate—if he didn't even *have* much of a soul? He was charming and funny, and sexy beyond what she'd ever willingly admit. And, most of all, he was *here*. And Asher wasn't.

The silence lingered, and Julia realized that for all her thinking, she still hadn't answered his question.

And in that moment, she knew that that itself was the answer.

She saw in David's eyes that he knew it, too.

He gave a miniscule nod. "Well, there you go."

They lay there in awkward silence a few more seconds, and then he said, "And besides..."

His trace of a smile sparked a flash of insight in Julia.

"Kat," she said.

He gave a sheepish shrug. "Yeah. Kat."

Chapter 24

Kat tiptoed into the bedroom of the honeymoon suite, doing her best not to disturb the sleeping Julia. As she approached the bed, her nose wrinkled.

No longer concerned about disturbing anyone, she flipped on the light. "Jules! Wake up. I smell sex."

Julia stirred slightly in the bed but didn't open her eyes. "Where have you been? What time is it?"

"It's late," said Kat. "I went to the hotel's sunset wine-tasting on the beach, and then I ended up going out for drinks with a travel writer named Robbie. Honestly, I was a little afraid to come back to the room—and I see I was right to be afraid! Where's David?"

Julia's eyes crinkled. "Back in his room. Can't we talk about this tomorrow?"

"No, we can't talk about it tomorrow!" said Kat. "I'm not sleeping in sex-soaked sheets without at least getting the full scoop. Couldn't you have called housekeeping to change the sheets? We're in a five-star hotel. They'll do anything."

Julia sighed and opened her eyes. "These are *not* sex-soaked sheets. Not by any stretch of the imagination."

"Well, you'd be entitled," said Kat, now placating. "You're on the rebound, after all. It's totally okay if you couldn't resist him—no judgment. David's very persuasive."

Uneager as Julia was to recount her rejection by the one person willing and eager to have sexual relations with just about anyone, except, apparently, *her*, she knew Kat wasn't going to leave it alone. "I didn't have to resist him," she told her friend. "He resisted *me*."

Kat's eyes widened. "What do you mean?"

"I mean he turned me down!" said Julia. "We were kissing, and, honestly, I probably would have. And then he told me it didn't 'feel right.' Can you believe it? *David Meadow* said it didn't *feel* right to have sex." She herself couldn't quite believe it, and she'd been there.

"No way," said Kat.

Indignant now, Julia said, "I was left at the *altar*. And then I'm turned down by David Meadow. *David Meadow*! How many women on the planet can say that? One, probably! Counting me."

From the look on her face, Kat's indignation rivaled Julia's. "Listen, do you want him to leave? I was the one who invited him. I take full responsibility. Want me to make him go home?"

Julia shook her head. "Oh, it's okay. Really, that was probably the best way for things to go. Now there won't be any more wondering, any what-ifs." She smiled slightly. "And on the plus side–I've been thinking about what this might mean for *you*."

"Why should it mean anything to me?" said Kat.

"Kat. Come on," said Julia.

"What? Seriously, why should I care? I mean, I'm sorry, I guess, that it didn't 'feel right.' Are you, like, disappointed?"

"*Kat*," Julia said again. "You don't care? Really? Not at all?"

Kat groaned and rolled her eyes. "All right, *fine*. I admit it doesn't make me entirely unhappy that you and David didn't have sex."

"I knew it!" said Julia. "It's been such a roller coaster what with everything that happened–and *didn't* happen. But if something good could come out of this for you..." Her voice caught. "That might make it all at least somewhat bearable."

Kat grabbed her by the shoulders. "Jules! This is not the end of the road for you. The universe didn't implode just because Asher turned into a frog. Pumpkin. Whatever. What happened to you wasn't happy. But it also wasn't the ending. You'll get your happy ending!"

Julia glanced down at the rumpled sheets, a reminder that David hadn't wanted her–just as Asher hadn't wanted her. "Kat, what if there's some legitimate explanation for all of this? What if Asher's dying or something?"

"And what if he is?" said Kat. "That justifies humiliating you? Seriously, at this point, would you even *want* him back?"

Yes, thought Julia. *Yes. Yes. Yes.*

In the next moment, she was sobbing uncontrollably.

With a sigh, Kat pulled her close, and Julia wept in her arms.

"We're really going to need the sheets changed tomorrow," said Kat.

Finally, after Julia seemed to have cried all her tears, Kat fluffed the pillows and guided her barely conscious friend into a prone position on the mattress. Julia was soon fast asleep, snoring lightly.

Kat reached for the bedside lamp and turned out the light.

So much for day one of the "honeymoon."

Chapter 25

Restless from the traveling and the tumult of emotions, Julia awoke before dawn. Unable to fall back asleep, she got up, thinking she'd go for a swim. As she was pulling on her bathing suit, however, she decided swimming was too pleasant; she needed something more masochistic. She threw on running shorts and a T-shirt and headed down to the beach. There, with hardly a glance at the aqua water and pink sky, she started running. As her bare feet pounded the sand and her tears mingled with her sweat, she was finally—*finally*—able to stop thinking and just be.

Later, relievedly physically drained, Julia returned to a vacant hotel suite—no sign of Kat. She took a leisurely shower, ate at the hotel's sumptuous breakfast buffet, and explored the lush tropical gardens surrounding the hotel. By midday, when Kat still had not yet reappeared, Julia began to wonder what in the world her "honeymoon" partner had gotten herself up to.

She dialed Kat's cell phone. To her surprise, a male voice answered.

"Hey, Julia," said David. "Kat's in the bathroom, but I saw it was you calling so I picked up."

"Oh, hey, David,' said Julia. "Where are you?"

"We're in the restaurant downstairs. We did a morning yoga class on the beach and then decided to go for lunch. We waited for you, but…"

"*Yoga?*" said Julia. "*You* did yoga? *Kat* did yoga?"

David laughed. "Yeah, we did. Kat says she'll do just about anything on a beach. And I'll do just about anything involving scantily clad women.

Afterward we decided to grab a bite. We're just finishing up. Sorry we missed you."

"No problem," said Julia. "I'll just eat lunch alone. While I'm here in Hawaii on my honeymoon. It'll be just the thing for my post-wedding PTSD. PWSD, I guess I should call it."

"Don't say that!" exclaimed David. "Come join us for a cappuccino or something." He chuckled. "I, of course, will be having black coffee. Or malt liquor. Or the two of them combined—as a real man should."

His words held a strange ring of familiarity.

"Have you said something like that before?" said Julia.

"Oh, Jules," said a beleaguered David. "As if I could possibly keep track of all the incredibly witty things I say. Be sensible."

"Right," she said, still thinking.

And then it came to her: Sean Harris. Ever-so-manly Sean Harris, who'd feared that a cappuccino might somehow compromise his masculinity—but who seemed to have no problem with lattes. Or yoga, for that matter.

She was suddenly extremely eager to talk with her friends.

"I'll be right down," she said. "There's something I want to run by you guys."

•   •   •

Seated at a four-person table with David and Kat, Julia eyed the empty chair next to her. The waitress hadn't removed the extra place setting, and she could almost imagine that Asher—her loving, devoted, *forever* husband—had just stepped out to take an important business call.

Stop it! she chastised herself. There was no husband.

And she might have figured out why.

David and Kat had finished their lunch and were awaiting a plate of raw, hand-rolled dark chocolate truffles for dessert. Julia scanned the menu quickly and ordered something. Strangely excited at having potentially solved the mystery, she waited until the waitress had brought their dishes before delivering her announcement.

"I think I know what happened," she said. "Why Asher left."

David and Kat looked shocked—and curious.

"Really?" said Kat. "You do?"

Julia nodded. "I can't believe I didn't think of it earlier. It must have been the thing with Sean Harris! Asher must have found out. What else could it have been?"

"No," said Kat, somewhat distracted by the dessert plate. As she'd explained to Julia and David, the antioxidants contained in all that raw cacao unquestionably more than counterbalanced any caloric overload.

"No, as in, you're shocked but it could have happened?" said Julia. "Or no, as in, it didn't happen?"

Before Kat could respond, David interjected. "Jules, I really don't think that was it. How could Asher possibly have found out? Did Sean send you dick pics or something? Were you guys sexting?"

"No, nothing like that," said Julia. "He doesn't have my phone number. Or my email address. I did run into him one other time, by the waterfront, but nothing happened. He hasn't tried to contact me at all."

She frowned slightly. Stated in such bald terms, it was evident that their kiss and their chance meeting had meant nothing—at least to Sean.

Kat sighed sympathetically. "Oh, Jules. I know how badly you want an explanation. But I honestly don't think that's it. For one, I don't see how Asher could have found out about Sean. And even if he did, I just don't see him reacting by ditching you on your wedding day. That's more David's style."

"Hey!" said David.

Kat ignored him. "Asher's more mature than to just abandon you like that. He'd have talked to you about it—and he would have forgiven you. I've seen how he looks at you, Jules. He'd forgive you anything."

Julia sat back in her chair, deflated. If her—*indiscretion*—with Sean wasn't the reason Asher had abandoned her, what could it be?

Meanwhile, Kat was ogling the last remaining truffle. This one was chocolate-raspberry, meaning, of course, that it contained *double* the antioxidants of the plain chocolate ones. She reached for the sweet—but David laid a hand on her wrist to intercept her.

"Hey babe," he said. "Save some sugar for me."

Julia braced herself for the explosion; coming between Kat and chocolate was a dangerous proposition.

To her astonishment, though, the explosion never came.

Incredibly, Kat only blushed—and, even more incredibly, ceded the truffle.

Julia rapidly put the pieces together: Kat's extended absence from their suite that morning; David's answering Kat's phone; his intimate reference to "sugar." It seemed her "honeymoon" had served as the launching pad for another couple's relationship.

Oh, the irony.

At the same time, she couldn't begrudge David and Kat their connection. She sensed it had been in the works for a long time.

Kat was looking at her, and Julia realized she'd been staring vacantly at the dessert plate.

"Jules?" said Kat. "Are you okay? Do you want the truffle?"

Julia laughed and shook her head. "No, I'm fine."

It was barely one o'clock. She had an entire afternoon and evening to get through—an entire day of third-wheeling it with David and Kat. And then more of the same tomorrow. She suddenly felt faint.

"I'm going to go back to the room and lie down for a while," she said.

Kat looked concerned. "Okay. You want me to come back with you?"

"No, no," said Julia. "You guys do your thing."

She left the happy couple and returned to the hotel suite. She lay down on the massive bed, curled up into a tiny ball, and hugged herself tightly. She knew that life didn't always go according to plan, that there would always be bumps in the road—but surely not like this! Her two years with Asher might as well never have happened. She was back to square one—in every possible sense.

He was her true love, her soul-mate. How on earth was she supposed to get over this one?

•   •   •

Julia was toweling off after a swim in the hotel pool when her cell phone buzzed—Kat.

"Where have you been?" demanded Kat. "I've left you like seven messages."

"I swam some laps. And then went for a walk on the beach. And then another swim."

"It's been *hours*," said Kat. "What's with all the exercise?"

"It calms me down," said Julia. "And it'll help me sleep. I need to be able to sleep, Kat. It's the only relief I get."

Kat sighed. "Listen, relief is good, but there are *much* more enjoyable ways to get it. For example, at this very moment, David and I are in the bar drinking margaritas. Those will also put you to sleep. And they're a whole lot more fun than exercise."

"Right," said Julia. "Speaking of David, when were you going to tell me that you two finally got your act together?"

There came an extended pause.

"Oh, *that*," Kat finally said. "It's nothing."

Julia didn't say anything.

"Just a little vacation fling," said Kat. "You can have him back when we get back to Boston. But for now, come have a margarita. Or a beer. Enough with the exercise for today. We'll be getting plenty of exercise tomorrow morning at the volcano, remember?" They'd made plans to view the sunrise from Haleakala, Maui's highest peak, and then to hike around the surrounding national park.

"Okay, okay," said Julia. "I'll be down in a little bit."

. . .

By the time Julia made it down to the hotel bar, the sunlight was waning, the shadows lengthening, another day of the "honeymoon" drawing to a close. She joined David and Kat on the outdoor patio.

A waiter approached to ask Julia what she'd like to drink.

"I'll have a beer," said Julia. "No, actually, make that a daiquiri. Strawberry, please."

"That's more like it, Jules!" said Kat. "Let's kick this vacation into high gear. Another round of margaritas for us," she told the waiter.

The hotel service was impeccable; they had their drinks moments later.

"Not to kill the mood, ladies," said David, "but keep in mind the high-gear portion of this vacation will be ending in just another couple of days. Of course, you *were* very lucky to have me for as long as you did–all good things, well, you know, that's just how it goes. Life, you know?"

Julia smiled. Who else but David would take a spur-of-the-moment trip to Hawaii for four days? She had to admit, though, that his company *had* helped her mood–and Kat's even more so, no doubt. "It won't be the same without you," she told him sincerely.

David shook his head regretfully. "No, it won't. But you must understand, there's interior design on the mainland that can't happen without me. People have no taste. And architects, they're the worst of all. There are a few exceptions, of course–Gareth, he's okay. But in general, it's bad. *Very* bad. I'm essential."

"We understand, sweetie," said Kat. "The world of high-end residential interior design is falling to pieces without you. Of course you need to get home."

"Yes," said David. "You get it. Although I won't actually be getting home anytime soon. I've got three site visits scheduled on my way back. The last one is to that monster project of Gareth's and mine in the Hamptons. It'll be *really* good to get home after that."

"I'll bet," said Julia. David truly *did* work like a maniac–which made sense, because David did *everything* like a maniac.

He sighed wistfully. "There really is no place like home. My home is my castle."

Kat shot him a look.

David glanced apologetically at Julia. "Oops, sorry, sensitive subject. I forgot."

"No problem," said Julia. "My home is *my* castle, too. A castle just won't be my home."

"It's better that way," Kat assured her. "Schloss Himmel, was it? What a stupid name. It would have just been cold and drafty and damp. And I didn't want to say anything before because I didn't want to hurt your feelings, but cupolas are *not* all they're cracked up to be. Yeah, overall, I think castles are one of those things that *sound* good but are really just a drag."

"In fact," said David, "the same might be said of marriage."

Julia smiled wryly. "In that case, I'm in *amazing* shape–no castle *and* no marriage. Thank goodness I still have my apartment!" Since her lease wouldn't be up for another few months, she'd planned to take her time moving her things to Louisburg Square. "At least I have somewhere to go home *to*."

"I'd say *that* calls for a toast!" said Kat.

They clinked their glasses together as David toasted, "To Julia's North End home–which is her castle!"

Julia couldn't help but laugh.

Now, that castle really *was* small.

• • •

Thursday night, David was on his way back stateside. The taxi driver tossed his suitcase into the trunk, the headlights gleaming brightly in the darkness. It was December nineteenth; Christmas was less than a week away.

"Adios, ladies!" said David, giving Julia and Kat a little salute. "See you in a couple of weeks. In another hemisphere. And a new year!"

"Thanks for livening up my honeymoon," said Julia. "And for not sleeping with me."

He laughed and hugged her. "My pleasure as to the former. As to the latter,"–he caught Kat's look–"I have no comment."

He let Julia go, and then looked at Kat. "You, my dear, don't get off that easily."

"Of course not," said Kat. "You never make *anything* –"

He cut her short by sweeping her up in his arms and kissing her for a *very* long time.

When they finally parted, Kat's face was flushed, and David's expression was smug.

"See you back in Beantown, babe," he said, stepping into the cab.

The taxi pulled away, and Julia turned to Kat. "Well?"

"Well, what?" said Kat, annoyingly reticent.

There was no point in pressing it, Julia knew. Kat would talk eventually. She suggested a walk on the beach.

Down by the water, the moonlight had turned the black sand a silvery gray. The air was fragrant with the scent of plumeria. They slipped off their shoes and walked barefoot in the light of the full December moon–the same moon that was shining down on Asher.

Wherever he was.

Julia again turned to look at Kat. "Look, you don't have to give me *all* the details, but there's one thing I'm *dying* to know."

"What's that?" said Kat.

"Just tell me," said Julia, "is the grass really greener in...the *Meadow*?"

Kat's grin was wider than the Pacific. "So green. *So* green."

•   •   •

In their remaining week on Maui, Julia and Kat traversed giant bamboo forests, snorkeled amidst green sea turtles, and rented a car to explore the towering waterfalls along the scenic Hana Highway. They celebrated Christmas Day with a swim in the open ocean with dolphins–lending legitimacy, they decided, to their throwaway toast on that questionable first night. They finished out their trip with a visit to a raw vegan café on Maui's North Shore, to try its world-famous kombucha. Abridged though the Hawaii vacation had been, they both agreed that their Maui adventure had been one for the books.

And then it was over.

In the early-morning hours of December thirtieth, the BartTech jet descended into Logan airport.

Kat looked at Julia. "We had fun, right?"

"Yes, we did," said Julia. "In fact, if not for the circumstances, I'd probably describe it as the best ten days of my life."

Kat grinned. "Me, too! It worked out so perfectly that I had vacation time I had to use up by the end of the year."

"It also worked out perfectly that you managed to orchestrate yourself some island romance–on *my* honeymoon. Thanks, friend."

Kat looked abashed. "I know, I know, no excuses. I'm a terrible friend. Forgive me?"

"Yeah, yeah," said Julia. "Eventually."

At that moment, the airplane touched down, jolting them both.

Another flight safely concluded, thought Julia, as she did every time she flew; another trip wherein she'd escaped her mother's fate.

Kat sighed. "Coming home is *not* going to be easy."

"You're telling me," said Julia.

PART 4

Marrying Myself

Chapter 26

Julia's first few days back home consisted solely of sleeping and avoiding reality–and the sub-zero temperatures. Boston winter was in full force.

She was in bed, fast asleep, when the old year slunk away and the new one officially arrived. Since she hadn't been expected home for another few weeks, few people apart from her immediate family and Kat had attempted to contact her. She would have to face the world at some point, of course, but for now she kept deciding to prolong her hibernation for just one more day. And there had still been no word from Asher. After multiple unsuccessful attempts to reach him by phone, she'd finally stopped trying.

Julia was dozing on the couch when her cell phone buzzed: Lacey, for the fifth time in forty-eight hours. Her stepsister was one of the few people who knew she was back from Hawaii.

She took the call. "Hey, Lace. Happy New Year."

"Right," said Lacey. "That. Anyway, he's alive. And working. Business as usual for the Bartletts, apparently."

Julia was immediately startled into wakefulness. "Asher? Really? How do you know?"

"I had a morning meeting in SoHo, so I figured I'd stop by BartTech's New York office."

Julia could scarcely formulate her thoughts. "You saw him? What did you say? What did *he* say?"

"*He* wasn't there," said Lacey, "but I talked to Enrique, their office manager. I've dealt with him before."

"Of course," said Julia, recalling that Lacey's firm had done some PR work for BartTech last spring. "What did he tell you?"

"Well, I didn't get much out of him, but honestly I don't think there was much to get. I just mentioned that I'd heard Asher's wedding didn't go quite as planned. Enrique said he'd also heard something to that effect. He told me BartTech has a huge new deal in the works–*huge*. They're acquiring some British telecommunications firm, and there are all kinds of antitrust implications. Apparently Asher and Dom and one of their associates are in London working on that. Enrique said he'll be back on Monday."

The associate had to be Odetta–who'd undoubtedly been delighted to learn that Asher was back on the market. "I'm so glad to hear BartTech's business hasn't been suffering," said Julia. "That also explains why I haven't heard from Asher. I don't think they have internet in London. Or telephones. Or probably even running water."

Lacey laughed sharply. "Yes, very backward place, London." She grunted. "That asshole. I knew you should have gotten a pre-nup."

"A pre-nup only helps if you actually marry someone," said Julia. "I would have needed a pre-pre-nup."

Lacey laughed again. "True. Next time, I guess."

"Yeah, next time," said Julia.

Her stepsister was quiet for a moment. "You doing okay, Jules?"

Now it was Julia's turn to laugh. David had asked her the same thing, and she still didn't know how to answer. "I don't really know how I'm doing. Or *what* I'm doing."

"You going back to work at some point?" asked ever-practical Lacey.

Julia sighed. "Yeah, at some point. I had told Carly and Franco that I'd come say hello when I got back from Switzerland, but they don't know I'm back early. And I don't think I'm going to tell them."

"In that case, why don't you come stay with me for a while?" said Lacey. "Forget Asher, forget Boston. Come to the Big Apple!"

"Thanks, I'll think about it," said Julia. "See how I feel once the dust settles."

"Once the *ash* settles, more like it. Jesus, what an asshole. What an *ash*-hole!"

"Good one," said Julia.

"Seriously, come any time," said Lacey. "And stay for as long as you like."

After they'd ended the call, Julia gave more thought to her stepsister's invitation. But what would be the point in going somewhere else? She didn't particularly want to be *here*, in Boston, but she didn't particularly want to be *anywhere*.

Beantown would do for now.

The afternoon suddenly loomed before her, a gaping expanse of solitude. She was suddenly desperate to get away from her thoughts, her emotions, herself.

And the only thing she knew that could reliably accomplish those things was painting.

Fighting back her creeping lethargy, Julia stood up from the couch. She gathered up her brushes and painting supplies and pulled out the painting she'd begun only a few short months ago–back when she'd still had a life, and a future. Any grand ambition of accomplishing anything remotely impressive or significant with her art had long since vanished. Right now, all she sought was escape.

And, blessedly, she found it.

Chapter 27

Julia's hibernation officially ended the Monday that she'd originally been scheduled to return to Boston. The first thing that morning, the Harts were already texting to find out when they'd get to see her. With a sigh, she texted Carly and promised to drop by the Hartland Travel office that Wednesday afternoon.

Then she went back to sleep.

•   •   •

When she stepped inside the Hartland Travel office on Wednesday, Julia was instantly transported to her early days as a college student, when she'd first started working there. She'd been so taken with the exotic reception area, with its teal walls, hardwood floors, and gold couch peppered with vibrant Bohemian cushions. Her bosses' offices, bright with natural light and overlooking the Boston Harbor, had seemed so grand. She'd even had her very own office, to use when she wasn't on reception duty.

Byron had since taken over that office. His presence was the primary reason that it had been months since she'd popped over here to visit.

Julia saw, to her surprise, that Whitley was occupying the reception desk today. Before she could ask why Whitley was here at Hartland Travel, instead of at JoH, the program assistant jumped from her seat.

"Welcome back, *Mrs. Bartlett*!" Whitley exclaimed.

Julia started. "Actually, I'm not Mrs. Bartlett. You see–"

A laughing Whitley cut her off. "Oh, I should have known, of course you kept your own last name. You're so *liberated*."

It was the sort of comment Byron would ordinarily have seized upon. Thank goodness he didn't seem to be around.

"Well, I wasn't exactly planning on it," said Julia, "but yes, I did end up keeping my last name. Where's Byron, by the way?"

"Jury duty," said Whitley. "It's a criminal case. He's the foreman!"

"Of course he is," said Julia. She hoped for the defendant's sake that he or she wasn't a socialist. Or a vegan.

"So tell me all about Switzerland!" said Whitley. "Wait, hold on, let me get Carly and Franco."

She ran off and returned a moment later with Julia's bosses.

Carly beamed at Julia. "Oh, honey! It's so good..."

Julia held up a hand to ward off the well-wishes. "Please, everyone—there's something..."

Carly shushed her. "Before you say anything else, come with us into the conference room. Whatever you have to say, you can say in there."

Ignoring Julia's protests, Carly led her into the large room they used for client presentations—which, Julia now saw, was decorated from floor to ceiling with silver and white streamers, sparkly hanging stars and moons, and silver and white balloons. At the center of the large oak conference table was a two-tiered, cream-frosted, strawberry-decorated cake, a masterpiece of culinary art. Perched on top were two tiny figurines bearing an unnervingly close resemblance to Julia and Asher.

"It's vegan!" said Carly.

Julia burst into tears.

The others laughed delightedly, clearly taking her tears for ones of joy.

Franco hugged her. "Julia, you're like the daughter we never had. Even though we couldn't be there with you in Switzerland, we are so, so happy that you finally got what you deserve."

If he'd known what *actually* happened in Thun, thought Julia, it would have been the cruelest of insults.

She tried to smile. "Oh, guys. This is so nice. And I feel the same way about you. You're like my second family. But there's something I have to tell you."

Whitley's eyes lit up, and she cast a meaningful glance at Julia's torso. "Preggers?" she said in a stage whisper.

Carly and Franco gasped their excitement.

"No, not preggers!" said Julia. "Not even close." She drew a deep breath. "The wedding never happened. I didn't get married."

It was evident she'd floored them all. Whitley, Julia could tell, was connecting the dots regarding their last-name conversation. And Carly looked about to faint.

Franco pulled out a chair for her to sit. The rest of them followed suit.

"Oh, Julia," said Carly. "What happened?"

Julia shrugged. "Nothing! Nothing happened. He didn't show up. He sent a text message two minutes before I was supposed to walk down the aisle."

Franco's blood was visibly boiling. "What kind of man ..." He shook his head, too worked up to finish the thought.

"An *asshole* man," said Carly. "That's what kind."

"*Total* asshole," said Whitley.

"Yeah, that seems to be the consensus," said Julia. "My stepsister called him an ash-hole." With dark amusement, she noted that Franco was eyeing the cake. Taking pity, she said, "But there's no reason we should let that stop us from enjoying this beautiful cake."

"Red velvet," muttered Franco, already reaching for the serving spatula. "Not even an asshole can ruin red velvet cake."

He cut them all gigantic slices, and they dug in. The creamy icing was blissfully sweet and incomparably rich—just like Asher, thought Julia. Could there be a more apt replacement?

Although the cake had fully occupied Franco's attention, Carly wasn't done with the Asher-bashing. She snatched the male figurine from the top of the cake, and, in one swift motion, tore off its head. "Screw that ash-hole!"

Whitley and Franco cackled happily, echoing, "Yeah, screw that ash-hole!"

Somewhat taken aback at the beheading, Julia felt compelled to join in. "Yeah, screw him!" she said, a beat behind.

Later, after they'd stuffed themselves, Carly packed up the rest of the cake for Julia. "Here, take this. It'll help you drown your sorrows—at least for a little while."

Before she left, Franco pulled Julia aside, out of Whitley's earshot. "Does all this mean you'll be coming back to work soon?"

Julia suddenly craved more frosting. Instinctively, she hedged. "Can you give me some time? I'd like to take a month or two to get my head straight."

Franco's brow furrowed. "Of course, honey, of course. It's just that there are a few work-related developments we'd like to discuss with you. Whenever you feel up to it."

Something was up, Julia could tell. And she wasn't sure she wanted to know what it was.

"Okay. I'll be in touch," she said.

Franco nodded. "Yes, just give us a call when you can. The sooner the better."

Chapter 28

That Saturday, Julia met Kat for lunch at Antico Forno, just a few blocks from Julia's apartment. The outing marked the second time that week that she'd left the house, the first being her visit to Hartland Travel.

Progress, she thought.

Sitting there in the restaurant, pleasantly warmed by the nearby blazing brick ovens, Julia was glad that Kat had talked her into getting out. The pumpkin ravioli had been well worth braving the cold for. Much more memorable than regular pasta, it was delicious–especially after two days of straight cake.

Kat was regarding her worriedly. "What's going on, Jules? I mean, I *know* what's going on, but tell me what's going on."

Julia laughed dryly. "The main thing that's been going on with me is cake." She'd told Kat about the surprise party at the office. "I still taste frosting every time I burp."

"Gross," said Kat. "Although I guess it could be worse."

"It's all just such a mind-fuck," Julia told her. "I was all ready to start my beautiful new life–my *real* life. And then, out of nowhere, my beautiful new life is suddenly out the window."

Kat nodded sympathetically. "Out the window of a cupola."

"That about sums it up," said Julia. "I mean, what happened to it? How could it just disappear? Is there another me, in some parallel universe somewhere, living the life *I* was supposed to have?"

"Well, I'm not a quantum physician. Physicist. Whatever," said Kat. "So I can't really speak to that. But was your old life really so bad?"

Julia immediately felt guilty. "No, of course not. My old life was–*is*–great. I have you. I have my family. I have my apartment. I have my...job." That said, she hadn't expected Franco to be so insistent on pinning down her work plans. Again, she wondered what was brewing at Hartland Travel. "I keep telling myself that what happened with Asher wasn't my fault, but I can't help wondering if there was something I missed. Was there some huge red flag I overlooked?"

Kat turned thoughtful. "Not that I noticed. He was away a lot, that was the only thing." She thought some more. "How was the sex?"

"Incredible," said Julia without hesitation. "It was so–*intimate*. When we made love, it was like we melted into each other. Like we truly became one. I've never experienced anything like it."

"Hmm," said Kat. "Sounds–*special*. How often did you do it?"

"Well, with him being away so much, not that often. I'd say, on average, once every two weeks. Maybe three? Definitely at least once a month. Unless he was away on business, then sometimes longer."

Kat was gaping. "Once a *month*?"

Julia suddenly felt defensive. "We would have done it more if we could. We both wanted to. It was just tough to coordinate."

"I didn't know that about you guys," said Kat. "That's, just, well–that's not a lot of sex."

"You don't understand," said Julia. "Asher doesn't do anything halfway. He likes to do things right. Quality over quantity."

Kat's skepticism showed on her face. "Well, the way I see it is, if the sex really *is* such great quality, you want a little more quantity. You make it happen."

The boost that Julia had gotten from leaving her apartment was gone. She was once again back to the depths of despair, where she'd all but taken up permanent residency. "I know, I know. I guess part of me thought the same thing. But I didn't want to seem too demanding. He was always so stressed out."

Kat nodded understandingly.

"I'm such a fool," said Julia. "I thought I'd found love–that I finally knew what true love was. And now I have no idea."

"Well, if it makes you feel any better," said Kat, "he fooled me, too. I thought he was the real deal—we all did! He pulled one over on *all* of us." She chuckled spitefully. "At least he won't be getting a castle. Serves him right."

Yes, thought Julia, Asher would have to make do with his Louisburg Square mansion, his Santa Monica beach house, his sprawling Jackson Hole family "cabin"—until he found someone he *did* want to marry.

They finished their meals and paid the check.

Outside, on the sidewalk, Julia didn't feel like going home just yet. "Want to catch a movie?" she suggested.

But Kat declined, explaining that she was meeting David.

"I'm sure it'll burn itself out eventually," she said, her eyes gleaming. "But honestly, at this point, I can't get enough."

"I'm glad at least *someone*'s getting some action," said Julia.

Kat grinned. "Yeah, for now you can live vicariously through me. Trust me, I'm getting enough for the both of us."

She hugged Julia goodbye and was off.

Julia stood there on the street a moment longer. She craved quiet—but not the depressing quiet of her empty apartment.

It came to her in a flash—meditation. Yoga minus the torture. But where?

Then she thought of St. Ignatius Church. It would be empty this time of day, she imagined, before the Saturday evening Masses.

Shivering in the biting cold wind, she briskly walked the few blocks to the church.

Inside, a frocked figure was placing hymnals in the wooden pews. Julia wondered if this was "her" priest—the one to whom she'd confessed her interlude with Sean. He was wiry-looking and short, entirely bald apart from two tufts of steel-gray hair above his ears. He glanced up as she approached.

"Hi," she said.

"Hello there, young lady," said the priest. "How are you?"

Julia immediately recognized that unmistakable Boston twang. It was him.

She smiled, feeling a kinship thanks to their shared confessional history. "I'm okay. I actually met you once before, sort of. I'm Julia."

He extended his hand. "Good to meet you, Julia. Liam Mahoney. I'm the pastor here."

"Yes, I was here a few months ago," she told him. "To confess something that happened while I was engaged." When Father Mahoney looked intrigued, she added, "I kissed another man."

The priest's eyes widened. "Ah, yes, I remember you!" He scratched at one of his tufts of hair. "Wasn't there something about a yoga class?"

Julia smiled. "Yes, there was."

He nodded. "Well, dear, I hope you didn't feel it necessary to abandon a practice you really enjoy, merely because of a single moment of indiscretion."

"No, I didn't abandon it," said Julia. She couldn't lie, though–not to a priest. "I wouldn't exactly say I *enjoy* it, though."

Father Mahoney looked appalled. "What do you mean? Who doesn't like yoga? I do it at least three times a week. It saved my back."

Julia grimaced inwardly. It seemed there was no escaping yoga's insidiously expanding sphere of influence, even in the realm of organized Western religion. It also seemed that disliking yoga was just about the most politically incorrect thing a person could possibly do.

"Well, I guess that's one more thing I ought to confess," she said. "I go to yoga and pretend to like it, but really I hate it. I'm also really bad at it. Not that I need to confess that. I think it's pretty obvious to everyone who sees me do it."

The priest smiled and ran a hand over the top of his bald head. "Oh, young lady, I think you're being much too hard on yourself. You can't be bad at yoga. No one's bad at yoga!"

"Yeah, I've heard that one lots of times," said Julia. "I think that's what they say to people who are bad at yoga."

Father Mahoney chuckled. "Maybe so, maybe so. Would you like to sit down for a minute, dear? You can tell me about your fiancé. Or is he your husband by now?"

Although she'd come here for contemplation, not conversation, Julia felt a sudden urge to confide in this down-to-earth man of the cloth. She took a seat beside him in the pew.

"He's neither," she told Father Liam Mahoney. "He dumped me right before the wedding. Not quite at the altar, but close."

The priest gasped. "Oh, Julia, I'm so sorry to hear that. It's his loss, of course. But that sounds very painful." He scowled and shook his head. "What a prick."

Julia smiled. "Thanks, Father. That actually means a lot, coming from a priest."

Father Mahoney looked penitent. "Dear goodness, my temper got the best of me. I shouldn't have called him a prick. He's clearly a very troubled soul. But how awful for you. How are you holding up?"

She shrugged. "I'm doing all right, I guess. The shock's just beginning to wear off. And I'm still adjusting to the idea of life without him. But I'm managing. Sort of."

He patted her hand. "Well, remember that God is a limitless source of comfort and consolation. No need to hold back. He can handle your pain, no matter how great."

Once again, Julia found she couldn't lie to a priest. "I don't really believe in God. I mean, I love the *idea* of a loving, all-powerful God, who answers prayers and has all these wonderful plans for us—who wouldn't? But I just don't think it's real. More like having an imaginary friend or something. But this church is so peaceful. It helps to just sit and breathe. That's why I came here, in fact—to meditate. To try and find some peace."

Unoffended by her candor, Father Mahoney again patted her hand. "Of course, dear, whatever helps. I'll leave you to it."

Julia smiled. "Would you mind calling him a prick just one more time?"

Father Mahoney glowered—not, she could tell, at her, but at the absent Asher. "He's not just a prick, he's a total—no, no, I won't say it." Glancing at the crucifix hanging on the wall, he crossed himself. "Father, forgive me."

He patted her hand one last time and left her to herself.

Chapter 29

As a dismal January collapsed into a just-as-dreary February, Julia's weeks seemed to fill themselves: painting, running, Tuesday-night yoga, the occasional outing with Jolene or Kat. To her relief, she'd snapped back into her old routines without hardly a pause. Unfortunately, they brought her little of the same joy they always had–although, to be fair, yoga had never brought her much joy.

The same seemed to be true for Sean Harris. She hadn't seen him at the yoga studio once.

On slightly more temperate days–when the temperature climbed into the double digits–Julia began venturing out to the Public Garden, to paint. During her college summers, she had loved setting up her easel and working amidst the lush greenery and waterways. Now, in the depth of winter, the scenery was quite different–the draping willows bare of leaves; the waterways frozen solid; the grass covered with snow. It was as if the park had gone from a Technicolor movie to a black-and-white photograph.

Still, the starkness of the wintertime park somehow suited her mood. She'd had her fill of clichéd springtime landscapes, brimming over with blossoms and sunsets and hope. No, there would be no more hackneyed tourist paintings from her. From now on, she was painting from the heart.

And these days, her heart was quite bleak.

• • •

Before she knew it, another week had passed, and then another, and another. All the while, the matter of work kept creeping unavoidably closer to the forefront of Julia's mind. Obviously, she'd need to go back eventually; at the very least, she needed to discuss her plans with Carly and Franco. But the prospect of sitting at a computer all day, churning out grant proposals for sums of money that were pocket-change to people like the Bartletts–while doing her best to deflect Byron's banter–all but made her want to slit her wrists.

Nevertheless, the inevitable wouldn't be put off forever. On a Friday afternoon in late February, she received a strangely formal email message from Franco, inviting her to lunch with him and Carly the following Monday at a neighborhood restaurant, Gennaro's. Reading the cryptic note, Julia felt a stab of premonition. Well, she'd sensed that something was brewing at Hartland Travel–and now she'd find out what it was. She sent off a short email confirming the lunch meeting.

And with that, she resolutely put work–and Byron Knowles–out of her head.

• • • •

Carly and Franco were already at Gennaro's when Julia walked into the restaurant on Monday at noon. She gave each of them a kiss on the cheek and took a seat. "I've never been to this place. It's so cute."

"We chose it specially for you," said Franco. "Because they have plenty of vay-gahn options."

"*Vee*-gun, honey," said Carly.

"That was so thoughtful of you," said Julia. "Thank you." The thought of old-school Franco researching North End vegan options was cute beyond words. It was also very out of character. Something was definitely up.

A waiter came to take their orders, and Franco insisted on ordering a bottle of wine–also unusual for a weekday lunch meeting. Now Julia's sensors were truly on high alert. What was going on at work?

Once their dishes had arrived, Franco wasted little time in getting to the point. He regarded Julia seriously from across the table. "Julia, as you've probably realized, this isn't just a social lunch."

Julia nodded. She straightened up in her seat.

"We've been in the travel business for twenty-five years," said Franco.

"Twenty-six," said Carly.

"Twenty-*six*," said Franco. "And we know the business inside-out."

"I know you do," Julia said. "And you've taught me so much. You were the first ones to give me a taste of a bigger world. I'd never even been overseas before I started working for you two."

Franco looked pleased. "I'm so glad that your experience with Hartland Travel has meant something to you. Because of everyone we've ever had working for us, you're the best. The *best*."

"Thank you," she said, surprised at the compliment. Really, all she'd done was keep showing up. But maybe that in itself was worth something. "That's so nice of you to say."

"The thing is," said Carly, "we can't keep doing this forever. We don't want to live our whole lives planning other people's vacations. We want to take our *own* vacations."

"Of course," said Julia, not sure what she was getting at. "You need to live."

"Exactly!" said Franco. "Which leads me to–"

Before he could continue, a waiter appeared bearing fresh baskets of warm bread, olive oil, and, of course, more wine–all of which were enthusiastically accepted by Carly and Franco. Julia had never known the Harts to turn down an offer of additional food or drink.

The waiter gone, Franco turned back to Julia. "Look, it's not going to be easy to tell you this. We know how committed you are to JoH. But operating a non-profit is tough in this economy. It's not your fault, but there's no getting around it: contributions are drying up. And it's a lot of financial pressure on Hartland Travel to keep it going."

Even though he'd said it wasn't her fault, Julia felt compelled to defend herself–and JoH. "That's not totally true. Donations were down slightly last year, but we have two major proposals in that I'm really optimistic about. If these come through, JoH will be in great shape, much better than last year. Don't lose faith in me yet!"

Franco shook his head. "It's not that we've lost faith in *you*. It's just that the pressure of keeping a non-profit going, in addition to a regular business, is more than Carly and I want to have to deal with in our golden years." He hesitated, obviously reluctant to continue. "I'll cut to the chase. We've decided to shut down JoH."

Julia's stomach dropped. Much as she'd been dreading returning to her job, it had never even occurred to her that she might not have a job to return to!

It hurt more than she'd imagined.

From the start, JoH had been her baby. She'd conceived the mission of the travel-focused non-profit, convinced Carly and Franco to fund it through Hartland Travel, and handled the paperwork for setting up the 501(c)(3) corporation. Although Hartland Travel was still the organization's primary contributor, she'd worked diligently to expand JoH's donor base. Most of all, she'd overseen the landmark Travel Sabbatical competition, whose third winner, Cruz Costa, would be embarking on his trip to Mexico in just a few months.

JoH had done good work—work that the other Board members, Carter and Sally, believed in enough to devote their limited free time to supporting. It crushed her to think of having to tell them that Franco and Carly didn't think it worth continuing.

She tried to view things from the Harts' perspective. "I understand. You two are businesspeople. It was never your idea to start a non-profit, and yes, it's a lot of work. And Sally and Carter are over-committed as it is." Julia glanced down at the table, feeling very lost but trying not to show it. She looked back up at the Harts and, with all the fortitude she could muster, told them, "Don't worry about me. Before everything happened with the wedding, I'd been planning to take a three-month sabbatical, anyway. So it's not like I wasn't expecting to be out of work for a while."

Carly and Franco looked at each other, then back at her.

"No, no, you don't understand," said Franco. "We're closing down JoH. But we want you to come back to work for Hartland Travel. Like you used to, in college. But this time in an executive role. As a principal."

Julia stared at him. "I thought you were laying me off. I thought I was getting fired!"

Franco guffawed, but Carly looked horrified. "Oh, Julia, of course not! To think that we would—at a time like this!"

"Nothing will change immediately," said Franco. "It'll take a good six months to wind down JoH. We just wanted to get your thoughts about coming back to Hartland Travel. You'd be a part-owner in the company, and between profit-sharing and bonuses, you should do very well."

Julia knew exactly the profits that Hartland Travel brought in. They were substantial.

"Like we were saying," Franco continued, "Carly and I don't want to work this hard forever. Which begs the question of who'll run the business after we retire. We'd like to begin grooming you to take over the company."

Take over the company?

Julia was at a loss as to how to respond. She knew how hard the Harts had worked to build up their business—and what an honor it was for them to want her to take over after they retired.

She just wasn't sure she wanted to.

She fumbled to say something. "It's strange to think about. To me, Hartland Travel is you two. And I've never been in charge of a business before. Well, not counting JoH."

"You'll have plenty of time to get used to the idea," said Franco. "Please know, we're not just being nice. You're the right person for this role. You'll be good at it." He settled back in his chair, his expression reflective. "Of course, the travel business has changed tremendously over the past decade. We were going over some figures with Byron the other day, and it became very clear that streamlining our focus is our only hope of staying profitable in the long term. JoH has been good for our corporate image, but at the end of the day, it's been a huge drain on company time and energy. As Byron put it, we need to get back to business."

Julia's skin prickled. Suddenly, things were making a *lot* more sense.

"This was Byron's idea?" she said.

"Yes," said Carly. "He's been so helpful breaking things down for us from a consultant's perspective. While you were away, he did a whole report comparing Hartland Travel's profitability before and after we established

JoH. It's very clear from the numbers that this is what's best for the company."

"Did you ask him to do that report?" said Julia.

"No, he took total initiative," said Franco. "And thank goodness he did."

Julia nodded slowly. It was clear she'd gravely underestimated her nemesis.

How long, she wondered, had Byron been plotting the demise of Journeys of the Heart? And to think how vehemently he'd fought for Cruz Costa to win the Travel Sabbatical competition, proclaiming his ability to "sell" Cruz in order to boost grants and donations to JoH! She could only deduce that Byron's real motivation for plugging Cruz Costa—apart from the teenager's overall adorableness—had been to keep *her* from getting the winner she'd wanted.

"So tell me," she said, "what does Byron think of the idea of me becoming a principal at Hartland Travel? And eventually taking over the business?"

"He doesn't know yet," said Franco. "We didn't want to say anything before talking to you."

Carly added, "But I'm sure he'll be thrilled. Especially since he'll also be playing a big role in the company."

More news to Julia. "He will?"

"Yes," said Franco. "We've offered him a full-time position at Hartland Travel. He'll be executive vice president of sales. Our number-two man. And, eventually, *your* number-two man. You, of course, will be our number-one man. Gal. Woman."

But even Franco's fumbling political correctness couldn't make Julia smile.

Working side-by-side with Byron, running Hartland Travel? Could there be a more hellish fate?

Another thought occurred to her. "What about Whitley? Have you told her you're shutting down JoH?"

Carly's face darkened. "Not yet. We thought that might be best coming from you. We'll certainly find a position for her at Hartland Travel."

Julia frowned. "Whitley's not interested in the travel business. She's a social worker. She wants to do non-profit work."

Franco sighed regretfully. "Honestly, you're probably right. Which is too bad, she's a good girl. But business is business. You can't please everyone."

While that was certainly true, Julia couldn't help but wonder why, out of all of them—her, Whitley, and Byron—*Byron* should be the one who ended up being pleased.

She looked squarely at her bosses. "I think you're making a mistake. JoH is a solid non-profit. As we continue to expand our donor base, we'll be much less reliant on funding from Hartland Travel. It'll take some time, but in five years, maybe less, JoH won't need a dime from Hartland Travel."

Her appeal had zero impact on her bosses. It was clear from their expressions that Carly and Franco had made up their minds: JoH was history.

"This is a lot for me to absorb," said Julia. "I've been immersed in the non-profit sector for the last three years. This would be a big change."

Franco chuckled. "Well, maybe it's about time *you* started making some profit. You ever think of that?"

Julia couldn't dispute *that* particular point. "Yeah, I could certainly use some profits," she said, feeling torn. "I'm sorry, guys, I just can't give you an answer right now. But please don't take my hesitation to mean that I don't genuinely appreciate your offer. I do. It's an amazing opportunity. I will give it serious consideration."

"That's all we ask," said Franco.

Carly reached across the table and clasped Julia's hands. "Whatever you decide, Julia, know that we just want you to be happy. We love you."

Julia smiled back at her longtime employers. "Thank you. I love you, too."

Kat was predictably beside herself with excitement when Julia called to relay the news. "You'll be a part-owner? And eventually in charge of the whole thing? How much does Hartland Travel make?"

Julia told her.

"That's like three or four times what you've been making at JoH!" Kat shrieked. "Fuck rich Asher! You're going to be rich on your own!"

Julia laughed. "Not exactly *rich*. That's gross income, not net. Besides, it would probably be five or six more years before I actually took over the company. Until then, I'd be sharing in the profits with Carly and Franco. Assuming I say yes, that is."

"Of course you're going to say yes! Why wouldn't you? What else do you have going for you?" Seeming to realize how that sounded, Kat added, "I mean, you have *lots* going for you. But you love art, you love travel. How is this not your dream job?"

"I love art, and I love travel, but that doesn't mean I love the travel *business*. Besides, there's more to the story. *Byron* is the one who convinced Carly and Franco to shut down JoH. This whole time, he's been plotting behind my back, getting his tentacles into Carly and Franco, and he somehow managed to convince them that JoH is sucking Hartland Travel dry. Which isn't true! Oh, and best of all, they just made Byron executive vice president of sales of Hartland Travel. How can I possibly work closely with someone who's out to get me?"

There came a long pause from Kat. Finally, she said, "Jules, no offense, but you're starting to sound a little paranoid. What's the big deal? Byron will do his job, you'll do yours. You can't let one annoying guy keep you from your dream job."

"My dream job is *painting*," said Julia. "Not sending people on tours to see *other* people's art. It's making art myself."

Kat sighed. "Look, you know I love your art. You know I believe in you."

Julia did know. Five years ago, when she'd had the show at the South End gallery, Kat had purchased one of her paintings for fifteen hundred dollars. Julia had been so appreciative that for Kat's next birthday, she'd given her another painting that, in her opinion, was even better. Both pieces were still prominently displayed in Kat's apartment.

"But with art," continued Kat, "it's almost impossible to control the profit that comes in. This is your chance for *guaranteed* profit."

"Yes, but–" Julia began to protest, but her voice was drowned out by the whirring of Kat's blender. Since those first early days of running, Kat had become a smoothie devotee.

A minute later, the whirring subsided.

"Mmm," said Kat, sounding like she was licking her lips. "You'll have to try this one–kale, avocado, almond milk, almond butter, and agave nectar. Which, I'll have you know, is completely different from refined sugar."

"That does sound good," Julia said.

"Not only that, it's super energizing. I worked out today at lunch, and I didn't have my running watch with me, but I could tell I was a lot faster. I'm pretty sure I doubled my pace. Or halved it. Whatever. You know what I mean."

"That *is* impressive," said Julia.

"Thanks. So what's the issue about going back to work for the travel agency? To me, it seems like a no-brainer."

"This wouldn't just be guaranteed profit," said Julia. "It would be my guaranteed *career*. I couldn't tell Carly and Franco yes, and then sell the company ten years later. They'd feel totally betrayed. Essentially, what they're asking me to do is marry their business. They want me to marry Hartland Travel."

"Ah, okay. I see what you mean. Another proposal."

Julia smiled. "Yeah. Not quite the one I was hoping for."

"Well, you'll figure it out," said Kat, with more confidence than Julia felt. "What'd you tell them?"

"As it stands right now, I told them I'd go back to work at JoH in April. But instead of doing my usual development work, I'll be focusing on winding down the nonprofit. I don't even want to think about it."

"In that case," Kat said, "I'll give you the same advice I've given you too many times to count..."

"I know, I know," said Julia. "Don't think. I'll try."

Chapter 30

For Julia, the ensuing weeks ran together in an impressionist blur. Every time she painted, she forgot that she had other career options. And every time she remembered the Hartland Travel option, she was overcome with a fresh desire to paint. What had resulted was her most prolific artistic period in years. In addition to the winter series from the Public Garden, she'd finished the large abstract painting she'd begun a few months earlier, as well as over a dozen smaller pieces.

"I think my artistic fire might be rechanneled sexual energy," she confided to Kat over dinner one Wednesday night at their favorite Indian restaurant in Somerville.

Kat chuckled. "That might explain why I'm *not* doing anything artistic. All my sexual energy is being channeled into David. I mean, I knew I was hot for the guy, but I didn't think I'd *stay* this hot."

"So is it still 'just sex'?" said Julia.

"Just sex," said Kat.

Her face was flushed, and Julia could tell it wasn't from the curry. "I think you're a fraud. You're claiming to be having a fling when what you're really having is a *relationship*."

Kat scoffed. "Don't be ridiculous. It hasn't even been three months. That's when things always start getting on my nerves. Anyway, he's going away this weekend. I'll see how I do without him. Will it be out of sight, out of mind, or will I actually miss him?"

"Where's he going?" said Julia.

"Oh, some site visit for one of his projects. Twelve-million-dollar renovation in the Hamptons or something crazy like that."

Julia smiled. "That sounds about right. Is that the project he's doing with Gareth?"

"Yeah, I think so," said Kat. "Hey, since David will be out of town, how about we do a girls' night out this weekend? Your sister will be up for it, I'm sure."

That much was true; Jolene was generally up for just about anything.

"Sure," said Julia. "And it'll give me a chance to catch up with Jolene. I haven't seen much of her lately. Did I tell you she got a job at Harvest Co-Op?" That was a grocery store in Central Square.

"No, you didn't," Kat said. "Good for her."

"Yeah, supposedly one of her New Year's resolutions was to focus on building up her jewelry business and her SunStar business. But for now she needed a more reliable way to pay the rent."

"I bet," said Kat, who shared Julia's view of SunStar Traditional Natural Eastern Remedies. "Is she still volunteering at the animal rescue?"

"Every weekend," said Julia. It was ironic that someone who never cleaned her *own* apartment volunteered to clean out cat cages for free. But her sister was committed. "Oh, and on top of her new part-time job, she's got a new *full-time* boyfriend. Jeff. She met him on her second day of work at the co-op. He's a doctor. He teaches at Harvard Medical School."

"Nice!" said Kat. "New job, new man—that girl works fast! Maybe she can give you some pointers. It's about time we got you back out on the scene."

About to protest that she'd never in her life been *on* the scene, Julia bit her tongue.

Maybe it *was* about time.

•   •

Saturday night, Julia knocked on the door of Jolene's apartment, to no response. She tried the door and, finding it unlocked, stepped inside her sister's predictably messy apartment.

"Jolene?" she called.

In the next instant, a dark bundle of fur darted between Julia's legs. She quickly swung the door shut before the tiny creature could escape.

His exit blocked, the kitten looked up at her questioningly. "Meow?"

Laughing, she bent down to scoop the black cat into her arms. "Jolene, who's this little guy?"

Jolene poked her head out of the bedroom. "*Girl*. One second, I'm on the phone with Jeff."

It was another ten minutes before her sister joined Julia in the living room. She was wearing a short, nearly sheer, spaghetti-strapped dress, chunky boots, and no stockings–hardly Boston winterwear. Although it was March, the frigid temperatures outside gave no hint of spring.

"Sorry about that," said Jolene. "Jeff's sick. And he's a *doctor*. It's so not fair."

"Poor Jeff," said Julia. "You're going to get sick yourself, wearing that in this weather. And you didn't tell me you adopted a cat! Did she come from the shelter?"

Jolene looked sly. "She did come from the shelter. But it's not *me* who got a cat–it's you."

Julia stiffened, which was enough to cause the skittish kitten to leap from her arms and disappear under the couch. "What are you talking about?" Much as she loved her sister, it drove her crazy how Jolene always acted so impulsively, without thinking through any of the consequences.

Jolene laughed at her discomfiture. "Oh, Jules, chill. I didn't *actually* get you a cat–unless you want her, that is. I'm just fostering her until she finds a permanent home. I'd keep her myself except there's a no-pets policy in this place."

The kitten had ventured out from underneath the sofa and was now diligently licking Jolene's boot. The sisters watched her, enchanted.

"She's so tiny," marveled Julia. "How old is she?"

"She's three months old, but the vet thinks her growth was stunted from malnutrition. Someone found her and four other kittens in a cardboard box on the Mass. Ave. bridge. She was the only one still alive. The others all froze to death."

"That's so horrible!" said Julia.

"Yeah, she's been through so much, poor thing. She may be small, but she's a fighter! And she's just *so* sweet. It's only been three days and I'm already head over heels. It's going to kill me to let her go. And I couldn't help thinking..."

Julia had a sinking feeling as to what her sister was about to say.

"I know how allergic Asher was to cats," Jolene continued. "But now that he's gone, I figured, why not take advantage of the situation? This sweet little kitty will get you out of your funk in no time."

There was no one who knew her so well–and could exasperate her so profoundly–as her sister.

"I'm not in a *funk*," Julia said. "I was dumped by the love of my life two minutes before my wedding. And now the non-profit I founded is dead in the water. My life is no longer a life. It's a Greek tragedy. A second-rate soap opera. Or a really lame reality show. It's like the first half of a motivational video, except that it's missing the second half..."

Her sister interjected. "Okay, okay, I get it. Look, do you want her or not?"

Julia smiled helplessly. "Of course I want her." She bent down and picked up the little cat, relishing the sensation of the tiny warm body pressing into hers. Her smile faded. "It's just that–what if..."

Her sister looked confused for a moment. Her expression then turned pitying. "Oh, Jules. Were you actually thinking he might come back?"

It was clear from her tone what Jolene thought the likelihood of *that*.

"No, of course not," said Julia.

"How's this?" said her sister. "We'll make a contingency plan. If Asher comes back, Olive can come live with me."

Julia smiled. "Olive?"

"That's what I've been calling her. Little black Olive. So, deal?"

Notably, Jolene wasn't explaining how, in such an event, she intended to get around her apartment's no-pets policy; clearly, this "contingency plan" was merely her way of allowing Julia to maintain, for just a little longer, the illusion that Asher's return was a genuine possibility.

Julia didn't call her out on the charade. "Deal."

Jolene squealed and kissed Olive on the head. "Baby girl, you've got a new home!"

Olive, however, had had enough of being held. She jumped from Julia's arms onto the couch and began batting at a set of keys hanging on a hook by the door—a setup suggested by Julia to keep Jolene from losing her keys, which worked very well, when Jolene remembered to use it.

"And by the way," said Jolene, "I have all the supplies you'll need. Litter box, cat carrier, cat food. You're all set. You can bring her home tonight."

"Wow," said Julia, impressed at this rare instance of forethought from her sister. "Great!"

Jolene smiled smugly. "How's that for thinking through the consequences of my actions? Planning ahead? All that good stuff? I know what you were thinking."

Julia laughed. "Yeah, okay, you did good."

Jolene's door buzzed, again sending Olive darting under the couch.

The other Kat had arrived.

A moment later, Kat, a gust of cold air trailing behind her, strode into Jolene's apartment, unhampered by her six-inch heels. "It's ridiculous out there!" Taking in Jolene's outfit, she said, "You're going to be freezing, Jo."

Julia gave her sister an I-told-you-so look, which Jolene ignored.

"Actually," said Jolene, "I think I'm going to be pretty hot."

Kat nodded. "Yes, Jo, you'll be the hottest person ever to die of hypothermia."

Jolene batted her eyes. "Oh, stop, you're just saying that." She glanced at Kat's shoes. "Anyhow, *you* are going to break a leg in those heels. That's why I stick to platforms. Much hipper—*and* safer."

Kat nodded airily. "Platforms are certainly the best choice for people like you, who lack an innate sense of balance. But for me, as a runner, my equilibrium has become rather unshakable. Athletics are really something, Jolene. You should give them a try sometime."

Julia's head was already pounding. The back-and-forth was typical of the way her sister and Kat interacted, each always trying to one-up the other. Their interpersonal dynamic could be taxing to be around.

The discussion was interrupted by a beep from Jolene's phone–Jeff again, no doubt.

Jolene glanced down long enough to read the message and then grinned back up at Kat. "Oh, believe me, I'm getting into *plenty* of athletics these days. I just tend to prefer the two-person variety."

Kat chuckled approvingly. "I can't argue with that. In fact, I'm getting in quite a bit of the two-person variety myself these days."

Jolene grinned. "Right on, Kitty Kat!"

As the two of them high-fived each other, Julia tried not to feel too pathetic. The only foreseeable athletics in *her* future were of the one-person variety; technically, perhaps, yoga was a group activity, but the torture felt supremely solitary.

A tiny black head was now peeking out from underneath the couch. Olive uttered a tentative, warbling meow.

Kat bent down for a closer look. "Meow," she said–one Kat to another. She then looked at Jolene. "Mission accomplished?"

Jolene gave her a thumbs-up.

Julia sensed a conspiracy. "Did you guys plan this?"

Jolene's eyes widened: her "innocent" look. "I just ran the idea by Kat to see what she thought."

"No fair!" said Julia. "You guys double-teamed me."

"Triple-teamed, if you count the cat," said Kat. "So what do you say, girls–should we get out there and wreak some havoc?"

"Let's wreak!" said Jolene.

They called a car to take them to their destination, the Cantab Lounge in Central Square. Minutes later, they climbed into the waiting SUV, Jolene clutching at her short dress to keep it from blowing up in the bitter wind.

"I really hope you're wearing underwear," said Julia.

"I plead the–what is it? Sixth?" said Jolene.

"Fifth," said Kat.

"Right, I plead the Fifth–as in fifth of vodka!" said Jolene, cracking herself up. "Speaking of which, who's buying? I vote for you, Kitty Kat. Remember, I work for a food co-op. Part-time. And Julia's back to being broke. Broken up and broke."

"Thanks for reminding me," said Julia.

"I'm trying to get you free drinks!" said Jolene. "You'll thank me later."

At the Cantab, however, things rapidly proceeded downhill. An hour into the live music show, Kat suffered a mishap in her high heels and twisted her ankle.

"What happened to your runner's equilibrium?" said Jolene, glancing—again—at her flashing phone. She'd been texting with Jeff all night.

"You obviously threw it off," said Kat. "I'm sorry, Jules, I'd better call it a night."

"You're *leaving*?" said Julia. "This whole thing was your idea!"

"I know, but I really need to start icing my ankle immediately. If I have to take more than a day or two off from running, I'll go nuts."

"You survived thirty-four whole *years* without running," said Julia.

"Barely. And I don't want to end up with permanent damage. You're a runner, too. I'm sure you understand."

"Sorry, Jules, I should also head out," said Jolene. "I told Jeff I'd bring him some soup. His throat is still a little dry." She gave an unconvincingly martyred shrug. "Relationships, you know? Duty calls."

Kat smirked. "You mean *booty* calls."

"It's medicinal, I swear!" said Jolene. "Medicinal booty. He's a doctor, remember?"

"Yes, I believe you've mentioned that once or twice," said Kat.

So much for their big girls' night out, thought Julia.

This time, they called for two cars. After helping Kat hobble outside to her waiting vehicle, Julia and her sister rode in the second car back to Jolene's. They asked the driver to wait while they ran up to Jolene's apartment, retrieved the cat supplies, and strong-armed the obstinate Olive into the cat-carrier. From there, they rode to Jeff's in Inman Square.

"Sorry about tonight, Jules," Jolene said as she exited the car. "Rain check?"

"Sure thing," said Julia. "Take good care of Jeff."

"I certainly will," said Jolene. "He says I have an *excellent* bedside manner. And he's a doctor, so he should know."

"I'm sure he does," said Julia. "And I'm sure you do."

The car pulled away from Jeff's and continued on toward the North End. It wasn't even eleven o'clock. Julia only hoped that tonight wasn't representative of her post-Asher social life.

As if reading her thoughts, Olive emitted a plaintive meow.

"I know how you feel," murmured Julia. She unzipped the carrier just enough that she could reach in and pet Olive directly. Nearly invisible in the dim light, the tiny bundle of darkness nuzzled her face into Julia's hand. Even her nose was black.

"That a critter in there?" barked the driver.

His backwoods accent startled Julia from her thoughts.

She laughed. "Yes, it's a critter. My new cat."

Uttering the words, she unexpectedly felt her spirits lift.

Yes, she'd lost her uber-wonderful fiancé and would be living out her near future not in a Louisburg Square mansion or Swiss castle with her Prince Charming, but in a tiny North End apartment, on her own—as Jolene had put it, broken up and broke.

But in the feline sense, at least, she was operating in the black.

Chapter 31

Another Tuesday night, another ninety minutes of yoga torture, and, at long last, the grand finale: lying sweaty and spent on her mat, vowing she'd never do it again—while knowing that in fact she most certainly would.

Clearly, she was suffering from some sort of New Age neurosis. Obsessive-compulsive yoga disorder, maybe?

On second thought, Julia decided, it was more like battered women's syndrome. After being brutally assaulted every Tuesday night and pledging to a subsequent bout of victimization, she'd experience a creeping amnesia that caused her to forget how awful yoga actually was. Her distorted thinking would culminate in an episode of grand denial on Tuesday afternoon, during which she'd manage to convince herself that it hadn't really been *that* bad, and might even be worth doing *again*. And the cycle of violence would begin afresh.

She groaned aloud. One nice thing—possibly the *only* nice thing—about yoga was that no one looked at you funny no matter what you did. Vibrational breaths, sighs, moaning, grunting, even crying were all regular occurrences. The crying was supposedly because yoga enabled people to tap into their previously repressed emotions. Julia herself suspected, however, that what brought on the tears was the traumatizing experience of yoga itself.

Even worse, if possible, than the prospect of next week's Ashtanga ordeal was the prospect of returning to work. She would have to break the news about JoH's demise to Whitley and the Board—and try not to punch Byron in the face. Worst of all, she'd have to be away from Olive for days on end. Since her unanticipated arrival just over a month ago, the tiny black cat had proven an outsized source of both trouble and delight. Julia's lower legs were covered in scratches; Olive liked to playfully pounce on her ankles in the early morning while Julia was sleeping. At the same time, the ruthless little predator was incredibly sweet, devotedly following her around everywhere she went, even to the bathroom in the middle of the night. Thanks in large part to little black Olive, the black pit of post-"wedding" despair hadn't quite entirely subsumed her.

Julia slowly became aware of a familiar voice drifting from above into her field of consciousness. "This is the last place I ever expected to run into *you* again."

She opened her eyes and gazed up into the blue-gray eyes of Sean Harris.

She experienced a flash of déjà vu, recalling their first unexpected encounter at the Ashtanga class. Why was it that he always caught her on her worst days? She'd been painting all day and hadn't even showered. Her shirt was spattered with green acrylic paint, which had probably also gotten in her hair.

She smiled nonetheless. "Hey. I didn't see you come in."

As he'd done that first time, Sean offered her a hand up. "I was a little late," he said. "They almost didn't let me in." He looked at her, amused, no doubt taking in her unkempt appearance. "So you're still doing yoga. *This* yoga."

Julia nodded sadly. "I was working on a painting and by the end of the day, I was desperate to get out of the house. This gives you an idea just *how* desperate."

Sean grinned. "I can tell. That you were painting, I mean. Your hair's a little green."

Julia shrugged. "New look. What do you think?"

"I like it," he said.

Sean waited while she rolled up her mat, and they headed out together down the stairs, pausing on the sidewalk on Hanover Street.

"I didn't expect to see you here again, either," said Julia. "I thought that one class made you swear off Ashtanga forever."

"What can I say? I like a challenge. And it's been helping with my plantar fasciitis. Nothing else did–physical therapy, acupuncture, nothing. But I've mostly been doing a morning class in the Back Bay, near where I live." He paused and added, "Even before that, though, I wasn't seeing you around here."

Of course he hadn't seen her; she'd been on her "honeymoon."

And after that–recovering.

"Yeah. I was away for a little while," said Julia.

Sean's eyes widened in understanding. "Oh, right, you were off getting married! Yoga can't exactly compete with a honeymoon. Where did you go?"

"Hawaii," she said.

Sean's face lit up. "How was it?"

"Beautiful. Volcanoes, beaches, tropical rainforests, the ocean. Good stuff."

"It sounds amazing. I've always wanted to go," said Sean. "So tell me, how was the wedding? How's the husband? How's married life?"

His expression was so kind, so open, so sincere, that Julia's heart just about broke in two.

She smiled pathetically, searching for words. "There's no husband," she told him. "There was no wedding. I never got married."

Sean rocked back slightly on his heels. "What do you mean? What happened? You called it off?"

"*I* didn't call it off," said Julia. "He did. Actually, he didn't even call it off–he just didn't show up. He sent me a text message right before the wedding saying he was sorry but he couldn't go through with it. That was it."

She gazed down at the icy sidewalk, fighting a flood of shame. This information would most certainly seal Sean's perception of her as a complete and total loser. But fortunately the awful Ashtanga had done its job; she felt that typical loosening of her inhibitions, the steadfastness that had quietly accumulated during the weekly hour-plus of extreme unpleasantness, allowing her to better deal with whatever *other* unpleasantness she might encounter in the outside world.

Even this.

Sean was looking at her expectantly, as if waiting for her to tell him she was kidding. When she didn't, he said abruptly, "Come on. Let's get a drink."

Sticky with sweat, green paint in her hair—perfect for a night out in the North End. Julia took in Sean's appearance. He was wearing a dark green T-shirt, which was dotted with sweat, and baggy black athletic shorts. Unlike her, though, he still managed to look adorable.

"Okay," she said. "A quick one, though. I want to get back to my cat. I've had her for just over a month, and I hate leaving her."

Sean grinned. "I understand. There's no telling what my cats will get into when I'm gone."

Julia stared at him in astonishment. "You have cats?" Two years with feline-avoidant Asher had almost made her forget that not *all* men were allergic to cats—that some men even *liked* cats.

He laughed. "I have two *wild* cats. I think they're slowly turning feral." They were across the street from Café Paradiso, and he gestured in its direction. "How about this place?"

All too vividly, Julia recalled the last time she'd been here, with Asher. She was on the verge of suggesting that they go somewhere else when she realized that there was virtually *nowhere* in the North End she and Asher hadn't been together. It would be physically impossible to avoid all their old haunts. There was little alternative than to begin rehabilitating them, so to speak.

She flashed back to the Schloss, her mother's dress, the excruciating brunch the morning after the non-wedding.

Asher to ashes.

"Sure," she said. "This place is perfect."

•　　•　　•

They were soon settled at a table by the window, yoga mats propped against the wall, steaming mugs of tea in front of them.

"So tell me the rest of the story," said Sean. "What did your fiancé–Asher–say when you finally talked to him?"

"I haven't talked to him," said Julia. "I called a few times and finally stopped trying."

Sean's face showed his shock. "You're kidding me. You still haven't talked to him?"

She shook her head, humiliated.

"That's ridiculous!" he said. "Where does he live?"

"Rowes Wharf," Julia answered automatically, before she remembered that the house renovation was now complete. "Actually, no, now he's in Beacon Hill. Louisburg Square."

"That's right around the corner," said Sean. "Let's go."

Julia found herself considering the proposition. "Seriously? I have been tempted to show up on his doorstep and demand an answer, but I didn't want to push him."

"*Please*," said Sean. "He deserves to be pushed–in fact, he deserves a hell of a lot more than that. Come on, I'll go with you. I'll wait outside while you talk to him."

"This is crazy," said Julia.

"Not half as crazy as not talking in person to the guy you were planning to marry," said Sean.

He had a point. Jolene and Kat done such a good job of acting like Asher no longer existed that that Julia had taken to following their lead.

But he *did* still exist, of course–and she deserved some answers.

"I'm all sweaty and gross," she said. "I can't go over there looking like this. I'm disgusting."

"What are you talking about?" said Sean. "You're beautiful."

Julia flushed, suddenly flustered.

He stood. "Come on. No time like the present. Let's do this."

She opened her mouth to argue, and then shut it again.

He was right. It was crazy that she'd let things stand at one text message.

"Okay," she said. "Let's do it."

They called a car, and minutes later they were pulling up in front of Asher's home in Louisburg Square. The lights were on; it looked like he was indeed back from London.

Sean squeezed her hand. "Good luck. I'll find a bar on Charles Street and wait for you there. Text me if you need anything. If I don't hear from you within the next half-hour or so, I'll head home."

He gave her his phone number to enter into her cell phone.

"Thank you for talking me into this," said Julia. "I should have done it much sooner."

"Of course," said Sean. "And don't worry, I'll take good care of your yoga mat."

A moment later, the car was driving away, leaving Julia in the heart of historic, gas-lamp-lit Louisburg Square, the epitome of old-money, blue-blooded Boston society.

She took a deep breath and walked up to the house. Despite all that had happened, she knew that Asher loved her. And she loved him. Surely, once they were in each other's physical presence, looking each other in the eye, everything would be okay.

She rang the front doorbell and heard the chimes echo through the hallway.

To her surprise, she heard a dog bark—it must be Rusty. Asher often dog-sat when Gareth was away.

A few seconds later, the front door opened and sure enough, there was Rusty, bounding at the screen door. And right behind the dog was Asher, in pajama pants and a white T-shirt, his wavy brown hair sexily disheveled.

It was clear from his attire that he hadn't been expecting visitors.

"Hi," he said, cracking open the screen door to prevent Rusty from getting out. His expression was bland, even...resigned. Hardly the welcome Julia had hoped for.

"Hi," she said. "And hi, Rusty." She rubbed the dog's head as Rusty eagerly butted up against her. Rusty really was a sweet dog, just absurdly energetic.

"Come in," said Asher.

Julia followed him into the living room. They took a seat on the couch.

"The place looks great," she said, absorbing the new décor.

"Thanks, yes, it's a relief to be done with the renovations."

There followed an awkward pause. Julia had never before had an awkward pause with Asher.

Finally, she broke the silence. "You're dog-sitting, I take it?"

Asher nodded. "Yes. Gareth left today for the Hamptons. He's got a project there."

"Right, David told me," Julia said. "He's doing the interior design."

She waited for Asher to say something—he missed her, he'd made a horrible mistake, *something*.

But he only sat there, silent.

She was suddenly all too aware of her grungy workout clothes and her own sweaty, un-sexily disheveled hair. She should never have come over here looking like this.

"What happened?" she blurted. "How could you do this? How could you just leave me like that?"

Asher closed his eyes, looking so tortured that she instinctively went to touch his leg in consolation.

At her touch, his eyes flew open and he recoiled slightly.

She drew her hand away, embarrassed.

"I'm sorry," he said. "I handled it all terribly."

She laughed sharply. "You didn't *handle* it at all. You just disappeared."

"I didn't know what else to do," said Asher.

"You didn't want to marry me?"

"I *wanted* to want to marry you. I just got so swept up in the wedding planning—"

"And the castle," said Julia.

"Yes, the castle." He sighed. "That was part of it. The closer we got to the wedding, the more I felt like I was just some Bartlett family pawn, playing out some role assigned to me generations ago. Get married, inherit the Schloss, work for BartTech, live out this totally predetermined existence. I felt like I was going to explode."

"Why didn't you just *tell* me all of this?" said Julia. "You knew I don't care about any of that stuff. We could have worked this out. *Together*."

Asher didn't say anything.

Another thought occurred to her. "Was it the vegan thing? Too much pressure? Are *you* still vegan?"

Incongruously, he smiled. "Yes, I'm still vegan. In fact, I've even made a convert or two in my inner circle."

Julia wondered vaguely who the "convert" could be. Asher's "inner circle" consisted primarily of his cousins, and she couldn't imagine any of them giving up meat.

"It wasn't your fault," he said. "Any of it. But the family pressure was like this poison, contaminating everything. Even us."

Julia felt a sudden flare of hope. "We can get it back! Now that those other distractions are gone, we can focus on *us*, on being together." Again, she touched his leg. "Asher, sweetheart, what we have is special. Don't let one moment of overwhelm overshadow all of that."

He wouldn't meet her eyes. "It's too late. It's just too late."

"No, it's not!" she said. "I love you. If you love me, it's not too late. It will *never* be too late."

Asher only shook his head.

Finally, when it became clear he wasn't going to say anything else, Julia stood up from the couch–still hoping he would protest. "Okay then. I guess I'll go."

Asher stood as well. "How are things at JoH?"

She chuckled darkly. "Not great, to say the least. But not your problem."

He looked concerned. "Why, what's going on? Are you back working?"

Work was the *last* thing she was interested in discussing with Asher. "Again, not your problem," she told him. "I go back on Monday. I'll deal with it then."

There was another awkward moment. Then, he held out his arms, and Julia all but leapt into them. Even after the painfully disjointed conversation they'd just had, it felt so natural, so *right*, to be back in his embrace. She would have remained there all night if she could.

But the hug was short-lived. A nano-second later, Asher jerked away, sneezing several times in rapid succession.

Olive.

Julia's mouth twisted. "I adopted a cat. Sorry."

Asher nodded, still sneezing. He gave her a little wave as she walked out.

Unbidden, the words of T. S. Eliot rang in Julia's ears. It had all ended not with a bang, but a whimper—or, rather, a sneeze.

She stepped outside and began walking toward Beacon Hill. Only then did she remember Sean. She couldn't bear to disclose this final humiliation. She paused on the sidewalk long enough to send him a text message.

Don't bother waiting around. I may be a while. Thanks for everything.

Sean responded within seconds.

I'll head home then. Hope it's going well. Talk to you later.

Cold as it was, Julia decided to walk the mile or so home to the North End. Confronting Asher hadn't given her any sense of closure or understanding. One thing, though, was crystal-clear.

It was over.

Chapter 32

"Well, it was certainly about time you talked to him in person," said Kat. "Even if he didn't have much to say."

Julia nodded and tried to smile. "It turned out to be futile. But I had to try."

As they had on countless Saturday mornings in the past, Julia and Kat had met at Veggie Galaxy in Central Square for brunch. This weekend, though, felt especially poignant, since on Monday Julia would be returning to work at JoH–while it still existed.

On the plus side, in the waning weeks of her "sabbatical," she'd crammed in a near-manic amount of painting. Finished pieces, some large, some small, lined the short hallway between her living room and the kitchen, making her small apartment feel crowded, as if another person had moved in. And, in a sense, another person *had* moved in: her artist self, who'd been largely exiled during the time she'd been with Asher.

"I have to say, I really like the sound of this Sean Harris," said Kat. "What he did, getting you to go over there like that–that takes balls."

"Yeah, it was sweet," said Julia. "Typical male response. I could tell he felt compelled to *do* something."

Kat jabbed a hunk of pancake with her fork. "I don't know how 'typical' that is. From what I've seen, most men will go to just about any lengths to *avoid* taking responsibility–let alone stepping up to help someone else."

"Guilty as charged," said David, sliding into the booth beside Kat and giving her a kiss on the cheek. A waitress appeared almost instantaneously. "What can I get you, darling?"

David scanned the menu. "Is everything here vegan?"

"Hundred percent," she told him.

He grimaced slightly. "I suppose I'll try the stuffed French Toast. Vegan–if you must."

"You got it," said the server.

He beamed up at her. "I really do, don't I?"

Julia and Kat exchanged looks as the waitress trotted off.

"We were talking about Julia's high school crush, Sean Harris," Kat told David. "He's the one who got her to go over there to talk to Asher. By the way, have *you* talked to Asher lately?"

David reflected. "Come to think of it, I did run into him a few weeks ago at an ICAA awards dinner." At their questioning looks, he elaborated, "Institute for Classical Architecture and Art. Not really *my* thing, but a guy I used to work with won a big award. I'm not sure why Asher was there, though. Some BartTech client probably invited him."

Kat glowered at him. "Why didn't you tell us?"

David looked defensive. "I only talked to him for two seconds at the bar!" Then, he sighed. "I'm sorry, Jules. I dropped the ball."

"Umm, *yeah*," said Kat. "Which only confirms my point about Sean. Who actually *has* balls."

"You didn't have any complaints about the hardware last night," said David.

Kat blushed and smiled, and the two of them shared an intimate moment.

By now, Julia was getting used to feeling like a third wheel. Each a handful individually, together, David and Kat were all but insufferable. At the same time, they made such a natural fit that, in hindsight, she wondered that it had taken them this long to get together.

The lovebirds' exchange was interrupted by the return of the waitress, delivering David's food.

"Here you go," she said, setting down the warm plate in front of him. "French toast stuffed with vanilla nut vegan cream cheese, topped with caramelized banana butter, strawberry basil sauce, and maple syrup. Enjoy!"

"Thanks, love," said David.

The server topped off their coffees and left.

David sampled his French toast, then shrugged at Kat and Julia. "All right, maybe not *all* vegan food is completely repulsive. Who knew?"

"Forgive him," Kat said to Julia. "He's still evolving."

He nodded earnestly. "Trying to, at least."

Kat looked again at Julia. "I think you should go for Sean. Have you heard from him?"

Julia shook her head. "Not really. He texted me the next day to let me know that he'd dropped off my yoga mat at the studio for me. We haven't been in touch since then."

Kat grinned. "So, ask him out!"

"Right," said Julia. "Ask out a guy who goes out of his way to try to help me get back together with my ex-fiancé? That's not usually a sign of romantic interest. He was just being nice."

At that point, David, who'd been preoccupied with his rapidly diminishing mound of French toast, spooned up his last remaining bit of strawberry sauce and settled back in his seat, his arm draped casually over the back of the booth. "Speaking of *nice*, I've got some good news. I managed to finagle you ladies an invitation to the event of the season. Please, don't thank me, I was glad to do it—it's just the kind of guy I am."

"Okay, we won't thank you," said Kat. "So what's the event of the season?"

He tittered casually. "Oh, just a little weekend bash in the Hamptons. Guest cottage for the two of us, and one for Julia. Fancy dinner Friday night, super-sleek gala Saturday night. No big deal, just a low-key weekend of rubbing elbows with film stars, Grammy-award-winning artists, maybe a sports legend or twenty."

He'd succeeded in garnering Kat's full attention.

"Are you serious?" she said.

"As a heart attack," said David. "And trust me, these two know how to party. This shin-dig is going to be one for the books."

"Which two?" said Kat. "What exactly *is* this shin-dig?"

"Remember those clients of mine in the Hamptons?"

"The project you have with Gareth?" said Julia.

David nodded. "That's the one. Danny and Camilla Durango are the clients, and the place is spectacular. They're hosting this event to unveil the new digs. Gareth and I drove up there last week for the photo shoot. It's going to be featured in *Architectural Digest*."

Kat grinned proudly. "That's my boy! Wait, the Durangos? Haven't I heard of them?"

Again, David laughed. "Umm, I would *think* so. Danny's a professional soccer player turned sports magnate. He owns half a dozen media networks. Total adrenaline junkie. Triple-D, they call him—Daredevil Danny Durango."

"My kind of guy," said Kat.

"And Camilla is a former model/actress, i.e., porn star," said David. "Now she's doing fashion. She just launched a new lingerie line. In fact, she also happens to be a triple-D, in a different sense. In a nutshell, they've got more money than they know what to do with, and they're both off-the-charts insane. It makes for quite a combo. Their parties are legendary. And don't worry, dear, there ought to be plenty of rock stars for you to woo," he added for Kat's benefit; she was always on the hunt for new music clients.

"When is the party?" Julia asked.

"First weekend in May," he told them. "It can still be a little chilly in the Hamptons then, but Camilla insists the gods are going to deliver us a perfect spring weekend. Quite honestly, I believe her; she has a knack for getting her way. So what do you say? You in?"

"We are *so* in," Kat answered for both of them.

Julia, however, wasn't so certain. "Do you think Asher will be there?"

David hesitated. "It's possible. He'll be on the invite list, for sure. But I doubt he'll show. This isn't exactly his scene. And don't worry, if he does come, we'll protect you."

"Yes, Jules," said Kat. "Don't you *dare* let the Chief Executive Ash-hole make you miss the event of the season."

Julia knew Kat was right. She couldn't let Asher, let alone the mere possibility of Asher, dictate her choices–not anymore. "All right then. I'm in!"

David grinned. "Excellent! Like I said, when it comes to partying, no one can keep up with Durangos. But we can try, right?"

Chapter 33

When Julia walked into work on Monday, the JoH office was the same as ever—the same faux leather couch, coffee table, and work desks, the same morning sunshine streaming in the street-facing window, the same street noises filtering in from Hanover Street outside.

What was different was the expression on Whitley's face when she greeted Julia.

"Welcome back, Julia," said Whitley, her voice tactfully lowered. "How are you doing?"

By now, the question—and pitying tone—were all too familiar to Julia. She summoned a smile. "I'm great! I've been doing tons of painting and other fun stuff."

"Good for you!" said Whitley, a little too vehemently. "I've been holding down the fort around here. I'm just finishing up our report to the Spring Foundation."

"Great," said Julia, her smile faltering just a bit. There would soon be no need for grant reports of any sort. But she couldn't bring herself to break the bad news about JoH to Whitley just yet.

"Also," said Whitley, "we need to start planning Cruz Costa's send-off. He leaves for Mexico June twenty-second."

Julia brightened. "Right! In fact, we've got a video session scheduled at two o'clock today. Do you want to join in?"

"Definitely," said Whitley with a grin. "Lots going on here at JoH!"

Of course, the biggest thing "going on" at JoH was that there soon wouldn't *be* a JoH.

She had to tell Whitley. "On that note," said Julia. "there's something I need to talk to you about."

Whitley's prominent nose twitched. "What's up?"

Julia sighed. "I'm not really sure where to start. As you know, I was the one who talked Carly and Franco into branching out into the non-profit world and starting JoH. But now they want to get back to their original focus, which has always been Hartland Travel. They've decided to shut down JoH. I'm so sorry to have to be the one to tell you. But I didn't want you to hear it from anyone else."

Whitley looked away, the tip of her nose slightly red.

"Wait a second," said Julia. "Did you? Hear it from anyone else?"

Whitley nodded reluctantly. "Yeah, Byron filled me in. He asked me not to say anything."

Julia exhaled, annoyed. "I should have known he would tell you! This whole thing was his idea."

As always, Whitley was quick to jump to Byron's defense. "He only wants what's best for the company. He showed me some of his spreadsheets. The company will be much more profitable if we take the resources we've been pouring into JoH and invest them in Hartland Travel."

It was no surprise to Julia that Whitley's justifications sounded like they'd come verbatim from Byron, as they almost certainly had. "I'm a little surprised at your reaction," she said. "I thought you'd be devastated about JoH. I thought you actually cared about our mission here."

Whitley's blue eyes bulged. "I do care! But the way Byron explained it, JoH is dragging Hartland Travel down. I don't want to be part of a sinking ship. If it's time for us to move on, then so be it."

"We aren't dragging anyone down," said Julia, now *really* annoyed. "We've been operating a financially viable non-profit. But if Carly and Franco are solely interested in being in the for-profit travel business, and it seems that they are, then it makes sense for them to focus exclusively on Hartland Travel."

At that moment, the office door opened–Byron himself. Dapper as ever in khakis, a crisp white shirt, pink vest, and navy blue sports coat, he flashed them a dazzling smile. "Good morning, lovelies! And welcome back, *Ms.* Jones."

He regarded Julia sorrowfully. "I'm *so* sorry about the wedding. You poor dear, to be publicly humiliated like that. Good for you for still showing up with your head held high. You're a trouper, no question about it."

Despite her irritation, Julia forced a shrug. "Yeah, just one of those things. Relationships, you know? Sometimes they just don't work out."

If anything, Byron's gaze grew still *more* pitying. "Yes, yes, of course, you poor darling. It could have happened to anyone."

His tone clearly suggested, however, that it would never have happened to *him*.

Whitley saved Julia from having to respond. "We were just talking about the decision to close JoH. Do you really think that's necessary? We've been surviving okay up until now."

Byron waggled a finger at them both. "Girls, girls, girls, *what* am I going to do with you? You're the sweet, gentle, bleeding-heart types. And me, I'm the big, bad numbers type. Granted, if people like you ran the world, it would be a much nicer place–but absolutely *nothing* would get done." He smiled grimly. "And frankly, if we'd been building up Hartland Travel these past three years instead of dumping dollars into the black hole that is JoH, poor Carly and Franco would have been able to retire long ago. They're getting up in years, you know."

Whitley nodded, but internally Julia was fuming. She knew full well that there was nothing stopping Carly and Franco from retiring; in fact, she was skeptical they'd even *want* to stop working in five years, as they claimed. But challenging Byron was like arguing with a tape recorder–an exercise in futility.

Again, she shrugged. "I see it a little differently. But they've made their decision."

"Yes, they have," said Byron. "It's out of our hands at this point. JoH is D.O.A.–Hartland Travel or bust!"

Julia's stomach clenched.

She was going to have to make that decision for herself. And soon.

• • •

Later, in her private office, Julia prepared herself to tackle the email correspondence that had piled up while she'd been away. One message in particular, however, immediately caught her eye. It was from her former future father-in-law.

She quickly scanned the message, which was dated the previous Friday. Then she read it again, to make sure she hadn't misunderstood.

Dear Julia,

I am delighted to inform you that the BartTech Foundation has approved a substantial increase in its annual contribution to Journeys of the Heart, in the form of an annual, automatically renewable grant of $250,000. Please let me know when you are available to sign for receipt of a check in that amount, and we will arrange for delivery at your convenience. Please know that we truly feel there could be no better use of our philanthropic funds.

Best,

Dom

Julia leaned back in her chair, absorbing the implications. In the past, the BartTech Foundation had made an annual twenty-five-thousand-dollar contribution to JoH–generous, but hardly game-changing. Ten times that amount, on the other hand, was enough to sustain JoH for an entire year, without any funding from Hartland Travel. And if, as indicated, this was to be an ongoing annual grant, JoH was *not* D.O.A.; it was set for life.

It was tremendous news for JoH.

Even so, Julia's chest burned with indignation. Clearly, this was a guilt grant. She should never have let it slip to Asher that JoH was having troubles. He'd obviously talked his father into funding JoH, possibly as penance for abandoning her in Switzerland–or simply to ensure the survival of her job, since she wouldn't have him to support her. But she'd rather starve than be beholden to him and his family. In fact, she was tempted to tell Dom to take BartTech's money and shove it.

Or go buy another castle.

The thought made her smile, but only for a moment. She'd just been presented with the golden opportunity to save JoH! This grant meant that Cruz Costa and others like him would continue to benefit from JoH's programs–and that she, Julia, wouldn't be forced to work with Byron at Hartland Travel. Perhaps best of all, she'd have the satisfaction of foiling Byron's backhanded scheme to destroy JoH.

Even so, none of it sat well.

Which prospect was worse, Julia wondered–working with Byron, or being professionally dependent on Asher and his family?

When it came to matters of large sums of money, the person to talk to was Lacey. Julia shut the door to her office and used her mobile phone to call her stepsister. She told her about Dom's email and the grant.

"A quarter of a million dollars?" said Lacey. "Annually? *Forever*? So your non-profit is saved in one fell swoop. Not bad!"

Julia frowned. "It's blood money. I don't want Asher's charity."

"Why not?" said Lacey. "Even if he *did* do it out of guilt, so what? You deserve to get *something* out of this miserable mess."

Julia should have known her stepsister wouldn't understand. "I don't want to be dependent on the Bartletts."

She could practically hear Lacey rolling her eyes. "Again, why not? If not them, you'd just be dependent on some other corporate foundation. That's the nature of being a non-profit. You're a whore to whoever decides to give you money."

Julia couldn't dispute that assessment; it was precisely what had always bothered her about her development role at JoH.

She sighed. "Ugh, I hate it. But you're right. For JoH's sake, I can't turn it down."

"No, you can't," Lacey said firmly.

"But I also can't keep working there. It would be like Asher was paying my salary. I just can't do it."

To Julia's surprise, her stepsister didn't protest. "Honestly, I'd probably feel the same way. So let Asher be the knight in shining armor for JoH–good for him. And good for JoH. And you'll move on to bigger and better things. Hartland Travel is a much better option, anyway."

"Hartland Travel or bust," said Julia.

"You know it!" said Lacey.

Julia said goodbye to her stepsister and walked next door to Hartland Travel.

"Julia!" said Carly, looking up from her desk. "What brings you to this side of the wall?"

"I've made my decision," she said. "I'll do it."

Julia returned to JoH a little while later feeling more sanguine. Carly and Franco had been elated to hear that she'd be coming back to work at Hartland Travel. Her own reservations aside, it felt good to be wanted.

And now she had some very happy news to convey to Whitley.

"Guys?" she said to Whitley and Byron, who were working quietly–for once–at their computers. "I have some news."

"Oh?" said Byron, not even bothering to glance away from his computer.

"It's about JoH," said Julia.

Byron groaned. "For the love of *God*, Julia, I know it's painful, but please, for all our sakes, *let it go*. JoH is D.O.A. Dead and buried in the cold, cold–"

"Will you just shut up for two seconds and listen?" she said.

Taken aback at her abruptness, he rolled his eyes but remained silent.

Julia directed her attention at Whitley. "A donor has just committed to an annual two-hundred-fifty-thousand-dollar grant to JoH."

Whitley gaped. "But that's enough ..."

Byron, too, was sputtering, at a rare loss for words.

"Exactly," said Julia. "JoH *isn't* dead and buried. Not if we don't want it to be."

Byron had recovered himself. "So who *is* this sudden miracle donor?"

Julia met his snake-like eyes. "The BartTech Foundation."

"Isn't that Asher's foundation?" said Whitley.

Julia nodded. "It is."

Byron cackled. "My, oh, *my*. Nice work, Ms. Jones! A little guilt goes a long way, eh? You took one big old lemon of a wedding and turned it into some *major* lemonade. And saved your own career in the process!" He made mock bowing motions. "Kudos. I couldn't have played it better myself."

Julia refused to let him get to her–at least visibly. "I can't speak to the motivation for the grant. But the person that this will potentially affect the most is Whitley." She turned to her coworker. "Now that JoH has the funding to keep it going, I wondered if you'd be interested in taking on a leadership role. Carly and Franco will still be stepping down as executive directors. You're the ideal person to take over."

Whitley's eyes were wide, her nose was twitching, and she was anxiously twisting a strand of her frizzy red hair. "Of course I want to stay at JoH! But you should be the one to take over as executive director. JoH is *your* baby."

Julia smiled, feeling bittersweet. Her "baby" was growing up–and she was moving on.

"I won't be staying at JoH," she told Whitley. "I'm going back to work at Hartland Travel."

For the second time in less than five minutes, she had the satisfaction of rendering Byron Knowles speechless.

. . .

Cruz Costa's video call came in promptly at two o'clock.

"Hi, Cruz!" said Julia.

Whitley waved to him from her chair.

From the video image that popped up on the screen, they could see that Cruz was in his bedroom. His bed was made, the room neat, almost Spartan. Visible were only a few typical teenage items: band posters, some schoolbooks, an acoustic guitar.

"Hi, guys," said Cruz, smiling broadly as he leaned forward toward the laptop computer on his desk. He was clearly keyed up, eyes sparkling, his muscular forearms tense.

Thank goodness Byron wasn't part of this exchange, thought Julia; he'd have been drooling at the monitor. "Can you believe you're leaving in less than a month?"

He laughed. "Not really!"

Having sworn off fossil-fuel-dependent air travel, Cruz would be taking the train to Mexico City. As they began discussing the logistical details of his trip, the teenager visibly relaxed. He sat back in his chair, and only then could Julia make out the slogan on his T-shirt, which hadn't been apparent when he was leaning forward.

It read, "*Vegan Is Justice.*"

"Cruz, are you vegan?" she said. Given the water-intensive, polluting nature of animal agribusiness, veganism would be a logical choice for someone as environmentally-minded as Cruz. But she knew that only a fraction of those who professed to care about the planet had made a corresponding shift in their own diets–and she'd never have expected a teenage boy from Albuquerque to have been one of them.

Cruz looked surprised at the question, until he seemed to remember the message on his T-shirt. He grinned and nodded. "Yeah. It's been almost two years now."

Clearly comprehending the momentousness of this information to Julia, Whitley gaped. She looked, open-mouthed, at Julia, then back at Cruz. "So's Julia! She's been vegan practically *forever*."

"That's so cool!" said Cruz. He asked Julia some questions, and they traded vegan stories.

"Honestly," said Julia, "it's probably good that I didn't know you were vegan before now. It might have unfairly influenced me in choosing the Travel Sabbatical winner."

Whitley hooted. "No, it *definitely* would have."

"What about you, Whitley?" said Cruz. "Are you vegan, too?"

"Not totally," said Whitley. "I'm mostly vegetarian, though."

Now Julia was the one to laugh. "Oh, really? I hadn't noticed that."

Whitley shrugged. "I'm taking a reductionist approach."

As they wrapped up the call, Julia found herself wishing that Byron had been part of this video session after all. Who better to nudge him in the direction of ethical eating than super-cool Cruz?

She dismissed the thought as quickly as it had come. Not even "Cruz-a-licious" could imbue Byron Knowles with a conscience.

• • •

Later, Julia sat down with Franco and Carly to talk shop. There had been significant developments in the travel industry the several years since she'd last worked at Hartland Travel, and she'd need to get up to speed.

"Again, we're thrilled you're coming back, but no pressure," said Franco, sipping a tiny cup of espresso—one of the approximate dozen he went through in the course of a day. "You're welcome to take all the time you need making this transition. Carly and I aren't completely useless just yet—well, at least Carly isn't." Carly was twelve years younger than Franco, and their age gap was a constant source of banter between them.

Despite his lighthearted tone, Julia could sense Franco's attachment to the business he'd spent his whole adult life building. "Are you having doubts about retiring?"

Carly shot her husband a look.

"Carly wants us to have more time for ourselves," said Franco. "She deserves that."

"*You* deserve that," said Carly. She told Julia, "He runs himself ragged. He needs a break."

"Or my wife will end up running off with some handsome young stud," said Franco. "That's my biggest concern."

That scenario wasn't outside the realm of possibility. Both the Harts were natural flirts, and Carly, in her late fifties, blonde and voluptuous and just a tad cosmetically enhanced, still garnered plenty of male attention. Franco, too, was charming and gregarious, but a lifelong diet of pasta, processed meats, cheese, and copious amounts of olive oil added to just about everything had given him an enormous belly, along with an extra chin or two. His shiny black hair, though, was still thick and lustrous. For that, he credited the olive oil.

"Like I said, Julia, you can take your time transitioning," said Franco. "But Carly and I have decided that your profit-sharing in Hartland Travel will begin next month. So even before you officially step into a salaried position at Hartland Travel, you should see a nice little boost in income."

Julia looked at him in surprise. "Wow, thank you! I wasn't expecting that."

Broken up—but maybe no longer broke.

"We're glad to do it," said Carly. "In the meantime, you'll have your hands full winding down JoH."

Julia gasped. "I completely forgot! There's been a new development. The BartTech Foundation is giving JoH an annual two-hundred-fifty-thousand-dollar grant."

"Holy shit," said Franco.

Julia laughed. "Yeah! Enough to sustain JoH indefinitely, without any support from Hartland Travel."

"BartTech," said Carly. "Isn't that Asher's company?"

Julia nodded. Thankfully, they didn't press her.

Franco ran a hand through his hair. "So does this mean you're going to stay at JoH?"

"No," said Julia. "It's time for a change. I talked to Whitley, and she's willing to take over as executive director of JoH. So you two can still completely wash your hands of the non-profit industry, and JoH will continue on its own. And I'll come back to this side of the wall."

Franco looked relieved. "Oh, good! Now let's get down to business."

With spreadsheets and annual reports displayed on the large computer monitor in front of them, Franco and Carly took Julia back through the previous several years of Hartland Travel's business activities. Profits had climbed fairly steadily over the past decade, but business had dropped off rather sharply during the final months of the previous year. Julia's bosses, who'd weathered all kinds of financial ups and downs in their lifetime in the travel business, seemed unfazed by the recent downturn.

"This economy is tough these days," said Franco. "People just don't have extra money to spend on travel and art."

"But business is usually up around Christmas time," said Julia, puzzled by the timing of the profit dip. The spiritual pilgrimages offered by Hartland Travel were extremely popular during the holiday season, when many religious groups planned trips to Jerusalem, Bethlehem, and Rome.

"Yes, usually," said Carly. "But last December, two of our biggest clients ended up dropping us. Do you remember Unity Guild and the Urban Faith Coalition?"

"Of course," said Julia. Both were religious organizations that sponsored tour groups of several hundred people to Rome every Christmas. Lacey, who'd gone to college with Urban Faith Coalition president Marianne

Miller, had been the one to refer the New-York-City-based group to Hartland Travel. Unity Guild had also been a referral—from Dom Bartlett, a long-time friend of Unity Guild director Tom McCormick. Julia felt a small jolt of pride that she, albeit through her personal connections, had been responsible for bringing in such substantial clients.

That jolt of pride was immediately replaced, however, by one of disappointment. It felt especially personal for these two customers to terminate their relationship with Hartland Travel.

"What happened?" said Julia.

"Apparently they found better deals elsewhere," said Franco.

Julia said, "Did you try to match the offers?" The Harts valued customer loyalty more than almost anything else, and they'd often gladly sacrificed profits in order to retain a long-term client.

"We tried," said Carly. "But UFC decided to work directly with a Rome-based travel group, essentially cutting out the middleman—us. And Unity Guild got a thirty-percent discount on their five-hundred-person tour from some new agency that's trying to boost its business. We couldn't beat that."

"Thirty percent!" said Julia. "That's quite the discount."

"No kidding," said Franco. "Honestly, I'd be a little worried about our profitability if we didn't have Byron on board. He's been developing a long-term sales strategy for Hartland Travel."

"He came along at just the right time," said Carly.

The right time for *whom*, wondered Julia—Hartland Travel, or Byron?

"Speaking of which," said Franco, "now that you've made your decision, we can let Byron know you're coming back to Hartland Travel."

"I'm afraid that cat's already out of the bag," said Julia. "I told him just now. Although I haven't told him I'll eventually be his boss."

Franco nodded. "No problem. The four of us can meet on Wednesday and really talk nuts and bolts. The first official meeting of our new executive team!"

Her and Byron working side by side, bouncing ideas off each other, sharing professional experiences, continuing to grow the business that Franco and Carly had conceived—somehow, she couldn't quite see it.

"Can't wait," said Julia.

And, so, Wednesday morning found her sitting around the same large conference table with Carly and Franco, this time joined also by Byron, who'd brought cappuccinos for the four of them. For Julia, the gesture triggered an unwelcome flashback to their very first meeting, when Byron had come for his interview and had brought her and Whitley drinks from Boston Common Coffee.

It seemed like decades ago—and her relationship with Byron hadn't improved in that time.

"Oops," said Byron, casting Julia a pseudo-guilty look as he distributed the drinks. "I blanked on the vegan thing. I forgot you have a thing against cows."

This, from the man who harped on her twenty-four-seven about the "vegan thing." Julia didn't buy it for a second.

"Actually," she said, "I *love* cows. That's why I don't like to see them pumped up with hormones and antibiotics, forcibly impregnated, robbed of their babies, and killed for cheap meat once they stop producing obscene amounts of milk. And, of course, the whole process starts with someone jerking off a bull for semen. Or maybe that's the part you like best of all, Byron."

But whatever fleeting satisfaction Julia had felt at lashing out at Byron evaporated when she noted that Franco and Carly were staring at her with amused disconcertion—as if *she* were the crazy one.

She should have known better than to waste her breath.

Byron's impeccable eyebrows were sky-high. He flashed Franco and Carly a pained smile. "Oh, dear. I think *someone* just had a vegan moment."

Franco chuckled. "Well, even if Julia opts not to partake, thank you, Byron, for the cappuccinos. Now, why don't we get down to business?"

The Harts proceeded to fill Byron in on the plan for Julia to take over the principal leadership role at Hartland Travel. To Julia's surprise, Byron's response to the news was ostensibly positive.

"Wonderful," said Byron in his silky-smooth, jazz-deejay voice. "I think Julia and I will make a great team. I'll look forward to working with you, Julia."

Working *for* me, she thought peevishly.

Byron continued sweetly, "I know we've had our occasional rough patches in the past, but I'll win you over, Ms. Jones, just you watch. You'll be eating out of my hand in no time at all." He looked coyly at Franco. "Maybe even eating *veal parmesan* out of my hand."

Franco chortled, and even Carly giggled.

And in that moment, Julia knew that she would never, *ever* enjoy working with Byron.

But what was a single working woman to do? She had to pay the rent.

Chapter 34

The next morning brought classic Boston "spring" weather: overcast skies, scattered April showers, and a dampness in the air that left an intractable chill in the bones. Reluctant to face the walk to work, Julia fixed herself a bowl of oatmeal and lingered on the couch with Olive.

"You're a mess," she told the still-skinny black cat, using a napkin to wipe away a bit of crust at the corner of Olive's eyes. Plucking a tuft of black fur from the sofa, she added, "And you're not the only one."

The fur situation was worse than she'd realized. While it was most noticeable on the white sofa, she now saw that cat hair had also accumulated in the corners of the living room and hallway and even on the edges of the dozens of paintings propped up against the walls. Somewhere along the line, she'd turned into a messy cat-lady artist—or Jolene!

And had she really been the one to create all that art? Apart from the winter wind in the Public Garden, she recalled little of the actual process. She'd been so desperate to escape her own thoughts and emotions that her flurry of painting now seemed like a dream.

Enough loitering, she told herself. Time for work.

She stood up from the couch, startling Olive, who jumped to the floor and bolted into the bedroom. She grabbed her jacket and handbag, called goodbye to the unseen cat, and headed for the door. On her way out, though, her bag caught on a precariously stacked cluster of paintings, and she paused to straighten them, thinking that she really ought to sort through them at some point. Maybe there were one or two decent enough to sell online. If nothing else, it would free up some space in her cramped apartment.

In the next instant, Julia decided that JoH—and Hartland Travel—could wait.

She tossed her jacket on the couch and used her cell phone to snap photos of each of the paintings—thirty-eight in total. She transferred the images to her laptop and then had to think to recall the password for the workspace she'd used to set up her art website, which she hadn't visited once in the past year and a half—and chances were no one else had, either. But she managed to remember the password, and it didn't take long to post the new images, which had turned out surprisingly professional-looking; cell phone cameras had come a long way.

Olive crept out of the bedroom and hopped onto her lap as she worked. Since she hadn't titled any of the paintings, she came up with names off the top of her head. It was unlike her to work so quickly and haphazardly, but the piles of artwork sitting in her apartment collecting dust—and cat fur—seemed to symbolize all the priorities she'd let slide over these past several years. She suddenly felt she couldn't bear the inertia a moment longer.

Julia posted the final photo and shut her laptop. All told, the entire process had taken under forty-five minutes. Sadly, it was more than she'd done in the way of marketing her art in years.

And now it was *really* time for work. She gave Olive a final snuggle, again donned her jacket, and set out.

The moment Julia stepped outside, however, the oppressive gray sky and chilly drizzle only made her long to be back *inside*. What rush was there, really, to get to the office—especially given her professional limbo, between two jobs? She decided to stop in at Boston Common Coffee for a latte on her way to work.

She hurried down Salem Street toward the coffee shop. Fighting a strong gust of wind, she tugged to open the front door of the café. In so doing, she nearly collided with Sean Harris, who was on his way out. He hadn't noticed her.

Julia waved to catch his attention. "Sean! I'm running into you everywhere these days."

Sean flashed her a startled smile. He was holding a cup of coffee and a small bag that probably contained a bagel or muffin. "Oh, hey, Julia. How's it going?"

She smiled back. "It's going!" Dismissive as she'd been of Kat's suggestion about "going for" Sean, it *was* starting to seem as if the universe was conspiring to bring them together. Looking at him now, his blonde hair windblown, his eyes a vivid charcoal gray contrasting with his navy blue sportscoat, she was struck again by how handsome he was.

The damp air suddenly seemed electric. He *had* to feel it, too; chemistry like this was never one-sided.

For the third time that day, Julia decided that Hartland Travel and JoH could wait.

"Want to sit down for a minute?" she said.

"Wish I could," said Sean, "but I'm on my way to cover an event at the Boston Garden." The sports arena, not far from the North End, was now officially the T.D. Bank North Garden, but most Bostonians still referred to it by its original name. Almost as an afterthought, he said, "Your talk with Asher went okay the other night?"

Julia's smile faltered. "I guess it gave me some closure. And closure is good, right? Anyway, I don't want to keep you."

She'd been hoping he'd protest, but instead Sean seemed almost eager to get away.

"Yeah, I need to run," he said.

"Sure, no problem," she said, trying unsuccessfully not to feel crushed at his obvious antsiness. His demeanor was all too reminiscent of Asher's the night she'd shown up at his house in Louisburg Square—as if he'd have preferred to be anywhere else than right here, right now, with her. She felt a stab in her stomach, which she knew all the soy lattes in the world wouldn't soothe. "I'll see you later."

"See you later," said Sean.

He'd gone only a few steps when he stopped and turned around. "Oh, and Julia?"

Her heart leapt. Maybe he'd changed his mind about staying for a coffee—or maybe, even better, he was going to suggest getting together.

"Yes?" she said, a little too keenly.

"Did you get your yoga mat? They told me they'd hold it for you at the studio."

Julia's smile vanished.

He was talking to her about yoga. *Yoga.*

"I got it," she said. "Thanks."

"No problem," said Sean. "Take care."

This time, Julia didn't bother watching him walk away.

As she unenthusiastically joined the dozen or so people waiting in line for coffee, Julia berated herself for having taken their kiss, and Sean's flirtatious repartee, to have meant *anything*. She'd been mildly appealing to Sean when she'd been attached to someone else, but now that he knew the truth–that she was a lonely, abandoned *reject*–he couldn't get far enough away. The same was true of David Meadow, whose romantic interest in her likewise hadn't survived her singlehood. Men just didn't want her–except when they couldn't have her.

She smiled darkly. She hadn't turned into Jolene after all. Unlike her sister, who was catnip to the male species, she, Julia, was reverse-catnip.

Except maybe to Olive. At least Olive loved her.

Which reminded her–she'd been meaning to ask Jolene if she would take care of Olive next weekend, while she was in the Hamptons at David's big event. She'd text her sister when she got to work.

• • •

Damp from the rain and jittery from the latte, Julia was just settling in at her desk when she realized, to her chagrin, that she'd been so caught up in being *offended* at the BartTech grant that she'd never responded to Dom's email message. Regardless of the motives behind it, the extravagant donation certainly warranted a personal acknowledgement. Not to mention, she had to arrange for the check to be delivered.

With some trepidation, she picked up the phone and dialed the BartTech office. The receptionist quickly transferred her to Dom.

"Julia," said Dom. "It's so good to hear your voice. How are you doing?"

"I'm doing fine," she said. "I got your email about the grant—two hundred fifty thousand dollars? Dom, are you sure? It's so much money! It's not that I don't appreciate it, I do, but I don't want to you to do this out of guilt—out of *Asher*'s guilt. Or because you think I can't take care of myself. I can. I *am*."

Dom chuckled. "I know that, Julia. But it's a done deal. BartTech is always on the lookout for worthy charities, and Journeys of the Heart is certainly one." He hesitated a moment. "And on top of that, I *despise* what my son did to you. Sage and I can hardly stand to look at Asher. It's impossible to overstate our disappointment at what he's become."

Despite herself, Julia was taken aback at his venomous tone. "Don't say that! He's your son."

This time, Dom's chuckle was harsh. "Yes, that's the unfortunate reality. But the bottom line is, we'd do anything to make this up to you, and this grant is by no means breaking the bank. It'll help a lot of kids, and we're happy to help make your job a little easier."

Julia felt a sudden flash of dread: what if he changed his mind about the grant once he found out she was leaving JoH? She had to tell him.

"You're absolutely right," she said. "This money will help a lot of kids. But it won't affect me directly, because I won't be staying at Journeys of the Heart. I've accepted a new position at Hartland Travel, where I used to work, before we founded JoH. My bosses, Carly and Franco, are starting to plan for their retirement, and they'd like me to eventually take over the business. It's a big opportunity for me, and I think I should take it."

Dom's extended silence made Julia wonder if she'd disappointed him almost as profoundly as his own son.

But then, to her relief, he laughed. "Well, Julia, you've obviously landed on your feet. Honestly, that means more to me than anything else. Look, if we weren't donating this money to JoH, we'd just be giving it to someone else. I'm glad it'll be going to the place you helped found. Will you be in the office this afternoon? I'll messenger over the check."

"Yes, I'll be here," said Julia. "Thank you so much, Dom. Really. This is just the nicest thing ever. And you have no idea how big a difference you've made for JoH!"

She hung up the phone feeling much better about the grant. Ironically, her talk with Dom had given her more closure than her conversation with Asher. She was still startled, though, at the animosity Dom had exhibited toward his only son. She felt an involuntary stab of compassion for Asher—which she ordered herself to quell immediately.

Asher deserved every bit of grief he got.

•   •   •

True to his word, Dom had the check sent over within the hour. Julia and Whitley looked at it incredulously, and then at each other.

It was official. JoH was saved.

Her eyes blurry with tears, Julia hugged her coworker. She hadn't fully processed the prospect of JoH's demise—but oh, how good it felt for that demise to have been averted!

"Thank you for hanging in there with me," she told Whitley. "I didn't realize how badly I wanted JoH to be okay."

"Me, too," said Whitley, hugging her back. "And now JoH is *more* than okay—we're rollin' in it!"

They spent the afternoon working through the details involved in cutting JoH's ties to Hartland Travel. Happily, Byron, who'd been spending the bulk of his time at Hartland Travel, wasn't around to distract them. Given the recent dip in profits, Julia imagined he'd be hitting the sales calls that much harder.

She smiled wistfully at Whitley. "It's like old times—just you and me. Although you'll probably want to hire some new staff for JoH, now that you have the funds to do it."

Whitley shook her head, looking dazed. "So many things to think about. Will you sit on the Board? It would feel too weird not having you around at all."

"I'd love to," said Julia. The thought hadn't even occurred to her—and it would be the perfect way for her to stay connected to JoH.

"It's incredible how fast things can turn around," said Whitley.

"Yeah," said Julia, although, in truth, she didn't find it all that incredible. Her mother's death had taught her how instantly *everything* could change. It was a lesson she'd learned yet again on the night of her almost-wedding. "It's already after six. You need to get out of here," she told Whitley. "And I need to go talk to Byron about the new payroll. Now that JoH is going to be independent, we'll have to formally separate all the bookkeeping."

Whitley grinned. "Hands off our dough, Hartland Travel!"

"You said it!" said Julia.

They packed up their things and left the office, Whitley for home and Julia for Hartland Travel.

Outside the travel agency, Julia could hear Bryon's silky-smooth voice saying something about travel pricing. Reluctantly impressed that her "nemesis" was still at it, she was about to open the front door when she heard him say, "Knowles Global Travel. That's K-N-O-W-L-E-S."

Feeling like the eavesdropper she was, Julia paused outside the door and continued to listen.

"Thank you so much," he said. "It's been a pleasure. We'll be in touch."

It didn't sound like a personal call, Julia noted. What could he be up to?

The last thing in the world she felt like right now was a confrontation. But if she was going to take on an executive role at Hartland Travel, she would need to learn to put out fires while they were still small.

She'd also need to get used to dealing with Byron–her number-two man.

She opened the door to the Hartland Travel office, and Byron jumped, confirming her suspicion that he'd been up to something sketchy. He recovered his composure so quickly, though, that Julia wondered if she'd imagined the guilty look on his face.

"How's everything going?" she said.

"Good, good," said Byron, standing up from his desk and collecting his tailored beige wool coat from the coat rack in the corner. "I'm off."

"Who were you talking to just now?" said Julia. "I heard you discussing travel pricing. New client?"

Byron sighed dramatically and held up his hands in mock surrender. "Okay, Ms. Jones, you caught me. I was making a personal call during working hours. I'm a bad, bad boy. I'll reimburse you for the company time. I was on the phone for"–he ostentatiously checked his watch–"just under twelve minutes. We'll call it an even fifteen. That's a quarter of an hour, and at an hourly rate of–"

Julia wasn't about to indulge his nonsense. "Byron, I don't care about the twelve minutes. I was wondering about the call itself. It didn't sound personal. It sounded like business."

"It was *personal* business," he said, as if that explained everything. "I still do some consulting work on the side, on nights and weekends. That was one of my consulting clients. But my apologies, it wasn't exactly kosher of me to speak with him on company time. It won't happen again, Ms. Jones."

"How much consulting work do you do?" said Julia. "You realize that Carly and Franco–and I–are expecting you to put in a full work-week at Hartland Travel. It's a full-time gig."

Okay, now she was being kind of a bitch, but at this point, she felt entitled.

"I know, I know," said Byron. "Again, my apologies. Never again, I swear. I am one-hundred-percent devoted to Hartland Travel. I won't work on work time again." He chuckled wryly. "You know what I mean."

"All right," said Julia, dissatisfied but unsure what else to say.

Byron finished buttoning his coat and nudged past her to the door. "A pleasure as always, Ms. Jones."

His smug manner made Julia's skin crawl. *Oh, how she hated him!*

"Good night," she said, smiling pleasantly.

Only after he'd gone did Julia realize that they hadn't discussed the payroll issue.

But no matter; Byron would be back tomorrow.

Unfortunately.

Chapter 35

"Good morning, Jules! Good morning, Olive!"

Never one for low-key entrances, Jolene burst into Julia's apartment, a duffel bag over one shoulder and a mammoth suitcase dragging behind her. She'd agreed to stay at Julia's place and take care of Olive while Julia was in the Hamptons for the Durangos' party. Olive, of course, was nowhere to be seen; she'd gone diving for cover under the sofa the moment Jolene had come barreling in the front door.

Her head spinning slightly from the cloud of chaos that invariably accompanied her sister, Julia said, "It's afternoon, remember?"

Jolene grinned. "Well, time is relative, right? I just got up, so it's still morning to *me*."

"That makes sense," said Julia. And it did—since just about everything was "relative" to Jolene. Her sister had promised to be here by one o'clock, and it was only a few minutes after. For once, Jolene had been—relatively—on time.

Jolene's suitcase banged the edge of one of the paintings propped up against the walls. "Yikes! You really *have* been painting."

Julia shrugged dismissively. "Honestly, I don't know if any of them are even any good. But hey, what I'm lacking in quality, I made up for in quantity. How about you, have you been making any jewelry?"

However, Jolene, who'd begun leafing through the artwork, wasn't listening. She paused at one of the Public Garden scenes. "Jules, I can't stop looking at this one. It's so—*existential*. But majestic, even...glorious." She shook her head. "I don't know how you do it."

"Yeah, me, either," said Julia. "Chalk it up to heartbreak and the thought of going back to work."

"Hey, whatever works," said Jolene. She flipped through more of the paintings. "You know, you've really evolved as an artist these past few years."

Julia chuckled. "Is it possible to evolve as an artist when you go almost two years without actually painting?"

"Sure, why not? Your subconscious artist-self was maturing that whole time."

"Right," said Julia. "And then my subconscious artist-self had her heart torn out of her chest. I think *that* was what triggered the evolution."

Jolene nodded sympathetically. "At least you didn't cut off an ear."

"True," said Julia. "By van Gogh standards, I'm doing well."

"And look at you now!" said Jolene. "Off to cavort in the Hamptons—aren't *you* special, living the life."

"That's me," said Julia. "Special and living the life."

Julia grinned. "And I'll be living the life, too! I can't wait to hang out for three days with little black Olive." She crouched in front of the sofa and called to the elusive black cat. "I've missed you, baby girl!"

Olive mewed loudly in response, and the sisters burst out laughing.

"She obviously missed you, too," said Julia. "I'm so glad she'll have you to take care of her while I'm gone."

"It'll be fun," said Jolene. "And besides, you're doing me a big favor, too."

Julia tried not to cringe. In exchange for cat-sitting, Jolene had extracted her permission to hold a SunStar sales party at the apartment the following night. The North End location was more convenient for guests than Jolene's Central Square apartment—not to mention, Julia's place was infinitely more presentable.

Of course, as Jolene had known full well, Julia's consent had never truly been in question. For one, Olive needed a caretaker. And, for two, Jolene would undoubtedly have gone ahead with the SunStar party regardless—with or *without* Julia's permission.

Taking in the gargantuan black suitcase which, she knew, contained Jolene's SunStar merchandise, Julia consoled herself that at least she wouldn't have to *attend* the SunStar sales party. While Jolene's captive audience was enduring a forty-minute SunStar video featuring SunStar founder/president/CEO Mrs. Catherine Lee making an intensive, hardline sales pitch culminating in a "one-time special offer"/demand for them to enroll in SunStar's convenient automatic monthly purchase program, she herself would be hundreds of miles away.

Cavorting in the Hamptons. Living the life. All that.

A thought occurred to her. "Are you going to also sell some of your jewelry at the party tomorrow night?" That was merchandise actually *worth* purchasing.

Jolene looked appalled. "Oh, no. Mrs. Lee is strongly opposed to dual-purpose sales parties. She says they distract people from the core issue."

Right, thought Julia, the "core issue" being that Mrs. Lee didn't want anyone's attention distracted from *her*. "You should at least wear some of your jewelry," she suggested. "That way people might ask about it, and it could lead to some sales."

"You know, that's not a bad idea," said Jolene.

Julia's cell phone buzzed; Kat was double-parked outside.

"I'd better go," she told her sister. "Good luck tomorrow night."

"Have an amazing time!" said Jolene. "I'll take good care of Olive. And your place."

"I know you will," said Julia. What she *really* knew, of course, was that she'd be returning to an apartment in shambles after three days of Jolene's "housekeeping"—and hopefully not to a products liability lawsuit arising from the sale of SunStar Traditional Natural Eastern Remedies out of her home. "Maybe just throw a blanket or something over the artwork, in case anyone spills anything."

"Sure thing," said Jolene.

It would be fine, Julia told herself. Most importantly, Olive would have a friend.

•

Julia and Kat had been driving for a few hours when Kat said, "We're almost there. Look for the Cliffside Villa sign."

"Okay," said Julia. Then she said, "Oh!"

In marked contrast to Boston's dreary April, this first weekend in May had brought spectacular spring weather to the Hamptons; maybe Camilla Durango really *did* hold sway with the gods. They'd turned onto a gently curving lane, lined with wildflowers and sculpted hedges, a seamless synthesis of wilderness and refinement. Pine trees towered overhead, glimmers of sunlight peeking through their needles, while puffy clouds of every conceivable shade of silver, white, and gray floated above. The backdrop was a breathtaking shade of blue.

"Holy crap," said Kat. "We have *arrived*."

They pulled into a semi-circular driveway in front of the manor itself, where there materialized an extraordinarily handsome valet. "Ladies, welcome," he said. "You are?"

"Kathleen Sullivan," said Kat. "And Julia Jones."

He glanced at his tablet. "Thank you. I'm Miguel. You'll be in the two cottages on the west side of the grounds. Ms. Jones, you will be in cottage number nine, and Ms. Sullivan, you will be in the neighboring cottage, number ten. Mr. David Meadow will be joining you, correct?"

Kat grinned. "Very correct."

"There's an informal reception happening right now in the main house," Miguel told them. "You're welcome to enjoy a glass of champagne and meet some of the other guests. I'll take your car and bags back to the cottages, about a mile and a half from here. Just let any of the staff know when you're ready to leave, and they'll arrange for a driver to escort you to your residences."

Needing no further encouragement, Kat handed over her car keys. "Gracias, Miguel!"

They stepped out of the car, and Miguel got in. Uncertain whether they should tip him, Julia looked to Kat, but she was preoccupied with her phone. Julia went to reach for her wallet, but Miguel held up a hand in polite refusal.

"That's very kind," he told her, "but we don't accept gratuities at Cliffside Villa. A guest is a guest, is what Mr. and Mrs. Durango say."

He gave them a friendly wave as he pulled away in Kat's car.

Kat finally looked up from her phone. "David's inside," she told Julia.

They walked up the short set of steps to the main house. The slight breeze carried a whiff of ocean, and the grand marble entryway glowed pink in the late-afternoon light.

They both stopped short and looked at each other, awestruck.

"We are *so* out of our league," said Julia.

"Speak for yourself," said Kat. "I'd say I finally *found* my league."

They entered the main hall, the focal point of which was a gushing champagne fountain.

A server instantaneously appeared. "Champagne or coffee, ladies?"

Kat pretended to think. "The former, please." She accepted a flute of champagne from the waitress and turned to Julia, "You know, I could get used to this. In fact, I already *am* getting used to this."

"And you, ma'am?" the server asked Julia.

Julia opted for the "former"–to Kat's obvious disapproval.

Even so, when the waitress poured the steaming coffee from a silver urn into a handcrafted ceramic mug, Kat's eyebrows went up. "I have to admit, that smells *really* good."

Julia took a sip. Earthy and aromatic, with notes of cinnamon and rum and a hint of cocoa. She closed her eyes for a moment, letting the flavors linger on her tongue.

The waitress smiled knowingly. "It's the best, right?"

Julia opened her eyes. "Incredible."

"It's Danny Durango's special blend, made personally for him," said the server. "He actually has a patent on it."

"A patent on coffee?" said Kat. "That's impossible."

The waitress laughed. "You obviously haven't met the Durangos. Not much is impossible for them."

She left them to attend to the other guests.

A moment later, Kat's eyes lit up.

Julia was learning to read the signs; her friend had clearly spotted David.

Sure enough, in the next instant, there he was, beside them.

"My girls!" he said, giving both of them kisses on the cheek. "So glad you could make it. And Jules, you'll be especially thrilled to hear that Camilla organized a sunrise yoga class for tomorrow morning."

"She's into yoga?" said Julia, surprised. Yoga didn't exactly jive with the former porn-star/professional-partier image she had of Camilla Durango.

David hooted. "Oh, dear God, no! Camilla would kill me if she thought I was spreading wholesome rumors about her. But last year, her personal assistant, Maeve, got clean and sober and discovered yoga, and fell in love. Yoga empowered her to come fully into her body and her true self–or something like that. Anyway, she'll be leading a class in the garden tomorrow morning at six."

"Ooh, a sunrise class in the garden!" said Kat. "Should we go?"

David tittered. "Oh, darling, you say the funniest things."

"I wasn't being funny," said Kat. "We did it on the beach in Hawaii, remember?"

David looked confused. "No, we didn't–oh, you mean *yoga*. Yes, that's true, we did."

Julia preferred not to think about her friends' non-yoga Hawaii activities.

"Well, as big a fan as I am of yoga," she said, "sunrise is a little ambitious for me. Besides, I didn't bring my yoga mat."

At that moment, a familiar voice, warm with laughter, came from behind her. "You and your excuses. Some yogi you are."

Julia turned to look–and there of all people, was Sean Harris.

She smiled incredulously–although perhaps she shouldn't have been so surprised. Boston was a small city, and given that Danny "Triple-D" Durango was an athlete-cum-sports-magnate, she supposed it wasn't *that* huge a coincidence that Sean was here. Recalling their last awkward meeting, she couldn't help but note that every single one of her encounters with Sean over these past months had happened completely by chance. He certainly wasn't making any intentional plans to see her.

She still hadn't responded to his greeting, she realized. "You're always sneaking up on me. What are you doing here? Job perk?"

"Perk and work," said Sean. "My editor's friendly with the general manager of the Celtics, and he knows the Durangos. That's how I got on the guest list." He added, voice lowered, "But the *real* reason I'm here is that my boss wants me to try to get an interview with Marcus LaBree. He's supposed to be making an appearance this weekend, and we're aiming to get his take on the domestic violence issue."

Although Julia didn't follow professional sports, even she had heard about the NFL's recent suspension of a New England Patriots player who'd been caught assaulting his girlfriend during a post-game party. A teammate, Marcus LaBree, had intervened, and the incident–which a party guest had recorded on his cell phone–had prompted a flood of media analysis of the speculated link between domestic violence and professional sports, especially football.

Kat and David were eyeing Sean with curiosity. Before Julia could make the appropriate introductions, David extended a hand in Sean's direction. "I'm David Meadow. You write about sports, I take it?"

"Good to meet you, David," said Sean. "Sean Harris." He and David pumped hands in an inordinately masculine fashion. "And, yes, I'm with *The Globe.*"

David gave an offhand nod. "Well, if LaBree doesn't show up, Tom Brady may make an appearance at some point. I've met him a few times. I can probably get you an introduction, if that would help. Maybe you can end up with *two* killer interviews."

"Wow, thanks," said Sean. "I will most definitely take you up on that."

"No problem," said David. "Not a big deal."

Julia and Kat exchanged amused looks. No one loved name-dropping more than David. But most of his name-drops were legitimate; he probably *did* know Tom Brady.

Smiling effusively, Kat gave a little wave to catch Sean's attention. "Hi, Sean! I'm Kat. I've heard all about you. I'm a big fan."

Julia grimaced. Leave it to Kat to make her feel even *more* awkward around Sean. And her "friend" had only begun.

"I went on Julia's honeymoon with her," Kat was enthusiastically telling Sean. "In fact, David and I both did."

"I did indeed," said David. "Just for a few days, in Maui–*on* Maui, I should say. But we had a grand old time, didn't we, girls?"

"Sounds like I'm the only one who didn't get to go on this honeymoon of yours," said Sean, looking at Julia. "Should I be offended?"

Julia did her best to smile, even though she'd come to the Hamptons with the aim of *forgetting* about her failed wedding and "honeymoon," rather than discussing them at length –especially with Sean. "Sorry. Next time."

"Oh, it was fabulous, simply *fabulous*," said David. "Summiting volcanoes, snorkeling in crystal-blue seas, lazing on black-sand beaches. And the best part of all–Julia Jones is still single! Now if *that* doesn't call for a toast, I don't know what does."

He smoothly lifted several flutes of champagne from a nearby waitress's tray, and before Julia knew it, her mug of patented coffee had replaced by a glass of champagne–and David was calling for a toast to her still-single status.

As the others clinked glasses, Julia wanted to crawl into a hole.

With friends like these...

She glanced at Sean, who also looked slightly uncomfortable.

If only they'd reconnected under different circumstances, she thought ruefully. If only he didn't think she was a pathetic, pitiful loser.

Thankfully, Kat had moved on to a less excruciating subject. "David, this house is gorgeous, breathtakingly gorgeous! You and Gareth must be so proud. Where *is* your better design half, by the way?"

"You're too kind, my dear, too kind," said a beaming David. "And Gareth's around. He's probably upstairs. He wanted to take some shots of the parlor."

Julia explained to Sean, "David did the interior design for the Durangos' house. And Gareth Knight was the architect."

"You'll get to hear all about that tonight," David told them. "After dinner, there's going to be a multimedia presentation showing the phases of the construction. Camilla and Danny asked Gareth and me to say a few words after the show."

"Oh, honey!" simpered Kat. "I'm so proud of you. How about another toast, to you, for creating all this beauty?"

"I was just a channel," said David, smiling modestly. "It's what I do."

"A toast, then, to channeling," said Kat, motioning to a server for more drinks.

Sean alone demurred, explaining that he had to get back to his boss's place in Southampton for a conference call. "Remember, I'm not one of you high-rollers. This is a working weekend for me."

He bid them goodbye and left the hall.

Julia couldn't help but think that every time she saw Sean, she ended by watching him walk away.

Kat had been watching, too. "He's got such a great butt," she whispered to Julia.

David sighed forbearingly. "Ladies, you're embarrassing yourselves. Besides, I'm so much hotter than that guy."

Kat patted *his* butt. "Yes, dear. You most certainly are."

Chapter 36

Later, back at the rustic whitewashed bungalow that was all hers for the weekend, Julia sat with a sketchpad on the cushioned wooden bench on the front porch. Pines loomed in the glimmering twilight, and a nearby brook was babbling. She doodled playfully, almost expecting to see fairies dancing across the horizon. She could happily have remained there all night.

Of course, David and Kat would never have stood for that.

She closed her sketchbook and stood up from the bench, taking one more moment to absorb the magical scene. It was time to dress for dinner.

Kat had insisted on a special Newbury Street shopping expedition in honor of their weekend at Cliffside Villa. Although it had seemed an extravagance at the time, Julia was now glad that Kat had urged her to splurge on something out of the ordinary for her first formal event since her "wedding." Her floaty chiffon dress was ethereal and romantic, perfect for spring. Donning it, she felt transformed.

A driver chauffeured Julia to the main house, where she rendezvoused with Kat and David. Kat's green sequined dress—another of their shopping trip acquisitions—matched the sparkle in her eyes. David, if possible, looked even *more* breezily stylish than usual. Tonight was but a prelude, David explained; the crowning event of the weekend would be the gala tomorrow night.

Even so, the grand dining room—the center of tonight's festivities—was packed with people. David led them to an eight-person table, where they joined three couples: an Oscar-winning actress and her much younger, intimidatingly well-muscled Brazilian boyfriend; a popular New York comedian and his even more famous podcast-host wife; and a Los Angeles couple who summered with the Durangos in the Hamptons. Seated next to Julia was the only other person *not* coupled-up: Russell, a retired Brown University professor who served on the Board of the East Hampton Historical Commission, which had been heavily consulted throughout the Cliffside Villa restoration.

With great animation, Russell explained that he was currently working on a book about the food eaten by the Confederate soldiers during the Civil War. Julia tried not to make too much of the fact that her apparent dinner partner was an eighty-something-year-old man—or that Sean Harris was nowhere in sight.

Thankfully, neither was Asher.

Fortunately, the packed dinner agenda left her little opportunity to ruminate. They were regaled with one exquisite, elaborately prepared course after another, with enough variety to satisfy any palate or preference. The foodstuffs were complemented by an endless flow of fine wine, all of which made it impossible to focus on anything but the immediate sensory pleasures before them.

And to think—as David kept reminding them—that the weekend had only just begun.

At shortly before nine o'clock, David nudged Julia and Kat.

"This is it!" he told them. "My moment of glory—well, mine and Gareth's. But mostly mine."

On cue, dozens of large media screens descended from the ceiling. The crowd quieted as Bud Rowan, a television actor and East Hampton neighbor of the Durangos, took to the podium to introduce the forty-eight-minute-long film documenting, in all its aristocratic majesty, the history of Cliffside Villa from its seventeenth-century origins to its modern-day restoration. Julia—and everyone else, from the looks of it—was riveted by the detail-rich, aesthetically compelling film, which would air on the History Channel next summer.

She thought of Jolene back in Boston. This sure beat watching a SunStar infomercial.

As the credits rolled and the final notes of the soundtrack faded away, Julia and Kat exchanged dumbstruck glances. While David was far from closed-lipped about his professional accomplishments, they'd had no concept of the historical significance of Cliffside Villa, the intensive nature of the restorations, or the legendary craftsmen with whom he and Gareth had collaborated on the multi-million-dollar project that had spanned more than three years. In hindsight, realized Julia, it was remarkable that the two of them had also, in that same time frame, managed to complete Asher's Louisburg Square house—though Asher's project must have seemed like small potatoes compared to Cliffside Villa.

The movie screens magically ascended back into their invisible locations in the ceiling.

David grinned at Julia and Kat. "Hang on to your hats. Here come our host and hostess."

Arm in arm, Camilla and Danny Durango seemed to glide together toward the podium. Danny, with olive skin and black hair streaming past his shoulders, was short and athletic-looking, his broad chest seemingly triple the width of his narrow hips. Camilla was practically his photographic negative: tall, fair, fine-featured, and preposterously thin, apart from her Barbie-sized bosom. She towered over her husband by a good six inches, seeming to Julia like a real-life comic book character—a fatally alluring villainess.

"She's really something," Julia whispered to David.

"*Something* is right," he replied. "But not much there that's real."

Danny began speaking. "Welcome, everyone. Welcome to our new home!"

The thunderous applause that broke out persisted for a full thirty seconds.

When the din had finally faded, Danny grinned. "My feelings exactly. Let me tell you, Cam and I were beyond excited to move into the newly renovated Cliffside Villa six months ago. Forget about cloud nine—we were on, maybe, cloud *ninety*-nine." He waited for the chuckles to die down before continuing. "Realistically, though, I figured that the excitement would start to fade pretty fast. You know how it is—you're all pumped up about your new Maserati, and six weeks later, it might as well be a Chevy Nova. Or a Dodge Durango, if you will."

There came more laughter from the guests, many of whom probably *did* know what it was like to own a new Maserati, thought Julia. She, on the other hand, hadn't owned a car in over a decade; she had no need of one in Boston.

"Those of you who know me know I'm not exactly an intellectual," said Danny, prompting still more laughter. "But I learned there's actually a psych term for it: hedonic adaptation. You get a jolt of pleasure from something at first, but then it dwindles over time." He grinned. "Those of you who know me *also* know that I'm a *big* fan of those pleasure jolts. They don't call me Daredevil Danny for nothing."

"Triple-D!" someone bellowed.

"Hell, yeah!" said Danny, pumping a fist in the air. "So even though Cam and I were over the moon when we moved into Cliffside Villa, part of me kept waiting for that hedonic adaptation to set in and the thrill to start fading. But the wild thing is, just the *opposite* has happened. Not a day passes that we don't notice one more ingenious design feature, one more brilliant little detail. And every day, we love it here more and more." He gazed out over the crowded room, looking, thought Julia, like a truly happy man. "And for that, Gareth and David, we have you to thank."

David, looking immensely gratified and–if possible–humbled, smiled and raised his wine glass to their host. Gareth, from another table, did the same.

Camilla Durango stepped up to the podium. "It's true! We love it here more and more every day. And we hope that you all love it here, too. This weekend, our home is your home." She paused. "Now, please help me welcome our men of the hour: genius architect Gareth Knight, and interior designer extraordinaire, David Meadow!"

David and Gareth joined the Durangos at the podium. The applause was now deafening.

Gareth took the microphone first. With great flair, he related various construction mishaps, zoning board fiascos, and myriad minor tragedies that had occurred over the course of the Cliffside Villa renovation, painting a vivid, hilarious picture of East Hampton local politics and the inner workings of the architectural process. He looked great, too, thought Julia. Gareth wasn't especially tall, but he was strong and fit-looking, the epitome of casual elegance in his pistachio green sports coat, hunter green trousers, and whimsical bow-tie. David often quipped that quirky bow-ties were *de rigeur* in the world of high-end residential classical architecture, and Gareth's–mossy green with white polka dots–more than fit the bill.

The architect concluded to enthusiastic applause, and then it was David's turn to speak. He smiled at the room full of guests.

"I'm going to keep this brief. You've got *much* better things to do here at Cliffside Villa than indulge the ramblings of a classical-fixture-obsessed interior designer–impossibly charming and handsome as he might be."

Kat looked sideways at Julia. "You've got to admit, he really is."

Julia rolled her eyes affectionately. "Okay, I admit."

The impossibly handsome interior designer continued, "More than anything else, I'd just like to thank Camilla and Danny for allowing me to be part of this once-in-a-lifetime project. Quite honestly, this was one project I never wanted to finish. Really, all I have to say is that I'm going to hate not having an excuse to come up here every weekend!"

At that, Camilla stepped toward him, clasped both his hands, and peered intently into his eyes. "Darling," she purred, "you don't need *any* excuse to come up here. You're welcome *any* time. Any time at all."

Kat's eyes had narrowed, noted Julia.

"Don't worry," she whispered. "Camilla's got nothing on you."

Kat nodded thoughtfully. "Yeah. You're right."

•　•　•

After dinner, the party moved to the spacious moonlit terrace at the back of the house. While Kat and David went in search of more champagne–a remarkably achievable mission at Cliffside Villa–Julia enjoyed a moment to herself, savoring the sumptuous evening. She gazed out at the Renaissance-style garden bounded by olive trees–and thought of that night in Florence, barely a year ago, when Asher had proposed.

It had been the best night of her life, or so she'd felt at the time. But since then, nothing–*nothing*–had gone according to plan.

A few minutes later, when David and Kat still hadn't returned, she decided to go say hello to Gareth, whom she'd spotted on the other side of the terrace, also alone. Granted, he'd been more Asher's friend than hers, but she was going to have to learn to stop seeing the world as two mutually exclusive universes. She'd really enjoyed his speech–and, besides, she had no one else to talk to.

Absorbed, as she had been, in the view of the moonlit garden, Gareth didn't notice her approach.

She tapped him lightly on the shoulder to get his attention. "Hi, Gareth."

The architect turned with a start. "Julia! David told me you would be here this weekend. Are you enjoying yourself?"

"Very much so," she told him. "Your talk was fantastic, by the way. You had us all rolling in the aisles. And needless to say, the house is incredible. You must be so proud."

He looked pleased. "Thank you so much. Yes, David and I and the rest of the team were very happy with how Cliffside Villa turned out. What matters most is that I think the Durangos are happy."

A sultry voice oozed from behind them. "Not just happy–*ecstatic*."

They both spun around to see Camilla Durango.

Up close, their hostess was even *more* striking. Her fair skin was like porcelain, and her flaxen hair cascaded down her back, shimmering in the moonlight, seemingly begging to be touched. The neckline of her form-fitting black dress plunged nearly to her waist, showcasing her spectacular bosom. Most striking of all, though, was her height. At five-foot-nine, Julia was generally accustomed to being the tallest woman in any room. However, Camilla, in her strappy, mile-high-heeled sandals, dwarfed both her and Gareth, while still managing to convey an impression of quintessential delicateness and femininity, her height more than counterbalanced by her utter...*narrowness*.

If she turned sideways, thought Julia, she'd disappear.

Gareth hugged their hostess warmly. His arms could have encircled her twice.

"Camilla, darling, meet Julia Jones," said Gareth. "Julia, Camilla." And then, before either of them had a chance to say anything, he said, "I'm afraid I must step away. Enjoy the weekend, Julia. Camilla, I'll catch up with you later."

He gave them polite air-kisses and was gone.

His departure seemed oddly abrupt to Julia.

Camilla caught her look. "I'm sure he's being pulled in a million different directions."

So it *hadn't* been her imagination, thought Julia.

"Your house is absolutely beautiful," she told Camilla. "And the guest cottages, too. Thank you so much for having me. I really appreciate your hospitality."

Camilla laid a hand on her arm. Her nails were scarily long, like talons. "I'm glad you could make it. Great dress, by the way. You look like a fairy princess."

Next to Camilla's drop-dead-sexy gown, Julia's chiffon dress, which had seemed so charmingly fanciful when she'd bought it, suddenly seemed childishly garish. "Thanks—just the look I was going for," she said. "Yours is great, too." She impulsively added, "By the way, you have the most beautiful hair."

"You're sweet," said Camilla. She tossed her head, sending her glossy locks flying and giving Julia a whiff of musky perfume. "You get what you pay for, right? And Felipe charges me out the ass. But since I'm his only client, I guess he kind of has to."

"You have an exclusive contract with your hairdresser?" said Julia. "You're joking."

"Oh, it's true," said Camilla. "I would never joke about hair."

"What about the coffee?" said Julia. "Is it true you have a patent on the blend?"

Camilla flashed her a private smile. "Honey, *everything* you hear about me is true." A vaguely predatory gleam came into her wideset eyes. "Not to be forward, but are you single? What's your cup of tea?"

"What do you mean?" said Julia, suddenly feeling cornered.

"Are you into women at all? I mean, I'm guessing you're not gay, but are you open to exploring?"

Julia's eyes widened, and she took a slight step back—which Camilla matched with a step forward. "No," she said. "Not really."

Camilla's predatory gleam intensified. "No? Or not really?"

"*No*," said Julia, more firmly this time. "I'm pretty non-lesbian. I mean, *totally* non-lesbian."

Camilla laughed and touched her arm. "I'm sorry, honey, I didn't mean to make you feel uncomfortable. It's just that Danny and I like to mix things up sometimes. And he loves your type." Her eyelashes fluttered, and she leaned in close. "And even more importantly, *I* love your type."

The time for subtlety was long past, Julia realized. She took a *big* step back.

"No, thank you," she said. "I appreciate the offer, but I'm not into that kind of thing. Sorry."

Camilla shrugged. "Understood," she said easily. "No problem."

Her hostess's casual air made Julia feel as if *she* were the one being unreasonable. Feeling compelled to explain, she blurted, "This is a weird time for me. I was engaged. And then I was dumped before the wedding—*right* before, as in two minutes. I went on my honeymoon with my best friend—and David Meadow. And this all happened pretty recently. I'm still trying to get used to the idea of not being with him."

A look of comprehension dawned on Camilla's face. "Oh, you're *that* Julia! Asher Bartlett's ex."

Julia laughed darkly. "Asher's ex—exactly."

Uh oh, she noticed; Camilla's gleam was back.

"Well, in that case," said Camilla, "this might be the perfect time for you to try something new—you know, take your mind off ..."

"Again, thank you, but no thank you," said Julia. "Listen, it's been lovely chatting with you, but I should really go find my friends."

Even as she made her escape, she could hear Camilla's sultry voice trailing behind her. "Open invitation."

Over an hour later, Julia still had seen neither hide nor hair of Kat and David. But it was a convivial crowd–and growing more convivial by the minute. Julia mingled with, among others, a congresswoman, a news anchor, and a Zen monk who'd published a best-selling self-help book. And several people had even expressed interest in her art, making her glad she'd thought to bring some of her artist business cards.

At one point, she caught sight of Sean. She tried to catch his eye, but he was engaged in intense conversation with a concrete block of a man, an African American male nearly as wide as he was tall. It must be Marcus LaBree, Julia realized. It seemed Sean had succeeding in scoring his big-time NFL interview.

Kat appeared beside her, holding two glasses of champagne. She handed one to Julia. "Some party, eh?"

Thirsty from all the chit-chat, Julia took a large gulp of her drink. "I'll say! Where have you been? I didn't know you guys were going to dump me for the night!"

Kat grinned guiltily. "Sorry. David was giving me a private tour of Cliffside Villa–*very* private, if you get my drift. What have you been up to? Have you been having fun?"

"Oh, yeah," said Julia. She told Kat about being propositioned by Camilla Durango. "Gareth left me with her all by myself–like prey! She told me she and Danny like to 'mix things up.'"

"I can vouch for that," said David, walking up behind them.

Kat looked at him suspiciously. "Oh, really? What does *that* mean?"

David shrugged, looking nonchalant. "So I might have participated in an orgy or two, way, *way* back in the day. So sue me. Who are you to judge anyone, anyway, missy?" He pointed. "Hey, isn't that Beyoncé over there?"

Kat's gaze didn't waver from David. "Don't try to change the subject."

Julia, though, couldn't resist a quick look. "I think that might really *be* Beyoncé," she told Kat.

David gave the supposed Beyoncé a little wave. "She's great. We go way back."

"Of course you do," said Kat. "Just like with the Durangos. Back in the *day*."

David chuckled dismissively. "We were just kids having some good clean fun. Well, maybe not *clean*, exactly, but healthy. Wholesome. Natural. Heavy petting, essentially. Not to imply that pets were involved. I draw the line at bestiality."

Now, Kat was laughing.

"That is to say, I draw the line well *before* bestiality," said David. "Although, there was one time things *did* get borderline inappropriate between me and –"

Kat put a finger to his lips. "Honey, *stop*. A little confession is good for the soul, but quit while you're ahead."

By now, it was well past midnight. As her friends' conversation continued to drunkenly devolve, Julia scanned the patio, wondering if Sean had finished his interview. To her disappointment, she didn't see him anywhere. He'd probably met a gorgeous single woman–one of Camilla's porn-star friends. Or maybe he and Beyoncé had gone off together somewhere.

Meanwhile, Kat and David had moved on to a new–presumably hypothetical–topic of discussion: whether David ever would, under any circumstances, participate in a threesome or even a *double*-threesome.

Time to call it a night, thought Julia.

"I'm going to turn in," she told her friends. "But let me know what you decide about the double-threesome. I'm happy to put in a good word for you with Camilla–or Jolene, if necessary."

Her friends' laughter echoed on the stone patio behind her as she made her way out, alone.

Chapter 37

Back at the cottage, sleep eluded Julia. Her thoughts kept returning to Sean. Could it be that he'd somehow known that she'd be here in the Hamptons this weekend—that that had been at least *part* of the reason he'd come all this way on the off-chance of garnering an interview with a famous football player?

She immediately chided herself for her baseless fantasizing. There was no conceivable way Sean could have known she'd be here. He was here because he was a *reporter* chasing a *story*—she'd even seen him talking with Marcus LaBree! Clearly, getting the interview had been more than a token excuse for making the trip. Besides, if he'd been interested in her, he would have sought her out during the party that evening.

She finally dozed off at around two a.m., only to be awakened a few hours later by the squawking of an especially boisterous crow.

She checked the clock: five-fifteen a.m.

She groaned. If only David hadn't mentioned the sunrise yoga class, then she could have lazed around and puttered away the morning to her heart's content. But despite her late night last night, she felt restless and jittery, and she knew she wouldn't be able to fall back asleep. Maybe the yoga would help calm her nerves.

She inhaled sharply, recognizing the insidious thinking pattern that invariably led her back into the vicious yoga cycle.

I really need help, she thought.

The sun was just starting to peek up over the horizon as Julia walked the mile or so to the main house, where the yoga class would be. There, a tall, toned, mocha-skinned woman with curly blond hair tenuously constrained by a pink headband was directing people toward the paved garden terrace–at the center of which was a multi-colored pyramid composed of dozens of brand-new yoga mats, each rolled up in its own carrying case.

"Please, grab a mat," said the woman. Her voice was husky and deep, causing Julia to suspect that Camilla's assistant, Maeve, had used to be a man. Maybe that was what David had meant about yoga empowering her to come into her true self.

"They're complimentary," said Maeve. "Yours to keep. So you can keep doing yoga at home."

"Fabulous," said Julia, choosing a dark green mat from the pile. "Just what I need, another yoga mat." Having two mats had better not mean she'd be expected to do twice as much yoga.

She unrolled her new mat and settled herself on the terrace, thinking how incredibly unfair it all was. She'd assumed–quite reasonably, she still felt–that her temporary escape from the trials and tribulations of ordinary life in Boston would also include an escape from the trials and tribulations of *yoga*.

But no, yoga had followed her all the way to the Hamptons. *It* was stalking her, not Sean Harris.

"Come here often?" said a male voice behind her.

She turned to see Sean Harris.

Of *course*, thought Julia. Of *course* he hadn't seen her last night, in her floaty, feminine dress. Instead, their paths were crossing *now*, when she was rumpled, slightly hung over, and operating on three hours' sleep.

"I can't believe you came for sunrise yoga," she said.

He shrugged. "Believe it or not, yoga's the latest thing with a lot of NFL players. They think it might help extend their careers. So when my boss heard that Camilla Durango had organized a sunrise yoga class, he made me promise to come. He has this theory that once the NFL guys are all loosened up from yoga they'll be more open to talking."

That had certainly been true of *her*, thought Julia. "Your boss sounds like a real bulldog."

"You don't know the half of it," said Sean. "Honestly, I can't imagine any of the pros'll show, but I guess you never know."

Julia smiled. "By the way, I noticed you got your interview with Marcus LaBree last night. Congrats, that's fantastic."

Sean shook his head regretfully. "No, I didn't. I did catch him at one point and he said he'd give me half an hour, but then he disappeared. I never managed to track him down after that."

Julia looked at him, confused. "But I thought I saw you talking with him. African American, not too tall? Built like a brick wall?"

Sean burst out laughing–loudly.

Julia had no idea what was so funny.

"That wasn't Marcus LaBree," said Sean. "That was my boss, Jimmy Taylor."

"But he looked like a football player," said Julia. "I could have *sworn* he was a football player."

"He used to be–fifteen years ago. No, Marcus LaBree is a six-foot-eight white guy." Sean shook his head, still grinning. "Julia, you may be the only person in New England –and possibly the planet–not to know who Marcus LaBree is."

"I told you I don't follow professional sports," she said. Was it racist for her to have assumed a black man to be a professional athlete? But Jimmy Taylor really *did* look like a football player–and, in fact, he *had* been, meaning that she hadn't been totally off base. "And I don't watch a lot of T.V."

"That's like saying you don't know who Oprah is because you don't watch many talk shows. Or who Donald Trump is because you're not into politics. Or–"

"Okay, okay, I get it," said Julia. "I live under a rock."

Sean laughed. "I didn't mean it that way. I actually think it's kind of cool to be oblivious about superstar professional athletes. Trust me, they're overrated."

She was saved from having to respond by the approach of another familiar figure—Gareth, toting his own yoga mat and looking quite sporty in loose-fitting black yoga pants and a V-neck white T-shirt.

"Julia!" he greeted her. "I didn't expect to see you here."

"Oh, I jump at any chance for yoga," she said. "Especially before daybreak."

"Me, too!" said Gareth, seemingly sincerely. "I need my yoga fix. Five times a week, minimum."

"You're much more dedicated than I am," said Julia. "Even just once a week is agony for me."

"Not to worry," he said. "I'm sure this class will be tailored to beginners."

Julia nodded, mildly offended at the implication. Just because she *hated* yoga didn't mean she was *bad* at it. Of course she *was*, but that was beside the point.

"So will you be here the rest of the weekend?" Gareth inquired. "Don't feel bad if you can't stay for the whole time. A lot of people are leaving early."

"No, I'll be here the whole weekend," said Julia. "Unless you're trying to get rid of me, Gareth."

"No, no, of course not," he said.

She'd been joking, but the chagrined look on Gareth's handsome face made Julia wonder if her joke had been exactly on target. It struck her that maybe he knew something she didn't. What if, contrary to David's assurances, Asher was planning to come this weekend after all?

An awkward pause ensued, broken only when Sean, who'd been observing the entire interaction, extended a hand to Gareth. "Good morning—good crack of dawn, that is. I'm Sean Harris."

Gareth pumped his hand. "Great to meet you, Sean. I'm Gareth Knight."

"Yes, I know," said Sean. "The presentation last night was amazing. And your stories were hilarious. I can only imagine what it must have been like working with Camilla Durango—and Triple-D." He grinned. "In fact, I bet you've got a whole lot *more* stories than the ones you told last night."

Gareth laughed. "I've got a few. But the Durangos were fabulous to work with. Very open to new ideas, good listeners. Just great."

Thankfully, the stilted conversation came to a halt as Maeve called for the class to begin. By now, there were over fifty people gathered on the terrace—an impressive turnout, considering the extent of last night's partying. That said, one of the attendees had already passed out on his yoga mat, snoring, a tiny puddle of drool accumulating by his mouth.

Depending on the intensity of the class, thought Julia, that could well be her in ninety minutes' time.

"Any NFL players here?" she whispered to Sean as they dropped to their mats in a restful child's pose.

He chuckled. "Of course not. I knew I was on a fool's errand."

Maeve proceeded to lead them through a series of postures and movements that, from what Julia could tell, incorporated several different styles of yoga, but fortunately no recognizable Ashtanga. Out of the corner of her eye, she noted how fluid and natural Gareth's movements were—especially in comparison to her own. Even so, the setting was so delightful, the early-morning sun so cheerful, and the garden vegetation so brilliantly green that the yoga class wasn't nearly as torturous as she'd feared. Maeve had shown them mercy.

The final notes of the Tibetan singing bowl faded away, signaling the end of the class.

From her prone position, Julia glanced over at Gareth, who was no longer lying on his mat. Now that class was over, he was doing his own free-form yoga moves: standing splits, headstands, handstands, even a back-handspring.

She sighed hopelessly. Gareth was the real yoga deal. She was just a yoga poser—who, ironically enough, happened to be terrible at poses.

She sat up on her mat and looked at Sean.

He was smiling. In this early morning light, his eyes matched the color of the sky—clear, blue, and very bright. "That was nice, right?"

"You know, it actually was," said Julia. "This teacher made me feel like I might not be *completely* hopeless at yoga. That is, until I caught a glimpse of Gareth! He's a pro. I'll never compare to him."

"Compare to me how?" said Gareth, who, Julia saw, was now standing right behind them. He'd probably back-flipped his way over.

"I was referring to your yoga prowess," she replied. "And how inadequate I feel when I compare myself to you."

Gareth frowned. "You have *nothing* to feel inadequate about, Julia. Not compared to me, not compared to anyone."

"Thanks," said Julia, somewhat taken aback by his vehemence.

Again, Sean broke the tension. He flashed his boyish grin. "I, on the other hand, have *plenty* to feel inadequate about. At least when it comes to yoga."

Gareth looked at him, surprised–and then laughed. "Right. Well, chin up, man! Yoga isn't everything."

He gave them a little wave and strolled off.

Julia was impressed that Sean had managed to evoke laughter from Gareth, who never seemed to loosen up around her. She rolled up her new yoga mat and slid it into its carrying case. "Did you pick up on any awkwardness with Gareth? I got a weird vibe."

Sean shrugged. "Oh, he's just a little uptight. He probably just needs to get laid."

It was a remark David might have made. *Men*, thought Julia. "Thank you for that insight."

Sean looking endearingly sheepish. "Sorry. Been hanging around too many pro athletes, I guess. That's their answer to everything."

"I'm not surprised," Julia said with a laugh.

"What are you up to now?" said Sean.

"I might grab a nap. But this afternoon, David and Kat and I are going into town for lunch. You're welcome to come," she offered.

Sean shook his head. "Thanks, but Jimmy–my boss–and I have a bunch of meetings lined up today."

"You'll be at the party tonight, though, right?" said Julia, trying not to think about the fact that, yet again, he'd turned her down.

"Yes, I'll be there," he said.

"Okay, then," said Julia. "See you later."

She slung her yoga mat over her shoulder and set off toward the cottage, thinking that, for once, their encounter had ended with him watching *her* walk away.

At least she hoped he was.

Chapter 38

Later that morning, Kat joined Julia for coffee on the cottage porch. Now, in the streaming morning sunlight, they could see the babbling brook, which was clustered with wildflowers and berry bushes, butterflies flitting amongst the blossoms. Like a scene out of a storybook, a bluebird cocked his head at them, looking as if he were about to speak.

"The only thing that's missing is the fairies," said Julia. "And David. Where is he?"

"The classical-fixture-obsessed designer is out fixture-shopping with Camilla and Danny," Kat told her. "Apparently they wanted some suggestions for their Manhattan apartment. David's going straight from one Durango project to another."

Julia's eyebrows went up. "Fixture shopping? Sounds sexy. Especially given their history."

Kat rolled her eyes. "Please, don't remind me." She grinned. "But on a happier note, I was of course *thrilled* to finally meet the famous Sean Harris. That's so crazy he's here! *What* a cutie."

Julia couldn't help but smile. "Yeah, isn't he? You should have seen him doing yoga this morning."

Kat's ears perked up. "He came to yoga this morning? Hoping to run into you, maybe?"

Julia shook her head. "If only. No, he'd heard that some NFL players might be there. He was just trying to get an interview."

Kat looked unconvinced. "And were there any? NFL players?"

"No, not from what I could tell." A thought occurred to Julia. "Hey, do you know who Marcus LaBree is? Would you recognize him if you saw him?"

Kat laughed. "Umm, yeah, I *think* so. Seven feet tall, looks like a Nordic god? I'm pretty sure I could pick him out of a crowd."

"Oh," said Julia, deflated. Apparently she *was* the only person on the planet unfamiliar with Marcus LaBree.

"That'll be wild if Marcus LaBree shows up this weekend," said Kat. "David wasn't kidding–this really is some extravaganza. Honestly, in terms of over-the-top, I'd have to say this weekend kind of puts your wedding to shame."

"You mean my almost-wedding?" said Julia. "But yeah, you're right. In a way, this weekend is a perfect antidote to Switzerland. Almost like a redo. Except, of course, that I'm here alone, with no one to marry. Except maybe myself. "

"Look on the bright side," said Kat. "At least you won't have to deal with Asher's neurotic nonsense the rest of your life. Honestly, I don't know how you put up with it as long as you did."

But Julia's thoughts were still on her last, off-the-cuff remark.

"Now that I think about it," she said, "that might not be such a bad idea."

"Not putting up with Asher's neurotic nonsense?" said Kat.

"No, not that," said Julia. "Marrying myself. Making a commitment to *me*."

Kat considered. "You know, you're right, that's *not* a bad idea. In fact, I'd say it's pretty fabulous!"

Julia grinned. "I'm going to do it. Screw Asher. I'm going to have my own personal wedding. Promise to love, honor, and cherish *me*. Why not?"

"Why not!" said Kat. "We'll make it a big party. We can have it on my roof deck."

"I was thinking something more intimate. With just the bridesmaids. Do you think they'll be into it?"

"They'll love it," said Kat. "But the main point is, *I* love it. That is, the main point is, *you* love it. But I love it, too! When do you want to do it? How about on your birthday, in June?"

Which also happened to be the anniversary of Julia's engagement.

"Perfect," said Julia. "All right, then, it's settled. I'm marrying myself."

"You're a great catch!" said Kat. "It'll be our *next* event of the season. Want to come over on Monday and we can start hammering out the details?" They'd both planned to take off that Monday from work, to recover from the weekend.

"I do," said Julia. "I do, I do!"

At that moment, a cream-colored convertible Bentley, top down, pulled up in front of the cottage: David. "Ladies! Spring has sprung!"

He hopped out over the top of the car door without opening it and trotted over. He squeezed in between the two of them on the bench and wrapped an arm around each of them. "*Such* a great weekend!" he crowed. "And it's only going to keep getting better and better."

•　　•　　•

At least in terms of the sheer extravagance of the festivities, David had been right, Julia reflected later. Tonight's party was outdoors, but not on the patio; the guests had been transported by car from the main house to a location several miles away: a remote clearing the size of several football fields, in the midst of thick, nearly impenetrable pine woods.

"This is the Durangos' 'wilderness' party space," David told Julia and Kat. He chuckled wryly. "Although when you have to knock down a few thousand trees to create something, I'm not sure it still qualifies as 'wilderness.' But it's something, eh?"

Julia blinked.

Kat, too, was taken aback. "So much for nature conservation."

David, for once, seemed genuinely morally perturbed. "Hey, remember I'm just the *interior* designer. This is the *exterior*. You can't blame me for this. Although I did pick out the couches."

"They're nice," said Kat.

It was a display like nothing Julia had ever seen: an abundance of outdoor couches and armchairs, rushing champagne fountains and already-bustling full bars, tables and tables of food, and three stages with three different bands. The only illumination–apart from a moon so full it might have been specially ordered for the occasion–came from bonfires and standing torches. The combination of the thick woods, moonlight, and flickering firelight created an overall impression of being in an enchanted forest in the middle of nowhere; maybe she should have saved her fairy princess dress for tonight. Tonight, though, she was wearing a long, strapless charcoal-gray dress–another of her and Kat's Newbury Street acquisitions–with silver jewelry, including the "wedding" bracelet Jolene had given her.

The other-worldly setting had clearly affected Kat, who was gazing dreamily at David. "Wanna go stare into the firelight, babe?"

"Anything for you, babe," he said. Almost as an afterthought, he added, "Julia, want to come?"

Julia shook her head. "That's okay. I think I'll go check out the food."

Unsurprisingly, the spread at the nearby buffet table was munificent. Julia soon had a plate piled high with food. She turned, looking for a place to sit, and saw that Kat and David weren't far behind; they'd been waylaid en route to the fire by Russ, their tablemate from last night. Julia caught a snatch of their conversation–from the sound of it, Russ was explicating on his Civil War food research.

She smiled–poor David, being roped into an esoteric intellectual conversation at an event like this one. But then Russ caught sight of her, and before she knew it, she, too, was part of the discussion regarding cornmeal, molasses, and salted meats.

As Russ energetically pontificated on the nuances of salt-cured pork belly as compared to uncut slab bacon, Julia's attention drifted. Not too far away, she noticed Sean sitting on one of the couches, his arm resting on its back. Next to him, her slender back only inches from his casually extended arm, was a delicate wisp of a woman with creamy skin and raven-black hair. In her short, sparkly silver dress–more of a slip, really–she looked like a pixie or a sprite. She was breathtaking.

Kat had followed Julia's gaze. "Wow, gorgeous," she said, nudging David. "Don't you think?"

David, who'd studiously been looking elsewhere, glanced in the direction she was motioning. He shrugged. "Sean? He's okay, I guess."

Kat grinned and kissed him on the cheek. "You're growing on me, babe."

"Let's get some grub," said David. "How 'bout it, Russ? I think they might have Civil War-style salt pork."

As the others raided the buffet, Julia waited, taking in the enchanted forest. There, at the very center of the forest clearing, was the most sprawling couch of all: a voluminous white wrap-around sofa. Reclining on it with her swarthy, swashbuckling husband, was Camilla Durango.

Camilla saw her looking. She waved. "Julia! Come meet Danny."

Julia glanced over her shoulder. David, Kat, and Russ were still occupied at the buffet; Russ was interrogating the chef about the molasses used in the baked beans. She set down her plate of food on a nearby table and went to join her host and hostess on the sofa.

Camilla's husband rose slightly at her approach and extended his hand. "I don't think I've had the pleasure. Danny Durango."

"I'm Julia Jones. It's so nice to meet you," said Julia. Danny's strength was tangible from his handshake, but his touch was light, even reserved; he clearly had great powers self-restraint. She caught herself thinking he was probably incredible in bed.

She'd better be careful. At this rate, she'd be agreeing to a threesome in no time.

"Julia's the artist I was telling you about," Camilla was saying to her husband.

Julia couldn't help but wonder what *else* Camilla had told Danny about her.

"Yes, of course," said Danny, eyeing her with new interest. "I used to love making art when I was a kid. Painting, sculpture, all of it. But then I got busy with other things."

"Like sports?" said Julia.

He grinned. "Yeah, among other things. But seriously, I'd love to check out some of your work."

Julia pulled a card from her tiny jeweled evening bag, which was big enough to hold lipstick, a few business cards, and not much else. "Well, in that case, here you go. All the information is on there."

Danny peered at the card. "Julia-jones-art-dot-com. Perfect. Thank you."

"Thank *you* for being interested in my work," she told him. "People sometimes get nervous when they find out I'm an artist. They think I'm either going to try to sell them something, or that I'm going to ask them for a job. They don't seem to understand that I already *have* a job–the last thing I want is another one."

"A job besides your art, you mean?" said Camilla.

Julia explained about the travel agency.

Danny nodded sympathetically. "Yeah, working sucks. Fortunately I'm at the point where my companies pretty much run themselves. Now I basically get to be a playboy."

"Yes," said Camilla, her voice husky, "but you're no *boy*."

The next thing Julia knew, Camilla and Danny were passionately making out on the couch, while she sat there silently, not knowing where to look.

A minute or two later, they seemed to remember her.

"Sorry," said Camilla. "We get a little trashy sometimes. Even after twelve years, I still can't keep my hands off him."

Julia smiled, strangely touched by their affection for each other.

A new band had just taken the stage, their opening chords reverberating in the forest space.

Camilla's face lit up. "I love these guys! Come on, Julia, let's go. Danny hates to dance."

She tugged at Julia's hand, and they ran together like little girls toward the stage. The music and the mystical setting–not to mention the steady stream of alcohol–were intoxicating, and Julia and her hostess danced with childlike abandon in the fairy-tale clearing in the woods.

Things grew still more fairy-tale-like a few hours later, when Julia was taking a break from dancing–and Camilla–by the fire, and Sean approached with a giant by his side.

"Hi," said Julia curiously.

"Julia Jones," Sean said formally, "I'd like you to meet Marcus LaBree."

Kat had been right. With his chiseled jaw, steel-blue eyes, and lion's mane of blond hair, Marcus LaBree looked like a Nordic god. He towered over everyone, his stature more comparable to that of the surrounding trees than of any of the other guests.

"Great to meet you, Marcus," said Julia, as she gazed up, up, *up* into those mesmerizing eyes. His giant's hand made her own seem like a child's.

Sean's expression was mischievous. "I had to prove to Marcus that there was a woman on the planet who didn't know who he was."

Julia smiled at Marcus. "He's just being silly. Of course I know who you are. I'm a *huge* Red Sox fan."

Marcus's laughter boomed throughout the clearing. "Close enough! And hey, I may not play baseball, but I still manage to bat a thousand every time."

Julia giggled, unabashedly enthralled. Sean's plan had backfired, she thought; Marcus LaBree had yet another adoring female fan. "So I take it you gave poor Sean his interview?"

"Yeah, this guy's relentless," said Marcus. "The final straw was when he told me he went to a sunrise yoga class this morning just to try to catch up with me. At that point, I felt too guilty to say no."

"I went to the sunrise yoga class, too," said Julia, feeling shortchanged. In exchange for *his* hour and a half of yoga, Sean had gotten an exclusive interview with a world-famous athlete. What had been *her* reward?

Marcus tipped back his head and laughed his booming laugh. He looked at Sean. "And to think I fell for that guilt trip! Now I get the *real* reason you went to sunrise yoga."

Sean grinned. "So maybe my motives were a little mixed. But hey, I got the interview, right? Mission accomplished."

"No worries, man," said Marcus. "All's fair in love and journalism." He smiled at Julia. "Great meeting you, Julia. I hope to see you again."

He stepped away, leaving Julia and Sean alone by the fire. It crackled pleasantly.

"So that's Marcus LaBree," said Julia, the firelight warm on her face. "Now I know."

"Yes, now you know," said Sean. "What you may *not* know, though, is that there are plenty of women who'd happily sacrifice their firstborn child to get as much time with him as you just did. He's got a pretty fanatical entourage."

Still a little weak in the knees from her encounter with Marcus, Julia could understand why. "In that case, thanks for hooking me up," she said. "Although, honestly, I don't really see what all the fuss is about. He wasn't *that* great."

"Yeah, right," said Sean. "Anyway, don't tell my boss that. He was over the moon that I got that interview. The story's going to run tomorrow. I cranked it out this afternoon and submitted it right before I headed over here."

It really *had* been a working weekend for Sean, noted Julia. "Congratulations! That's quite the coup."

"Well, I don't know about *coup*," said Sean, "but it does mean I probably have a job for another week. The newspaper industry isn't exactly the business to be in these days. But this will certainly help."

As caught up as she'd been in her own work drama, Julia had almost forgotten that she wasn't the only one faced with professional challenges. "Well, I'm glad it worked out." She peered at Sean in the firelight. "Were you really stalking me at yoga this morning?"

He started. "Of course not! I was stalking Marcus." Then he smiled and shrugged. "Okay, maybe I was stalking you both."

Julia looked at him, astonished. "I thought you were avoiding me. You acted so weird when I saw you in the coffee shop that day–like you couldn't stand to be around me for one more second."

Sean colored slightly. "I'm sorry. It's just that that night, when we went to Louisburg Square, you seemed so excited to see Asher again. I thought you were still in love."

Julia sighed. "Yeah, I probably was, a little. But I told you the conversation didn't go well. That it was over."

"Yeah, but what kind of creep asks a woman out after something like that? Moving in on you the minute your first choice didn't work out? No one wants to be someone's plan B."

"I don't think you could ever be anyone's plan B," said Julia.

Sean frowned. "Look, I like you, Julia. But our timing has always been off. And you know what they say. Timing is everything."

This was a send-off, Julia realized. He'd written her off already!

But she wasn't about to give up that easily–not after all that happened.

"Our timing *was* off," she said. "But it's not anymore. And just because Asher happened to be my first choice chronologically doesn't mean he's *still* my first choice–not anymore."

Sean searched her eyes. "You sure about that?"

She met his gaze. "I'm sure." Although she still didn't understand exactly what had gone wrong with Asher, it was obvious in hindsight that something had been off–*way* off.

"All right then," said Sean. His face relaxed into a smile. "And if you want to get technical, chronologically, it was *me* who came first. I knew you long before you ever met Asher."

Julia smiled back. "You make a good point."

And in the next moment, he was kissing her.

Julia was instantly transported to the sweaty post-yoga kiss they'd shared, months ago, in the North End. In fact, she realized, the sensory memory of it had never left her. Even though there had been just that one kiss, she'd missed kissing him.

It was true. Sean *had* come first.

Chapter 39

By the time the first streaks of dawn appeared in the sky, many party guests were passed out on couches or even the ground. Others were still going strong, daybreak simply prompting a shift in beverage choice from beer to Bloody Marys and mimosas. Tipsy, exhausted, and more than a little disheveled, Julia couldn't remember the last time she'd partied literally all night long.

Or when she'd last felt so happy.

She glanced at Sean. He looked just as drunk, just as sleepy, just as disheveled–and just as happy.

A new crew of servers had cleared the tables of last night's offerings and replaced them with a lavish selection of breakfast items: fresh fruit, fresh-baked baguettes, muffins, croissants, pastries, and fresh-made juices and smoothies. Interspersed throughout the "wilderness" space were stations for made-to-order Belgian waffles and omelets made from eggs or–Julia was thrilled to see–tofu. And, of course, there was the Durangos' patented coffee, its enticing aroma wafting over the crowd.

Sean had noticed it, too. "How about some java?"

"You read my mind," said Julia.

They joined the short line at one of the nearby coffee stations. There, in front of them, looking notably put-together in a lime-green and white seersucker suit, was Gareth, holding out a mug for coffee.

Julia opened her mouth to greet him, and then closed it again, not wanting to startle him. She'd hate to be responsible for causing him to spill coffee on his pristine summer suit.

"Milk or cream?" she heard the server ask.

"Oat milk, please," said Gareth, waiting while the waitress reached below the table to retrieve the container.

Julia's jaw all but dropped. The "cheese snob" who'd thought it sacrilegious to hold a vegan wedding in Switzerland was now requesting non-dairy milk for his coffee?

Wordlessly accepting the cup of coffee that Sean was handing her, she felt a jolt that had nothing to do with caffeine. It was clear she'd stumbled onto Asher's "inner circle" conversion–and his inner *secret*.

"Here you go," the server was saying, holding out a ceramic pitcher, but Gareth didn't notice. He'd noticed Julia, and the expression on her face must have clued him in to the fact that she'd finally–*finally*–figured it out.

Although obviously nonplussed, he summoned a smile. "Julia. How are you?"

She couldn't look at him. She turned and walked away, not sure where she was going but wanting only to be far, far away.

In her shock, she'd forgotten about Sean, who, naturally, was confused by her abrupt departure. He called after her. "Julia, where are you going? What's wrong?"

Gareth was calling to her, too, but Julia didn't respond to either of them. Instead, she kept walking, until she reached the forested edge of the party space. Spotting a narrow, winding dirt path into the woods, she was contemplating taking it when she heard footsteps behind her. Assuming it was Sean, she turned her head slightly and said, "Please, just leave me..."

She stopped mid-sentence when she saw that it wasn't Sean.

It was Asher.

"So you made it after all," she said.

"Yes," said Asher. "I came up yesterday afternoon." He didn't make a move to touch her.

Standing there, next to him, Julia had never felt so alone.

She glanced behind them toward the coffee station–where Gareth was still standing, anxiously looking their way.

"The oat milk gave it away," she said. "I'm such an idiot. It was right there in front of me the whole time. I honestly believed it was all about Rusty."

Asher had recovered himself. "Let's sit down for a minute."

She allowed him to direct her away from the woods, to a green vinyl couch a few feet away that was littered with empty beer bottles. He cleared away the rubbish, and they sat.

The sun was now up, casting everything with a golden glow. Julia waited for Asher to speak. After an extended, uncomfortable silence, he cleared his throat.

"I'm sorry, Julia. I'm so sorry."

He'd said it before, of course–in his pre-wedding text message, and again when she'd gone to see him in Louisburg Square. This time, though, the apology was different–because Julia at last understood what he was apologizing *for*. This additional insight changed everything.

There were a million things she could say, a million and one questions she had every right to ask. But she didn't want to pry it out of him. More than that, she didn't want to make it one bit easier for him. Why should she?

Then, to her shock, Asher smiled. "Oh, Julia. I know it's ridiculous, but I just can't help being happy to see you."

She sat there, truly at a loss for words.

He gave an almost lighthearted shrug. "And, honestly, it's a relief for you to finally know. I'm gay."

A bitter bubble of laughter escaped Julia. "It may be a relief for *you*. But not for me. How long have you and Gareth..." She shook her head. "Months? Years? Were you hiding this from me the whole time we were together?"

"No, not at all," said Asher. "For most of the time we were together, it was just you." He gazed out at the woods. "I loved you, Julia, I really did. I wanted to marry you. If it hadn't been for Gareth, I think I *could* have married you. And I think I could have been happy."

She tried unsuccessfully not to feel offended. "I don't understand."

"If it hadn't been for Gareth, and how we are together–if I hadn't found out that *that* existed, I would have gladly gone through with our wedding."

He sighed. "I wasn't plagued with doubts about marrying you. I was *thrilled* to be marrying you."

Julia laughed darkly. "Well, clearly, at some point that changed."

Asher ran a hand through his hair. "Julia, I didn't even realize I was gay. Actually, that's not completely true. I just did a really good job of denying it, even to myself. Especially since the whole fate of the Schloss hinged on my getting married."

The explanation left Julia unimpressed. "In case you haven't heard, gay people can get married these days. You could have married a man and still gotten the Schloss."

He shook his head. "It's not that simple. Gay marriage is a fairly recent development. And the trust language refers to a *wife*, not just a spouse. Also, there's one other trust provision I didn't mention to you." He hesitated. "Not just a just a wife, but a 'suitable' wife. As determined by my parents."

That made more sense. Julia could readily imagine just how "suitable" Sage and Dom would deem a male partner—but still. "I know they're not exactly open-minded, but would they really let you lose the Schloss? Over that?"

"I honestly don't know," said Asher. "But it's not just them. The City of Thun would almost certainly challenge the will on that same basis, since the museum is the alternate beneficiary. Our lawyers tell us that opposing counsel would argue that the term 'suitable' should be interpreted based on the intent of my great-grandparents and the standards of their generation."

Julia was beginning to get a sense of the complexity of the legal issues at play. "What a mess."

"To say the least. It would be a legal shit show. Chances are we'd end up settling with the museum. Paying them off. Anyway, regardless, I'm not getting married anytime soon. Gareth and I aren't at that stage yet."

Yet, noted Julia with a frown. "So it was true after all. You really *were* marrying me just for the castle. Everything you said about your grandparents, about believing in love, believing in *us*—it was all a complete load of bull."

Asher again shook his head. "It wasn't like that. I loved you. I wanted to be with you. That's all I wanted."

"But you're *gay*," said Julia. "Didn't it occur to you that that might not be fair to me?"

"Of course it occurred to me! That's why I didn't go through with the wedding."

"How noble of you," she said, even as tears flooded her eyes.

"Oh, Julia," said Asher, his voice flat. Julia could tell, even without looking at him, that he, too, was about to cry. "I certainly don't purport to be noble. Just please try to understand. The 'me' I'd cultivated–and thought I really was–didn't exist. *Doesn't* exist. Gareth told me he wouldn't keep seeing me if I got married. And *not* getting married meant putting the Schloss at risk." He chuckled bitterly. "On top of all that, how do you think my parents were going to feel about having a 'homosexual' son? How do you think they *do* feel?"

A fierce–and unwelcome–pang of sympathy pierced Julia's chest. She recalled her conversation with Dom. He'd told her he could hardly stand to even look at Asher–and that Sage was on the verge of disowning her own son. It was evident that Dom hated Asher not for what he'd *done*, but for what he *was*.

"When did you tell them?" she said.

"The afternoon before our wedding. They told me I was just confused, that it was just an extreme case of cold feet–and that if I didn't go through with the wedding, they'd never forgive me for the shame I'd brought on the family."

Dom and Sage had known the whole time, realized Julia. They'd looked her in the eye and lied to her face.

"I'm so sorry," she said. "Do you think they'll come around?"

Asher shrugged. "My father, maybe, eventually. My mother–unlikely."

Again, Julia could tell he was doing his best not to cry. She felt a burst of fury at Sage, who could so coldly reject her only son over something that wasn't wrong, that wasn't even intentional, that was simply part of who he was.

Still, she felt a masochistic need to hear the full truth, in all its gory details. "When did you and Gareth first–you know?"

Asher nodded slightly, clearly having expected the question. "It was in September. We met in Louisburg Square one Friday afternoon to go over some things at the house. He'd brought Rusty with him, and later we decided to take her to the park. That was when things first turned romantic." Even though he was clearly embarrassed, he was smiling slightly; this was clearly a cherished memory.

Julia smiled wryly. "So this is all Rusty's fault. I should have known."

Asher chuckled. "Yeah, I fell in love with Rusty first. Gareth and I joke that he seduced me with his dog."

Julia wondered what other private jokes he and Gareth shared. "And to think I was worried about Odetta. Before Gareth, you'd never suspected? You'd never had a relationship, or even just a fling, with a man?"

Asher shifted uncomfortably in his seat. "There were a few incidents in boarding school, but that's just kind of how it was in that environment. I never really counted those. And then in college and grad school, there were a couple of times that things got a little crazy sexually. HBS parties were out of control." He was referring to Harvard Business School. "But there were generally women in the picture, too. It wasn't usually just me and another man."

Generally, noted Julia. *Usually*. It was a pretty packed homosexual history for someone in such supposed denial.

"Why didn't you tell me when I came to see you a few weeks ago?" she said. That was the part that *really* didn't make sense.

Asher sighed. "My parents were deep in discussion with the lawyers at that point. They made me promise not to tell anyone until they figured out the legal ramifications for the Schloss. They also convinced me it was better for you not to know. Otherwise, they said, you'd feel like you'd been living a lie."

Of course, it *had* been a lie–a two-year-long delusion.

"I had such faith in you," said Julia. "I don't know how I can ever trust anyone again." She exhaled slowly, looking at the ground. "All I've got is myself."

Even as she said it, though, she realized she felt okay. Alone, but all right.

She looked back up at him. "Since we're coming clean, I might as well tell you that I kissed someone while we were engaged. It only happened once, but I felt terrible about it. I even went to confession." She gave a short laugh. "Given everything that's happened, I no longer feel quite so guilty."

Asher blanched. "I understand. I didn't give you everything you needed."

The enormity of the understatement made Julia's heart go cold.

She stood up from the couch. "No, you didn't. You lied to me, you lied to your parents, and you lied to yourself. And all because you wanted a castle." She laughed harshly. "Until you realized you didn't want the castle *that* much."

She turned and strode toward the line of cars waiting to take the guests back to their lodgings, wondering what lesson she was possibly to take from this experience. Kat, Asher, *everyone* had urged her to believe in the purity and perfection of Asher's love—which, as it happened, hadn't been worth believing in.

She motioned to one of the drivers, and he opened the rear door of his vehicle for her to enter. As she did so, Julia saw that Sean was climbing in behind her. She gave him a questioning look but didn't protest.

It was barely seven o'clock in the morning, and all she wanted to do was to go to sleep. In fact, she wondered if she'd ever want to get out of bed again.

Whatever perverse satisfaction she'd felt at having the last word with Asher was fading fast, leaving in its place only guilt. She knew that Asher had done his best. Of course, his best had been nowhere *near* good enough, but it had still been best. He hadn't willfully tried to hurt her.

She closed her eyes and rested her head back against the seat.

She felt Sean's hand on her thigh. "Was that Asher I saw you talking with? Are you okay?"

She forced herself to open her eyes and look at him. Sean hadn't done anything wrong. It wasn't fair to shut him out.

For having been up all night, his face looked remarkably fresh. His blue eyes were clear and alert, the faint stubble on his cheeks and chin adding a touch of rakishness to his sporty, all-American good looks.

So this was what Sean looked like in the early morning. This was what he would look like if she woke up next to him.

"Yes, that was Asher," she said. "And I'm fine."

Sean looked alarmed. "You didn't get back together with him, did you? Oh, God, don't tell me you're engaged again."

Julia laughed hollowly. "No, we didn't get back together. I finally found out the real story of why he ditched me on our wedding day. He's gay. So's Gareth. They're both gay."

"As in, gay *together*?" said Sean.

"Exactly," said Julia. "They're a couple. Gareth stole my man."

Sean let out a breath. "Well, that explains a lot, I guess."

"Yeah," she said, still processing. "It does."

The car was now pulling up in front of Julia's cottage. She thanked the driver and stepped out of the car—as did Sean.

They stood there a moment in the early morning sunlight. The picture-postcard cottage, its window-boxes overflowing with pink petunias, the brook babbling cheerfully in the background, gave the moment that same fairy-tale feel she'd been experiencing all weekend.

This moment, though, was no fairy tale. It was real.

Sean touched her arm. "All I can say is, Asher must be *really* gay."

Julia smiled faintly. "Why? Because he's so good-looking? Because he has such a great sense of style?"

"It's not *that* great. And he's not *that* good-looking," said Sean, about as convincingly as she'd downplayed Marcus LaBree's appeal. "No, what I meant is that if he'd had any heterosexual tendencies whatsoever, they'd have multiplied exponentially when he was with you."

Julia gazed into his blue eyes. "Oh, you think so?"

"I know so," he said.

He pulled her to him and kissed her for a long, long time.

Again, Julia had the thought that she might never again want to get out of bed. This time, though, it no longer seemed such a gloomy proposition.

Chapter 40

Not until Sunday afternoon, in the car on their way back to Boston, did Julia have the chance to fill Kat in on Asher's revelation.

"Gay?" screeched Kat, almost swerving off the road. "How the *hell* did we miss that? I mean, I never thought my gay-dar was perfect, but I thought it was generally on target." She sighed hopelessly. "How wrong I was!"

"How wrong *I* was," said Julia. "I was sleeping with him and I had no idea." Asher had always poured heart and soul into their lovemaking, an emotional investment she'd interpreted as a commitment to quality over quantity. In hindsight, though, it was clear that it hadn't been about quality over quantity but about Asher gearing himself up in order to make love to her. How much energy he must have expended in order to muster such a convincing level of ardor!

And convincing it had been. She'd never once suspected.

"You never had *any* inkling?" said Kat.

"No, never," said Julia. "I mean, he's incredibly sensitive and sweet. And artsy. And much more emotional than his father. And, of course, he's definitely a little obsessive-compulsive. But those are all just stereotypes..."

Kat was shaking with laughter. "Right, but apart from those five *billion* signs—okay, stereotypes—there was absolutely no indication whatsoever!"

Julia looked at her, startled. Then she started laughing, too. "I was blind. A total idiot. A complete and utter fool."

"We both were," said Kat. "Not to mention, my boyfriend! How could he not have picked up on this?"

This was the first time that Julia had heard Kat refer to a specific relationship status with David. It had been an eventful weekend in *many* respects.

Kat grabbed her cell phone and called David, who had gone directly from the Hamptons to the Durangos' Manhattan apartment.

"It's all your fault!" she said.

Julia could make out vague sounds of protest from David.

"What do you mean, what do I mean?" said Kat. "You set Julia up with a gay man!" After a brief pause, she said, "Okay, introduced them, whatever." Another pause. "Yes! Asher is gay. How could you not realize this? You worked with him. You work with Gareth. They're a couple! How could you not have figured it out?" Finally, following the most prolonged pause yet, Kat guffawed. "Got it. Okay, sweetie, we forgive you. Mostly. Talk to you later."

She clicked off the line and rolled her eyes at Julia. "Oh, my lovable little narcissist. Asher never hit on *him*; therefore, Asher must not be gay. That was the extent of David's reasoning."

Julia laughed. "Well, he did say gay men love him."

"Yeah, well, mystery solved, I guess. So is Asher officially out of the closet?"

"I'm not sure how 'out' he wants to be," said Julia. "From what he told me, his parents didn't react well to the news. But then again, he and Gareth are a couple, so I think it's all pretty official."

"How did your conversation end?" said Kat. "Did you hug him goodbye, or did you tear him a new one?"

Cringing at the memory, Julia gave Kat the details–about Sage and Dom, the trust provision, the legal issues with the castle.

"I was pretty mean to him," she concluded. "I feel bad now."

She pulled out her phone and tapped out a text message to Asher.

Sorry I flew off the handle. I know it must have been hard for you. I hope we can be friends. I still miss you. xoxoxo

Less than a minute later came a response:

You have nothing to be sorry about. I'm glad we talked—I should have talked to you much, much sooner. Please forgive me. Of course we can be friends. I'll always love you, angel.

"Well?" said Kat.

Julia shrugged. "All is forgiven. He'll always love me. We're going to be friends."

"Happily ever after," said Kat.

"Yeah," said Julia, uncertain whether to laugh or cry. "Not quite the happy ending I'd envisioned, but under the circumstances, I guess it'll have to do." Then she had another thought, and smiled. "So, this weekend was an ending—but also kind of a beginning."

Kat looked intrigued. "Oh, really?"

"With Sean," said Julia. "Sean Harris."

Kat grinned and shook her head. "Good God, girl. *Finally.*"

Chapter 41

"Don't be mad," said Jolene when Julia walked into her apartment.

Apart from the expected general disarray, there didn't appear to be any major damage—no red wine stains on the couch, nothing visibly broken. Julia took a seat next to Jolene on the sofa. Olive immediately jumped up onto her lap.

"What shouldn't I be mad about?" said Julia.

"Well, don't tell Mrs. Lee," said Jolene. "But I had a dual-purpose SunStar party."

"That's great!" said Julia. "You sold some of your jewelry?"

Jolene looked sly. "No, I sold some paintings—*your* paintings."

"What do you mean?" said Julia, confused. "How did that happen?"

Her sister grinned. "When I was setting up for the SunStar party on Saturday night, I started to move some of your paintings out of the way, into your bedroom. And then I figured, why not leave them out for people to see? So I set them out along the walls. And it turned out that some people were much more interested in your art than in SunStar."

Julia laughed. "That's quite the compliment. Which ones did you sell? And how much did you get for them?"

"One of the Public Garden paintings—the small one with the George Washington statue in the background. That one went for eight-fifty. And the other one was a scene of the North End at night—the view from your bedroom. I got twenty-five hundred for that one. I went by the prices you had listed on your website, then added a few hundred just for the hell of it, since these guys seemed pretty eager. Not bad, eh?"

"You made me three-thousand-something dollars?" said Julia.

"I did!" said Jolene. "I told them they were getting a bargain–which they are. They paid you electronically. You should see the money in your account."

Without warning, Olive leaped from Julia's lap onto the floor, sprinted around the living room, jumped onto Jolene's lap and then off again, and then bolted into the bedroom.

The sisters looked at each other and started laughing.

"She's in a spazzy mood," said Jolene.

Julia was still mentally processing the art sales. "I'm giving you twenty percent. For being my agent."

"Sweet!" said Jolene. "I'll take it. Oh, and one more thing I forgot to mention. Again, don't be mad."

Uh oh, thought Julia.

"You know that big painting of yours, the abstract one? I think you called it 'Expression' on your website."

Julia nodded. It had been one of her off-the-cuff titles, for lack of anything better. In many ways, though, the title was apt, for the painting *had* been more expressionist in style than her usual realist work.

It had also been an expression in another sense–an expression of the chaos and despair she'd felt in the wake of Asher's abandonment.

"My friend Jessica's husband's friend wants it," said Jolene. "For his gallery in Provincetown. He's going to call you tonight."

Julia gaped at her sister. "He wants it for his *gallery*? Jolene, do you realize what this means? I'm an artist! After all this time, I'm really an artist." And then, to her sister's great amusement, she proceeded to hug her for about five minutes.

Jolene hugged her back. "Don't be silly," she said, laughing. "You've *always* been an artist. Now you're just an artist whose time has finally come."

Amidst the excitement over the artwork sales, Julia had almost forgotten that she had some rather major news to relate. "Jolene, Asher was at the party in the Hamptons. He explained everything to me. He's gay."

Jolene looked at her for a long moment–and then erupted into laughter. "Of course he is! Of *course*."

Julia told her about Asher and Gareth—and Rusty.

All of which only caused her sister to cackle even harder.

"Moral of the story," gasped Jolene, "never trust a man who can't hang with cats! That's the true test—can he handle pussies?" She shrugged unabashedly at Julia's shocked expression. "Hey, you know me! I tell it like it is."

Julia simultaneously laughed and groaned. She thought of Sean and his two cats; he certainly passed that test. "Oh, yes, my dear sister. You most certainly do."

• • •

As promised, Jolene's friend's husband's friend, a man named Morty Gold, called Julia that evening. For more than twenty years, Morty told her, he and his partner, Kevin McAuley, had owned and operated the Gold Alley Gallery in Provincetown, Massachusetts.

Before he went any further, Julia asked him what in on *earth* he'd been doing at a SunStar Traditional Natural Eastern Remedies sales party.

Morty laughed. "Right! Not my typical scene. My friend Noel's wife dragged him there. Noel knows I'm always on the lookout for new artists, and when he saw your paintings, he texted me to see if I wanted to come take a look. I happened to be in Boston for the weekend, so I popped on over. I'm really intrigued by your art and the way you inject jarring abstract notes into realist works while still managing to maintain aesthetic appeal. In other words, your paintings hurt a little, but they're still pretty! They're very well-suited to the gallery. Do you know P-town? We're on Commercial Street."

After some discussion, they agreed that Morty would send someone over Monday evening to pick up the "Expression" painting, which he was so enthusiastic about that he wanted to buy from her outright rather than sell on commission. He also requested that she turn over to him two of her Public Garden pieces, which he'd put up for sale in his gallery.

"I don't want to have too many of your paintings on site for now because I'd like to develop an air of exclusivity around your work," Morty explained—a remark that made Julia smile. *Exclusive? Her?* "I'll use those three pieces to pique some initial interest. Over the next couple of months, they should generate a nice little buzz, and from there, what I'd love to do is launch into a full show of your work at the end of July." He gave a little laugh. "That's appropriate, right? Julia in July? How does that sound to you?"

Julia was momentarily at a loss for words.

Her own show—and in July, at the height of Provincetown's high season.

And to think that she had her sister—her flaky, messy, borderline-alcoholic, vitamin-supplement-selling sister—to thank.

"Thank you," she said, a wholly inadequate expression of what she was feeling. "That sounds amazing. It's been years since I had any of my work in a gallery."

She immediately worried that confessing her obscurity might cause Morty to second-guess his proposal. Instead, he said, "Well, it's about time you did! The big event we had planned for July recently fell through and I'd been frantic trying to figure out what in *hell* I was going to do instead, and then you come along! Just to warn you, though, it's going to be a *boatload* of work to get things ready. We're already into May, so that gives us under three months to get our ducks in a row."

"Sure," said Julia. "Just let me know what you need from me."

"Well, first off, I'd like you to come see the gallery ASAP. Any chance you can make it down here within the next couple of weeks? We have plenty of room, you can stay with us. Bring your sister if you like. In fact, a friend of mine has a gallery that displays jewelry. She'd be a great person for Jolene to meet."

"That sounds fantastic," said Julia. "And I'm sure I can talk Jolene into it."

"Good, good. And ideally, I'd like to have at least another two or three paintings from you by mid-June. Can you do that?"

"Sure," said Julia, thinking of what that would mean for her weekends between now and June: all painting, all the time.

But she could do it. In fact, she'd be *thrilled* to do it.

Morty continued, "You'll also need to meet with our PR woman and a couple of local reporters that I work with. And I'll need a compelling artist bio—I'll put you in touch with someone. Also some written descriptions of your work in general, and one for each of your paintings. We'll need to go over each of your paintings piece by piece and work out the pricing. I know you have some prices listed on your website, but I probably have a better sense of the market rates. Oh, and the guest list. We'll publicize the show in all the usual places, local papers, social media, all that, but we should also send out some personal invitations. So I'll need the contact information for people you'd like to invite. The bigger, the better."

The barrage of information had left Julia feeling a bit stunned.

Before she could respond, Morty shrieked, "Good Lord! How are we going to get all this done by July?" He laughed. "Don't mind me. I always get this way. We'll get it done. And it'll be fun. Crazy, but fun. What's your schedule like? Are you free on weekdays?"

"No," said Julia. "I have a full-time job."

Morty inhaled sharply. It was as if all the gears that had been frantically turning in his head had come to a screeching halt. "Oh, dear. I didn't realize that. That could be tough."

"I'll make it work," said Julia. "My employers are very understanding."

"Are you sure?" said Morty, his doubt apparent. "Julia, I need to know that I can count on you. This is going to require a real commitment, we can't half-ass it. And no offense, but I've dealt with enough unreliable, over-committed artists in my time—like this last one who just went belly-up on me. I'm not taking on another one. Maybe you'd like to take a couple of days to think about it?"

"I don't need any time to think about it," said Julia. "I'm in. I'll talk to my bosses tomorrow." While she hated to let Franco and Carly down, she wasn't going to allow a misplaced sense of loyalty to them, and to a job she'd never loved, stand in the way of this opportunity. She owed this to herself.

Especially since she'd soon be *marrying* herself!

"All right then!" said Morty. "Strap yourself in and hold on tight, Miss Julia Jones! We are in for one hell of a ride!"

Chapter 42

As Kat and Julia discussed Julia's personal wedding plans the next day, in Kat's apartment, Kat was becoming increasingly fired up. "Who says single women can't take a binding oath? We're going to start a revolution!"

"Power!" said Julia. "Taking it back!"

Kat's expression turned slightly worried. "Just to clarify, though, you're not ruling out marrying an actual man someday, right? Assuming Mr. Right comes along?" She grinned coyly. "Or maybe even came along this past weekend?"

Julia's smile faded. Mr. Right *had* come along–and then turned out to be gay. And she hadn't heard from Sean since she'd gotten back from the Hamptons. Granted, it had been only one day, but she couldn't help but wonder if their connection, special as it had seemed in the moment, might have been merely the product of the outlandish setting and her own heightened emotions.

Only time would tell.

"No, of course not," she said. "But in the meantime, no more waiting around for someone else to make me feel like I matter. I matter to *me*."

Kat nodded her approval. "I like it, very progressive. What a summer it's going to be for you–your own wedding in June, and your own art show in July!" Julia had, of course, told her all about Morty Gold and the Provincetown gallery. "Although, if you wouldn't mind waiting on *me* for a just a second, I'll be right back."

Kat disappeared into the kitchen, and, for the next few minutes, the whirring of her Vitamix blender prevented further conversation. Smoothies seemed to have become Kat's answer to just about everything–a sort of panacea for all of life's problems. And they kept getting greener.

She returned to the living room a short time later bearing two tall glasses brimming over with greenness. She handed one to Julia. "This one is pure greens–kale, collards, parsley, celery, lemon, and half a green apple for sweetness."

Julia took a tentative sip. "It tastes like spring."

Kat beamed. "I know, don't you love it?"

Julia took another sip. On second thought, it tasted more like grass.

In many ways, she reflected, this greenest-of-smoothies epitomized the monumentality of the changes that had transpired in Kat's life over the recent months. The running, smoothie-guzzling, and occasionally-yoga-going Kat was trimmer and healthier than ever before–and, most of all, no longer avowedly single.

Of *course* she was happy for her best friend. She wasn't green with envy, she was just green with...smoothie.

"You don't think it's pathetic?" said Julia. "Marrying myself after I was practically left at the altar?"

Kat scoffed. "It's not pathetic, it's revolutionary! Remember?"

"Right," said Julia. "Revolutionary."

After some discussion, they decided that the wedding would take place at sunset on Kat's roof deck. Only the "bridesmaids" would be present for the ceremony itself. A larger party would follow afterward.

"The regular guests don't need to know the backstory," said Julia. "To them, it'll just be a birthday party."

"The point is," said Kat, "this soiree will show everyone that the Asher thing isn't keeping you down. You're like a phoenix, rising from the ashes–no, the Asher! Asher to ashes, dust to dust–but *you* still have plenty to celebrate." She drained the last of her smoothie. "What are you going to wear? Should we do another shopping trip?"

Julia thought about it. "Maybe Marissa can do something with my mother's gown–assuming Jolene's okay with that. Let me call them."

She first called her sister and filled her in on her plans for *another* wedding. "I was thinking of having Marissa redo Mom's wedding gown for me to wear," she told Jolene. "But I didn't want to start chopping it up until I checked with you, since you might want to wear it at *your* wedding someday."

It didn't take long for Jolene to think about it. "Thanks for checking with me, Jules.. But don't worry about me. I know Mom would have *loved* this idea–and she would have loved the idea of your wearing another version of her dress. So go ahead–chop it up! Just save me a snippet, okay?"

"You got it," said Julia.

She next used her cell phone to dial Marissa. She put her friend on speaker phone as she filled her in on everything: Asher, Gareth, the castle, the art show, and her *new* wedding plans.

Ever-steady Marissa absorbed the information compassionately and without fanfare. "Well, *you* had a busy weekend. I turn my back on you for a second, and no telling what you've been up to!"

"Never any telling with me," said Julia. "So what do you say? Are you up for getting creative with my mom's dress? Maybe make it a little more casual, quirkier, more...*me*?"

"Ooh, am I ever!" said Marissa. "This is going to be fun. By the way, who's going to officiate the ceremony?"

Julia hadn't thought of that.

"Maybe one of your yoga people?" suggested Kat. "They're into all kinds of cheesy, self-helpy stuff, right? Not that that's what this is, of course."

Julia had a flash vision of Pepper, the Tuesday-night yoga teacher, in her form-fitting short-shorts and pink halter top that showed off her flat, muscled abs, presiding over her personal wedding. "Umm, *no*."

Kat and Marissa both laughed.

"Point taken," said Kat. "Well, we've pinned down the date and the location–"

"And the dress," said Marissa.

"Yes, and the dress," said Kat. "Those are the essential things. We've got over another month to figure out the rest."

Camilla's sunshine-on-demand hadn't made it to Boston. As Julia walked home through the North End, raindrops spattered her face. She had to dodge the springtime tourists crowding the sidewalks, determined to experience New England's finest gnocchi, cannoli, and/or gelato despite the drizzly day. As she rounded the corner onto North Bennet Street, she caught sight of St. Ignatius Church, home of the salty Boston friar. Did people still use the word "friar"? But "priest" sounded so formal. Yes, she decided, "friar" suited the down-to-earth Father Mahoney much better. Dreary weather had never seemed to dampen *his* spirits—and he'd always succeeded in lifting hers.

She spontaneously turned and walked into the church.

Inside, the church was dark and still, a world apart from the bustle outside. Today marked her third visit here in a manner of months. And to think that a year ago, she'd scarcely anticipated ever setting foot in a house of worship again.

Then again, this year had brought any *number* of things she hadn't anticipated—not all of them pleasant. Father Mahoney had been one of the more welcome additions.

Julia scanned the darkened room, wondering if he'd be here.

Sure enough, there he was, straightening a crucifix hanging on the wall.

"Hi, Father Mahoney," she said.

He turned to look, and his face lit in recognition. "Well, hello, Miss Julia! Nice to see you again. What can I do for you today? I can't offer you much in the way of physical refreshment—well, apart from a Communion wafer or two, although those aren't really meant to be given out as snacks—but I can offer you spiritual sustenance! Will that do?"

In fact, thought Julia, some crackers might be just the thing to settle her stomach after Kat's smoothie. She could still taste the greenness. But of course he'd been kidding about the Communion wafers. "Spiritual sustenance will do wonderfully," she told him. "No one does spiritual sustenance like you."

Father Mahoney beamed. "I try, my dear, I try. So tell me, what have you been up to?" He eyed the crimson smudge on her jeans. "Been painting the town red, have you?"

Julia only now noted the paint smear. She laughed. "Yes, you could say that." She thought of the artwork cluttering her hallway at home. It had been an eventful year in *many* respects. "I've been a little possessed," she told him. "In a good way, mostly."

The priest gave her a crooked smile. "So no exorcisms required?"

"I think I'm okay on exorcisms," said Julia. "But there are some new developments I wouldn't mind getting off my chest, if you have a minute."

Father Mahoney was instantly all ears. "Of course, dear. Do tell."

Julia explained about her encounter with Asher and what she'd learned.

When she'd finished, Father Mahoney shook his head sympathetically. "Oh, my dear, what a difficult time you've had of it. Him, too, no doubt." He smiled and squeezed her hand. "But you'll be all right, dear. Your spirit is like a light, it shines through, I can see it on your face."

He went on to murmur some words about God and Jesus, and the blessings washed over Julia, not quite registering but somehow seeming a fitting denouement for her and Asher's story–the fairy tale gone so terribly awry.

That story was over, Julia realized.

And a new story–*her* story–was only just beginning. Her painting-cluttered hallway at home was evidence of that.

Father Mahoney was still speaking. "Healing takes time. So be very gentle and patient with yourself." He regarded her warmly. "And if there's ever anything I can do for you, anything at all, just let me know. You know where to find me."

Julia felt a sudden surge of gratitude for this uncommon man of the cloth.

And the twinkle in his blue eyes had sparked an idea.

"You know, there *might* be something you can do for me," she told him. "It's kind of a strange request."

Father Mahoney chuckled. "Oh, my dear, you don't know strange requests until you've served as a Jesuit priest in South Boston for thirty-two years. Compared to Southie, the North End is a piece of cake. But sorry, dear, I didn't mean to go on. Tell me, what can I do for you?"

For a moment, Julia hesitated, uncertain whether he would understand, let alone agree.

Then, she told him. "Well, to help me heal over what happened with my *other* wedding, I've decided to have my own *personal* wedding. To commit to love and honor *me*. In other words, I'm marrying myself."

The delighted expression on Father Mahoney's face told Julia that he'd more than understood. "What a lovely idea! People these days have no idea how to love themselves. The shame, the self-loathing I see, it's criminal. And it's at the root of so much ugliness and evil. How can we possibly love anyone else if we don't even love ourselves?"

"Exactly," said Julia. "And I've *been* one of those people, with the shame and self-loathing." She hesitated. "So this is my strange—or not-so-strange—request. I wondered if you would officiate my personal wedding ceremony in June. It won't be anything too formal, just me and the four women who were going to be my bridesmaids at my other wedding. Can you do that? Are you priests allowed to do that sort of thing?"

Father Mahoney's brow furrowed. "Well, it wouldn't be an official Catholic marriage ceremony, of course. The Church does impose some limitations there—not all of which I agree with, I'll have you know. But that's another matter."

"Oh, that's fine," said Julia. "I'm not looking for anything official. It's just for me."

"Lovely, lovely," said Father Mahoney. "In that case, Julia, I would be honored to officiate your personal wedding. It's not the strangest request I've gotten, not by a long shot. But it is one of the nicest."

Julia could only grin. "Thank you. Thank you very much."

•   •   •

She stepped outside the church a few minutes later to find that the overcast sky now held a faint glow–a hint of sun to come. She felt a glow of accomplishment as well. Talking to Father Mahoney had put into place the final necessary piece.

This wedding was happening.

Chapter 43

As she was walking to work Tuesday morning, Julia's cell phone buzzed in her bag. She grabbed it and glanced at the display, not recognizing the number. "Hello?"

"Julia? This is Camilla Durango."

"Oh, hi," said Julia, wondering why in the world Camilla would be calling her. "How are you?"

"Fabulous," said Camilla. "I have a proposition for you."

"Oh, really?" said Julia, instantly wary. She was *not* going to be part of the Durangos' next sexual adventure.

"It's about your art," said Camilla. "David's going to kill me—he's so controlling when it comes to interior decorating. And I know he doesn't trust my taste. But this can be our little secret."

In the morning North End rush, Julia strained to hear. She stepped off the busy sidewalk into an alley to better converse with Camilla. "What are you talking about?"

"Our Manhattan apartment. David's doing the interior design, and he's great, don't get me wrong, but sometimes his style can be a little clichéd. Do *not* tell him I said that! But Danny and I would like to find a few pieces that are a little more outside-the-box—you know, not your typical run-of-the-mill, classically-trained-interior-designer-selected stuff. We took a look at your website, and we love your paintings. Well, some of them, at least."

"Oh, thanks," said Julia.

"Are you in a gallery?" said Camilla. "Where can we see some of your work in person?"

Julia grinned. Talk about serendipity!

"Actually," she told Camilla, "there's a gallery in Provincetown that's going to be showing a few of my paintings. I'll be having a show there in July. I can add you to the guest list for the opening if you'd like."

"P-town, how fun!" said Camilla. "Yes, add us to the list. In the meantime, I'll let you know the paintings we're interested in and if you could set those aside for us, we'll send you a deposit. We'll come pick them up next time we're in Boston, which should be within the next couple of weeks. Can we come see some more of your stuff then?"

"Sure," said Julia. "Any time. Just let me know."

"Wonderful! I'll have my P.A. confirm a date with you next week," said Camilla. She clicked off the line.

Julia remained standing dazedly in the alley, her head spinning with all that had transpired over these past forty-eight hours:

Asher and Gareth.

Jolene's unexpected sale of three of her paintings.

Father Mahoney's agreement to officiate her wedding ceremony.

The promising inquiry from a wealthy art collector—even if that art collector happened to be an ex-porn-star going behind her interior designer's back.

Her own show!

She laughed giddily. It had already been an action-packed day, and she hadn't even arrived at work.

"Ms. Jones!" Byron greeted her when she walked into the Hartland Travel office.

"Mr. Knowles!" said Julia. "How's business?"

"Bustle, bustle," said Byron, his eyes not leaving his computer screen. "Loads to do before our four-thirty management meeting."

"Looking forward," said Julia. The weekly meeting would no doubt be merely the latest episode of the Hartland Travel sitcom, starring debonair firecracker sales star Byron Knowles, with cheesy laugh track provided by Carly, Franco—and, of course, Byron himself. On impulse, she added, "I've got a ton to do at JoH. I'll be over there most of the day. See you at our meeting."

Without even setting down her bag or taking off her jacket, Julia turned on her heels and walked out of the office.

"Later," Byron said, his snide voice trailing after her.

Julia ignored him. It probably didn't bode well that she'd not managed to withstand even a full five minutes in Byron's presence. But she really did need to finish up the paperwork establishing JoH's changes in leadership.

By comparison to Hartland Travel, the Byron-free JoH office was blissfully quiet. Absorbed in her tasks, Julia was startled by the sound of the office phone. She picked up the receiver. "Journeys of the Heart."

"That annoying guy you work with," said Lacey, without preamble. "Your nemesis. What's his name?"

"Byron," said Julia. "Byron Knowles. But according to Mimi and Franco, he's going to be my friend, my colleague, my right-hand man. So I really need to stop thinking of him as my nemesis."

"Maybe not," said Lacey. "This morning I ran into Marianne Samuelson from the Urban Faith Coalition. Remember them? They organize an annual trip for high school students to Rome. I referred them to you."

"Yes, of course," said Julia. "They're one of our biggest clients—or were. Apparently now they're working directly with a Rome-based travel agency. So they no longer require our services."

"Yeah, Marianne told me," said Lacey. "Too bad. But Marianne *also* happened to mention that she'd been contacted by a Boston travel consultant named Byron Knowles, who tried to make her a better offer."

Confused, Julia said, "Byron was trying to get her to stay with Hartland Travel?"

"No, no, that's the weird thing," said Lacey. "According to Marianne, Byron thought that UFC was *still* with Hartland Travel, and he was trying to get her to switch over to *his* company, Knowles Global Travel. She told him that everything was already settled, and they were going with the Rome people."

Julia processed this information. So *this* had been Byron's game all along.

Lacey voiced the conclusion she'd also reached. "It sounds to me like Byron's been poaching Hartland Travel's customers—or trying to, anyway. Unbelievable."

Julia smiled darkly. "Actually, I have no trouble believing it. Thank you very much for this information, Lacey."

"My pleasure," said Lacey—and Julia knew that it was. "Keep me posted."

Julia hung up the phone, still thinking. The obvious question was whether Byron had tried the same tactic—this time successfully—with Hartland Travel's other recently-lost longtime customer, the Unity Guild. She needed to talk to Unity Guild President Tom McCormick.

As she pulled up Tom's contact information on her computer, Julia realized that she ought to have reached out to him long ago, even in the absence of this new information about Byron. The fact that contacting him hadn't even occurred to her before now made her wonder if she had what it took to take over the travel company. She was an artist, not a businesswoman.

Well, she told herself, she'd learn. And in her art career—now that she had one!—some business savvy would serve her very well.

Tom McCormick answered on the first ring.

"What can I do for you?" he said, after she'd identified herself.

"We were obviously disappointed to lose Unity Guild's business after all these years," said Julia. "I was hoping to get a sense of what happened. Were you unhappy with our travel services?"

"No, of course not. But another agency was able to give us a substantial discount on the same package, and it simply didn't make sense for us to say no."

"May I ask *which* agency?" said Julia.

"I suppose so. It's a small local business, Knowles Global Travel. They offered us a package for forty percent less than we'd have had to pay Hartland Travel for the same services. I couldn't turn it down. I have a responsibility to give Unity Guild members the best deal possible."

"I understand," said Julia. "Just out of curiosity, what was the quote they gave you?"

Tom gave her the number, and Julia nodded to herself. Exactly as she'd suspected. The quoted price was lower than what Unity Guild had been paying Hartland Travel, but by less than ten percent. Byron had falsely inflated Hartland Travel's prices in order to make his own offer to Unity Guild that much more attractive.

"We could have matched that price," she said. "And in fact, we still can. I'll even go one step further and offer you five percent *below* that price."

She'd barely finished her sentence before Tom said, "Done."

Julia was grinning when she hung up the phone.

Maybe she *did* have what it took to make it in the travel business after all.

• • •

As Byron strolled into the afternoon meeting, Julia examined his face for any signs of guilt or trepidation—and found none. By all indications, he hadn't a care in the world. And, as usual, he was bearing coffee drinks. Julia had come to think of it as his bread-and-circuses tactic: he used sweet treats and flamboyant mannerisms to distract people from what truly mattered.

He distributed cappuccinos to Carly and Franco and then made a show of setting down an enormous cup in front of Julia, announcing, "Extra-large almond milk latte for the vegan queen!" He flashed Franco a look. "I, of course, am the *non*-vegan queen."

Franco laughed heartily, proud, Julia could tell, to show off that he was "with it" enough to know what Byron meant by "queen."

Byron's bread-and-circus temporarily complete, they proceeded to get down to business. Naturally, the first item on the agenda was Byron's "aggressive new marketing plan" for Hartland Travel.

As he began launching into his spiel, Julia held up a hand. "Byron, if you don't mind, before we discuss your aggressive new marketing plan for Hartland Travel, I wondered if we could discuss your aggressive new marketing plan for *Knowles Global Travel*."

Three heads jerked simultaneously to look at her.

Franco and Carly looked confused. Byron's face was bland, revealing nothing.

Julia addressed her bosses. "Earlier today, I spoke with Tom McCormick from Unity Guild. He told me that the company that offered them a better deal was Knowles Global Travel. And apparently Byron tried the same thing with Urban Faith Coalition, but they'd already decided to go with a Rome agency."

It took Carly and Franco only a moment to absorb the implication.

"You were trying to take our clients?" said Carly. "Byron, how could you?"

Franco's gaze was thunderous. "And to think we let you talk us into closing down Journeys of the Heart."

"Closing JoH was a solid business decision," said Byron. "It still is. Julia's bleeding heart was bleeding Hartland Travel dry."

Carly was shaking her head. "We never understood why you wanted an unpaid internship."

"Or why you wanted a full-time job when you had your own company to run," said Franco. "What you wanted was a ready-made client list!"

On his part, Byron looked barely discomfited. He still thought he could talk his way out of this, realized Julia.

"Darlings, you've got it all wrong," said Byron. "Everyone, take a deep breath and relax. And Julia, if you could *possibly* refrain from being a drama queen for thirty seconds, we'll be able to get this all sorted out."

Julia laughed. "Don't sell yourself short, Byron. I may be the vegan queen, but the drama queen title goes to you, hands down." She'd jotted down the figures that Tom McCormick had given her on a notepad, which she pushed in front of Carly and Franco. "These are the prices Byron quoted Unity Guild. He jacked up Hartland Travel's price by almost fifty percent so that he could pretend to beat it by forty percent and steal one of our best clients."

Carly gasped—and Franco looked about to explode.

Julia grinned. "But I took care of it. I stole them back."

Now, Byron was the one who looked about to explode.

"That's right, Mr. Knowles," said Julia. "Knowles Global Travel just lost a client."

Before Byron could say anything else, Franco said, "And needless to say, you just lost a job. Get out."

"Guys, please!" said Byron. "Can't we discuss this? I can *help* Hartland Travel. We can help each other."

"Get out," Franco said again. "*Now.*"

The look on his face was enough to send Byron scrambling for the door.

He glanced over his shoulder and shot Julia a dark look, clearly unable to resist taking one last jab. "You are one class-A *bitch*. Wannabe artist who can't keep a man—I see right through you. Good luck to you, honey. You'll need it."

Franco shot up from his chair and bellowed, "Out!"

Byron scurried out of the office, slamming the door on his way out.

Franco shook his head and sighed loudly. "Well, he certainly took us for a ride."

"Not for long, though," said Carly. "Thanks to Julia."

"Yes, that's our girl," said Franco. His forehead wrinkled in thought. "We'll need to get in touch with all our customers. There's no telling who else he contacted."

"Or what he told them," said Carly.

"We also need to tell Whitley," Julia said. "She's going to be upset."

Franco nodded. He used his cell phone to call Whitley. "Can you come to the other office, please? Yes, now."

Whitley arrived less than a minute later, her red hair frizzing around her, prominent nose twitching anxiously. "Is everything okay? Where's Byron?"

Franco told her what they'd learned.

Whitley's entire nose had turned a fiery red. "I can't believe this."

Julia couldn't help but wonder if Byron had confided at least part of his underhanded scheme to her. "You really didn't have any idea?"

"Of course not!" said Whitley. "He told me he hoped to feast on Hartland Travel's crumbs. In other words, if we turned anyone away, he'd snatch them up."

"He was more than feasting on our leftovers," said Carly. "He was stealing our bread and butter." She glanced at her husband. "And olive oil."

Franco grunted. "Well, he won't be doing business in this town much longer, I can tell you that."

At these words, Julia felt a small—*very* small—stab of pity for Byron. Franco had brought down foes far more formidable than Byron. He would make short work of Knowles Global Travel.

In fact, she now noticed, Franco looked all but inspired. Having a business rival seemed to have sparked something inside him.

Carly had noticed it, too. "Honey, why do you look so *happy*?"

Franco shook his head thoughtfully. "This brings me back to the early days. Remember, honey, when we were young and hungry and killing ourselves to make it in the travel business?"

"I remember," said Carly, smiling. "Every day it was something else. Who'd have thought we'd ever be where we are today?"

The Harts fell silent, reminiscing, and Julia realized how deeply they must love this, their travel company, which they'd built from the bottom up, with only each other to rely on.

"You know," she said, "I don't think you two are ready to retire just yet."

Franco opened his mouth to protest, but Carly laid a hand on his leg to quiet him.

"You may be right, Julia," she said. "If I can just get him to take a vacation once in a while, I'll be happy."

From the look on Franco's face, he might have just won ten million dollars. "I love you, dear!" He leaned over and kissed Carly on the lips, while Julia and Whitley looked on, amused. A moment later, he turned his attention back to Julia. "Don't get us wrong, we still want you to take over the business. But maybe not just yet."

Julia grinned. "Well, that works out pretty perfectly. Because believe it or not, I'm not just a 'wannabe' artist anymore. In July, I'm going to have an art show at a gallery in Provincetown. It's going to take a lot of work to get ready, so I may need to take some time off over the next few months."

Whitley clapped her hands. "Julia! Your own show? That's so exciting."

"And of course we believe it," said Carly. "What's hard to believe is that it hasn't happened *before* now."

"Wonderful news," said Franco. "And that's fine about the hours, we'll figure it out. In fact, this incident with Byron has given me a few new ideas I wouldn't mind exploring."

Carly rubbed his leg affectionately. "Of course it has." She smiled at Julia and Whitley, "I should have known I'd never get him out of here. But it's okay. It's where he belongs."

"I think you're right," said Julia.

· · ·

Sean wasn't at Ashtanga class that night. Walking home, Julia wondered glumly whether, after all the anticipation, their romantic interlude would prove to be but a flash in the pan. It was looking like Sean might turn out to be only the next man whose interest hadn't survived her singlehood.

But when she turned the corner onto Salem Street, there he was, waiting in front of her apartment building.

"What are you doing here?" she said. "And how did you know where I live?"

"I walked you home from yoga one night, remember?"

"Right," said Julia. "Stalker."

Sean grinned. "Hey, whatever it takes. Like Marcus LaBree says, all's fair..."

Julia looked at him doubtfully. "Is this what it's come to? Quoting professional athletes?"

"This is *exactly* what it's come to," said Sean. "No, actually, what I wanted to do was invite you on a real date–beyond yoga."

Julia felt a thrill down to her core–and her pants. She smiled faintly. "You mean you're not just a flash in the pan?"

His eyebrows went up. "Oh, I'm much more than that," he said. "You just watch. Dinner Friday night at my place? I got a vegan cookbook. I'll knock your socks off with my culinary abilities."

"That sounds lovely," Julia told him. "I'd love to experience your...culinary abilities. Thank you, I accept your invitation."

"Excellent!" said Sean. "I figured what better spot to properly ask you out than where we first kissed. When you were engaged."

"That's so sweet!" said Julia. "And by the way, I'm no longer engaged."

He leaned toward her. "So I heard. I'm so sorry..."

Chapter 44

"Dearly beloved," said Father Mahoney.

Julia, Kat, Jolene, Lacey, and Marissa were gathered on the roof deck of Kat's apartment. The setting sun cast everything with a rosy hue. Julia was wearing her mother's wedding dress, its sleeves cut off, skirt shortened, and redesigned by Marissa into a breezy, beachy frock that Josie would have loved—and that made Julia feel like an angel.

Or, not like an angel exactly, but like...*herself.*

Her feet were bare.

"In order to live, and live well," Father Mahoney continued, "we must divine what is truly important in life. Those of us who earnestly ponder this question invariably discover that what matters most is not professional success, social status, or material possessions. Because they are not what's real."

Real, thought Julia. She'd believed that her future with Asher was real. It had turned out to be anything but. What else might she be wrong about?

"What is real," said Father Mahoney, "is kindness. Integrity. Truth. And all of these can be summed up in a single word: love. Love is what matters. Love is what is real. Love is *all* that is real."

Julia regarded the little priest fondly. Other than providing him with the basic concept, she'd entrusted the wording and ceremony details to him. Clearly, that trust had been well-placed.

"We seek love in so many places, and often the wrong places. We don't find love in worldly possessions or fleeting sensory pleasures. We do find it, at times, in our relationships with others. And in art, and yoga, and other activities we truly enjoy."

Julia felt a twinge of irritation that yoga—blasted, insidious *yoga*—had somehow wrangled its way into her personal wedding ceremony. On second thought, perhaps she ought not have entrusted Father Mahoney with *all* the ceremony details.

"But sometimes," said Father Mahoney, "we get so caught up in our worldly activities that we forget the one place love can *always* be found: within ourselves. We have a responsibility to cultivate the love inherent in us, because that love is who we are. That's right. We, my friends, are love."

He cleared his throat, and Julia could tell that he, too, felt the effect of the words he was uttering. "Today, we have the privilege of witnessing Julia Jones undertake a sacred promise to be true to herself, and to the love within her. What nobler vow could there be?"

Father Mahoney nodded to Julia to step forward.

She did so, her heart pounding.

The priest smiled. "Do you, Julia Jones, promise to love yourself, to be true to yourself, and to honor the love that is within you?"

"I do," she said.

"Do you promise to allow love to govern your life, to be your compass and guide in all things?"

"I do."

"Do you promise to nurture and attend to yourself, as tenderly as God would care for his most beloved child?"

"I do."

"Love without forgiveness is barren. Do you promise to forgive yourself for all things done or undone, to allow forgiveness to heal all your wounds, past and present?"

"I do."

"Do you promise to care for your body, to nourish yourself physically, to always remember that it is your body that harbors your precious, perfect soul?"

"I do," said Julia, relieved that she hadn't been specifically asked to vow to keep doing yoga.

"Do you promise to care for your mind, to seek only truth and wisdom and light?"

"I do."

"And do you promise to care for your spirit, to guard and protect it at all costs?"

"I do."

Father Mahoney held out his hands to her, and Julia clasped them warmly.

"Now, take a moment to reflect upon this most sacred commitment you are undertaking here today. In these final moments, I encourage you to privately acknowledge any additional promises that you would like to make to yourself."

The glowing pink sun dipped below the horizon. Soon, the birthday party guests would be here–fifty-plus people in total, according to the RSVPs. Her father and Stephanie. Franco and Carly. David. Even Asher and Gareth. And, of course, Sean.

It wouldn't be quiet for long.

Julia closed her eyes, the fading sunlight flickering across her face. She felt the air on her skin, the warmth of her friends close by, the simple wonder of being here, now, with herself, *for* herself. She vowed never to abandon that self again.

When she opened her eyes, Father Mahoney was smiling at her.

"Julia, know that in the days and years ahead, in times of joy and in times of sorrow, you will always have *this* moment: the moment that you promised to love yourself always. And know that this moment will live beyond today, forever providing you a place of refuge, a place of solace, a place of peace."

Father Mahoney nodded to Jolene, and Julia's sister stepped forward with the hand-crafted silver ring she'd made especially for today. She slipped it onto Julia's righthand ring finger, and Father Mahoney said, "I hereby pronounce you, Julia Jones, married to yourself."

There came applause and cheers from the bridesmaids, bouquets tossed into the air, hugs and kisses and laughter.

Yes, thought Julia, her heart full, she would indeed remember this moment. She'd been searching for so long, a quest that had taken her from the alleyways of Boston to the highest peaks of Switzerland and beyond–and back to Boston yet again.

Now, that search was over. She'd found what she'd been seeking, right here, inside her.

Here it was. Here was love.

Acknowledgments

The narrator of T. S. Eliot's poem "The Love Song of J. Alfred Prufrock" says, "I have measured out my life by coffee spoons." I, on the other hand, have in many ways happily measured out my life by coffee *shops*, which have served me in equal parts as office, meeting place, refuge, and escape. Thank you in particular to these cozy, quirky, independent coffee shops, where much of *Marrying Myself* was written, rewritten, tweaked, and lovingly nudged into the novel it is today: Boston Common Coffee (Boston), Ninth Street Espresso (New York City), The Bean (New York City), Ost Café (New York City), Ugly Mugs (Nashville).

Thank you to my mother, Motria Benson, the first person to read the completed manuscript of *Marrying Myself*, whose love and support for my writing has never wavered, notwithstanding her also never-wavering urgings to get a real job. Thank you to my sister, Terry Pittman, whose insightful feedback and real-time reactions to the characters and events in *Marrying Myself* helped me make the novel more heartfelt, more real, and more fun. Thank you my brother, Mickey Benson, whose architecture stories inspired many of the fictional design tales in this book. Thank you also to my steadfast, loving father, Michael Benson. Thank you to Elijah Shaw for keeping me consistently on track, with my eye on the prize and my heart in good hands. And thank you to my dearly departed vegan cat, Sammy, who was not a reader but loved books and whose blackness, litheness, sleekness, and sweetness will forever remain the stuff of legends.

A special thank you to Jenny Villalobos, Lisa Padden, Amy Sibulkin, Cindy Martin, and Amy Nathan, whose comments and constructive criticism were integral to the revisions that made this book better in its final form than its original. Thank you to Boston friends Melanie Cerio, Allison Jones, Monika Pauli, Nancy Radford, Woody, Brad, John, David(x3), Justine, Sarah, Lucille, Paul, Donna, Mary Beth, and Lynne for their love and support during both my best and darkest times. Thank you to Albert Smegal for believing so earnestly in *Marrying Myself* that he even dreamed of its final cover. And thank you to Laureen Evans Granger, without whom this novel would never have been conceived.

A special thanks to author friends and mentors Jaden Terrell and Carrie Classon, an invaluable source of support during what seems to me the most challenging part of writing a book: that which comes *after* writing the book. Thank you to my vegan community in New York City, Nashville, and beyond, and especially to Victoria Moran and Dr. Will Tuttle for the education and inspiration they have provided me and countless others over the past decade-plus. Thank you to artist Lauren Markham, portrait photographer Karen L. Richard, and graphic designer Kostis Pavlou for their noteworthy professional contributions. Thank you to Jerry Wise and Gordon Moffat for their efforts to ensure that this book saw the light of day. Thank you to Yoga to the People of New York City, where I sweated, complained, and learned more about myself every day on my mat. Thank you to Sandy Coomer, founder of Rockvale Writers' Colony, an oasis in the hills of Tennessee, where I retreated to trim *Marrying Myself* from a massive tome to a readable, accessible novel.

My most sincere thanks to my literary agent, Jane von Mehren, and my unofficial assistant agent, Maggie Cooper, of Aevitas Creative Management, for their faith in this book and for their annoyingly on-target nitpicky suggestions as to how to make *Marrying Myself* a story people would love reading. Thank you to Reagan Rothe of Black Rose Writing, a publishing company whose independent mettle matches my own, for bringing this book and my beloved characters out into the world. Finally, thank you to that quiet voice within, that spirit that would not be extinguished, which revealed to me this story of a woman's search for love and where she found it.

Most of all, I would like to acknowledge all of the suffering animals, human and non-human, who desire, as we all do, safety, happiness, and the freedom to live out their lives without interference. May each and every one of us be free.

About the Author

An attorney who's been running from the law her entire professional life, Christine Melanie Benson is also a news satire writer, short story author, legal writer, and host of the Vegan Posse podcast. Her experience includes over a decade as a regular freelance legal writer for Baltimore's *The Daily Record* law digest, and her fiction works have been featured in *An Eclectic Mix Anthology*, RomanticShorts.com, *The Binnacle Maine Literary Journal*, and satire website *The Spoof!*. Formerly of Boston and New York City, Christine now makes her home in Nashville, Tennessee. *Marrying Myself* is her first novel.

Note from the Author

Word-of-mouth is crucial for any author to succeed. If you enjoyed *Marrying Myself*, please leave a review online—anywhere you are able. Even if it's just a sentence or two. It would make all the difference and would be very much appreciated.

Thank you!
Christine Melanie Benson

We hope you enjoyed reading this title from:

BLACK ROSE
writing™

www.blackrosewriting.com

Subscribe to our mailing list – *The Rosevine* – and receive **FREE** books, daily deals, and stay current with news about upcoming releases and our hottest authors.
Scan the QR code below to sign up.

Already a subscriber? Please accept a sincere thank you for being a fan of Black Rose Writing authors.

View other Black Rose Writing titles at
www.blackrosewriting.com/books and use promo code
PRINT to receive a **20% discount** when purchasing.

CPSIA information can be obtained
at www.ICGtesting.com
Printed in the USA
LVHW090548151122
733124LV00021B/260/J

9 781685 131463